SEE THE DEAD BIRDS FLY

ANDY MASLEN

TYTON PRESS

In memoriam
Richard Harry Maslen 1935 - 2022

No bird soars too high if he soars with his own wings.

—William Blake

1

Ted Sondersson didn't always enjoy hauling a load of timber from the forests of northern Sweden to the mid-country sawmills.

Too much anxiety about the price of diesel. The risks of being bushwacked by a biker gang.

Even the temptations of lone female hitch-hikers worried him. Suppose they suddenly turned out to have strung-out boyfriends with hunting knives and a wayward look in their red-rimmed eyes?

But today was different. The run had been long, but quiet. And, most importantly, profitable.

He was on his way home with a fat bank transfer sitting snugly in his account. Enough to pay for the repairs to the summer house and maybe even a little left over for a new set of skis.

He thought of Inga, wearing an embroidered peasant top with no bra beneath it, and those jeans she knew he liked. The low-slung ones that showed off her arse. His cock stirred and he allowed himself a brief but enjoyable fantasy of taking his wife of thirteen years from behind.

He glanced in his mirrors. The road was clear. Ahead, too. One of those rare but exquisite moments when the motorway seemed his and his alone. Truckers had a name for the phenomenon. *The ghost road.*

You could imagine, for a brief while, that all the other vehicles that slowed you down or made you hiss in anger as they chopped and changed lanes without indicating or even keeping pace with the rest of the traffic, had simply vanished. Removed from the road by a friendly god who looked down kindly on those who drove the big rigs for a living.

Ted glanced across at his iPhone, resting atop the paperwork fanned out on the passenger seat. No cop cars in sight. Nobody to see him making a call and wag a finger up at him. Maybe he'd call Inga.

He leaned sideways for the phone. He grunted with the effort: the Scania had a wide cab and the passenger seat was a stretch. Finally, taking his eyes off the road for as little time as he could possibly manage, he snagged the phone and hauled himself back into an upright position, juggling the phone into position so he could thumb the icons that would dial Inga.

He glanced up at the road as the call connected.

'What the fuck!' he yelled.

Was it an angel, staggering onto the smooth, dark tarmac of the E18? The outspread wings must have been two metres across at least. Three, even. But what kind of angel had wings that colour? Black as sin. Black as night. Angels weren't real, anyway. And why would an angel be making that face? Eyes panicked circles. Mouth an 'O' showing white teeth and red tongue. Black fur of pubic hair against bone-white skin. Did angels even have genitals?

While these brief, chaotic thoughts raced around Ted's brain, his body was performing other movements, without any conscious control. He'd dropped the iPhone and grabbed the wheel with both hands. His right foot had leaped from accelerator to brake and his thick, muscled right leg was extended, exerting fierce pressure on the pedal.

His arms were locked out at the elbows. It was one of the things you learned early on driving a big rig. You absolutely did not swerve to avoid animals in the road. Maybe in a sports car or even a family saloon, you might wrench the wheel over and give a moose or a wolf the scare of its life as you slewed around it before regaining the carriageway, heart hammering, adrenaline making your knees shake and your leg muscles tremble.

But in a forty-tonne Scania eighteen-wheeler? Even without a couple of hundred pre-processed pine logs on the trailer? No. You did not swerve. Not unless you wanted the whole damn rig ending up on its side with you smashed up in the cab like a raw egg in a blender.

Ted hit the angel at sixty three kilometres an hour. The bang reverberated through the cab. Blood and feathers flew up and coated the windscreen. A giant wing cartwheeled crazily left to right trailing long streamers of red and white…stuff…before landing in the field of sunflowers to the right of the motorway.

The airbrakes screamed and whistled like a locomotive entering hell. Ted yelled in horror as the angel's face slammed into the windscreen right in front of him and bounced away, leaving a bloody imprint in which he could clearly see the outlines of the eye sockets.

He brought the truck to a stop. His heart felt like it

might burst free of his rib cage and leap, pumping blood, out onto the dashboard.

'What the hell? What the shit-Godammit-to-hell?'

He swung himself down from the cab and ran around to the front of the truck.

Gobbets of flesh, wet and stringy, were stuck between the chromed teeth of the Scania's vast grille. He saw a penis and turned aside to vomit onto the ground. The black feathers were everywhere, clinging to the grille, the headlights, the air intakes beneath the licence plate. Most were attached to thin white bone fragments. Others adorned the metalwork, glued there with dark, sticky blood.

Ted ran up and down the verge, searching desperately for the rest of the angel, yet terrified by the thought he might find it.

'Oh God,' he wailed, as he saw the ruined remains of the body ahead of his truck, splayed and broken.

The ghost road was full again. But Ted was oblivious to the cars and trucks passing him, heads turning, curious, to see what was causing this burly trucker to stumble on rubber legs back to his rig. He scrambled up into the cab and grabbed his phone.

'Come on, come on, shit-of-the-devil, come on!' he shouted as his fingers, suddenly as dextrous as work gloves full of sand, refused to obey his instructions to call the police. Finally, he managed.

'Hello, Emergency. What service do you require?'

Ted swallowed.

'All of them,' he croaked.

2

The detective in charge of CID at the district station in Vällingby, a suburb on the western side of Stockholm was, in Stella's opinion, a rare kind of policeman indeed.

Kriminalkommissarie Daniel Magnusson had gone out to the crime scene in person. But on being shown what had occurred, he'd called her immediately, requesting she come over from HQ to help him out. No territoriality. No hogging a *'bloddig biff'* – a 'rare steak' in English but Swedish cop-slang for a case with lots of blood and plenty to get your teeth into.

'I know my way around a murder scene, Stella,' he'd said once he'd been put through by reception, the wind at the crime scene setting up a loud rustle on the line that made it hard for Stella to hear him. 'But I also know when I'm looking down the barrel of a weird one. So I thought I'd get the opinion of the—'

Stella took a moment to translate the Swedish phrase he'd just used. What the hell did *konstigheternas drottning* mean? She hadn't come across it before, even though she'd been speaking Swedish for two years since moving from the UK.

Her eyes widened as she mentally translated his colourful phrase.

'"Queen of Weirdness." Is that what they're calling me in Vällingby these days?'

Daniel laughed. 'Actually, that was your receptionist. Maybe you should have a word.'

'No. I like it,' she said with a smile. 'We'll be with you as soon as we can.'

She grabbed her murder bag. The black nylon holdall held everything she might need for the first day of a new case, from a forensic suit and bootees to notebooks, power pack for her phone, torch and even a spare pair of knickers and a washbag.

'Jonna, with me, please,' she called out to her assistant. 'Body on the E18 out at Vällingsby. Weird, apparently.'

She and Jonna had become friends since Stella's first case in Stockholm. They went running together most days and had even double-dated with Jonna's new girlfriend Emmelie, and Magnus, a Danish journalist Stella had been seeing. Neither relationship had survived the six-month mark, which, as Jonna had remarked caustically at the time, left the two female detectives with, 'less time for sex, but more for catching weirdos'.

Yet for all her excellent qualities as a friend and a cop, Jonna had one fault. She needed more whip than a two year old at Solvalla racecourse to exceed the speed limit. Unless there was a genuine emergency and not just her boss's characteristic eagerness to reach a new crime scene as quickly as possible. Stella was already thinking she'd better drive before Jonna got her tight little bum in the driver's seat.

Sure enough, 'He's dead, Stella,' she said as they were leaving the rear of the station on Kungsholmsgatan towards the force's small fleet of pool cars. 'No emergency. We can get there in plenty of time without breaking the law.'

In response, Stella held her hand out for the keys to the Volvo.

'Ever hear of the Golden Hour, Jonna?'

'But you said Daniel told you the truck hit the victim at 11:00 am.' She checked the time on her phone. 'And it's after twelve now.'

Unsure if Jonna was being overly literal on purpose, Stella simply blipped the fob and swung herself in behind the steering wheel.

'All the more reason to get there in a hurry.'

They made the fourteen-kilometre journey along the E18 in a brisk twenty minutes, blue lights acting on slow-moving traffic ahead like a municipal snow-plough on a winter morning.

Stella pulled up behind a white forensics van after a uniformed officer lifted a flapping length of yellow crime scene tape. Traffic had put a diversion up at junction 155 on the E18, but the other side of the motorway was slammed with crawling vehicles.

Phones held up like magic amulets, drivers and passengers alike craned to get a look at whatever horrors lay behind the white nylon tent the forensics officers had erected directly in front of the truck. A second tent bellied and snapped in the breeze about thirty metres further down the road. In the field of sunflowers beside the motorway, the CSIs had set up a small, white-roofed gazebo.

A couple of media helicopters clattered overhead, and Stella was grateful for the CSI tents. The last thing they needed was pixelated footage of a murder victim hitting social media and the evening news before they knew what they were dealing with.

She stepped out of the car and wrinkled her nose as the faint spring breeze wafted a stench of blood and shit in her direction.

Traffic cops knew that smell and they weren't shy about sharing the details with their colleagues in plain clothes. It was the inevitable result of a collision between a body and a fast-moving vehicle whose plastic bumpers, crumple zones and air-bags were designed to protect those on the *inside*. Anything more than a glancing blow would rip and tear through soft tissue, mixing and spilling body fluids and waste products before splashing them all over the road.

Wordlessly, Stella and Jonna slid into their white CSI suits. Each discreetly smeared oil of camphor onto her top lip, out of sight of Traffic, who were always ready to sneer at the faint hearts of the *rena händer* – 'clean hands' – brigade.

Ahead, the big truck sat on the hard shoulder, leaning at a slight angle where its nearside wheels had begun to dig in to the soft earth beyond the tarmac.

Stella turned to Jonna. 'Ready?'

'Ready.'

They rustled their way over to the big tent at the front of the truck. Inside, out of the breeze, the smell intensified, making Stella's eyes water. CSIs, dressed identically to the two detectives, were collecting scraps of flesh in clear plastic evidence bags, laying down numbered yellow plastic evidence markers, taking photographs and tweezering material from the tarmac into debris pots.

One of the white-suited figures detached itself and

made its way over to Stella. She recognised the gait, and the generous build: Signe Arrhenius, Head of Forensics.

Signe pulled her mask down to speak.

'Hey, Stella. Good to have you here. This is right up your street. Want to come and see?'

'Show us.'

Signe resettled her mask and led Stella and Jonna to the front of the truck. A Scania, Stella noted, taking in the red griffon wearing a silver crown. Inside the tent, Signe pointed to the bloody grille.

'The victim was hit dead-on, excuse the pun, and thrown thirty metres. He's in the next tent.'

'Victim?' Jonna asked. 'That implies homicide. Are you sure this wasn't just a road traffic accident?'

'I think you'd better just come with me,' Signe said. 'Vällingsby CID would hardly have called you out for an RTA, would they?'

Fair point, Stella thought, her detective's senses already sharpening as they approached the second, larger forensics tent.

Stella gasped. Partly it was the smashed remains of the body. But mainly the dozens of ink-black feathers plastering the scene. What had happened here? Some sort of motorway bird-strike? Was that even a thing?

The man – the *victim*, Signe had called him – or what was left of him, lay on his back. Several gaping parallel wounds disfigured the front of his torso. Stella thought back to the Scania's grille. The blood-smeared chrome bars told their own, eloquent story. Hit head-on by the truck and mashed into the grille by the force, then flung to the ground as the brakes finally brought the rig to a stop. She made a mental note to check with a traffic cop before they left.

Stella checked out his face first, trying to avoid

thinking about the arms just yet. The nose was broken, mashed flat between his cheeks. Both eye sockets were broken and rimmed with blood. The mouth just a pulpy mess of flesh and teeth.

Dark hair, worn longer than the average office worker. Strong jawline, stubble beneath the blood. Maybe he'd been good-looking, once. She shook her head. It was one of the random observations that homicide cops puzzled over for a second or two before parking it to return to the horror of the scene in front of them.

Her gaze kept flitting from the corpse's face to his shoulders, then back again. Finally, like a nervous bird alighting on a dangling feeder in a suburban garden, her eyes came to rest.

At first, Stella couldn't understand what she was seeing. Gradually, as her eyes and brain started collaborating, she inhaled slowly through her mouth and let it out in a controlled breath.

'What the devil is that?'

'Is that a *wing*?' Jonna asked, beside her.

Stella squatted beside the body. The left arm was missing, ripped out of the shoulder joint. Presumably beneath the forensics gazebo in the sunflower field.

But the right was present. Or at least a limb was present. Human from the midpoint of the upper arm to the shoulder, but below that, as Jonna had exclaimed, it was a huge black wing.

'It must be a metre or more,' Stella said.

'One-point-five, as far as I can tell with it folded like that,' Signe confirmed.

'How's it fastened on? Are those stitches?' Stella asked, peering at the mess of bloody tissue at the intersection between human and avian anatomy where she could discern black threads knotted along the join.

'I think so. Now you see why I said we had a victim, yes?'

'Is it real?' Stella asked, leaning closer and swallowing her gorge down as the smell of fresh blood and oily feathers threatened to overwhelm her.

Signe knelt beside Stella and lifted one of the long primary feathers with the tip of a narrow Perspex rod.

'I'm not an expert in matters ornithological,' she said, 'but if you observe the way this feather is embedded into the skin of the wing, it does appear to be, at the very least, remarkably realistic.'

Stella turned aside to Jonna. 'Can you make a note? We need a bird expert from the university on standby. Presumably in birds of prey. Larger species, anyway.'

Jonna nodded. 'I'll go and make a few calls.' She left the tent.

'Have you called the pathologist?' Stella asked.

'I managed that task, yes,' Signe said. 'Even without consulting a checklist.'

Stella felt her cheeks heating inside the forensics hood.

'Sorry, Signe. Of course you did. This is just a little shocking, that's all.'

'Shocking? For the Queen of Weirdness? Then this is, what would you say in English – a *red letter* day, yes?

'Something like that.'

'Have you ever encountered anything similar? Perhaps in your work in the UK?'

Stella cast her mind back over a career spent catching all manner of murderers, from contract killers who regarded more than two 9mm rounds as a waste of resources to deranged serial killers who liked to recreate Old Master paintings of martyred saints.

Each, in their own way, was as bad as the other. They involved the taking of a human life. Yet imagine a spectrum where green was 'bad but not horrifying', amber was 'bad and horrifying' and red was 'bad, horrifying and what-the-actual-fuck?'.

A wife snapping after years of her husband's coercive control and bashing his head in with a golf club? Green. (And surreptitious nods of approval in the canteen.)

A drug lord torturing a rival for hours before administering the coup de grâce with a ballpeen hammer? Amber.

A grief-stricken cop, out of her mind with thoughts of vengeance, slicing a CPS lawyer's head open with a cast-iron skillet before getting naked and cutting her body into manageable pieces with an electric carving knife and stashing it in her own Miele FN28262 freezer?

Sweat flashed across Stella's chest, neck and face. And it had nothing to do with the heat inside the forensics tent. The vision she'd just had was not of a psychopathic serial killer with delusions of grandeur and a narcissistic personality disorder.

It was of herself.

Or the version of herself she'd dubbed, a long time ago, Other Stella. A violent alter ego consumed by homicidal rage that had finally been defeated by a shaman on a First Nations reservation in Western Ontario. Even then, Stella had gone on to murder her former boss, Detective Chief Superintendent Adam Collier.

She'd never been able to work out which deaths troubled her more. The sixteen that came before, when she'd been able to apportion blame to Other Stella. Or Adam's. A cold-blooded execution that was strictly unnecessary, given that, at the time, he was sinking to his death in an ice-cold lake.

'Stella?'

Stella started, took an involuntary step backwards and tripped, tumbling onto her bottom, hands instinctively spread out behind her.

'Sorry. I was thinking,' she said, getting to her feet and wiping blood off her left glove.

'And?'

'And what?'

'And is this a first, or have you seen anything similar?' Signe asked, a hint of impatience adding an edge to her normally soft voice.

'No. Nothing like this. Sorry. I need some air. I'll be outside.'

Stella hurried out of the tent. What the hell had just happened? She hadn't thought about Other Stella in years. Living in Sweden might have been forced on her by the woman now living in 10 Downing Street, but it had turned out to be a fantastic move.

She'd managed to put her past where it belonged. Behind her. And she made new friends as well as the beginnings of a new career. She'd even welcomed her sister- and brother-in-law and their kids to Stockholm. Elle and Jason had stayed in a nearby hotel, Stella's two-bedroom flat not having the space for a family that now included two teenaged girls.

There was just one person who didn't quite view her move with unalloyed joy.

Jamie.

They'd been on the point of moving in together.

But after telling him exactly how many people she'd killed – more than any of his patients – he'd gone cold on the idea.

3

Stella saw a white-faced man talking to a traffic officer. His beer belly overhung his jeans, which were held up by a pair of red elasticated braces clipped to their overstressed waistband. He was gesticulating at the truck, then holding his arms wide and flapping them, before swiping a palm over his face.

The driver. Had to be. She made her way over to join them.

'Hi,' she said, holding up her SPA ID. 'I'm Detective Inspector Stella Cole. Call me Stella. Are you the driver?'

He shook her outstretched hand.

'Yeah, that's right. Name's Ted. Sondersson. I already gave my statement to one of these guys,' he said, nodding at the traffic officer.

Stella turned to the uniformed sergeant. 'Thanks, I'll take it from here. But I would like to talk to you when I've finished with Ted, OK?'

'Sure,' he said. 'I'll be over there in my car.' He rolled his eyes. 'Got some paperwork to start.'

Stella turned back to the truck driver.

'I know you've been over this, but I'm with a different team. Can you tell me exactly what happened? Try not to leave anything out, even if it seems trivial to you.'

'Trivial? That's a laugh. I mean, it's not every day you're on your way home and this, this damn great *thing* just launches itself at your windscreen. I could have been killed!'

He fished a tin of General snus from his pocket, opened it and inserted one of the little flat bags of dry tobacco under his top lip. He offered the tin to Stella, who shook her head.

She could feel herself getting impatient. A violent urge washed over her: she wanted to shake him. An image clouded her vision: a smirking version of herself wielding a sawn-off shotgun. She blinked and it vanished. She took a breath, wishing her heart would stop cantering along like a horse in a trotting race.

'It must have been very shocking,' Stella said. She tried to keep her tone sympathetic. 'But if you could manage to tell me what happened. Maybe start a few minutes before the collision.'

The trucker nodded and smiled. His upper lip bulged around the snus and Stella wondered whether the nicotine was calming him.

'I'm on my way home, right? The road's clear. Nothing in sight in either direction. The ghost road, that's what we call it. Then this guy with wings just runs out in front of me. I hit him and there's blood and feathers everywhere. I slam on the anchors and get the rig safely to a stop. I get out, go and check, but he's dead. Obviously. Then I call your lot.'

Stella made a note. Looked at the trucker.

'Where did he come from?'

'I told you. Out of nowhere!'

'Well, he must've come from somewhere, mustn't he? I mean, if he was standing in the carriageway, you'd have seen him in time and you could have stopped before you hit him.'

There it was again. A sharpness in her tone and an urge to slap him. What was he hiding?

'In the sunflowers, I guess.'

'You guess? Didn't you see him?'

'Yeah, I saw him. He was in the sunflowers then he just launched himself out in front of me.'

Stella looked back at the pair of traffic officers measuring the black rubber skid marks tailing back up the motorway from the rear of the truck.

'Can I ask how fast you were going, Ted? When you hit the man?'

'What, I'm under suspicion now? Is that it? Well, for the record,' he said, as his eyes dropped to her notebook, 'I was doing no more than seventy, maybe even less. Well under the limit for a heavy truck.'

'I'm sure you were, Ted, and I'm not accusing you of anything. Just trying to build a picture of the dead man's last moments. Did my colleague from the traffic division ask for your phone?'

'Yeah. First thing he did.'

'Let's go back to the man. What sort of state was he in as he ran out in front of you?'

Ted's reply was in two parts, both of which confirmed her fears. The first part was an eloquent expression, eyebrows raised, mouth dropping open. The second was verbal.

'What state do you *think* he was in? I mean, he wasn't looking very happy, if that's what you mean.'

17

Stella was tiring of the trucker's mix of belligerence, self-pity and sarcasm.

'Ted, just so we're clear, you just killed a man while driving your truck. So, no, I don't suppose he was happy about it. But you could be a lot more helpful if you'd just drop the attitude and answer my questions, OK?'

Ted folded his brawny arms across his chest, so that they rested on his belly. He shot Stella a belligerent look.

'One, you're supposed to say he was "in collision with" – that's how we do things here. Unless you can prove I set out to kill him, it was a collision. I didn't "hit" anyone. Second, he looked scared. No, not scared. He looked terrified. I mean, frightened out of his damn mind. He's stark naked and he just ran out in front of me, what do you expect he looked like?'

'All right, Ted, thank you. That's all for now. We'll be in touch if we need to ask you any more questions.'

Free of the truculent trucker, Stella made her way over to the traffic cop's car. He looked up from his ruggedised laptop and smiled.

'Not often we get the homicide squad out here,' he said. 'Mind you, after seeing that, I can see why they sent for you.'

'Because of my incisive mind and stratospheric investigative skills, you mean?'

'Yeah, and because they call you—' He grinned.

She smiled down at him. 'Yeah, yeah, I know what they call me. So, have you checked the driver's phone?'

He nodded. 'First thing I did. Nine times out of ten when a truck's involved in a collision, it turns out he was texting or gaming or checking his social media. This guy was old school. He was making a call.'

'Who to?'

'Someone called Inga. I'm guessing wife or girlfriend.'

Stella squatted so they were eye to eye. 'What's your take on it? I saw your guys measuring the skidmarks.'

He rubbed his nose.

'The way I see it, he's on the phone, not looking at the road ahead. The birdman comes out of the sunflowers, staggers into the carriageway, Ted looks up, sees him but it's way too late. He slams the brakes on but hits him anyway. The guy's killed outright, probably. Thrown backwards, lands in the road with the truck bearing down on him. Lucky for us, well, you, really, the truck stops before it catches up with him. Otherwise you'd be scraping strawberry jam into a bucket and good luck autopsying that over at RMV.'

RMV was *Rättsmedicinalverket*. The National Board of Forensic Medicine. Which reminded Stella. Henrik Brodin should be here soon. She really wanted to speak to the forensic medicine doctor. Henrik was only in his thirties, but his balding head and horn-rimmed glasses gave him the appearance of an older man.

'Where do you think he came from?'

'He'd just delivered a load up in Jamtland.'

'Not the trucker, the victim. It's odd, don't you think. He must have been in so much pain.'

'Well, the nearest building's probably the Dollarstore on the east side of the road. It's only about three hundred metres away. But you've got industrial estates and more big-box stores all over the place here. It's not exactly remote.'

Stella thanked him and went to see what was inside the tent in the field of sunflowers. The CSIs had finished their work and the tent was hers.

She stared at the bloody object on the ground.

Nothing could have offered a starker contrast to the cheerful blooms nodding their heads in the sunshine all around it. A gigantic black wing was attached to the upper part of a human arm, which had clearly been ripped out of the shoulder joint.

Shaking her head and wondering who had done this and why, she went to find Jonna.

She stopped off to accept the offer of a coffee from a flask one of the traffic officers was offering round. As she sipped, and stared at the stationary cars on the other side of the E18, she let her eyes drift out of focus.

What *were* they looking at? More than an RTA. Less than a homicide. In fact, come to that, which statute had been flouted here? She knew her way around the Swedish penal code, but this was a new one on her.

In 2018, the British Court of Appeal had ruled that body modification such as tongue splitting fell foul of the law on assault, regardless of whether consent had been given. Stella was fairly sure their lordships would consider stitching a bird's wings onto a human being's arms to be within the realm of body modification.

Jonna came up to her.

'Ready to head back?'

'Yep. Nothing we can do for now. We need an ID on the victim and then we can track down next of kin.'

On the drive back to Stockholm centre, Jonna asked Stella the question that had been revolving around her head since she'd first clapped eyes on the body.

'What the fuck was that, Stella?'

'Honestly? I have no idea.'

'Is it even a homicide?'

'That's a very good question. I don't think it is. According to Ted the trucker, the guy was alive when he hit him.' Stella frowned. 'Sorry, when he was "in collision with him". So cause of death's going to be something like massive blunt force trauma caused by a forty-tonne Scania eighteen-wheeler.'

'But it's more than just an accident, right?'

'Exactly. I think we're looking at something under Part Two, Section 6. I'd be going for exceptionally gross assault.'

'The criterion for that being?'

Stella had memorised the Swedish Criminal Code's section on offences at the same time as she was doing the Foreign Office's intensive Swedish course. No point having the lingo if you got tripped up on the jargon was how she saw it. She tested Jonna now.

'You be the perpetrator.'

'OK. I'm a twisted psycho who gets off on making hybrid birdmen. I blame my parents. They never showed me enough love.'

Jonna added a throaty cackle for good measure.

'Very good,' Stella said, grinning guiltily. 'Did you inflict severe bodily injury?'

'I'd say so, yes.'

'Was the act life-threatening?'

'Another yes.'

'Sure about that? The injury didn't cause the trucker to hit Birdman, did it?'

'But he must have been bleeding heavily, no?'

'I don't know. We'll have to wait for the autopsy. Next question, did you display particular ruthlessness or brutality?'

'Definitely.'

'Right, so we've passed the threshold for a charge of gross assault. Let's move on,' Stella said, finding it helpful to work in this way with Jonna. 'Was the bodily injury permanent?'

'Yes.'

'Did you cause exceptional suffering?'

'I think I did. Even if he'd survived, I mean, Christ, Stella,' Jonna exclaimed, her voice suddenly shaky, 'he had his arms removed and replaced with wings.'

'Which leads us to the final question, taking the charge up from gross assault to exceptionally gross assault.' Stella decided to answer for Jonna, suddenly finding their role-playing in bad taste. 'Did the perpetrator display *exceptional* rather than just *particular* ruthlessness? Yes, the sadistic bastard did.'

'Do you think it was a one-off?'

Stella glanced across at Jonna, catching the tightness around her eyes, before returning her gaze to the road ahead. Because that was the big question, wasn't it?

If it was a unique event, then the motive could be some warped idea of vengeance and the victim's identity would probably yield the perpetrator's. There was also the outside chance that the victim really was some sort of extreme body modification enthusiast. If he were, then she'd bet on his having a diagnosed mental illness, for which he might have stopped taking his meds. Maybe he'd approached an unscrupulous practitioner to turn him into a bird.

If.

Could be.

Probably.

Outside chance.

Might.

Maybe.

So many assumptions. So many unlikely events that would have to occur in a precise sequence for this to be true.

Yes, those were both possibilities. But another option

was screaming to be heard. Something with cold, dead eyes and a gaping void where its sense of empathy ought to be. Something for which remorse was as foreign a concept as flight to an alligator.

She sighed deeply. Hoping the truth lay within the realms of the normal. Of options one and two. Yet suspecting, knowing, if she was honest, that the reality was that option three would claim their time and energy over the coming weeks, possibly months.

Jonna deserved an answer.

And then, as Stella tried out a number of phrases that might reassure her assistant without offering false hope, a quiet voice spoke up from somewhere deep in her psyche. A voice she'd forgotten existed except in the occasional nightmare.

If this is a one-off, babe, then I'm the Queen of Sweden.

A cold shudder rippled across Stella's rib cage before scuttling, like a newly-hatched brood of spiders, down into the pit of her stomach.

The real Queen of Weirdness had spoken.

4

Mikael was not supposed to escape.

He nearly ruined everything. Lucky for me, he found his way onto the E18.

Next time I will have to use a larger dose of ketamine. I need them alive for their transformation, but I still want to kill them afterwards. Me. Not some overweight trucker.

Still, Stella saw my work. So we're connected.

I know she doesn't think of me as an integral part of her life. I'm little more than a stranger to her at the moment. But that will change. I'll help her catch the killer. And when I do, she'll recognise the truth. We are meant to be together.

I could make a direct approach, of course I could. But what if she falls back on the boring official rules of her job, rather than embracing her destiny, and the role I have created for her? The role that will transform _her?_

To be quite frank, I do not handle rejection as well as I used to. Let us just say that, as an adult, I have become a little less tolerant of being abused than I used to be.

Look, all I mean to say is that when I reveal myself to Stella, *she must accept me for who I am. I would find it hard to entertain any other answer but a wholehearted 'yes'.*

I shouldn't depress myself with such negative thoughts. Of course she will accept me! And she will acknowledge my love. Acknowledge, and reciprocate. Anything else would simply be – I don't want to sound like one of those deluded psychopaths – but it would be rude.

And Stella is not rude. Look how she has adapted to life in her new home. How she learned the language. The customs. Even the whole fika thing. All that coffee and cake and she retains an enviable figure. When we are together, we can go cross-country skiing. That way she can eat as much cake as she wants without putting on so much as a gram of surplus weight.

I will do anything to make her want me.

Desire me.

Love me.

Anything.

5

Stella dropped Jonna off back at HQ and headed straight home, pleading a headache. She parked outside her block, a modern apartment building on Mariebergsgatan clad in salmon-pink and buttercup-yellow panels. Normally they cheered her up even on the darkest of days, but today they looked sickly, nauseating.

As soon as she was inside her flat, with the door locked behind her, she ran for the bedroom and stripped off her clothes. Her vest and knickers were soaked in sweat and she was trembling as she peeled them off and lay back on her bed. She drew in a breath and then, suddenly fearful she might start screaming, let it out again in a long, slow groan.

The voice in the car was Other Stella's. But it couldn't be. Could it? That side of her character had been erased, and with good reason. Back when Stella was still pursuing bloody vengeance against the people who'd murdered Richard and Lola, Other Stella had gradually assumed control. Stella had felt powerless to stop her continuing to expand the list of targets.

'No,' she said aloud. 'She's gone. She's dead. There's only me.'

She closed her eyes, half-expecting to hear that sardonic voice contradicting her. Mercifully, she heard nothing but the blood pulsing in her ears. Stress, then. The horrific scene on the E18 had overloaded her emotional circuitry. Her mind had conjured up a fleeting memory of the dark aspect of her personality that she could all too easily imagine perpetrating such an assault on another human being.

She resolved to see one of the SPA's psychology team. Just for a check-up.

Feeling better about the aural hallucination she'd experienced, she dressed in her running gear and was out on the street ten minutes later, heading down to the waterside running track.

After twenty minutes, she was in the zone, almost flying over the tarmac as she added mile after mile to the distance under her feet. Her mind entered the state of clarity she used to break through blockages in the most intractable cases.

Instead of having Jonna play the perpetrator, she simply conjured up a spectral figure with whom she could talk.

— Did he *ask* you to do this?

— *He* needed *me to do it.*

— Don't avoid my questions.

— *You mean was he one of those freaks with split tongues or horns growing out of their foreheads?*

— Yes.

— *No. It was my decision.*

— Did you mean for him to survive it?

— *It's hard to say. He had to die, I can tell you that.*

— Why wings?

— That's for me to know and you to find out.

Stella shook her head free of her new imaginary friend. What she needed right now was hard evidence and maybe some psychological insight. In fact, scratch that. What she really needed was a drink.

As it turned out, the occasion was about to present itself. In a way that would solve two problems at once.

Turning the corner from Friskvårdsvägen into her own street, she saw a man loitering, no other word for it, outside her building. His head was bent over his phone. The dark curly hair, streaked with grey, looked familiar. There was something about the stance, too, that kindled a mixture of surprise, excitement and anxiety in her chest.

As she jogged closer, her pulse, already bustling along at well above its resting rate, leaped skywards. Had he sensed her approach? The vibration through the pavement, or just possibly through the air? At any rate, he looked up, turned his head to the left and their eyes locked.

He smiled, and raised a hand, a little hesitantly.

She stopped a little way away from him, just to check it was really him.

'Jamie! What the fuck?'

'Nice to see you, too, Stel,' he said, the smile faltering but still clinging on by its fingernails.

She smiled. 'Sorry. What I meant to say was, 'Oh my God, Jamie! Look at you! What are you doing here?'

'Can I get a hug, then I'll tell you?'

Stella looked at him. She'd forgotten, since moving to Sweden, just how good-looking her former boyfriend was. He was in rugged good shape and if he had a few more silver hairs among the black, they only added to his charm.

She moved closer and hugged him quickly.

As she drew back, he held up a plastic carrier bag that clinked promisingly. 'I brought some wine. Your favourite. Sancerre. Can we—'

'Oh God, sorry, yes of course. Come in, come in.'

She fumbled her keys out of the little teal leather wallet zipped into a pouch in her running vest and immediately dropped them. Finally, after a little more of this rigmarole, she managed to get the door open.

Inside her flat, she held Jamie at arm's length. 'I want to hear all your news, but I think I should take a quick shower first. Open the wine, OK? There's olives in the fridge and breadsticks in the cupboard to the left of the cooker. The balcony's nice this time of year.'

Jamie laughed. 'Leave it to me. Just don't be too long. God, I've missed you.'

After showering, Stella slipped into her bedroom and closed the door.

'Now what?' she asked her reflection in the wardrobe mirror and then experienced a frisson of nervous energy, half-expecting the reflection to answer back of her own accord.

Nothing happened. Stella stood there, wrapped in a fluffy white bath towel, feeling reassured. Two people from her past visiting her in Mariebergsgatan on the same day would have been too much to cope with.

Wanting to be back with Jamie as soon as she could, but seized with doubts about what to put on, she pulled open her underwear drawer. Plain and practical from Bread & Boxers? Or something a little more feminine from Sofía Luzón? She frowned. What did it matter? It wasn't as if Jamie would be seeing it.

Her hand hovered above a rolled pair of plain white knickers and a simple cotton bralette. Then, as if it had a mind of its own, it moved leftwards and picked out a cream lace bra and matching briefs. Not tarty, not at all, but it would make her feel good.

She slipped into her favourite Levi's 501s, faded, and starting to fray at the hems, and a white T-shirt from Arket. Dragged a brush through her hair and caught it up in a ponytail with a scrunchie, applied a dash of red lippy and some mascara and consulted her reflection a second time. She nodded.

'You'll do,' she mouthed, then winked at herself.

With several dozen butterflies fluttering in the pit of her stomach, she went to find Jamie. He'd taken olives and breadsticks out onto the balcony, along with the bottle of Sancerre, from which he'd poured two glasses. Less than half-full. Not trying to get her pissed, then. But this was a decent bottle, and Jamie had always loved to show off about his wine knowledge.

He turned towards her and smiled. 'Wow!'

Trying not to deconstruct the scene in front of her with a detective's eye, she took the glass he was holding out.

'What are we drinking to?' she asked.

'How about second chances?'

That felt right. The flying insects in her belly quieted.

'To second chances,' she said.

They clinked glasses and drank. The wine delicious. Dry, tasting of apples and sunshine. She popped a green olive stuffed with an anchovy into her mouth.

'You look amazing,' he said. 'I mean, really good.'

'Thank you. You've scrubbed up pretty well yourself.'

'Not sure I have after my journey, but I'll take that.'

'So?'

'So, what?' Jamie replied, grinning.

'Do I need to contact my colleagues in the anti-stalking team? I mean you're a long way from London and, as far as I remember, we hadn't made a plan to meet.'

She heard the edge in her reply and reproached herself for it immediately. Jamie was a lovely man, trying, clearly, to make amends for the way they'd left things the last time they'd been together.

'Sorry, Jamie, that came out all wrong. I just meant, it's lovely to see you,' she said, taking another, longer sip of her wine and feeling the alcohol begin to work its magic on her. 'I'm a bit on edge, that's all. Been a bit of a weird day.'

'Which I would love to hear about. But you're right. I do owe you an explanation.' He took a pull on his own wine, half-emptying the glass. Was he nervous? He didn't look it. He sighed. 'Letting things end like they did between us was the worst thing I ever did.'

'You mean, after I told you I'd killed seventeen people and you had trouble coping? It seems pretty reasonable to me.'

Jamie poured more wine, topping up both their glasses.

'I mean, when you told me you were moving out here and I just, I don't know,' he ran a hand over his face, 'let you.'

Stella raised her eyebrows. 'I'm not sure anyone "let" anyone else go anywhere.'

'Sorry, that was a bad choice of words. Christ, I'm making such a mess of this.'

Jamie looked so distressed, Stella suddenly felt a rush of emotions: part love, part desire, part an urgent need to end the tension between them.

She stood up.

'Come here.'

He complied, rounding the little steel table with its blue-and-white mosaic top and stood in front of her.

Stella put her glass down and wrapped her arms around him. She kissed him, gently, on the lips. Then with more pressure. She drew back and stared up into Jamie's dark-brown eyes. She kissed him again, and this time he responded. As he embraced her, she felt as though someone had just lifted a rucksack full of stones off her back halfway around a long run through the forest. She felt lighter, freer than she had for a long time.

'Well, I was not expecting that,' Jamie said when the kiss finally ended.

'Too much?'

'No! Not at all. I've dreamed of that moment ever since you left England. I just didn't know how to get back in touch with you.'

Stella smiled. 'Well, I suppose what with you being a psychiatrist, navigating the spectrum of human emotions must be, I don't know, unfamiliar territory?'

Jamie grinned. 'Guilty as charged, detective. Is that right? What's your official title over here?'

'You're addressing *Kriminalinspektör* Cole,' Stella said, standing to attention.

She knew the posture would push her chest out, just a little, so the lacy bra might become visible through the thin white cotton of her T-shirt. Not the subtlest of moves. But then, men weren't the subtlest of creatures. A frequent topic of conversation between Stella and Jonna whenever they went out drinking.

Jonna complained that having a relationship with another woman was twice as complicated as it was with a man. 'It's all nuances, Stella! Nuances, feelings and misunderstandings. With men it's,' she dropped into a

33

comically deep voice, 'uh, baby, like, I really love you. Now let's have sex.'

Stella smiled at the memory.

'What?' Jamie asked.

'Nothing. Are you hungry?'

'Starving. I haven't had anything to eat since lunchtime.'

In the kitchen, Stella manoeuvred Jamie towards a chrome barstool topped with a shiny red vinyl seat.

'Sit. You can watch me cook.'

Stella peeled a couple of garlic cloves and laid them on a wooden chopping board with a generous pinch of some sea salt.

'You didn't answer my question,' she said over her shoulder as she smashed the garlic with the flat of the blade and began mashing it into a gritty paste with the salt.

Jamie took a sip of his wine.

'What question?'

'What brings you to Sweden? A conference?'

'It's a long story.'

'I've got plenty of time. And I'm a good listener, remember?'

Wondering for one crazy moment whether Jamie was about to confess to being a murderer too, Stella began reducing a red onion to a pile of tiny, regular cubes.

'The job with the Institute of Forensic Psychiatry and Neuropharmacology didn't work out,' he said. 'I naïvely thought they'd share my vision of helping people recover from the severest forms of mental illness, but it was just bullshit to get me to sign on. Their board of directors was focused solely on the profit motive. I think I was really there to lend a little gloss of respectability.'

'Oh, Jamie, I'm sorry. What happened?' she asked, sniffing as the vapour from the onion hit her eyes.

'I had a massive row with my boss in her office. In full view of the rest of the team. I think it's fair to say my behaviour fell outside the norms of professionalism,' he said. 'Then I quit. We agreed that if I didn't push for any kind of severance pay, they'd not insist I worked out my notice. A clean break, you might say.'

'God, are you OK?'

'I had a rough couple of weeks, but then I realised, I have some money saved. Plus the money from my house. And I was only renting in London. I could get consulting work pretty easily, I'm sure.'

'You wouldn't consider going back into clinical work?'

'Maybe. I'm actually happy to be exploring my options. At least for a while. So, in answer to your question, I wanted to see you. A lot. I realised there was nothing stopping me, so I booked a flight and here I am.'

'Hang on. Where are you staying?'

Jamie laughed.

'Don't worry, I'm not pushing to stay here,' he said. 'I booked a nice Airbnb. An apartment overlooking the water.'

For a second, Stella's heart sank. She realised she'd been hoping Jamie had been seized with such a fit of impetuousness that he'd just got on a plane in the clothes he was wearing and that was it.

She could only think of one reason why.

Because she still loved him.

6

With the dinner things cleared away, Stella led Jamie to the sofa, a new piece of furniture purchased – where else? – from Ikea in the leafy northern suburb of Järfälla.

They sat at opposite ends, but turned in towards each other. As it was only a two-seater, the gap between them wasn't large. Perhaps the length of a kiss, if they chose. Stella tucked her feet under her and sipped her wine.

'It's good to see you, Jamie.'

'Me, too. I mean, yes, it's good to see you too.'

'We left things in a mess. I did, I mean. I'm sorry.'

He frowned. 'What happened? One day you were here then it was like you just vanished.'

Stella debated, briefly, how much to tell him about Gemma Dowding's threats. Was there a downside to total honesty? She'd already told him about her kill tally, after all, so what was she worrying about?

'When she was still the home secretary, Gemma Dowding sent for me,' she said. 'She told me, in no uncertain terms, she wanted me gone.'

'Why?'

'Because of what I know about Pro Patria Mori.'

'I thought that conspiracy was all wound up?'

'It is. But she still wanted an air-gap between her and it. She said I had to leave the country or Elle, Jason and the girls would be hurt,' Stella said. 'She arranged my permanent transfer to the SPA, sent me on a deep-immersion Swedish course at the Foreign Office, and here I am.'

When she finished speaking, Jamie said nothing. His eyebrows had drawn together, though, and his lips were set in a straight line. She could see the machinery whirring inside his skull, as he tried to process the second devastating story she'd told him in two years.

His lips parted as if he were about to speak. In the silence, the click was audible. He frowned, then drew in a sharp little breath, as if he'd stepped on a shard of glass in bare feet.

'Please tell me you're not going to kill her,' he said.

There was a pause, then they both burst out laughing. The absurdity of Jamie's question, yet its utter plausibility as a concern, meant they kept setting each other off.

'Because –' Jamie began, as another fit of hilarity convulsed him, ' – because, I really don't think I can see myself,' he paused, composed himself, 'spending the rest of my life with a woman who offed the PM.'

His voice dissolved into a manic giggle as he finished speaking.

Stella's laughter died in her throat.

'Pardon?'

Jamie sat up straighter and took a gulp of his wine.

'It's why I came here, Stel. I love you. I think I always loved you,' he said. 'I want to be with you. Forever. I can't bear the thought of losing you a second time. Please can we pick up where we left off?'

Stella put her glass down on the coffee table.

'Maybe where we left off isn't such a good place.' Jamie's face fell and she hurriedly continued. 'But I love you, too. So why don't we start afresh? Right here? Leave the past where it belongs.'

'In the past?'

'Exactly.'

He placed his wine glass next to hers, then shuffled closer until he could take her in his arms.

'Give us a kiss.'

'Oh, you big romantic.'

After a few minutes rediscovering just how good a kisser Jamie Hooke was, Stella pulled back.

'Time out. This is good, but I need a moment. I wasn't expecting my day to end like this.'

'But it's all right, isn't it? I mean, you're happy we're back together?'

'Yes, of course. But, like I said, it's been a weird one.'

'Par for the course for the Queen of Weirdness, I'd have thought.'

Stella's good humour evaporated like mist on water beneath the summer sun.

'How did you know my nickname?'

Jamie smiled. 'Relax, I swear you don't need to call the anti-stalking team. I called your station. I wanted to find out where you were. A very helpful officer let it slip. Said something like, "the queen always likes to go running after work". I asked her, "Queen? Of what?" And she told me. I hope you don't mind,' Jamie said with a half-smile. 'If it's strictly a cop-thing, a work name you keep for insiders, I totally understand. It's the same at Broadmoor. When I was working there, the inmates used

39

to call me Doctor Strange. Nobody else, not even the warders. Just them. It was a bonding thing.'

Stella's antennae stopped vibrating. She reproached herself. Here she was, in the throes of rekindling her relationship with the nicest man she'd ever met, apart from Richard, and she was putting on her *kriminalinspektör* hat. No. The clothing that mattered tonight was underneath her T-shirt and jeans. She thanked Sofia Luzón and took another little sip of wine.

'Weird, how?' Jamie asked. 'Your day, I mean.'

Stella sat straighter and resettled her right foot under her left thigh.

'Long story short, we got called out to an RTA this lunchtime. A truck hit a pedestrian.'

She paused, injecting some timing into her tale, wanting to shock Jamie, who probably thought he'd seen everything. Or at least heard everything.

'Okaay, so far, so not weird,' he said.

'Said pedestrian had wings where his arms should have been.'

Jamie frowned. 'That *is* weird. Pushed into a harness, you mean?'

She shook her head, then touched her left temple as the motion set off a moment's dizziness. She put her wine down.

'Not a harness. I mean, someone cut off his arms and replaced them with actual wings. Massive bird's wings, must have been seven or eight feet across.'

Stella was gratified to see Jamie's reaction. His eyes widened and he let his head drop back on his neck until it touched the back of the sofa.

'Well, that's a new one on me,' he said to the ceiling. 'Was he dead when the truck hit him?'

'Nope. He was shortly afterwards, though.'

'Not a homicide, then.'

Stella explained about the likely offence under Swedish law. Then asked the question that she'd so far failed to answer to her own satisfaction.

'What's going on, Jamie? I mean, what am I dealing with here?'

He looked at her, rubbing the back of his neck.

'What have we got here? Somebody who feels that human beings, as they are, fail to meet some idealised vision. They're not living up to his concept of what a perfect human would look like.'

'And once he's done it once, he's going to want to do it again, to make improvements.'

'*Absolut*, as your new colleagues would say.'

'Is he going to kill the next one, do you think?'

'Do you want him to?'

'No! Of course not. It's just, I feel somehow that the first guy was a mistake. Not creating him. But letting him escape. I mean, where was the showmanship aspect? Guys like this, they want people to see what they've done,' she said. 'I would have expected him to be displayed in the centre of Stockholm, somewhere everyone could get a good look.'

'That's a very good insight. We'll make a forensic psychiatrist of you yet.'

Stella raised her glass. 'Thanks, Doctor Strange, but I'll stick to policework, if it's all the same to you.'

'You know, as I'm a free agent at the moment, I could assist you on the case. I mean, if it would be helpful,' he added. 'I don't want to be pushy.'

Stella smiled. She'd been thinking along similar lines. There was just one problem.

'I'd love that. Problem is, our budget has been cut to the bone. Malin's just about OK with overtime for the uniformed cops, but outside consultants? Especially highly qualified British shrinks with top-level experience? Forget it.'

Jamie shook his head.

'Sorry, I should have made myself clear. I meant, I'd do it for nothing. I don't need the money and it would be good to get back into some kind of public service after my bruising experience in the private sector.'

'Really? You're not just saying that?'

'Honestly? My life has lacked a sense of purpose in recent months. I think working with you could go a long way to restoring it. If you'll have me, that is?'

'Oh, I'll have you, Mister Jamie Hooke,' Stella said. 'In fact, why don't you bring another bottle from the fridge and maybe we could take it through to my bedroom.'

Jamie passed a hand over his eyes and then gave Stella a look she found hard to read. Was he uncomfortable? Sad? Reluctant?

'There's nothing I'd like better, but I'm absolutely shattered. My day started earlier than it had any right to,' he said. 'Would you mind if I just went back to my place tonight? But I could come round tomorrow? Maybe we could drink that second bottle then?'

'Oh, OK. If you're tired, that's probably best,' Stella said, trying to hide her disappointment. 'Or, you could come next door anyway and we could just cuddle. I've missed you, too, Jamie.'

Too pathetic? Too needy? Where was her feisty persona that had half the cops over at Kungholmsgatan treating her like some sort of avenging angel and the other half desperate to secure a place on her team?

'Let's have a cuddle right here,' Jamie answered. 'But

then I should be going. I've got a few things to clear up back in England. Online,' he added.

And then, seemingly only a few minutes after he'd popped up outside her building's entrance like the ghost of relationships past, Jamie was gone, leaving a faint smell of his aftershave and some indefinable smell Stella thought of as 'essence of Jamie'.

'I must be losing my touch,' she said to the empty apartment.

As she cleared up from dinner, she mulled over the things Jamie had said about the person who had transformed another human being into that grotesque hybrid creature.

If the dead man had failed to live up to some idealised concept of a human being, what was the desired end result? It was all about the wings: you didn't need to be a genius to see that. Even the most junior member of her squad would draw that conclusion.

She took the remains of her wine out onto the balcony and sat there, watching the sun go down, trying not to imagine what it would feel like to have her arms cut off while alive and replaced with wings.

She made a list of actions for the morning.

ID the dead man.

ID the species of bird.

Find out where the wings came from.

Check local CCTV.

Contact Henrik Brodin about getting the autopsy done.

Talk to Signe Arrhenius about forensics at the scene.

Because while this specific incident might not meet the criteria for homicide, if Jamie was correct – and her copper's instincts said he was – there would be another birdman flying before too long.

7

Stella has an assistant.

They're working the case together. But now I'm on her team, too, what fun we'll have.

I can provide first-hand insights into the behaviour and thought processes of psychopaths. It will help her close in on the perpetrator of these heinous crimes.

Crimes plural? Yes, that's right.

You see, Mikael was merely the first in this series.

I'm sure at this point, Stella's hoping it's a singularity. A one-off. Some fucked-up weirdo who just needed to get it out of his system.

But I bet, deep down, where our darkest desires fester, far away from the light, like those gross deep-sea fish, all transparent teeth and bulgy glass-ball eyes, she's praying it's not.

And good girls always get their prayers answered.

I know what they call her. It's not a public nickname. But I found out ages ago.

I just made a couple of calls. Put on the charm. Mentioned I'd soon be working with Stella and wanted to try to fit in.

Some helpful, over-sharing halfwit in Traffic told me.

The Queen of Weirdness.

So, what does a member of the royal family want more than anything else? Justification.

That's what I'm giving her. I will help her in the greatest case of her career, and she'll show appropriate gratitude at the correct moment.

8

Sara Marksson stood up, her pulse fluttery, feeling light-headed, as she always did before speaking in front of a group. Today was especially difficult. The charity's charismatic frontman, a famous writer and even more famous as a recovering addict, had dropped in to lead the session.

'Hi, everyone, my name is Sara, and I am an addict.'

'Hi, Sara,' the other addicts chorused, under Sven-Arne Jonsson's benevolent smile.

'I've been clean and sober now for nine months and three days. But,' she dashed away a tear that popped out from the duct in the corner of her left eye like a bullet from a gun, 'it's so hard. I feel like I've failed. As a mom, as a wife, as a human being. Every day, I wish I could go down to the river, under the bridge, find my dealer and score.'

Sara sat back down heavily, as though she weighed twice her fifty-seven point five kilos.

Her killer-to-be led the applause before leaning

forwards and speaking softly, as if the comforting words were meant just for her.

'We all feel like failures some of the time, Sara. Just take it one day at a time. You'll soon feel totally different. You could even say transformed.'

Sara smiled. It was good that people here were so unjudgy. She felt a renewed sense of optimism. Sadly it would prove insufficient defence against the insult that would befall her within hours.

After the meeting, once they'd drunk the coffee – good, strong – and eaten the supermarket biscuits – oversweet, stale – the person for whom the media would shortly be scrambling to find a catchy nickname approached Sara as she was about to leave.

'Sara?'

'Oh, hi.'

'I was wondering, would you like to get a quick bite to eat? There's a nice cafe round the corner. Vegan. We could talk.'

Sara smiled. 'Sure! I'd love that. Thanks for what you said earlier. It really helped.'

'I've been where you are. I know it's hard.'

'Did you mean it? That I'd be transformed?'

'I guarantee it.'

9

Natalie Eriksson was on earlies all week.

One of the other emergency room nurses had come down with a bug, and the ward sister had swapped all their shifts around. Eyes crusty with sleep, she sipped from the aluminium mug of coffee before slotting it back into the cup-holder.

The only consolation was the empty roads. Later in the day, Sjättenovembervägen would be choked with traffic. As she approached the roundabout where she would take the exit onto Götalandsvägen, she slowed, flicked on her turn signal and changed down into second gear. As she did so, the seat belt cut into her belly. She frowned as she remembered the extra portion of takeaway she'd helped herself to the previous evening.

'Not sure how that fits with your diet, hon,' Karl had said.

He was smiling though. Karl liked her body. Too much, she sometimes thought. He was no help whenever she decided she needed to lose a few kilos.

She looked across the rounded hump of grass

surrounded by silver-grey granite setts to her exit onto Älvsjövägen, and frowned. What the hell was that?

Dead-centre on the roundabout, amidst three spindly birches, a naked woman was standing with her arms outstretched. Only that was wrong, wasn't it? Because human beings' arms were basically long, slender limbs ending in hands.

The naked woman's arms weren't arms at all.

They were wings.

While these thoughts were chasing each other around Natalie's sleep-numbed brain, her body was executing the movements necessary to pilot her five-year-old VW Lupo onto the roundabout and flick on the turn signal for her exit. Muscle memory.

Which was just as well, because Natalie's eyes were no longer on the road. As her own arms turned the wheel, her eyes were locked onto the face of the winged woman.

What was she then? An artist? One of those street performers who imitated statues in the Old Town? But why out here? This was hardly tourist-land. Or anywhere an artist could reasonably hope to get an audience.

Her front wheel hit the edge of the granite kerb and the car jolted up onto the circular surround. She was heading straight towards the woman.

With a cry of alarm, Natalie fought to control the little car and managed to make it off the roundabout before pulling onto a slip road bordered by shops and takeaways. She killed the ignition with the car still in gear and opened the door to leap out, even as the Lupo jerked backwards on its springs.

Looking both ways, even though she was still the only car on the road, she darted across the tarmac and onto the grass.

Was the woman even real?

Yes. She was definitely human. Not a mannequin. Natalie had seen enough traumatised human flesh to know the real thing when she saw it.

Nearing the woman, she could see that she had been wired onto a T-shaped wooden framework that had been erected between two of the birches.

Her eyes were closed. Natalie looked in horror at the huge wings that were, she could now see, crudely stitched onto the stumps of the woman's arms.

'Hello!' Natalie shouted into her face. 'Hello! Can you hear me?'

She lifted the right eyelid. The edge of a pale-blue iris was visible, just peeping out from under the top lid.

'Christ, what happened to you?' Natalie asked the woman's impassive face.

She pushed two fingers into the soft place under the jaw, noticing as she did so a crust of black blood blocking the left nostril.

No pulse. Natalie got her phone out and hit 122.

'Hello, what is the nature of your emergency, please?'

'I have a dead woman on the roundabout at the junction of Sjättenovembervägen, Älvsjövägen and Götalandsvägen in Årsta.'

'Are you sure she is dead?'

'I'm an ER nurse. She has no pulse and somebody has cut her arms off and put wings on instead.'

'Can you repeat that, please?'

Natalie did as she was asked, then supplied her number to the sceptical-sounding operator, who told her she should wait at the scene. Police and paramedics would be there shortly.

* * *

Stella was fast asleep when the unusual circumstances of the call pushed it through several departments and ranks of police officer, before somebody had the wit to call her.

She'd programmed a special ring-tone for despatch into her phone. So when the cave where she was talking to a lioness with her sister-in-law's face suddenly boomed with a discordant jangle, she was awake and fully alert in seconds.

'This is Stella. What's happened?' she asked, realising with a brief flash of pleasure that she spoke Swedish even on being brutally summoned from a dream by work.

'A member of the public discovered a body in Årsta,' the guy on despatch said. 'She's got wings. Like—'

' – the guy out at Vällingby. Can you text me the location, please.' Her phone beeped a few seconds later. 'Got it, thanks. Have you alerted Forensics and the RMV?'

'They're on their way.'

Five minutes later, having washed her face, cleaned her teeth and dragged on a T-shirt and a pair of jeans, Stella was out the door and heading down to the parking garage. Ten minutes after that, she was pulling up on the approach to the roundabout in Årsta.

Uniformed officers had blocked off all roads, and the backed-up traffic was already building, despite the early hour. She climbed out, unzipped her murder bag and, once she was kitted out in her Tyvek forensics suit, strode from her car across the road and onto the roundabout. Showing her badge to the officer logging entries and exits from the crime scene, she ducked under the tape and walked over to the body.

No sign of the CSI van yet. Or of Henrik Brodin. Well then, she'd just have to make a start on her own.

She stood face-to-face with the dead woman. As she did so, she made a mental adjustment, labelling her, 'the second victim'. A single dead body with wings instead of arms could, just, be considered a one-off in the section of case files reserved for the truly weird. But two constituted a pattern. A pattern that pointed in one direction, and one direction only. A serial killer. A particularly demented serial killer. Unlike the official definition, Stella didn't require a third victim.

She called Jonna.

'Hey, Stella, what's up?'

'I need you.'

'Where?'

Stella gave her the location and ended the call.

She walked around the body. Though decay started at the point of death, there was no smell. The flesh looked healthy, with none of the frost-damage that might indicate freezing followed by thawing. So she had been murdered recently. Within the last twelve hours, Stella was willing to guess.

The joins between avian and human body parts resembled those from the scene out on the E18. Crude black sutures and a crusty white residue that looked like dried superglue.

The killer had used some kind of garden wire, bare greyish metal, to secure the woman's outstretched form onto a wooden T. Two lengths of brand-new softwood timber, pine most likely, bolted together and plunged into the soft earth. More wire extended left and right from the crosspiece to loop round the trunks of two birch trees.

Was it supposed to be a crucifixion? Were they dealing with a religious nutcase? Or, what had Jamie once told her was the medically correct parlance? Yes, 'a person suffering from religious delusions within a psychotic framework'.

Stella thought that might just about cover it.

The woman was youngish. Early thirties, anyway. Slender build, small breasts with pale-pink nipples and a flat belly free of stretch marks. Hopefully not a mother. Apart from the grotesque mutilation her killer had inflicted on her, she was in perfect shape. Although, looking closer, the skin on her face was marked with the scars of old sores of some kind, or maybe adult acne. One for Henrik. She made a note to ask him about them.

She turned away from the body, scanning the apartment blocks and shops that ringed the road junction. Had anyone seen anything? She couldn't see any CCTV cameras but maybe one of the residents was an insomniac and had been looking out at the time the killer had been working. She snorted. Yeah, right. Because that was how *all* major crimes got solved. A reliable, drug-and-alcohol-free witness with 20/20 vision and an eidetic memory.

She saw Jonna climbing out of her silver Ford Focus. She raised her hand to wave to Stella, then put on a crime scene suit. Suitably dressed now, she hurried across the road to join her inside the cordon.

As she took in the bizarre corpse, Jonna employed a particularly Swedish oath that summed up the sight confronting them both.

'The Devil in Hell! He's done it again.'

'Yep. And this time there's no doubt about whether he meant her to die.'

'This is a serial killer.'

'You're on fire this morning.'

'Sorry.'

'No, no. It's me. Just a shit way to start the day, that's all,' Stella said. 'It's not even six o'clock yet, I haven't had my first coffee of the day, and we've got two corpses with wings where their arms should be.'

'What do you want me to do?'

'Can you get a door-to-door started, please? Usual questions. Anyone acting suspiciously in the neighbourhood recently, especially casing the roundabout. And if anyone saw anything last night, bring them in to the station and buy them a nice coffee and a cake.'

Jonna nodded. 'You got it.'

Stella turned at the sound of a noisy diesel engine. A white van marked with the three crowns logo of the National Forensic Centre had joined the ragtag caravan of vehicles transforming the roundabout into a makeshift police car park.

A trio of forensics specialists climbed out and donned protective gear. Stella left them to it. She returned to her car and stripped off the Tyvek suit, inside which she was sweating, despite the early hour.

She called Henrik Brodin. He was five minutes away.

Stella sat behind the wheel of her car. She wanted Henrik to pronounce the woman officially dead as quickly as possible for two reasons. Even though it was still early morning, pedestrians and those cars who had made it as far as the blocked-off road junction were already capturing the scene on their mobiles. And judging from the azure sky, it was going to be another hot day. She wanted the dead woman on ice well before the heat accelerated the process of putrefaction.

While she waited for the pathologist, she turned her thoughts to the two linked crimes. What did the wings signify? Two avenues of enquiry presented themselves without the need for any creative thinking.

Birds.

Angels.

Was that it? Or could she dredge her mind for other references? People with wings…

Where had she seen that image, whether as disturbingly rendered as the woman on the roundabout or not?

Everyone dreamed of flying from time to time. She herself had had one only recently, levitating in front of the whole department and demonstrating how she could hover over crime scenes to get a literal bird's eye view.

She pulled out her notebook and jotted down the first three ideas.

Something was knocking from her subconscious mind. An image of a man with wings soaring into a blue sky, a beatific smile on his face. Below him, raising a finger in warning, an older man, similarly outfitted.

Of course! The myth of Icarus. The voice of her history teacher floated down to her through the years. *As I'm sure you remember from your summer reading, ladies and gentlemen, master-craftsman Daedalus fashioned wings from wax and feathers, so he and his son could escape Crete. Ignoring his father's warnings, Icarus flew too close to the sun. The wax in his wings melted and he fell into the sea and drowned.*

She added a fourth line to the list.

Birds.

Angels.

Flying dreams.

Icarus.

What else? She tapped her temples with the pads of her index and middle fingers as if she could dislodge shy thoughts from the dark recesses of her mind.

Imprecise images of winged woman sculptures swam in and out of focus. She was sure she'd seen at least one in the National Museum, that classical pink-stone hall of culture on *Södra Blasieholmshamnen*.

She added a fifth item to her list.

Winged sculpture.

She closed her eyes. Figuring out what went on in the twisted corridors of the psychopathic mind presented her with the most testing challenges as a homicide detective. Even though the places it forced her to visit were the most unpleasant, deviant locations in the human psyche, she always felt a guilty thrill as she arrived at the answer. The key to the murderer's motivations that would help her catch them.

She stared through the windscreen. Thankfully, the CSIs had erected a popup white tent around the grotesque tableau in the centre of the roundabout.

'Why do you do it?' she asked the car's empty cabin.

She closed her eyes and repeated her question.

'Why do you give them wings?'

She adopted a deeper, gruffer voice than her own and answered.

'Because I want them to fly.'

'Why?' Stella asked.

'Because *I* can't,' the psychopath said.

She shook her head. 'Get in a plane. Then you can fly.'

'It's not the same, and you know it. Babe,' she added in a deep growl.

A sharp rap on the glass startled her and she swore as her eyes flew open.

Henrik Brodin was leaning down and peering in at her. He was smiling and poking down on an imaginary button. Stella dropped the window glass.

'Morning, Henrik. Sorry, I was miles away.'

'Morning, Stella. I hear we have another flying man on our hands.'

'She's a flying woman, actually. Although she's decidedly earthbound. I'd like to get her out of there as soon as possible, please.'

'Before she starts to cook, yes?'

'Yes.'

'I'll need to take some photos and run a couple of quick tests but then, yes, I'll pronounce life extinct and we can get her over to the morgue.' He paused. 'Are you feeling all right? You look pale.'

'No breakfast.'

He smiled. 'Ah. Well, get some coffee and crispbread and call me when you're ready. I assume you'd like to observe the autopsy?'

'Please.'

'I have the results of the first autopsy, by the way. Maybe we could discuss them afterwards. See where the points of similarity and difference are.'

'It's a date,' she said with a half-smile.

She twisted the key in the ignition and turned the car around. What she needed to do next was get the team together and up to speed.

10

Sven-Arne Jonsson stood in front of the full-length mirror in his bedroom.

He had to admit it, he looked good. No. He chided himself. Better than good.

'You look fantastic!' he told his reflection, winking.

Especially given that five years earlier he had been a junkie. A washed-up, washed-out writer of critically ignored but massively popular thrillers that had gained him a measure of youthful fame. Then alcohol, pills and cocaine had sunk their claws into him and dragged him, not even screaming, down into the abyss of addiction.

The money helped. He could afford better-quality drugs.

The coke, for example.

It was cut, of course it was. But with inert white powders whose job was to stretch the coke, and thereby the dealer's profits, but not to poison the client. No rat poison or washing powder for Sven-Arne Jonsson, thank you very much.

His trajectory, though fresh to Sven-Arne, was all-too-familiar to observers of the celebrity circuit. The fall had taken a scant nine months. From darling of the celebrity party circuit to prey for the sub-group of paparazzi who specialised in capturing their subjects toppling, drunk and red-faced, from nightclubs.

And worse.

An arrest for violent behaviour. Accusations of spousal abuse. A very public online lynching by a Twitter mob. And, finally, the destination for all those who could afford it. A stint in Sweden's premier rehab facility for those with deep-enough pockets.

During his time at Saint Ingrid's, he had undergone not just a chemical detox, but a spiritual conversion too. Not to God. Not as such. Sven-Arne had been a vocal atheist when clean and sober, and had not changed his views since. But he had come to realise that his mission – his life's purpose – lay, not in purveying cheap thrills to his readers, but in salvation to his fellow addicts.

That, at least, was the story.

He emerged to a clatter of whirring digital shutters and fit-inducing electronic flashes (because who left Saint Ingrid's without making sure their agent had tipped off the media?) to announce in an apparently impromptu press conference that his writing days were behind him.

'From now on, I dedicate my life to helping addicts overcome their demons and transform themselves, as I have, into our better angels.'

One or two of the more cerebral journalists who wrote up this extraordinary conversion on the road to Damascus weighed in with the opinion that perhaps this die-hard non-believer had been affected by the eponymous saint's views after all.

In fact, Sven-Arne had lifted the final three-word phrase from Abraham Lincoln's first inaugural address.

A detail that either passed them by or was felt not sufficiently interesting to be worth mentioning.

Within a year, Sven-Arne was the charismatic leader of a new anti-addiction programme called 'Ingrid's Way'. It helped that many of his former acquaintances had started attending the first group he set up, in Stockholm.

The resultant buzz on social media ensured that the mainstream media climbed aboard the bandwagon and provided Sven-Arne with all the free advertising he needed. He didn't need to take a salary. His book sales, already healthy, rocketed upwards like a space probe, propelled by his newfound status as a wellness guru.

Occasional sniping from older, more established addiction charities, especially those offering some sort of twelve-step programme, only served to raise Sven-Arne's profile still higher. His growing band of devoted followers, who called themselves, apparently without irony, Disciples of Ingrid, swung into action in his defence every time.

With groups springing up all over the country, Sven-Arne devoted the greater part of his time to dropping in and leading meetings, offering personal testimony, and counselling.

Media interviews, of course. Chat shows. Even the odd appearance on *Aktuellt*, the nightly news show, where the fawning interviewer would send lowballs his way about the effects of drugs on Swedish society.

He'd recently set up a private detox clinic. It was doing spectacularly well.

A book deal loomed. No more of what one sniffy *Aftonbladet* literary critic had once sneeringly referred to as 'middlebrow torture porn,' either. The publishing director of Kattuggla AB herself had asked Sven-Arne if she could publish his autobiography.

He was still considering her offer. By Swedish standards it was magnificent: a 4.4 million krone advance plus royalties two points above industry norms.

But that was for another day. Right now, he had a meeting to prepare for.

The Central Stockholm Ingrid's Way group was holding a session in the basement of a church favoured by the upper echelons of the city's society. The people who hummed their 'i's in the posh Östermalm accent without embarrassment or displays of false modesty. They came to genuflect before God at *Stirka Kyrkan* on a Sunday before resuming praying to Mammon the following day.

While the programme had been established to provide aid and succour to all, it had very quickly become a hangout for celebrities. Perhaps not those at the pinnacle of their professions. They still preferred to keep their problems far away from the prying eyes of the media, checking in to clinics either in Sweden's remote forested regions, or out of the country altogether. Britain's Priory was a favoured destination.

Ingrid's Way had proved a draw for that level of person who had managed to parlay an appearance on a reality show into a job presenting daytime TV. Or a viral TikTok video into a spot doing backstage interviews with the starstruck contestants on *PopStar!*

D-listers, basically.

A couple of proper stars would have been nice. But he was raking it in catering to the tier fours and the wannabes below them on the celebrity ladder. The brand-new Ferrari on his drive attested to that. On the whole, he felt he could manage without the A-listers.

He flipped open another button on his soft white shirt, shrugged on a midnight-blue linen jacket and went downstairs. He grabbed the keys for the Ferrari from the hall table and called out to Sofia, his current girlfriend.

'I'm off, darling. Be back about ten. Love you!'

'Love you, too!' Sofia called back from the sitting room.

Sven-Arne frowned. Would it have killed her to get off her expensively re-upholstered arse and kiss him goodbye? Apparently, yes, it would.

Inside the scarlet sports car, he shook his mane of blonde hair and then revved the engine up to a scream before nosing out through the electronically controlled gates and making a left turn towards *Stirka Kyrkan*.

Fifteen minutes later, he was standing outside the door to the basement meeting room, peering in through a small circular window. The head of the group had arranged the chairs in a circle, as always.

Sven-Arne always gave the same instruction to the group leaders. Explain they would be welcoming a very special person to join this session of Ingrid's Way. Yes, an addict, but an addict who was now clean, sober and ready to help them advance further on their own journeys.

Then they would nod to him. He would enter, walking slowly enough that those with their backs to him could swivel in their seats to see who would be addressing the meeting.

The group leader nodded. Sven-Arne pushed through the double doors. Hesitated for a moment, as if he might have forgotten something. Really a ploy to allow everyone to register his presence.

Then, as the applause swelled, he would paste on that famous, self-deprecating smile, hold his hands up as if to say, *'Oh, no, please. Not for me. I'm just like you,'* before making his way to the seat beside the group leader.

'Hi, everyone,' he said, in a soft voice that encouraged people to lean forwards to catch his words. 'My name is Sven-Arne and I am an addict.'

This brought forth smiles, and even the odd chuckle. Then he continued.

'I founded Ingrid's Way because I did not believe that I had to surrender to a higher power to face down my demons. My views on religion are well known, so I won't bore you with them here.'

More appreciative laughter. One woman, a pretty brunette with dancing blue eyes and a low-cut T-shirt, offered him a smile that lasted just a fraction too long. Noted.

'I brought them forth,' he said, looking straight at her. 'It was my job to send them back to Hell.'

Sven-Arne delivered the rest of his speech on autopilot. It wasn't hard. It was exactly the same as the hundreds of other times he'd given it.

He spent the time checking out the women in the group, especially the delicious brunette, who he finally placed. Her name was Annigret Johansson and she had moved from Instagram to national TV seemingly without displaying any talent whatsoever. Great body, though.

Once the personal testimonies had concluded and a Q&A session likewise, the local leader pronounced the meeting closed and suggested everyone mingle and take the opportunity to get to know 'our too-modest founder' a little better.

Sven-Arne moved to the side of the room, where a table had been laid with a mouth-watering selection of open sandwiches and soft drinks, plus flasks of coffee. In his haste to make contact with Annigret, he collided with a small, mousy woman who was moving against the flow of people to begin stacking the chairs.

'Sorry,' she mumbled.

'No, my fault,' Sven-Arne said, flashing the trademark smile.

She muttered something else, an apology, it sounded like, but his focus had shifted.

While the Ingrid's Way meeting was progressing, Stella was in a meeting of her own. The SPA psychologist had suggested they meet at her apartment as it was after hours.

'Plus, my home consulting room is a lot more comfortable than the one they give me at work.'

Her name was Alyssa Sondergard and Stella warmed to her immediately. They were about the same age, which helped, but more than that, when Stella had booked the appointment, Alyssa had talked like she really meant what she said and wasn't just going through the SPA-prescribed motions.

The room they were sitting in was bright, with evening sunshine streaming in through a picture window that gave onto a leafy square. She could hear the sound of children playing – high-pitched squeals and shouts.

Alyssa smiled. She balanced a notebook on her knee.

'So, Stella, how can I help you today?'

Stella had lost her inhibitions about spilling her guts to therapists many years ago. She didn't waste time now, either.

'Some years back, more than ten, actually, I suffered a breakdown after my husband and daughter were murdered,' she said, nodding as Alyssa mouthed, *I'm so sorry.*

'Anyway, because of the trauma, I developed a dissociative personality disorder where a part of me split off. I called her Other Stella. She was…not a good person. I had a lot of therapy, drug treatment and so on, and she disappeared.'

Stella paused for breath.

'I'm scared she's back.'

Alyssa sat a little straighter in her chair. Stella wondered where the brief story she'd just told her sat on the spectrum of tales of woe she heard from SPA officers.

'Two questions come to mind,' Alyssa said, carefully. 'First of all, what makes you think she's back?'

Stella ran her ponytail through a clenched fist.

'Because a couple of days ago, I heard her voice in my head.'

Alyssa made a note, nodding as she wrote.

'We'll come back to that. Second question, why is it scary if she's back?'

This time Stella tugged so hard on her hair it hurt. She unclenched her fingers and let her ponytail drop. Yes, why *was* she scared? Could it be because that way madness lay? That the last thing Sweden needed was a cop with more kills under her belt than most of the murderers currently incarcerated in its comfortable, socially progressive prisons? How about that for a start off? She gave Alyssa a slightly less terrifying answer.

'Like I said. She's not a nice person. You could say she's the worst version of me, if that doesn't sound too much like therapy-speak.'

Alyssa laughed, showing small white teeth. 'You're allowed to use therapy-speak if it conveys what you want to say, Stella. I won't write you up for it. But anyway, let me go back a little bit. You say you heard...' She checked her notes. 'Other Stella's voice in your head.'

'As clear as I'm hearing yours now.'

'Did you experience anything beyond hearing her voice? Did you see her? Smell her? Did she touch you?'

'No. Nothing like that.'

'And how long did she talk to you?'

'It was a single sentence, then nothing.'

'I see,' Alyssa said, making another quick note. 'Can you tell me what she said?'

Stella nodded. 'She said, "If this is a one-off, babe, then I'm the Queen of Sweden".'

'What was the context?'

'I was on the way back to HQ after going out to see the dead guy with birds wings who got hit by the truck over in Vällingby?'

Alyssa nodded. 'Go on.'

'I was discussing the case with my assistant and I think she'd just said something like, did I think it was a one-off? That was before we found the dead woman on the roundabout at Årsta.'

'How would you describe your reaction to seeing the dead man?'

'Oh, God,' Stella said, tugging her ponytail again. 'It was horrific. I mean, can you imagine it? It's bad enough when a pedestrian gets hit by a car, but this was a Scania eighteen-wheeler doing about seventy kph. And he had these huge wings...you know, grafted on to his arms.'

'Pretty shocking, then?'

'I think that would cover it,' Stella said with a weak grin.

'You see, Stella, what I'm wondering is whether, in reaction to this incredibly traumatic event, what you heard was simply that inner voice we all have, expressing perfectly understandable shock and horror.'

'But it was *her* voice! And her phrasing.'

'Maybe Other Stella used to borrow *your* phrasing. Have you thought of that? After all, she is a part of you, even if not a very nice part.'

Stella shrugged. Alyssa had a point. It had been over ten years since she'd last shared headspace with Other Stella. And nobody could deny that seeing the smashed corpse of the birdman had been shocking.

'You see, if this *were* a recurrence of your dissociative personality disorder,' Alyssa said, 'I would have expected there to be other manifestations beyond a single sentence you heard internally.'

Stella frowned.

'You mean I'm not mad, just traumatised?'

Alyssa smiled, closing her notebook. 'Don't play it down, Stella. There's nothing "just" about traumatic experiences. I see too many cops struggling because they won't allow themselves to admit that their job gives them nightmares, let alone full-blown PTSD. Being strong doesn't have to mean denying how much you're emotionally affected by the things you see.'

They ended the meeting with an agreement to meet again for a short follow-up a week later.

Jamie called towards the end of the day, pleading a migraine and crying off their date. Part of her was disappointed, but another part, the detective part, was glad that she'd have more time to devote to the case.

***

As she lay awake in the small hours of the morning, listening to the traffic in the street outside her bedroom,

Stella returned to Alyssa's closing words. The trouble was, if you opened yourself up to your innermost feelings your colleagues might find you running down Mariebergsgatan, stark naked and screaming at three in the morning.

11

The following morning, Stella drove straight to the RMV building where Henrik was due to conduct the autopsy on the woman from the roundabout.

Garbed in blue surgical scrubs, her face obscured by a matching mask, Stella stood to one side while Henrik gestured to the parts of the corpse he wanted the photographer to capture.

In the background, a computer's fan whirred noisily. It sounded as though it was dying. Stella frowned at the thought. Bit incongruous, wasn't it? She smiled grimly to herself, glad her mouth was concealed behind the mask. Because when it came to incongruous, wondering about minor pieces of PC hardware came a long way behind watching an RMV pathologist autopsy a body to which bird's wings were attached.

'Ready?' Henrik said.

'Whenever you are.'

Henrik nodded and clicked on the mic suspended above his head.

'We have the corpse of a white female,

approximately thirty to thirty-five years old. The most notable feature is the substitution of what appear to be the wings of a large bird for the arms.' Henrik peered at the woman's face. 'A dark substance that is probably dried blood is present in the left nostril. Also, facial scarring that could be acne or some other autoimmune disease.' He turned to Stella, clicking off the mic. 'Now for the fun stuff.'

Henrik was part of a group of newer pathologists at the RMV who had been labelled the Young Turks. As much for their attitude as their youth. Their older colleagues may have bestowed the nickname from a sense of outrage, but the group had adopted it gratefully and even held monthly dinners under the rubric.

Stella felt her age at this precise point – forty had passed a few years earlier – since she couldn't see anything 'fun' about dissecting a young murder victim's corpse.

'Normally, I would begin with the classical Y-incision,' Henrik intoned, lifting his head fractionally towards the mic, which he'd reactivated. 'But given the unusual condition of the body, I am going to start with the upper limbs.'

His mortuary assistant passed him a pair of stainless-steel scissors, which he used to snip the stitches holding the right wing in place. Stella was pleased to see him cutting through the plain section of thread, preserving the knots for later analysis by Forensics.

'Could you hold the wing out at right angles to the body, please, Linda,' Henrik asked his assistant, revealing her gender, which had been hidden inside the de-sexing autopsy outfit of cap, mask, gown, gloves and rubber boots.

'Need a hand?' Stella asked, as the assistant lifted the wing away from the body.

It was almost two metres long and threatened to become unwieldy for the young woman. Standing side by side, the two women held the monstrous wing out so Henrik could see what he was doing. It weighed barely anything.

'It's light,' Linda said.

'Hollow bones,' Henrik said as he bent over the sutures, snipping them methodically, all the way round the join.

One by one, he dropped the cut sutures into a stainless-steel kidney bowl, tapping each one off the long-handled tweezers with a rhythmic *tink-tink*.

Next, he selected a small scalpel and began cutting away the glued-together edges, creating a ragged armlet of tissue. He cut through it and dropped it into a second kidney bowl.

'So, how has he put you together?' Henrik murmured, then, as if remembering he was recording, he spoke up. 'I am resecting the long-head biceps brachii.'

Stella watched, fascinated, as Henrik cut into the muscles and tendons of the dead woman's arm, eventually revealing the bone – *'the humerus,'* a voice from her school biology lessons piped up.

'I am going to remove the skin from the proximal end of the wing now,' Henrik said, before going to work with a scalpel.

Gradually, as Henrik cut and pried, noting how the arteries had been clamped shut, the killer's handiwork became visible. Somehow, he had joined the wing bone to the humerus. More glue, Stella suspected. Would that have been strong enough to support it in the outspread position she'd observed on the makeshift crucifix at the roundabout?

'How are they joined?' she asked.

'Exactly my question,' Henrik answered. He placed his hands around the two bones and gently twisted them in opposite directions. There was a sharp crack that set Stella's teeth on edge, and the bones began to move freely against each other. The rest of the wing moved in Stella's grasp, creating the unsettling sensation that they were restraining a living bird.

'Ah, I see,' Henrik said. 'Stella and Linda? If you could just pull, gently, please.'

The two women locked eyes for a second then, working in synchrony, began pulling the wing away from the dead woman's shoulder.

With a muted pop, the wing came free.

'On the other dissection table, I think,' Henrik said, gesturing to a second stainless-steel platform.

They laid the wing down and returned to the woman's body.

'Our killer is something of a craftsman, I would say. That looks like aluminium to me,' Henrik said.

He pointed with the scalpel to a narrow silver-coloured rod protruding from the stub of bone disappearing into the woman's deltoid muscle. He picked up a pair of pliers and started pulling and twisting on the metal rod.

He grunted with effort.

'Stella, could you steady the shoulder for me, please? Linda, can you stabilise the humerus, please?'

With all three exerting force on the various parts of the woman's upper body, Henrik was able to retract the metal rod from the bone and place it, with a clank, onto the second dissection table.

Stella couldn't resist: she bent down and peered into the hole left in the humerus by the rod.

'He's drilled out both bones, then fabricated a piece of aluminium to peg them together,' she said.

Henrik nodded, then lifted his visor to push up his glasses, which had slipped down his nose.

'I think the killer has spent quite some time thinking through the best way to achieve his aims,' he said. 'He hasn't just ripped or pulled off the arm, what we medics call avulsion. He's worked out he can use the existing joint and upper portion of the humerus to create a scaffold with the flesh pared back.'

Stella had a nightmarish vision of a French-trimmed lamb cutlet.

'And that gives him a ready-made wing-stub,' she said.

'Exactly. The rest is just stitching and the liberal application of superglue.'

'I read an article about a case in the US where the killer was gluing body parts together with meat glue,' she said. 'That stuff cheapo restaurants use to turn offcuts into quote-unquote steaks. Why didn't he use that, do you think?'

Henrik nodded. 'Transglutaminase: the serial killer's adhesive of choice. But why bother? OK, so superglue doesn't give such a neat and invisible bond. But who knows under all those beautiful feathers?'

'Tell me you're not actually admiring this, Henrik.'

'Sorry. Occupational hazard.'

'It looks like he's burned it,' she said, pointing to an area that looked like seared meat.

'Yes, he's cauterised the minor blood vessels and the cut edges of the muscles. From the size and shape of the burn marks, I would say he used a soldering iron. I'll run some comparative tests later.' He caught her eye. 'On a steak, Stella! Don't worry.'

'So we have a killer who knows his aero-engineering *and* his anatomy,' Stella said.

'A Renaissance man,' Henrik said, with what Stella felt was a slightly unhealthy level of admiration.

'He's also a certifiable nutcase, Doc, let's not forget.'

'You mustn't call him that, Stella,' Henrik replied.

'Because it's not the Swedish way?'

'Because we want him in prison, not some nice psychiatric unit.' He paused. 'Maybe there are sections of the intelligentsia who think it can all be explained away by child psychologists and analysis of social ills, but I happen to believe in evil. I see the results too often not to. The people who commit acts like this? They need locking up. For good, preferably.'

'Agreed. Listen, can you let me have your report as soon as possible please? I've seen enough. I need to set up a murder inquiry.'

'Of course.'

Stella stopped as she reached the door.

'Sorry, Henrik, you said you were going to tell me about the first body.'

'Yes. Same MO as this one. It's the same perpetrator. I'd stake my career on it.' It was one of the things she liked about this Young Turk. His willingness to stick his neck out.

'Oh, and in your report, can you let me know your thoughts about any of the implements he used on her, please?'

'Sure.'

As she made her way across town to police HQ, she ran through lines of enquiry. And she felt it. That indefinable sensation. Part excitement, part fear – was she up to it *this* time? – and part the hunter's instinct for her prey.

Because this was real

This was happening.

Again.

12

The conference room could hold eight comfortably. For the twelve people currently inhaling the coffee-tainted air, it was a tight squeeze.

Those officers who had arrived early had grabbed the chairs. But now they had to endure the uncomfortably close presence of their brother and sister officers, looming over them from behind. Not so bad if the person sharing your personal space had had a shower that morning, or not just pulled a double shift. Or was wearing nice perfume, or subtle aftershave. So half were OK. The rest suffered in silence.

The detectives in Stella's team had taken one side of the square of tables. Sitting between Jonna and Oskar Norgrim was her latest recruit.

Tilde Enström had shown herself to be resourceful, smart and hard-working during a case Stella had worked in the town of Söderbärke. After passing the national investigators' exam she had applied to join Stella's team and, after a few strings were pulled, been appointed as a *kriminalinspektör*. Nominally the same rank as most of them working there, but equivalent to the UK rank of detective constable.

Alongside the detectives sat Signe Arrhenius from Forensics, several uniformed cops and two civilians employed as data coordinators and analysts. Malin Holm, the big boss, occupied the centre seat at the far side of the square of tables. Facing Stella. Imperceptibly, she nodded. Showtime.

Stella cleared her throat. 'This morning, at 5:57 a.m., a member of the public reported a body on a roundabout in Årsta.' She gave the location, allowing people time to make a note. 'This is what she saw.'

Stella clicked the remote control for the PC projector.

In the calm of the conference room, the image of the dead woman seemed theatrical somehow. A poor taste prank by some art students, perhaps. Or a shot from a low-budget folk-horror film.

'What the devil is that?' one of the detectives asked.

'It's the same as that bloke who got smashed by the truck over in Vällingby, isn't it, Stella?' Oskar asked.

'Exactly. Right down to the method used to attach the wings. Technically, that one was accidental death, but it's clear to me that whoever did it had other plans.'

'What's cause of death for the woman, Stella?' Tilde asked.

'I'm still waiting for the autopsy report. All I could see on the body in the way of wounds – apart from the obvious – was some dried blood in the left nostril.'

'Weird,' someone muttered.

'Good job Stella's on it, then,' came an even quieter reply.

'Right. Jobs,' Stella said. 'I want to know who the two victims are. Check missing persons. Once we know that, we can start connecting the dots to figure out why and where they were chosen.'

'You think they were selected specifically?'

This was Malin. At her question, the room stilled. Stella knew why. Not because of her authority. Because Malin, as a good senior detective should, had put her finger on the central question. Even her choice of words had purpose.

She could have asked why they'd been *attacked*. But that would have conjured up a vision of a madman racing around the streets with a bottle of chloroform and a scalpel, snatching random victims off the street before butchering them.

But no. Malin had asked how they'd been selected. *Chosen*. Which implied a scheme, a plan of some kind.

Stella nodded.

'In my experience, crimes with this level of *weirdness*,' she aimed a half-smile at the officer who'd muttered about her aptitude for the 'difficult' cases, 'are committed by an individual who is trying to say something.'

'Yeah, like, I'm a damned nutcase,' one of the uniformed cops said spiralling a finger at her temple, to laughter.

'Can we keep this serious, please,' Stella said, pointing at the grotesque image behind her. 'There's a dead woman in the morgue right now missing her arms.'

'Sorry, Stella,' she muttered.

Stella smiled to soften the reprimand.

'What do we know about serial killers?'

Tilde's hand shot up, to chuckles from the older cops.

'Serial killers come in two basic flavours. The cunning kind with plans, however surreal or ridiculous. And the more instinctual kind, driven by uncontrollable urges, happy to kill using whatever comes to hand before moving on to their next victim,' she said. 'Both enjoy killing and they may get sexual fulfilment from it. But while the second group are what you might call thrill-killers, the first are always working to some interior design.'

'Bit early to be talking about a serial killer, isn't it? I thought there had to be three murders?' This was Lars Stenmark, a detective constable.

Tilde turned her head to address him directly.

'Normally, that would be true. But I think we can see that the distinctive features of the two crimes Stella has linked leave little doubt we're looking for a serial offender,' she said, primly. 'Nobody who goes to that much trouble is going to be happy with just two victims. Especially since it looks to me like the first one escaped before he could be posed according to the plan.'

Stella could only nod. It was an impressively concise explanation of her thinking from the most recent, and junior member of the team. She congratulated herself on spotting Tilde's potential back in Söderbärke.

'Thanks, Tilde,' she said, earning herself a radiant smile from the new girl. 'That's basically it. We're all experienced enough to know that one-off murders don't look like this. Spouses use whatever comes to hand. They're usually found covered in blood beside the corpse. They might even have called it in themselves.'

Her remark set off a chain of intersecting observations among the assembled officers.

'If it's gang-related it's a stabbing, a bullet to the head—'

' – or torture if someone's trying to make a point.'

'This is too – what's that word the kids all use these days?'

'Gnarly?'

'Nah. Performative, that's it. You know, the big show. Like, look how clever I am.'

'How sick and twisted, you mean.'

'Yeah, but I'm right, aren't I, Stella?'

'You are. So, let's get identities for our two victims. Usual routes, please. And as soon as we do, I want to start looking for connections,' she said. 'Somewhere in their background they will have met their killer. Signe, anything interesting on the forensics front?'

'Nothing, I'm afraid. Either the killer was extremely forensically aware or extremely lucky. But we'll keep checking.'

'Thanks. Next, CCTV. Check municipal cameras on all four approaches to the roundabout. Plus shops, restaurants, all the commercial and residential premises for say five hundred metres in every direction. Remember to ask about doorbell cams, dashcams, birdbox cams, even kids in the house making TikToks.

'Henrik Brodin found ketamine in the first body. It could have been recreational, but I'm betting our guy uses it as an anaesthetic,' she said. 'Jonna and Tilde, can you start checking out vets, please? Colleges, university courses, vets new to the city or with blemishes on their record.'

Jonna nodded. Tilde followed suit, scribbling furiously in her notebook.

'What about the wings?' Tilde asked, once she'd finished her note.

'I was coming to that. They're big. And they looked real to me. So, where did they come from? The wild? The zoo? Private aviaries? There can't be that many places with the space to keep birds of that size. Someone must have reported something, even if it's a gamekeeper on some estate calling in big birds of prey going missing. Oskar, can you look into that, please? And I want to know the species our second victim's wings came from.'

Her perpetually harassed-looking second-in-command nodded his head.

After issuing a general instruction to keep her informed and requesting everybody's presence at 5:00 p.m. for a catch-up, Stella dismissed them.

Malin lingered, and, when they had the room to themselves, sat again.

'We need to talk about how we handle the PR side of this. There's already some noise on social, but the mainstream media haven't got wind of it yet. But it won't be long. Not with something this bizarre.'

'How about we issue a press release stating the bald facts and sketch round the mutilation?'

Malin's finely arched eyebrows curved upwards. 'Sketch round it? How do you propose we do that, Stella? They had birds' wings grafted onto their bodies.'

'Good point. How about, we say something like,' Stella looked over her shoulder at the image of the crucified birdwoman. Back at Malin again. 'Police are investigating two suspicious deaths in the greater Stockholm area. It appears the killer may have employed elements of theatrical costume.'

Malin nodded, pulling her lips to one side as she thought.

'It's not an *outright* lie. That is certainly what it *appears* like.'

'We can always backtrack if it comes out before we're ready. Say that we can't know for sure until we receive the RMV autopsy reports. Plus there's so much weird shit on the internet these days, nobody will think it's genuine until there's incontrovertible evidence. A few out-of-focus phone images won't cut it.'

'Have you had the reports yet?'

'Nope. Should be later today.'

'Good. I can work with that. Tell me, do you agree with Tilde? Who seems like a bright young woman, by the way.'

'Like I said, I've seen too much of this sort of thing before. It's a serial, Malin, I can feel it. One of the bad ones at that. Clever, resourceful, able to master their urges. They'll think they're superior to us. It could work in our favour. It's a krona to a kanelbullar they'll write a letter to the media before too long, boasting about their crimes.'

'God, I hope you're right. That's when they start getting sloppy. So what about you? What's your next move?'

'One, I'm going to head back out to the first crime scene. I want to see what's nearby. Two, I want to bring in a profiler.'

This time, Malin's eyebrows practically jumped right off her forehead.

'Stella! We discussed the budget only last week! You know the Ministry is on an efficiency drive.'

Stella smiled. Malin was normally so composed. Her nickname was 'the Ice Maiden'. But when riled, or blindsided by a particularly upsetting suggestion from one of her team, she could blow her top spectacularly. At which point her other moniker came into use: *Grímsvötn*, for the active Icelandic volcano.

'You don't have to worry about the Ministry. I have an offer from a respected British forensic psychiatrist. He's willing to work for nothing.'

Malin's eyebrows drew together. 'And this eminent

shrink from your home country. He wouldn't happen to be a Dr James Hooke, would he?'

Was that a hint of a smile tweaking the corners of Malin's lips up? Though often perceived as aloof, she made it her business to get to know each member of her team personally. She'd shared a couple of glasses of wine with Stella one evening after work, listening while she explained about her breakup with Jamie.

'None other,' Stella said. 'He's…' She felt her cheeks heating up all of a sudden and wondered why. It wasn't as if she had anything to be embarrassed about. '…He's over here on holiday. Taking a career break.'

'A break to repair a break?'

Damn! That was what made Malin such a good manager. She always saw the truth behind her subordinates' evasions.

'I think so. It's early days.'

'Well, good for you if it is, Stella. From everything you said, he seems like a nice guy.'

'He is. A really nice guy. And right now, a resource I could really use. He offered, by the way. I didn't ask.'

Malin shrugged. 'I see no problem bringing him as a consultant. His record speaks for itself. Looking way down the line, when you catch the guy and we get him in a courtroom, would Jamie be willing to testify as an expert witness?'

'I'm sure he will, but I'll ask him tonight.'

'Dinner?' A beat. 'More?'

What? Where had this mischievous sense of humour come from? Stella looked at her boss anew.

'Definitely dinner,' she said, finally.

'Well, enjoy it. Just don't let your resurgent love life interfere with the case.'

'Never.'

'OK, then. I have a press release to issue. I'll see you later. Call me if you need anything, yes?'

With that, Malin was gone, leaving Stella in an empty conference room, staring at the grotesque image of the birdwoman's mutilated corpse.

13

Stella had no intention of waiting until dinnertime to speak with Jamie. She called him from her office.

'Morning. How did you sleep? Did you get your sorting out done?'

'Morning. Yes, all done, thanks. I'm guessing from the TV news you're busy this morning.'

'I am. But I was wondering whether you wanted to meet me for a coffee?'

'Of course. When and where?'

'Now and *Cafe Björkar* on Scheelegatan.'

'I'll be there. If I arrive first, shall I get you something? Do you still drink a flat white with an extra shot?'

'Nope. I've gone native. A large Americano with a splash of hot milk please. And a pastry.'

'What kind?'

'Surprise me.'

He paused. 'Oh, I think I can do that. See you in a bit.'

Stella walked to the coffee shop, pausing only to

smell the heady scent of a huge rambling honeysuckle planted outside a sleek apartment block.

Jamie was already there. He was sitting at the window on a high stool, with a brown leather messenger bag on the seat beside him, reserving it. He smiled at her as she reached for the door handle and pointed out the mug beside his own. A plate bore a couple of kanelbullar.

Inside, she was plunged into the hubbub of a cafe full of rich Stockholmers doing what they did best. Talking at high volume about real estate prices, their kids' nannies, work or just the weather, while consuming sweet cakes and coffee that, together, they called *fika*.

Jamie slid off his stool to kiss her and then swept his bag off the neighbouring stool for her.

'So, what's up with this new case?' he asked.

It was such a relief to be able to talk to him again, she plunged straight in.

'He's a serial, no question in my mind. He's taken two people already. We're only not calling number one a homicide because he escaped somehow and got hit by a truck.'

'The TV news were vague about the details, but on Facebook there are images that look like this morning's victim had wings.'

'She did. Look, before we go any further, I need to get a little bit official with you.'

'I'm guessing you want me to sign some sort of secrecy document?'

'Actually, it's not that bad. No Official Secrets Act or anything. I just need you to promise you won't reveal details of the case to anyone outside the investigation. In fact, can you not reveal them to anyone unless I'm present, please?'

'Worried about a leak?'

'No. It's just, what with you being here in an unofficial capacity, I'd prefer to keep control of the narrative, that's all.'

'Sure,' he said, smiling easily. 'If anyone asks me about the case, how about I just play the dumb Englishman and refer them to you?'

'Works for me.'

'Great. So does that mean I'm on the team?'

'If the offer's still open.'

'Of course. I know I shouldn't say this, but it'll be fun working together again.'

Stella drew her head back and raised her eyebrows.

'Fun?'

'Bad choice of words. But you know what I mean. We make a great team, darling, that's all.'

She smiled, then covered her embarrassment by taking a sip of the coffee and a bite of one of the sugary cinnamon buns.

'What do you think?'

'I'll need to come in and view the crime scene photos. And if the bodies are still in the morgue—'

'They are.'

'Then I'd like to see them, too.'

'I'll get you a temporary ID. It'll help you move around at HQ, although be prepared for people to call me first.'

'It's fine. Like I said, I just want to help.' He took a bite of the other bun, then sipped his coffee and winced. 'My God! Do you get *any* sleep?'

Stella's first months in Sweden had been a tumultuous time of high-octane cases and even higher-octane coffee. Her sleep patterns had adjusted, though, and now she could drink the stuff like water. She laughed.

'You get used to it, I promise.'

'I hope so. What was it old Nietzsche said? *"That which does not kill us makes us stronger"*?'

'Speaking of which…'

'Right, right. Your killer. What can you tell me about him from the two bodies?'

Stella outlined her thinking, in much the same language as she had used with Malin earlier. When she'd finished, Jamie dragged his fingers through his grey-tinged curls.

'That's pretty amazing for a non-specialist, especially based on such flimsy evidence,' he said. 'I'm not sure you really need me at all.'

She poked him in the chest. 'Quit with the false modesty, Doc. Come on, where did I go wrong?'

'Nowhere. Not really. But maybe I can flesh things out a little. I'll be able to do more once I've immersed myself in the case but for now, how about this?'

He sat straighter and leaned towards her, so that he could speak in a low murmur. Probably best. She didn't want some innocent cafe-goer losing their breakfast as they discussed mutilation techniques or the psychosexual pathology of serial killers.

'He appears to be organised. He's got somewhere private to work. He's very controlled. He feels Godlike. He's creating, no—' Jamie frowned, 'he's *re*-creating his victims, isn't he?'

'Meaning?'

'They start off as complete humans but he removes their arms and replaces them with wings. He's transforming them into something else. Something he regards as better. Probably as perfect.'

'I was thinking today's victim, the young woman, she looked like an angel.'

'Which would speak directly to a person suffering from religious delusions.'

'But it could just as easily be that he's excited by the Icarus myth.'

'Yes, or maybe he just loves large birds. You did say the wings were to scale?'

'Yeah.'

'He might feel like he's a bird inside. Maybe something big and predatory like an eagle.'

'And he doesn't want to cut his own arms off, so he projects his feelings onto his victims.'

Jamie nodded excitedly. She could see the old fire igniting behind his eyes. Loved him for it.

'Yes! Exactly! He feels that his victims, or maybe the whole human race, are his inferiors. Dumb, earthbound animals, whereas he is some kind of higher being.'

Stella grinned. 'Like a consultant forensic psychiatrist in a room full of cops, for example?'

Jamie's eyes flashbulbed. 'How dare you! I am an extremely humble man. In fact, I am probably the most humble consultant forensic psychiatrist in the world.'

She laughed. It felt good to be back with him. Yes, there was work to do. She didn't need a couples counsellor to tell her that, but, finally, she could see a route back to a life with Jamie at its heart. A good life. Just as soon as she caught the maniac stitching birds' wings onto innocent Stockholmers.

'So, Mister Olympic-level humblebragger, how is any of this going to help me catch him?'

'Hmm. I think we need more caffeine if we're going to delve into investigative strategy.'

Five minutes later, during which time Stella had

93

checked in via text with the various teams she'd set up, Jamie reappeared at her side with two more coffees.

'I think animal cruelty might be a route in,' Jamie said as he took his seat again. 'Look for anyone with a criminal record for mutilating birds. And it takes a degree of surgical knowledge to remove someone's arm if you're going to sew a wing on in its place. I mean, anyone can take a saw or an axe and chop off a limb.'

'Delicately put,' she said dryly.

Jamie shrugged. 'Sorry. I've been away from the clinical setting for too long.'

'No, I'm sorry. You're only trying to help – *pro bono*, at that – and I'm taking the piss. I'm thinking about the aluminium support,' she said.

'More evidence you might be looking for a surgeon. Maybe a specialist in orthopaedics.'

'Except they use titanium for artificial joints, don't they?'

'That and cobalt alloys. Carbon fibre. Ceramics, too, and ultra-high-molecular-weight polyethylene if you're really going to do a deep-dive.'

Stella fished out her daybook and jotted down a note.

Check with orthopaedic dept at hosp.

Stella's phone buzzed. She glanced down. It was a text from Henrik.

Can you pop into RMV? Interesting findings.

She turned to Jamie. 'I have to go. Can you come in to the station later? Say around 5:00 p.m.? We can get you accredited and I can introduce you to my team. They're a great bunch.'

He smiled. 'Sure. Now, go and catch your serial killer.'

'What about you? Any plans for the rest of the day?'

He tapped the side of his nose. 'Oh, I'll keep myself busy. Now go, go!'

She left him finishing his coffee. He waved as she exited the noisy cafe and she raised her hand in response. 'Later,' she mouthed to him through the window.

14

Carola Vilks nodded with satisfaction at the resume on screen before her. A young woman wanting to be an engineer.

Working as an engineer hadn't always been seen in Sweden as a respectable career for women. Even in a country renowned for its enlightened outlook on gender equality, some jobs, it seemed, were still for the boys.

As for running an entire aerospace engineering company? Well, people supposed it *could* be done. But would it be done *well?* That was the question.

Carola Vilks didn't have time for those people. Nor for their stupid questions. If they wanted an answer, let them consult Vilks Luftrum AB's financial performance in *Svenska Dagbladet.*

She had taken the controls as CEO three years earlier, after her father retired on health grounds. During her brief but highly successful tenure so far, sales and profits had climbed steeply – like a jet whose engines incorporated her company's aluminium-based weight-saving technology.

Gottfrid Vilks – the Old Man, as the family called him – had made no secret of his disappointment in having produced no male heir. But the terms of a family trust dating back to the 1930s were absolute. A Vilks must head the company, regardless of their sex. No outsiders were to be allowed to run things unless the current CEO died childless. In the event that any surviving heir was younger than eighteen, a board of advisers comprising family lawyers and trusted lieutenants would run things until they reached their majority.

Carola had returned from the Old Man's funeral and begun making calls that very evening, outraging those who felt a decent period of mourning – or even restraint – might have been more seemly. That Carola appeared to feel no remorse for her actions, or empathy for those she'd offended, only compounded her sins in their eyes.

Those who immediately lost their jobs were the most outraged of all. They took to the business TV shows and serious newspapers and magazines to opine on the likely trajectory of the company now Carola was flying solo.

Wrongly, as it turned out.

Even without the blood coursing through her veins, Carola was uniquely qualified to run Vilks Luftrum AB. For a brief period she had worked as a test pilot, taking new fast jets to the limits of their performance envelope, and sometimes beyond. She appeared to feel no fear and could maintain a running commentary on avionics, performance and atmospheric conditions, even as this prototype or that was tumbling, leaf-like, towards the ground.

It was said by her enemies, who had multiplied since her elevation to CEO, that Carola was, in fact, a psychopath. Not one of those sadistic murderers who occasionally flared bright as a jet's afterburners in the popular press. Of course not! That would be silly. But somebody who scored highly on those traits characteristic of psychopaths and said to be common among top business executives, politicians and senior surgeons. Risk-taking. Lack of empathy. Ruthlessness. Narcissism. Extreme calmness under pressure.

Carola knew all about the rumours. Enjoyed them. Fanned the flames occasionally if they seemed to be dying down. Her profile had never been higher. Her remuneration kept pace with her reputation. She saw to that, brushing aside the objections of the board like so much swarf clogging a lathe.

One of the traits her enemies might have been less willing to recognise was Carola's ability to make friends. Carola had contacts in many different spheres of Swedish society. They ranged from pool-hall hustlers (thanks to a habit acquired in her university days and never lost) to the MPs and political aides who populated the corridors and committee rooms of the Riksdag.

She also had friends in the SPA. Amongst the top brass, of course, whom she made sure to invite to her annual Midsommar party, famous in Stockholm both for the lavishness of the refreshments and the breath-taking spectacle of the flying display. But also in odd little corners, like the forensics department. And even rank-and-file cops, especially in the airborne division, where she could talk sprag clutches and swash plates with the chopper pilots like an old hand.

On this particular morning, Carola had taken one of her mid-level contacts, a lonely single man who worked in forensics, out for coffee. He enjoyed (apparently without questioning it) his unbelievable good fortune that a beautiful, unmarried woman who ran a major Swedish company appeared to find him fascinating. Carola enjoyed pumping him for gossip, information about cases, anything that might help her get along in life. Much as a carefree angler will drop a baited hook in the water and be content to land whatever finds the bait attractive.

Towards the end of their assignation – *I'm so sorry but I have a meeting in half an hour. You understand, Nils* – he had first looked left and right, rather theatrically Carola felt. Then sworn her to secrecy. Before revealing, in a low murmur, that the killer had used aluminium struts to assemble their grotesque human-avian hybrids. *I thought with your background, you might find it interesting.*

Oh, she'd found it interesting all right.

And now she saw an opportunity to raise her profile still higher. By helping the police investigate the murder in Årsta.

Not just any police, either. The British super cop who'd been building quite a reputation of her own in her adopted country, putting away serial killers like it was no more difficult than stacking a dishwasher.

Carola wanted to get to know Stella Cole better.

A lot better.

She picked up her phone and called her assistant.

15

Henrik rose from behind a cluttered desk to shake Stella's hand. He ushered her to a seat at a small round conference table in a corner of the office. A human skull sat in its centre.

'What's up?' she asked him.

'I know you prefer to discuss my topline findings directly. I agree, by the way, although I have just sent you my reports.'

'What have we got?'

'Let's deal with time of death first. Obviously our male victim we can pinpoint to the minute thanks to the trucker's mobile phone: 11:01 a.m. yesterday. If only we were always so lucky.'

'And today's?'

'Judging by her stomach contents and a few other indicators, body temperature, rigor mortis, the usual, I'd say somewhere between six last night and the early hours, say 3:00 a.m.'

'She was found at 5:45 a.m. So that fits our timeline. How about cause of death? I saw dried blood in her left nostril. Was she stabbed up there? Something long and thin. A screwdriver? Or a meat skewer?'

Henrik nodded. 'Maybe you should come and work here with me. Yes, that's pretty much what happened.'

He fetched a folder from his desk and withdrew a black and white X-ray on which was overlaid a dotted red line.

'That's the wound track,' Henrik said. 'The blade enters the left nostril here,' he said, tapping the glossy paper. 'Then it moves in a perfectly straight line up through the nasal cavity until it meets the suture joining the cribriform plate of the ethmoid bone and the lesser wing of the sphenoid bone. With me so far?'

'Just about.'

He nodded, then pushed his glasses higher up his nose. 'It fractures the bones, which are fairly thin, although you'd still need to give it a good hard shove. Then it travels upwards through the frontal lobe of the brain before coming to a stop against the underside of the frontal bone.'

'Can you ID the weapon?'

'You were on the money with your first guess. A PZ2 Pozidrive screwdriver.'

'That's very specific. How can you be so sure?'

'Simple. Look here.'

Henrik took out another photo. Stella looked at the image. It might have been a satellite photo of an X-shaped industrial facility in a rose-pink desert.

'Is that the tip?'

'Yes. The blade was travelling at sufficient velocity for the tip to become embedded slightly in the interior surface of the bone. I took measurements.'

'So we have the murder weapon. Excellent. What else can you tell me?'

'I just got the first victim's tox screen back from our specialist lab.'

'And?'

'He'd been given a massive dose of ketamine recently. But there's some other stuff that's really interesting.' He pushed a sheet of paper towards her.

The technical Swedish was in some ways easier to read than the less formal everyday words she sometimes still grappled with. But science was a more universal language, and that of toxicology, doubly so.

'Was he an addict?' she asked after scanning down the list of prohibited substances on the report. 'That's quite a shopping list.'

Henrik shook his head. He tapped a line towards the top of the report, buried in a long paragraph Stella had only skim-read.

'That says "microscopic traces". You've got heroin, cocaine, methamphetamine, cannabis – but it's all by-products of decay. The histopathology – sorry, that's lab-speak. Let me start again. His tissues bear signs of long-term, heavy drug abuse at the cellular level. I also found significant cirrhosing of the liver, what I could find of it.'

'So he was a boozer, too.'

'Recovering, or reformed: he was clean for alcohol.'

Stella paused for a moment, giving her brain time to assimilate this new information.

'What about this morning's victim?'

'Still waiting on Toxicology, but there was evidence of past alcohol abuse and traces of cocaine and prescription tranquilisers. Some sort of benzodiazepine.'

'Like Xanax.'

'Yeah, Xanax would account for it. Also Librium, Klonopin, even our old friend Valium. Though that's a bit of a blast from the past these days, recreationally speaking.'

'You don't think she could have been prescribed it?'

Henrik spread his hands wide. 'That's your department, not mine.'

'And there was I thinking you Young Turks weren't afraid to stick your necks out.'

Henrik grinned, the expression transforming his normally owlish looks into those of a charismatic if naughty schoolboy.

'On its own, it doesn't tell us much. But in combination with the other signs I found, and the fact that the other victim appears to have been a user at some point, I'd say no. Not prescribed. There was something else, too.'

Stella's mind flashed to the scene that had greeted her on the roundabout. The scars on the young woman's face.

'She had odd marks on her face. Like acne scars.'

Henrik's eyes lit up. 'Yes! She did. It took me a while, and a couple of calls to colleagues, but eventually I nailed it. They're a reasonably common side effect of Antabuse. That's—'

'— a drug they prescribe for alcoholics. It stops them enjoying the buzz or something.'

'Well, technically, it prevents the body from processing ethyl alcohol. There's no buzz to enjoy at all. Instead a range of unpleasant side effects, from chest pain to nausea.'

'So we have two recovering addicts-slash-alcoholics. Killed within a few days of each other. Both mutilated with the birds' wings. Both found in Stockholm. One killed by accident, presumably before he could be murdered, the other stabbed through the brain with a screwdriver.'

'It looks that way, yes.'

'What about the mutilations themselves? What can you tell me?'

'To incise the skin and cut through the soft tissue, I would lay money on it being surgical instruments. Scalpels, basically.'

'How about the bone?'

'That's where it gets more interesting.'

'Not a bone-saw, then. Something from a hardware store? An angle-grinder?'

'I think so. It's probably not much help. They must sell in their thousands, but...' He shrugged.

'It's all helpful. Thanks, Henrik. Are there photos of the cut marks in your report?'

Henrik grinned. 'Many photos. If you find the right kind of implements at a suspect's place, you could easily run a comparison on the tool marks.'

'Can I ask one last question?'

'You can ask as many as you like. I enjoy our chats. Not every police officer is as interested as you are in the technicalities.'

Stella nodded her acceptance of the compliment.

'Would they have suffered, do you think? I mean, would they have been conscious while he was mutilating them?'

Henrik steepled his fingers under his nose, a curiously donnish gesture, as if he were delivering a university seminar.

'I can't say for certain. They each had plenty of ketamine in their systems. But obviously the male victim woke up after the...' He hesitated. 'I don't know what to call it. Procedure? Operation?'

'Stick with mutilation for now. This was brutal. He's a brute. Let's not dress it up like he probably does in his sick mind.'

'Fair enough. He woke up afterwards. The ketamine might've dulled the pain, but he would still have been in agony. I suspect our female victim didn't regain consciousness. There were no signs of struggle on her body. I think he put her out with the ketamine, mutilated her, then killed her.'

'Thanks, Henrik. Call or text me if you get anything else.'

She left the RMV facility and walked the twelve minutes back to HQ, trying not to imagine how terrifying it must have been for the male victim to wake up and realise what had been done to him.

But she had new information. Henrik's results would help her steer the investigation into its next phase.

She had time of death for both victims. She had cause of death. She had a description of the murder weapon. And she had the beginnings of a profile for both victims, not to mention some fledgling insights into the killer's warped psychology.

What she wanted more than anything else now was the victims' identities.

Later that day, at the 5:00 p.m. briefing, she would get half her wish granted. But not before an old enemy put in an appearance.

16

A staccato knock at her open office door made Stella look up from the report she was writing.

The man occupying the doorway was thin and hungry-looking, eyes burning with the feverish intensity of a true believer. Perhaps being head of the *Avdelningen för särskilda utredningar* – the Special Investigations Division – would do that to a body over the years. Certainly, being the internal affairs bogeyman made Assistant Police Commissioner Nikodemus Olsson probably the most unpopular man at HQ.

'Hello, Nik,' she said, dreading whatever came next. 'What can I do for you?'

He came in, closed the door behind him and folded his rail-thin frame into the visitor chair.

'You have a new case, I hear.'

'That's right. What looks like the beginnings of a serial killer's activities.'

'Which the media will love, naturally.'

'Indeed. Though they're only doing their job.'

'And which will involve re-erecting the pedestal they put you on last time, I expect.'

And there it was. Nik's first barbed arrow aimed directly at her. For if he was Most-Hated Officer at Kungsholmsgatan overall, Stella fulfilled that role for Nik himself.

'The trouble with pedestals, Nik, is the higher they build them, the farther you have to fall,' she said, swatting the arrow away. 'Was there something specific you wanted to talk about, or is this just a social call to discuss my unlooked-for media profile?'

He aimed for a smile. Stella pictured micro-Niks perched on his cheekbones, hauling miserably on thin steel wires attached to the corners of his mouth.

'There was, actually,' he said. 'This is your first big case after the business over in Söderbärke.'

'If you don't count the regular murders I've been clearing in the interim.'

'Quite. But we both know what I mean. The thing is, Stella, last time out, you shot the main suspect. What was his name?'

She knew Nik knew. Refused to play his game. Stayed silent. Stared at him.

Nik cracked first, as she'd known he would,

'Will Andersson. You put a nine-millimetre round into his right calf.'

She shook her head. 'Incorrect.'

Nik's lips pursed. His habitual expression.

'The records are quite clear.'

'It was his left calf. If you only skimmed the report, let me refresh your memory,' she said. 'Having confessed to an earlier killing spree, Will murdered seven women, including a priest and a national politician. He then tried to kill Jonna Carlsson by driving straight at her. Then me, by pushing me into a frozen lake. I shot him to prevent him escaping. *After* issuing the requisite warnings, a decision that the investigating panel ratified when they cleared me of misconduct.'

'Goodness me, Stella, that's quite a speech, It almost sounds like you have it memorised. Or was it your legal experience speaking?'

'Pardon?'

'Well, I gather you used to be married to a lawyer. Did he coach you in how to avoid scrutiny?'

Stella rounded her desk without being aware of making any conscious decision at all. Heart pounding, she grabbed Nik by the narrow lapels of his suit jacket and dragged him towards her so that he fell forwards off the chair and onto his knees.

She bent over him and thrust her face into his, teeth bared.

'Don't you *ever* mention my family to me again, do you understand?'

His normally pale complexion had turned bone white. He gripped her wrists.

'Stella, you're being irrational. Let me go.'

She shook him.

'I said, do you understand?'

'Yes, yes, of course I understand. Now let go of me.'

Shaking, Stella unclenched her fists and released Nik from her grip. Still white with shock, he sank back into the chair.

'I could have you on a disciplinary charge for this,' he said, his voice trembling.

'And I could make an official complaint against you for making slanderous insinuations about my dead husband.'

'I did no such thing,' he spluttered.

'It's your word against mine, Nik. Now unless there's anything else, I suggest you get the devil-to-hell out of my office.'

Brushing away invisible lint from his trouser leg with a vigorous slapping motion, he eyeballed her. Some of the dark fire that had momentarily dimmed in his eyes had returned.

'Just make sure you don't shoot anyone else on *this* case, Stella. Once might have been justified. Twice would start to look like a habit.'

He got up and left. His right hand shook as he reached for the door handle.

With the office to herself again, she dropped her head into her hands. What had she just done? Despite her fighting talk, she'd assaulted a fellow officer. No doubt, given the glass walls of her office, in front of witnesses. Nik would be well within his rights to make a complaint. Hell, he could even make a criminal complaint and leave Internal Affairs out of it altogether.

Maybe she ought to see Alyssa again. But there was a briefing to attend first. Once everyone was assembled, Stella tapped the table to get their attention.

'OK. What have we got? Jonna and Tilde, can we hear from you first, please?'

Jonna turned to her new partner. 'Do you want to go?'

Tilde smiled and nodded, then turned back to Stella. She glanced at her notebook.

'There are thirty-one veterinarian practices in the greater Stockholm area. Between them they employ ninety-eight vets, one hundred and five veterinary nurses and forty administrative staff. There are one hundred and seventeen students studying veterinary medicine at the...' she checked her notes again, 'Swedish University of Agricultural Sciences, Uppsala University, Linköping University and the Karolinska Institute in Solna. We started calling them. Nobody has reported any ketamine going missing.'

'That was Tilde's idea,' Jonna chipped in.

Tilde smiled quickly before continuing.

'Also, I contacted the Swedish Veterinary Association. We need a warrant to inspect their disciplinary files. But I spoke to a very nice lady in their records department. It turns out we both like cross-country skiing. Anyway, off the record, if you will forgive the pun, she said that she couldn't remember any cases where a vet had been reported for mutilating birds. However, Jonna did find something interesting, didn't you, Jonna?'

Stella turned to her friend. This was great, seeing the established detective and the new girl slotting together into a really efficient team.

'There've been a string of break-ins in the last month at zoos and bird sanctuaries. A bunch of birds were killed and guess what?'

'Their wings were removed.'

'I went out to a bird of prey conservancy over in Fagersta. They showed me the corpses. They had them on ice. A...' she consulted her notebook, 'cinereous vulture, a martial eagle and a cape vulture. All with wingspans of two to three metres plus.'

'We've requested CCTV,' Tilde added, 'even though their security people said the local police had already reviewed it. Just in case.'

'You said a string,' Stella said. 'Where else? More importantly, what else?'

'A marabou stork, a great white pelican and a kori bustard were killed at Stockholm Zoo. Wings removed.'

'And a goliath heron was attacked at Kolmården Wildlife Park in Norrköping,' Tilde added.

Stella swiped her hand over her face. 'So that's seven birds that we know of. We can assume he's planning at least that many murders. Every day we don't catch him is a day when we could be seeing more corpses turning up with wings where their arms should be.'

She turned to Oskar.

'Any news on identifying the species of birds he used on the two victims? It would be good to match them to the dead ones.'

Oskar frowned, making his always lugubrious expression look even more forlorn.

'I sent bone and feather samples to the zoology department at the university. Still waiting for an answer. I'll chase them up.'

A civilian staff member knocked on the conference room door and poked his head in.

'Sorry to interrupt, Stella, there's a Doctor Jamie Hooke in Reception. He says he's working for you on the Icarus case.'

'The what?'

'Sorry. They called him that on the lunchtime news. Icarus. Even though, technically, it was Daedalus who made the wings.'

'Great. That's all we need. Anyway, er, Oskar, could you take over, please? I'll go and sign Doctor Hooke in and bring him up for an introduction.'

'Sure, Stella,' Oskar said, rising from his chair.

She left as he was asking the other teams for their reports in his slow, deep voice.

Jamie was sitting in a low armchair upholstered in stain-proof dove-grey fabric. Where other visitors were scrolling through their social media feeds on their phones, Jamie was watching everyone else.

In her turn, Stella spent a few moments watching him. How he kept his face neutral while observing the people coming and going. Melting into the background, not so much drawing attention to himself as repelling it, like the cloth he was sitting on.

She called out to him then explained to the receptionist that they could admit her guest through the glass barrier.

'Hi, how's it going?' he asked, as they walked towards the bank of lifts. 'I'd give you a kiss, but I guess that would probably be inappropriate. Even for Sweden.'

Stella grinned. 'Probably. But who cares. I just beat up the head of Internal Affairs, so a kiss is probably the least of my worries.'

A frown flitted across Jamie's brow, then cleared. He leaned in and kissed her briefly on the cheek.

'You want to talk about it?'

'Later. Not now.'

The lift doors opened, and once the car's occupants had spilled out, talking animatedly or checking their phones, she led him inside and thumbed the button for the fifth floor.

'Ready?' Stella asked Jamie as they walked down the corridor to the conference room.

'As I'll ever be.'

'You're not nervous, are you?'

'What, because I'm about to tell a roomful of Swedish cops how to catch a serial killer about whom I know virtually nothing, you mean? Why would I be nervous?'

She grinned. 'Just give them that old Hooke charm and a bit of psychobabble and you'll be fine.'

As his mouth dropped open in mock-outrage, she opened the door. Oskar glanced over and nodded to her. 'We were pretty much done, Stella,' he said.

'Thanks, Oskar.'

She led Jamie to the front of the room like a teacher bringing a reluctant pupil out to read his work aloud.

'Everyone, this is Doctor Jamie Hooke. Jamie has offered his services free of charge to help us catch our killer. Jamie is accredited by the British Home Office as a forensic psychiatrist and was head of Clinical Services at Broadmoor, one of the UK's secure psychiatric hospitals for the criminally insane,' she said, then inhaled quickly. 'And, just to forestall any canteen gossip, Jamie and I are in a relationship. However, I can't think of anyone else who knows more about deviant psychology than him. I promise you our relationship will in no way colour this investigation or my evaluation of any insights he provides.'

After this speech, which left her short of breath, she turned to her left.

'Jamie? Anything you want to say?'

'Yes. Thanks for the glowing commendation and for embarrassing me with the revelation we're seeing each other.'

The assembled cops, analysts and civilians chuckled indulgently. She had to admire him. The quip about the 'Hooke charm' was only partly a joke to reassure him. When he needed to, Jamie could turn it on like a tap.

He faced the roomful of law enforcement personnel. As he did so, his posture and stance altered slightly. She saw the way his back straightened, his shoulders widened and his head seemed to sit a little back on his neck. A classic power pose. Was he going to assert his authority with a cheap management training course trick? But then he did something that surprised her.

He turned his back on the room, sat on the table, then swivelled round on his bottom with his knees tucked in until he came to rest facing the cops again, with his legs dangling down. The image of the schoolboy returned, only now he looked like the cool kid.

'*Hej! Du letar efter en galning. Låt mig hjälpa dig fånga honom,*' he said, enunciating every one of the Swedish words with care.

Stella frowned. As far she knew, Jamie couldn't speak Swedish.

17

I think it's fair to say I have Stella's attention now.

Sara played her role to perfection. Prettier than Mikael and, of course, not staggering out in front of a truck to be turned into pie filling.

Soon she'll realise how much she needs me.

And I will be ready.

Together we'll solve the case that will make her name live for ever.

She'll be gracious as she accepts the praise from the high-ups and the adulation of the media. But she'll mention her team and, as she stares into the lens of the camera, she'll shoot me a quick glance that only I will be able to interpret correctly.

— I couldn't have done it without you.

— I can't live without you.

That's fine, my darling.

You won't have to.

All I need is my fall guy.

18

Stella shook her head. Jamie had just said, *'Hi. You are looking for a madman. Let me help you catch him.'*

He smiled. 'Sorry. I learned that from Google Translate. I'll have to switch to English now.'

'You called him a "madman",' Oskar said. 'I thought people in your profession didn't use that kind of language.'

'We don't,' Jamie said. 'But I'm a long way from home,' a beat, 'as you can probably tell.'

More indulgent laughter. Stella had forgotten just how good Jamie was.

He continued. 'If he ends up in a psychiatric facility I'm sure my Swedish colleagues will employ the technically correct term. But for us, right here, right now, and the general public, who will be understandably frightened, I think "madman" fits the bill.'

'I've seen profilers in action,' one of the older detectives said. 'Are you just going to tell us he's white because his victims are? Eighteen to thirty-five years old. Loner. Troubled childhood. Bed-wetter. Problems relating to women? Medical professional. The usual guff?'

'Do I need to? It looks like you have that side of things covered,' Jamie said with a smile, earning an answering grin of acknowledgement from the cop. 'Look, I get it, I do. I'm an ivory tower psychiatrist with no frontline experience. I write my reports and spray around enough ambiguous phrases that when you catch this guy – and I know you will, by the way – I can say, there you are! What did I say! He *is* white. *And* single. OK, he's forty-eight and works in a paper mill, but I was mostly right.'

'Give him a chance, Henk,' Jonna said from the other side of the room. 'Let's hear what he has to say.'

Jamie turned in her direction. 'Thanks. It's Jonna, isn't it? Here's my pitch.' He turned back and swept the assembled law enforcement officers with a level gaze. 'You are dealing with a narcissist. He thinks he's smarter than you. Superior in every way. But that's his fatal flaw. His weakness. He needs to keep proving that to himself. He needs that validation. Psychopaths can appear supremely self-confident, but often it masks a psyche as fragile as a blown egg.

'I would expect him to make contact with you in the next few days. Either directly via a letter or indirectly by contacting the media. He will taunt you. This is the beginning of the end for him. He is reaching out to you, but those stretching fingertips will lead you straight back to him.

'I won't bore you with any of that "guff" about his race or sexual leanings. His relationships with his mother or women in general. Instead I can offer insights into how men like him *think*. If, when, you arrest him, he may decide to confess or he may decide to deny everything.

There, again, I can help. I can suggest potential approaches to the interview that will encourage him to go for the first option.

'I can't say much more until I have seen the case file, but let me finish by saying this. You must feel free to question, to challenge and even to reject anything and everything I say. You're the cops. Not me. Thank you.'

To Stella's astonishment, the fifteen or so hard-bitten investigators burst into applause. Led, she was even more surprised to see, by Henk, who'd been so cynical just minutes earlier.

Jamie made great play of clumsily clambering back over the table and regaining his place beside her. As he turned away from the cops, he winked at her.

'Still got it,' he mouthed.

'Thanks, Jamie. That was, er, illuminating,' she said. 'I just want to add one more thing. In my experience catching these weirdos, they love to get close to the action. They might mingle with the onlookers at a crime scene, offer to distribute posters in a neighbourhood where someone's gone missing, that kind of thing. Accept all offers of help as well meant, but get names and addresses if possible. OK, thanks all. That's it.'

Jamie stayed behind as the room emptied.

'I've booked a meeting with Malin. I want to introduce you,' Stella said.

Her phone rang. She looked down. Unknown caller.

Stella answered warily, half-expecting some murmuring psycho to start telling her about his next victim.

'Stella Cole. Who is this, please?' she asked.

A woman replied, instantly putting her mind at ease.

'Hi Stella, my name is Carola Vilks. You may have heard of me.'

'I'm afraid not. What can I do for you, Carola? I'm in the middle of a homicide investigation.'

Stella rolled her eyes for Jamie's benefit. He smiled back at her.

The woman continued as if Stella hadn't spoken. Something about her tone compelled Stella to listen. To make time for her.

'I am the CEO of Vilks Luftrum AB. Does your excellent Swedish extend to translating the name?'

'Vilks Aerospace. Could you get to the point, please?'

'Very well. I believe the dead woman found in Årsta and also the dead man out in Vällingby both had aluminium…what shall I say, fitments?…in their bodies.'

Stella's body went onto high alert. Her pulse began bumping in her throat, she had butterflies in her stomach and her hands felt sweaty. The fact she was speaking to a woman no longer made her feel comfortable. Not at all.

'How did you get that information, Carola?'

'Is it true?'

'That's classified.'

'Of course it is. Well, I could be a nosy journalist after a scoop, so I forgive your need for secrecy,' Carola said silkily. 'Let's assume it is. Aluminium is used widely in my industry. I myself hold several patents for novel fabrication processes. It is lightweight, you see, and strong, perfect for fabricating many aircraft components. I just wondered whether this man you are searching for, this Icarus, might work in the industry. Perhaps I could help you track him down. If I could see these aluminium components, it might point in a certain direction.' A beat. 'Assuming they exist, of course. Well, what do you say, Stella? Could you use a little external expertise or do you have everything wrapped up?'

'Where are you based, Carola?'

'Our headquarters is in Stockholm, but it's largely a financial and marketing office. I work out of our materials research centre down in Norrköping. Take the E4 to junction 119 and follow the signs. Our facility occupies half of the industrial park. We are hard to miss.'

'I was hoping you could come here. I can't release evidence from our own facility just at the moment.' *And I don't like being ordered about by entitled Swedish businesswomen, either.*

'Well, I have quite a busy diary this week, but it is a citizen's duty to help the police. I suppose I could be with you tomorrow? Say at noon?'

'Let's make it eleven. I have a meeting at noon.' *I don't. But we're playing on my turf. My rules.*

'Of course. I can make that work. Until tomorrow, then.'

The line went dead.

Stella sat down. Was this actually happening? She'd barely finished lecturing her team about people inserting themselves into the investigation and it had just happened to her.

She shook the mouse on her desk to wake up her monitor and searched for Carola Vilks. Thousands of web pages promised interviews, analyses, backstories, profiles, listicles of Sweden's most influential women. Even an interview in one of the lifestyle magazines about 'Sweden's glamorous girl bosses showing style and savvy do go together'.

In the article, Carola reclined, catlike, on a scarlet suede sofa, in a distressed olive-green flight suit paired with a pair of ridiculous heels. Some stylist's idea of ironic contrast, Stella assumed. White-blonde hair caught up in a chic up-do. A half-smile suggesting amusement at the silliness of posing for magazine photographs. And large, wide-set intelligent eyes of a startling bright blue.

Interestingly, the brief profile that accompanied the photo mentioned Carola's unusual background as a former test pilot, and fully qualified aerospace engineer, a rather brilliant one at that. It chimed with her boast about holding patents.

Next, Stella visited the Vilks Luftrum website. Everything checked out. Carola was listed as CEO. The picture on the Our Team page matched those on her web search. LinkedIn, Twitter and Facebook all confirmed her identity. Carola Vilks, if a little arrogant, was the real deal. And she was offering to help. Stella nodded to herself. She'd be a fool to turn it down. Plus, following her own instruction, she had both the name *and* the address.

19

Later that day, as she wrestled with the wording on yet another report for Malin, Nik Olsson stopped by her desk. He smiled coldly down at her.

'Can I help you, Nik?'

'I imagine you've been wondering why I haven't filed an official complaint against you after you attacked me.'

'Well, you imagine wrong. Believe it or not, I have one or two more pressing matters to deal with.'

He leaned over her.

'Most police officers make mistakes, most very minor transgressions. They generally need nothing more than a friendly verbal warning. Others flout not just the regulations, but the *law*.' He paused. 'For them, I see no point in handing out what the Americans call "nickel-and-dime" sanctions. The truly corrupt police officer is too wily to be caught by trivial complaints. And bosses can protect their favourites, too. So, I'll bide my time, Stella. But one day, when I have the evidence I need, I will come for you. And I'll bring your high-flying antics to a stop, once and for all.'

'Please don't threaten me, Nik,' she said.

'Why, are you going to assault me again?'

Slowly, she rose from her chair and faced him. They were toe to toe. She hadn't so much invaded his personal space as annexed it. He swallowed. Stepped back.

* * *

After finally closing down her PC at 7:56 p.m., Stella met Jamie outside SPA headquarters. Their meeting with Malin had gone well. He was officially a member of the investigative team and had spent the afternoon ensconced in a small office with the files.

He'd changed into faded jeans, a clean white shirt and an old brown leather jacket she always liked him in, creased, comfortable, with the odd scuff here and there. It summed up how she felt about their relationship.

As they kissed, she felt the smoothness of his newly shaved cheeks. He smelled nice, too: a hint of a woody, spicy aftershave and, more than that, clean, sexy Jamie Hooke.

Stella knew where the evening was heading. She hoped Jamie did, too, despite his sudden departure the previous evening.

So when Jamie asked her where they were eating, she leaned close and whispered, 'Bed first, then dinner.'

He smiled back at her. 'Sounds delicious. I'm starving.'

Her stomach flipped. Partly through her own desire and partly because whatever had taken Jamie from her the night before, it hadn't been the lack of it on his side. She threaded her arm through his and led him round to the car park.

Outside her apartment, Stella was able to get the

door unlocked without any repeat of her earlier clumsy fumblings with the key. She stood aside for Jamie, followed him inside and bumped the door closed with her bottom.

The latch had barely clicked before Jamie turned so that she walked straight into his arms. The kiss was long and lingering. When it ended, she drew back.

'Wow! That was vintage Hooke.'

'I want you,' Jamie said, his voice thick. 'Right now.'

They practically ran for the bedroom, clothes flung to each side as they went. Jamie's leather jacket caught a table lamp in Stella's bedroom and brought it crashing to the floor. Stella laughed at the broad comedy of the moment, then Jamie's shirt was off and he was spinning her around to unclip her bra.

Moments later, they were both naked and in bed. Stella felt herself softening, warming, tingling as she held Jamie against her.

'I've missed you,' she breathed. 'I've missed *this*.' She squeezed him and he groaned in response.

'Me, too,' he said, moving on top of her.

The sex was good – exciting and swoony, both – but it was over too soon for Stella. She held Jamie close, winding his curls around her fingers, feeling his chest heaving against hers as his breathing settled. She heard the breeze rustling the tree branches outside her window. Birdsong made the apartment feel more like a woodland clearing. Somewhere, just beyond the trees, she thought she saw a woman preening long white wings.

'Ready to go again?' Jamie murmured.

She started. Had she dropped off? She felt him against her and grinned.

Stella shrugged off his enfolding arm and pushed

him over onto his back. She straddled him. It felt good. It felt right. It was as if the breakup had never happened.

And now, finally, they could be totally honest with each other. He knew she'd killed. And he didn't mind.

No more secrets.

* * *

Sitting at a candlelit corner table in a one-room seafood restaurant only the locals knew about, Stella reached across and covered Jamie's left hand with her right.

'Thank you.'

'What for?'

'For not giving up on me. On us.'

'How could I? I love you, Stel.'

'I love you, too.'

'I think I was only part-me without you. I need you. I hope you feel the same way about me.'

As an undeclared but fervent feminist, Stella's mother had always warned her daughter against putting herself in a position of need with regards to a man.

Love a man, or a woman for that matter, darling, she'd said once. *Love him, cherish him, live with him, marry him. But don't ever make yourself* dependent *on him.*

Stella had always tried to follow her mum's advice. Before she married Richard, afterwards – and since his death. But something had changed. It felt good to accept the truth. She *did* need Jamie. She felt more complete somehow when she was with him.

'Yes.'

He looked anxious. 'Yes, you need me or, yes, something else?'

'Yes, I need you, Mister Needy-pants. Now let's order. I'm hungry.'

Jamie smiled. 'I'm glad. I'm hungry, too.'

Later, as they picked among the wreckage of a seafood platter, scattering prawn heads and crinkled black oyster shells, Jamie asked Stella the question she'd been waiting for.

'Do you think he's going to do it again?'

'I'd be a fool not to, wouldn't you say?'

He tilted his head on his side, smiling briefly as he spotted a clam shell still containing its morsel of garlic-scented flesh.

'It's too ornate to be the work of a two-and-I'm-out killer. He's perfecting his method. There'll be more. Until you stop him.'

'And you're sure it's a him? I know the stats, and that's what my gut is telling me, but I'd like to hear it from you.'

'Am I one hundred per cent certain? No. No scientist ever can be. But even going by the practical aspects of this morning's display, that suggests a male offender.'

'Because of the strength needed to get a body into position like that?'

'Basically, yes.'

'It could be a female body-builder. Or just a woman with a working knowledge of levers. There were no signs of sexual assault.'

'Agreed. So, it *could* be a woman. But, as you say, serial killing isn't exactly a shining example of an equal opportunities field.'

'You're right. I just wanted to check my assumptions. Did anything leap out at you from the photos? Anything that might suggest how the victims are connected? I think they were both alcoholics-slash-addicts, by the way.'

'Connected other than by their killer, you mean?'

'Well, that's my number one priority, obviously,' Stella said, finishing her wine and refilling both their glasses. 'Once we can ID the victims, we can start piecing their lives together, especially their final hours. Even if they have nothing in common at all, there's always that one point of intersection: they both met the same man, and he killed them.'

Jamie pressed his hands together in front of him, resting his chin on the tips of his middle fingers. For a moment, Stella saw him as a priest. A priest of the perverted ways people's minds worked and the deviant behaviours into which those workings led them.

'What I saw was a man who puts a great deal of care into what he's doing to his victims,' Jamie said.

It was the same line Henrik had come up with at the autopsy. Wanting Jamie's take on it, Stella raised her eyebrows. 'Care? How?'

'It's the way the wings were joined on to the bodies. For a start, he fabricated those aluminium struts. Then he drilled out both bones to the precise diameter needed. He clamped the major arteries and even cauterised the wounds to minimise bleeding. Finally, he sealed the wounds with superglue and sutures. That's the work of someone who, however disordered his thinking about human life, cares deeply about what he's doing.'

Stella nodded, putting Jamie's observations alongside her own at the autopsy.

'He could have just hacked the arms off with an axe and duct-taped the wings on.'

'Exactly. What does that say to you?'

'Huh. I was hoping you were going to tell me that.'

'I will. But let's hear your view first. You're the cop who catches them, after all. I just treat the ones the courts judge to be insane.'

Stella didn't speak at once. She looked at a spot on Jamie's right jacket sleeve midway between the shoulder and the elbow. Imagined the shirt inside the lined leather, and the flesh inside that. Skin, fat, muscle, bone, tendons, ligaments, nerves, veins, arteries. Such a complex piece of engineering. No wonder religious believers cited the human eye as evidence for God's existence. It was hard to imagine such structures arriving by chance.

Was that it? Was she dealing with someone who thought they were God? Or was that a distraction? A too-convenient line of enquiry that could derail the investigation and waste scarce resources chasing imaginary deities down metaphorical rabbit holes?

She flashed on the phrase that had passed through her mind microseconds ago: *a complex piece of engineering*.

And who had just offered her help with the investigation? One of Sweden's most influential aerospace engineers. A supremely confident, even arrogant woman, who clearly enjoyed being the centre of attention *and who had just inserted herself into the investigation*.

Was it really going to be this easy to apprehend Icarus? She refocused. Jamie was looking at her, a smile on his face. Had she been gone long? It didn't seem so from his expression.

'I think our guy is a great respecter of engineering. Human or otherwise. He sees the human body as a wonderful machine. A complex machine...' She paused, a thought tapping quietly at the door of her conscious mind, asking to be let in.

'But,' Jamie prompted.

Stella swung the door wide.

'But not a perfect machine.'

'Explain.'

She nodded to him, listening as the newly admitted thought spoke.

'For some reason, he believes that human beings are physically imperfect. He sees it as his job to fix that imperfection.'

'By replacing arms with wings.'

'Yes. He thinks we should be able to fly.'

'Sure about that?'

Stella frowned. She'd been voicing her inner thought, but now her copper's brain took back control.

'OK, let me back up a bit,' she said. 'No, he doesn't think we should be able to fly. He's too intelligent for that. Even with the wings he's used, there's no way the victims could get airborne. Alive, obviously.'

'Sooo?' Jamie gave the extended syllable a Swedish sing-song quality.

'So for him, the wings represent the *idea* of flight,' she said, suddenly feeling on surer ground. 'They symbolise perfection, as he sees it. That could be birds, it could be angels, it could be something we haven't thought of yet.'

'That's where I've got to, as well,' Jamie said. 'I think he is trying to tell us we're imperfect and that we ought to be as he is suggesting with these grotesque hybrids.'

'Which is all very well, but how does it help me catch him?'

Now it was Jamie's turn to fall silent. Stella didn't mind. She used the time to scrutinise the dessert menus their black-clad waitress had just brought over with a smile.

'In case you have a little room,' she said with a smile that popped an attractive little dimple into her left cheek.

Stella opted for a mango panna cotta and a double espresso and showed the menu to Jamie. He nodded and pointed at the chocolate mousse.

'We know our guy must have at least some familiarity with surgical procedures. We also know that...' Jamie adopted a 'TV host' voice, '...pop quiz, which job has one of the highest incidences of psychopaths?'

'Surgeons. Also politicians, top executives and law enforcement.'

'Yes, which is mildly worrying for those of us currently dining with a member of the latter,' Jamie said with a wink. 'But it's the first one that interests me.'

'So we look for a surgeon, presumably specialising in orthopaedics—'

'Yes, and maybe upper body, within that general field.'

' – who has, what, published an article saying how the human body is badly designed?'

Jamie shrugged. 'That sounds like a long shot, but it would be a good sign, wouldn't it?'

'Chance would be a fine thing!'

Stella paused while their waitress placed the two small but delicious-looking desserts before them.

'I'll be right back with your coffee,' she said brightly.

'You know what Henk said earlier, in the briefing?' Stella asked, spooning out a delicate little oval from the quivering panna cotta.

'About all that profiling guff?'

'That,' she said with a smile, before placing the just-cooked cream and mango sauce into her mouth. 'Oh, that is so good,' she said inadvertently.

'But do I have any thoughts on who we're looking for?' Jamie supplied helpfully.

'Mm-hmm,' Stella mumbled through another mouthful.

'Sure, why not. Let's say we have a male. He is strong and fit enough to get a female corpse weighing around nine stone into a vertical position. Psychopaths rarely start killing before their eighteenth birthdays and usually in their twenties. And as these appear to be our guy's first two kills, we'll assume he hasn't been long in the field. So we'll go for an age range of twenty to thirty.'

'What else?'

'I think he's smart. Probably educated to university level. This level of symbolic mutilation is the preserve of the more cerebral killer. High-school graduates or those who never even finish tend to blitz-killing or cruder mutilation. For the record, I think he is likely to be white.'

'Because his victims were?'

Jamie wrinkled his nose. 'Because Sweden is mostly white. Basic demographics, no psychological voodoo needed.'

Stella smiled. 'He'll have a workshop, too,' she said. 'If it's at his house, it'll be remote. I can't imagine him risking a neighbour catching him unloading condor wings from his pickup, can you?'

'No. So an industrial unit, or a shack somewhere in the forest. Unobserved anyway.'

Stella nodded, running her teaspoon around the glass bowl, scraping up the last of the dessert. Someone was coming to see her the next day who had an entire factory to play in. But Carola Vilks didn't fit their impromptu profile in one important regard. She was a woman.

They settled the bill and, as the evening was warm, took a leisurely route back to Stella's apartment via the waterfront.

'Come on, there's somewhere I want to show you,' Stella said, linking arms with Jamie.

She led him down to the stretch of water known as Lilla Värtan. They walked to where the river split around Helgeandsholmen, the small island housing the Swedish Parliament building.

They walked halfway across the bridge with its grey granite setts, mingling with tourists who were either unaware of the killing that morning or unconcerned. Selfies. Now, they *were* important.

'You want to get one of us?' Jamie asked, nodding towards a couple posing with their backs to the parliament building.

'Really?'

Jamie's face fell. 'We don't have to.'

'No, of course I want to. Come on.'

Stella pulled her phone out, flipped the camera round and held it aloft, as so many people around them were doing.

'Wouldn't it be great if I caught the killer in the background,' she said, before grinning into the tiny lens and thumbing the red shutter button.

'I can see the headline now,' Jamie said with a grin. 'Stella catches killer on camera.'

But when she tapped the tiny thumbnail, the image was just her and Jamie, smiling to the lens with the magnificent rugged stone facade of the Riksdagshuset behind them.

'Oh well,' he said. 'Better luck next time.'

'Come on,' she said, steering him back towards home. 'All that food has given me an appetite.'

20

Carola Wilks arrived at SPA headquarters ten minutes early for her appointment with the British super cop. This would give her time to cool off and ensure she presented a sweat-free appearance to her hostess. Not that she was over-given to perspiring.

For their meeting she had selected a stylish, though austere, steel-grey suit in a linen-cashmere mix. It was the creation of one of her favourite designers. She had spotted his potential early, when he was still a student at the Institute of Fashion and Textiles, and nurtured his talent.

The jacket was unbuttoned, the better to show off the cerise silk shirt she wore. Just before entering the building, she'd undone a second button to reveal a modest amount of cleavage and a three carat diamond pendant set in a lightweight ingot of aluminium created through one of her own patented processes.

At 10:55 a.m., Stella appeared in the reception area and approached the central desk. Carola watched as the young man who'd asked her to sign in pointed her out to Stella.

Stella was definitely better-looking in the flesh than the scant photos on the web had suggested. Shorter than Carola had imagined, but then, she was wearing low-heeled boots. A decent pair of heels would add three inches easily.

Carola rose from the chair and extended her hand as Stella drew near.

'Carola?' Stella asked.

'Yes. And you must be Stella. I am thrilled to meet you. Truly. And honoured you would allow me to help with your investigation.'

Carola employed the tone and gaze that had men with far more power and money than her eating out of her hand. Stella seemed oddly unmoved. Too busy with the case, Carola decided. Which was understandable. Serial killers must be so hard to catch.

* * *

Jamie was sitting at the kitchen table in his Airbnb, proofreading an article, when the doorbell rang. Sighing, he got to his feet. It would be a cold-caller selling double-glazing, or a politician canvassing for votes. Easy enough to get rid of.

But when he opened the door, he got a surprise. It was the tall, strongly built female cop on Stella's team, standing there with a shy smile.

'It's Tilde, isn't it?' he asked with a smile. 'Do you want to come in? I was about to make myself a coffee.'

'Sure, thanks,' she said in English.

Back in the kitchen, he fiddled with the fancy coffee machine while making small talk with Tilde. When he had the coffees prepared and, remembering how fond the Swedes were of 'a little something to go with your coffee?', some crispbreads, he sat opposite Tilde.

'What brings you all the way out here, Tilde?'

She sipped her coffee and regarded him over the rim. Was she shy? Embarrassed? A worrying thought came to him. He'd been booted off the case already. *A problem with SPA protocol,* she was about to say. He felt a flash of anger. The rookie had been given the dirty job. Her answer confirmed one of his guesses.

'This is a little bit embarrassing,' she said, putting the chunky white mug down on the table. 'It's just, I don't know if Stella told you about me, but I'm really, really new.'

'To what?'

Her eyes widened. 'Everything! New to Stockholm, new to being a homicide investigator. New to major crimes. And definitely new to hunting serial killers.'

'I'm sure Stella wouldn't have brought you onto her team unless she was confident you'd be an asset.'

She bobbed her head in acknowledgement of his praise. 'Yeah, but this case. It's just so weird. That's why I'm here, actually. I was wondering if you could give me some pointers.'

'Well, I'm not an investigator, Tilde, you know that.'

'But you know about psychopaths, right?'

'Oh, yes, I think we can safely say I know a little about them.' Tilde frowned. He wondered whether his irony had lost her. 'I know *a lot* about them,' he added.

She smiled. The expression transformed her. She was rather pretty, in a milkmaidish sort of way. Rosy cheeks and twinkling blue eyes.

'So can you give me, I don't know, a crash course?

Like the basics. The type of person we're looking for, what drives them? That kind of thing?'

Now he understood, he felt the ground firming under him. The rookie wanted to impress her new boss without being seen cribbing from textbooks in the office. What better way than to consult the forensic psychiatrist brought in to help them?

'Of course I can,' he said.

For the next hour, during which they only paused once, when Tilde needed the bathroom, he outlined the fundamentals of psychopathic thinking and behaviour. He placed special emphasis on what he called in lectures, 'pathways to deviancy' rather than non-threatening forms like over-achievement in business, sport or politics.

Finally, just as he was thinking he'd miss the deadline to send his corrections to the article back, Tilde checked her watch. Her eyes popped wide.

'Oh my God, I've kept you far too long,' she said, getting to her feet. 'I'm so sorry. I had no idea, but it was all really interesting, Jamie. Thank you so much.'

He saw her out and then, shaking his head and wishing all his challenges could be met so easily, went back to the article.

He grimaced. He'd written 'cabalistic' instead of 'cannibalistic'. A quick stroke with the red pen and it was fixed.

* * *

Stella led her guest up to the major crimes department, and her office with a view down over Kronobergsparken, the public park at this time of year a beguiling mixture of lush grass and wooded areas, rich in birches, oak, ash and elm.

Coffee offered and accepted, the two women sat facing each other across Stella's desk.

'First of all, Carola, I want to thank you for offering your assistance with our investigation,' Stella began. 'I'm sorry if I was curt with you on the phone. It's been a hectic couple of days, as I'm sure you can imagine.'

Carola smiled. It was the expression of a woman who was used to receiving apologies, perhaps from inefficient underlings, or unsatisfactory lovers. Receiving them and brushing them aside.

'Please, it's me who should apologise. Thrusting myself forward when, as you say, you were setting up a full-blown murder inquiry.'

Honour satisfied on both sides, Stella decided to get down to business. She intended to benefit any way she could from Carola's offer, and also from close observation of her behaviour.

Earlier, she'd paid a visit to the evidence locker and retrieved the aluminium rod that Henrik had extracted from the dead woman's left humerus bone. He'd cleaned it before bagging it, so it presented a rather more innocuous appearance than when it had been smeared with blood.

She offered Carola a pair of white nitrile gloves.

'If you'd just put these on, I'll open the evidence bag for you.'

While Carola slipped her manicured fingers into the flimsy gloves, Stella took a scalpel she kept in her office drawer and slit the tape sealing the bag. She replaced the scalpel and, with her own gloves on, withdrew the aluminium rod and passed it to Carola.

Carola picked up the rod and turned it in the sunlight streaming in through the window to her right.

'What is that, twelve millimetres in diameter? A little more?'

'Twelve point one,' Stella said, impressed with the other woman's perception. Or her nerve in guesstimating the dimensions of a piece of metal she had milled herself.

'And it was inserted into an arm bone to provide a mounting post for the wing?'

'Exactly.'

Carola bounced the rod lightly in her palm, closing her eyes as she did so and lifting her chin, just a little, as if listening to distant music.

'Disappointing.'

'What is?'

'It's solid all the way through. The ends are blank, as you can see, but I had thought maybe the interior would be honeycombed.'

Stella tried to imagine how a person might produce honeycomb cells in a piece of solid metal. Couldn't. Asked instead.

'How easy is that to do?'

'Oh, not hard,' Carola said, breezily. 'If you have access to the right equipment. There are a number of processes that all come under the general heading "honeycombing". Some are basic, for construction work. Others, such as those used in the automotive industry or aviation, are rather more sophisticated.'

'The sort of processes your company specialises in?'

'Absolutely. The kind for which I hold patents, as I mentioned on the phone yesterday. If he'd used one of them, I think we could have narrowed down your suspect pool to somebody working in this highly specialised field. But, sadly, it's a piece of stock you can pick up anywhere.'

'And by anywhere, you mean?'

Carola shrugged. 'Metal merchants, specialist builders merchants, even eBay. You could get a piece like that, say three hundred mils long with a twelve-mil diameter for, what, a hundred and fifty krone? It's very cheap.'

Stella frowned. She realised that despite her fanciful conjecture that Carola might be the killer, she now desperately wanted something to go on. She wracked her brain for another question.

'Does aluminium have a different chemical signature depending on where it was produced?'

Carola smiled.

'An excellent question, Stella. I'm impressed. The answer is yes, everything from calcium and sodium to zirconium and hydrogen. I won't bore you with the details, though I always run that risk when I start talking about aluminium...' She paused like a stand-up comedian waiting for a laugh. Stella smiled, dutifully. 'But there are various oxides and intermetallics that can alter the physical properties of aluminium. They do vary from foundry to foundry, but, if I sense correctly where you are going with this, the amounts are absolutely minute and they vary more from batch to batch than foundry to foundry. They're always kept within prescribed limits, but within those, there are always variations.'

'So we couldn't, for example, track this rod back to a specific foundry?'

'Oh, you *could*. If you had enough money. But what would it tell you? Probably that it came from Norsk Hydro in Sunndal. It's where we get all ours from. They probably supply half the industrial consumers in Scandinavia.'

143

'Shit,' she said feelingly. 'Sorry.'

Carola laughed, a husky sound full of good humour. If she was a psychopath, she was a very affable one.

'No problem. Look, I'm sorry I couldn't offer you any more help. But maybe I could be something else for you.'

'What?'

'Well, this man, he's attaching wings to people, correct?'

'Correct.'

'Well, I am an expert in flight. If you need a sounding board, you know, if it's relevant, I would love to help you.'

'Thank you. I'll bear that in mind.'

After a few pleasantries, Stella showed Carola out and returned to her desk. Offers of help, however well-meaning, weren't what she wanted right now.

More than anything else, she needed names. Two to be exact. One for her male victim currently on the board as 'victim 1' and the other for her female, 'victim 2'.

21

Two days passed.

Every morning and every evening, Stella pushed her team for ideas, for answers as to the identities of their two victims.

'Somebody must know *something*,' she said. 'They've been missing for a minimum of a few days now. Have they been reported missing by a loved one? What about employment? Are they being missed at work? Have they missed dates with partners or friends? Tilde, any news on DNA?'

'We're still waiting on the RMV, I'm afraid. I've called every morning but it's a long queue and priority jobs keep bumping us lower down.'

'I'll ask Malin if we can find some budget from somewhere to push us higher up. Anyone else got anything?'

'I've been thinking about the tox screen reports,' Oskar said. 'Apart from the ketamine, both victims were clean for drugs or alcohol, yes?'

'Yes.'

'But the autopsy reports said both victims had internal damage caused by alcohol and drug abuse.'

'So they were recovering addicts-slash-alcoholics.'

'Yeah. So what if they were attending AA meetings? That would be a connection and we might get IDs.'

'Fantastic. Thanks, Oskar. Can you get onto that, please? Jonna, any update on the vets?'

Jonna twisted her mouth to one side, like she'd bitten on something sour.

'Here's the non-surprising news. Every vet practice in Stockholm holds stock of ketamine. None of the ones Tilde and I have spoken to have reported any break-ins or thefts of drugs. We're asking them all to recheck their stocks.'

'How about any disciplinary reports for animal cruelty?'

'Nothing.'

Stella sighed. 'That bit's a long shot. Keep on it, please. OK. Thanks, everyone. Let's get back to it.'

Later that day, Henk knocked on her door and stuck his head in through the gap. He was smiling.

'Stella! Got some good news.'

'Come in, then. Don't keep me in suspense.'

He stood in front of her desk, practically at attention. He thrust out a sheet of paper. She recognised the official crest at the top. The state DNA archive.

'We got a hit. The male victim. He's on the system,' Henk said.

Stella scanned the sheet of official language looking for the only field she cared about.

Name: Mikael Matthiasson

She read on.

Offence: drunk and disorderly, criminal damage: 15.1.17

Address: NFA

No fixed abode. Was he homeless? Sofa-surfing at mates' houses? A traveller? They'd find out soon enough.

She looked up at Henk.

'Can you get started on a trace? And get a media release together. Use his official photo from the crime records database. We want anyone who knew Mikael to contact us ASAP.'

He nodded. 'I'm on it.'

Stella grabbed her bag. She wanted to follow up on Oskar's idea.

The main office was humming as Henk shared the good news. 'Victim 1' was no more, henceforth to be known as Mikael Matthiasson. Stella looked around for Jonna. Her desk was vacant.

'Anyone seen Jonna?' Stella called out.

'She left about ten minutes ago,' someone answered.

Stella looked around. Tilde was talking animatedly on the phone. As soon as she replaced the receiver, Stella went over.

'Tilde, you're with me this morning. Get your things.'

Tilde jumped up so fast she knocked a half-empty cup of coffee. But before it spilled its contents, she grabbed it and set it straight on the desk. A small amount of liquid still slopped over the edge and soaked into a sheet of paper.

'Damn the devil!' Tilde muttered.

'Nothing important, I hope,' Stella deadpanned.

Tilde bit her lip. 'Part of my list of vets. But I hate mess,' she said, swiping at the little pool of coffee with a paper tissue.

'Leave that,' Stella said. 'We're going out.'

'Where?'

'I'll tell you on the way.'

As Stella drove towards *St Agnes Kyrkan*, a Lutheran church in the centre of Stockholm, she explained her idea to Tilde.

'Oskar said they might have attended AA meetings, right? Well I happen to know that the priest at Saint Agnes leads a group. It's one of the biggest in Stockholm.'

'Do you attend?' Tilde asked.

'Do you think I'd tell you if I did?' Stella said, laughing. 'The whole point of those groups is they're confidential.'

'I'm just curious,' Tilde said.

'Well I don't. But I've talked to Frida Strandberg before, on another case. She might be helpful.'

'I wouldn't judge you if you had, Stella. Everybody has problems, after all.'

'They do. But that isn't one of mine.'

'I hope you don't mind me asking. Only they taught us on the investigators' course never to be afraid of asking questions,' Tilde said. 'And I find people fascinating anyway, so…'

She tailed off. Stella wondered whether the young detective next to her without any filter might be on the spectrum. Not that it mattered, but it might explain some of her behaviour.

'It's fine. If you cross a line, I'll tell you. Your instructors were right. A good detective should never be afraid of asking questions. Of anyone, about anything. Remember that.'

'I will. Thanks. Guv.'

Stella turned her head to glance at her new assistant for the day.

'Guv?'

'I overheard Jonna call you that. It's OK, right?'

'It's fine. Although I prefer plain Stella. Here we are.'

Stella pulled off the road and into a small gravelled car park in front of the church. The doors were wide open.

She led Tilde from the bright sunshine into a dimmer but colourful interior. Children's paintings adorned the walls of the vestibule. Trees, landscapes, zoo animals. One picture caught Stella's eye. A huge bird standing between a man and a woman and two small children, its black wings extended around them.

She shuddered involuntarily.

'Let's see if we can find Frida,' she said, casting an uneasy glance over her shoulder at the artwork.

She saw the priest in the main body of the church, talking in a low voice to a young man who kept rubbing his bare arms and scratching at the back of his head. To Stella he looked like a drug user. Meth, most likely. The jerky body movements characteristic of that particular poison's side effects led to the addicts' nickname: 'tweakers'.

She laid a hand gently on Tilde's arm. 'Let's wait here till they're finished.'

Tilde frowned. 'But this is a homicide investigation, Stella. A *double*-homicide,' she hissed.

'I know. And this is a church. Frida's church. We won't get anywhere by barging into private conversations. Look, just take a few minutes off. See if you can find us a couple of coffees.'

Tilde jerked her head up and down. 'Call me, though, as soon as we're good to go.'

Stella smiled. 'I promise. You won't miss anything.'

Tilde offered another staccato nod and spun round to go in search of coffee.

Shaking her head, Stella wandered over to a

noticeboard. On her way, she caught Frida's eye. The priest smiled. Stella nodded back. The wordless communication was as clear as the plain glass filling the arched windows above them.

I'll be with you as soon as I can.

Take your time. I'll wait.

After a few more minutes, Stella heard shuffling footsteps. She turned to see the young man walking away from Frida, his head down, still scratching. She let him pass then walked down the aisle to Frida.

'Hey, Stella, how are you?' Frida asked, brushing a lock of unruly auburn hair away from her eye.

'I'm good, Frida. How are things here?'

The priest rolled her eyes, which were large and set wide apart.

'Oh, you know. Part priest, part social worker. Too many people needing too much help. I sometimes wonder whether God enjoys seeing His faithful suffer.'

Stella smiled. 'I think it's the same the world over. Certainly in England.'

Frida shook her head, dislodging more of the thick wavy hair.

'Now, unless this is a social call…'

'I'm afraid not.'

'What can I do for you?'

Stella heard hurrying footsteps. A completely different rhythm to those of the meth-head. Fast, brisk, light. Tilde.

'Here you are,' she said, thrusting a cardboard cup into Stella's hand. She turned to Frida. 'Good morning. I'm *Kriminalinspektör* Tilde Enström.'

Frida's eyes twinkled. 'Hi, Tilde. I'm Frida.'

'I haven't missed anything?' Tilde asked Stella.

'No. I was just about to ask Frida about the AA group she runs here.'

Frida frowned. 'Let's talk in my office, then. I think it would be better to be somewhere private, don't you?'

Frida's office was a clean, white-painted space filled with dozens of house plants. 'My babies,' Frida said with a smile, brushing her finger along one glossy, waxy leaf.

Once they were seated, and Frida had poured herself a cup of coffee from a drip machine popping and hissing quietly in a corner, Stella reached into her bag for a notebook.

'Have you seen on the news about the two deaths? The ones the media are attributing to Icarus.'

Frida nodded. 'So awful. And so bizarre, too!' Her eyes widened still further. 'I wonder where these people get their ideas from. Such wickedness.'

'Sadly, they do not see it that way,' Tilde said, surprising Stella. 'To a psychopath, human beings have no value other than in satisfying their needs, however unusual they may appear to others.'

'Unusual?' Frida echoed. 'I would say that cutting people's arms off and replacing them with wings is a little more than unusual.'

Tilde smiled. 'Of course. I just meant that in catching serial killers, it helps to understand how they see the world. Nothing more.'

Stella wanted to stop her new, and, she began to think, definitely temporary assistant before she could upset the priest further.

'Deviant psychology aside,' Stella said, 'we're working on the idea that one or both victims may have been recovering addicts or alcoholics. Possibly both. I was wondering whether you knew either of them. And if not, whether you might have contact details for other groups in the city.'

Frida looked down at her hands, which had knotted themselves into a bundle of bony knuckles in front of her.

'I can't reveal details of our members, Stella, you know that.'

'I know. But they're dead, Frida. No more harm can come to them, and you might be helping to prevent more deaths, especially if it's attendance at AA meetings that links the victims.'

'Do you think it does?'

'It's a possibility, that's all. Does the name Mikael Matthiasson mean anything to you?'

Frida blew out her lips, flapping them like a horse.

'No, but many of our service-users give false names. We don't mind. What's important is that they come and keep coming. We did have a Mikael once. But it's a common enough name. People don't usually reveal their surnames, though.'

'Can I show you a picture?'

'Of course. If it will help.'

Stella reached into her bag and withdrew the photo of Mikael Matthiasson from the criminal records database. She turned it round and pushed it across the desk to Frida.

'Recognise him?' she asked.

Frida reached for a pair of glasses in an open case and slid them onto her nose. 'For reading,' she said apologetically. 'I'm getting old!'

She picked up the sheet of paper and peered at it.

'No. That's not him. Our Mikael was completely different-looking. This man is bony. Mikael was fat, not to put it unkindly.'

'People's weight can fluctuate,' Tilde said.

'Yes, I know, but still, this is not my Mikael.'

Stella sighed. It had been a long shot. 'Can I show you one more photo? It's not pretty, I'm afraid.'

'That's OK. Maybe in my line of work I don't see quite the grotesque side of life you do, Stella, but I have a strong stomach.'

The headshot of the dead woman was really not too bad. She had the pallor of death on her skin, but her killer had not beaten her or mutilated her, not above the neck, at any rate. Stella wanted to over-prepare Frida so the reality would come as a kind of relief. Then she might be better able to concentrate on her face.

Frida gave the photo a quick glance, then studied it more closely, before handing it back to Stella.

'I'm sorry. I don't know her. But I can share my list of other group leaders in Stockholm.'

'That would be great. Thanks, Frida.'

Outside the church, Stella handed the list to Tilde. 'Right. Let's make a start. Which one's closest to here?'

Tilde studied the list then stabbed a finger at a name halfway down.

'This one.'

'Call him and tell him we're coming over.'

While Tilde phoned the group leader, Stella put the car into gear and pulled out from the church car park. It was tenuous, but at least they had a lead. Something would shake loose soon.

22

Stella feels frustrated that she's no nearer to catching the killer. Me, I mean. That's about to change. Because I'm going to help her solve the case.

And when it's all over, and the bodies have been buried, and the celebrations are over, it will be just the two of us. Like it was always supposed to be.

But not yet.

I'm having too much fun to stop.

23

Jens Kashani checked his messages for the hundredth time that day.

Nothing.

He'd left dozens of voicemails, texts, even a video-call to Sara's Instagram account. Talk about desperate.

Christ! Where was she? He'd been round to her flat. But despite leaning on the doorbell until that bitch of a neighbour came out and complained about the noise, she hadn't answered.

Jens wasn't a big guy; he'd never been one for hitting the gym. Or not with the free weights like those pathetic steroid-heads with obscene over-developed muscles and tiny, shrunken penises. But he'd even considered trying to kick down the door.

He got as far as leaning back and drawing his leg up like some cut-rate, mixed-race Bruce Lee. Then good sense, and a vision of him queueing at the ER with a broken foot, made him replace his sneaker-clad foot on the floor.

After shouting through the letterbox and receiving

another evil glare from the bitch queen next door, he'd left, stomach squirming with anxiety.

He knew all about Sara's history. How could he not, when that was how they'd met? Through the group. But they'd been instantly attracted to each other, and their relationship really worked in terms of helping both of them stay clean and sober.

He'd been due to meet Sara for dinner two nights ago, but she hadn't shown. Since then, he'd heard nothing from her and he was really worried. If she'd fallen off the wagon, he thought she might fall hard. She was never one for half-measures. Not with drinking, or drugs or even sex. God, the sex was fantastic. Sometimes it scared him: her hunger for it. It was as if giving up one craving had simply made room for another.

And now she'd vanished.

He'd called her parents. But neither Norbert nor Maria Marksson had heard from their daughter for two weeks. They weren't worried, Norbert had explained, because Sara rarely called them more than once a month and they'd spoken on the phone three weeks earlier.

He'd even called her work, to see if they knew where she was. But the boss at the warehouse had no clue. He was just as worried as Jens. But, as he ruefully explained, it wasn't uncommon. About a quarter of the people he hired from the halfway house programme would just disappear one day and either not come back or return, shamefaced, drunk, or both, weeks or months later.

Jens wasn't much of a reader, certainly not of the news. Unless it was about sport, or celebrities. Sara was a celebrity. Maybe not a big one. But she'd been on *Talented Sweden* and opened a couple of supermarkets off the back of it. She was on her way, as she liked to tell him. As soon as that big break came along, she'd been flying.

Because of his limited reading habits, he hadn't seen anything about the winged woman on the roundabout in Årsta. He might have caught a snippet on the radio, or as he scrolled through his Insta. But it hadn't registered. What was one more instance of weirdness in a world full of singing huskies, babies born with full sets of teeth and Russian porn stars with breasts bigger than basketballs?

But after his failed attempt to raise her in person, he'd finally cracked. He didn't really trust the cops. Too many friskings and illegal stop-and-searches when he was a teenager – OK, a teenager with an attitude, but still. Who else could he go to now? An influencer?

The cop at the police station had been polite. Called him Jens. Taken a description of Sara, her last known whereabouts, her contact details, *his* contact details. Finally, he'd advised Jens to try not to worry.

'Sara's probably just off somewhere having a good time. She'll come home when the money runs out.'

Jens had nodded dumbly and walked back out into the sunshine. He did not feel reassured. Sara having a good time was exactly what he was worried about.

A day later, he was sitting at an outside table in Stortorget, the prettiest square in Stockholm. Behind him, tall, narrow buildings in rainbow colours – red, tangerine, sunshine yellow, sky-blue – loomed over the cafe awnings. Their ornate rooflines looked as though a child with an eye for detail and a steady hand had cut them out of brightly coloured card with sharp scissors.

His soy latte was growing cold as he checked his messages every thirty seconds or so, between calling anyone he could think of. Two girls – they looked like tourists – ran across the square, filming each other on their phones and squealing with what looked like genuine delight. A flock of pigeons took to the air in a clatter of flapping wings.

His phone rang, a melodic counterpoint to the rattle of feathers, startling him. He looked at the screen. No caller ID.

'Hello?'

'Jens Kashani?'

'Yeah. Who is this?'

'My name is Stella Cole. I'm a detective. Could you come down to SPA headquarters on Kungsholmsgatan, please? I'd like to talk to you about the woman you reported missing: Sara Marksson.'

Jens crinkled his forehead. The woman was English. And she was familiar. He knew her name. He struggled to place her. Then it came to him.

She was a celebrity. The British super cop who caught serial killers and turned up on the gogglebox on Aktuellt.

Oh, Jesus. This wasn't good.

24

Stella went down to reception to collect Jens in person.

The girl on the front desk pointed him out to her. He was young. Late twenties, maybe early thirties. Dark-skinned, with amazing ginger corkscrew curls. She imagined parents of vastly different appearance. One Swedish in the classic style, the other from somewhere on the Indian subcontinent.

He looked like a fashion plate. Skinny, with his long limbs encased in tight-fitting lime-green jeans below a silk shirt of the purest white.

Stella approached him, clearing her throat so as not to startle him as he was facing away from her.

He turned.

She smiled.

'Jens?'

'Yeah, that's me.'

She held out her hand. 'I'm Stella. Would you like to come with me, please?'

'What's this about? Have you found her? I didn't know they put, like, senior people on missing persons.'

'Come with me. Let's get a coffee then we can talk in my office.'

All the way up to Major Crimes he kept up a stream of questions, observations about Sara, remarks about seeing her on TV. The poor guy was so nervous, she could smell the fear-sweat on him. Hoping for the best, fearing the worst: only talking could keep it at bay.

She arranged for someone to bring them coffee then took him into her office and closed the door softly behind her.

'Please, take a seat.'

He sat, crossed his legs then uncrossed them. Ran both hands over his hair and around the back of his neck before clamping them between his knees.

'Well, have you found her or what?' he asked.

'Jens, I need to ask you to look at a photograph. I don't know if it's Sara or not, but I hope you can tell me one way or the other. Can you do that?'

'Yeah, of course I can. You're the serial killer cop, aren't you? The super cop, that's what they call you on telly. Is she dead?'

Stella smiled. 'I investigate homicides. And I don't know about being super. I just ask a lot of questions and look at a lot of evidence. So I'm going to show you a photo. It's not pretty, I'm afraid.'

His lips twisted to one side. 'Shit, man, is it, like, a dead body?'

Stella nodded. 'Yes, it is.'

'Oh God! Is it all cut up, you know, like tortured or whatever?'

'No. Just dead. Ready?'

Jens nodded, biting his lower lip.

Stella opened the plain grey cardboard folder in front of her and withdrew the A4 photo of victim two. She spun it round and pushed it towards Jens with her fingertips.

'Is that Sara?'

Jens looked down at the image of the dead woman's face. Stella monitored his reactions closely. The husband, the boyfriend, the ex: the top three suspects when a woman was murdered.

At first Jens was frozen. As if someone had paused the movie of his life with him in the centre of the frame. Slowly, a tear emerged at the corner of each of his dark eyes and crawled over his cheeks.

His head started shaking from side to side. Slowly at first, then faster and faster.

No,' he said. 'No. Nononono, please, no!'

The last negative came out as a cry. He pushed the photo back across the desk and turned away.

'Jens,' Stella said, as gently as she could, though his verbal confirmation of victim two's identity was now just a formality. 'Is that Sara?'

'Yeah,' he said in a hoarse whisper. 'It's my Sara. Is she really dead?'

'I'm so sorry. Yes, she is.'

Tilde knocked and entered the office, two coffees in her hand. At the sight of Stella's guest sobbing, she placed the mugs on a side table and squatted beside him. She looked at Stella over the top of his head, eyebrows raised in mute enquiry.

Stella nodded back.

'Hey, hey. Listen, Stella is the best in the business,' Tilde said. 'She'll catch this guy, OK?'

Somehow, Tilde managed to calm Jens down. His sobbing grew quieter then stopped altogether. It was an impressive performance. The girl had cop smarts and a soft touch with grieving partners. Maybe the tension with

Frida had an innocent explanation. She might just have been nervous partnering Stella.

'Jens, are you up for answering a few questions about Sara?' Stella asked. 'It would really help us.'

He sniffed and blew his nose on a tissue from the box Tilde was holding out.

'Sure. I just can't believe she's gone, you know? She had everything going for her.'

'It's a huge shock. I'm so sorry for your loss,' Stella said, opening her notebook and picking up a pen.

An hour later, she had pages of notes on Sara's background. Her job, her friends, her hangouts and, crucially, the name of the addicts' group she attended on Wednesday evenings. Not part of AA at all. A new and more fashionable set-up called Ingrid's Way.

Tilde asked a few questions of her own, and again impressed Stella with her ability to keep the witness focused and talking without tiring him out.

Finally, closing her notebook, Stella readied herself to ask the final question. The question she'd been saving until this moment.

'One last question, Jens, then I think we're done for now,' she said, softening what was to come with a sympathetic smile. 'Can you tell us where you were between 6:00 p.m. on Thursday night and 6:00 a.m. on Friday morning?'

His head jerked up like a marionette operated by a clumsy puppeteer.

'Pardon?'

Stella repeated her question. 'It's just a formality. We'll be asking everyone we talk to about Sara.'

'Shit! You people never change, do you?'

'I'm sorry. What do you mean?'

'This is racism, man. Same today as it's always been.'

Stella frowned. She hadn't expected this and now she felt unprepared. The last thing she needed, or wanted, was a potential witness bringing a complaint. Especially with Nik Olsson hot to file more charges against her.

'Jens, I assure you, your race has absolutely nothing to do with this,' Stella said. 'I don't know what your past experience with the police has been, but I'm sitting here with you, promising you I will not stop until I find Sara's killer. You are a witness, not a suspect. But I have to ask you about your whereabouts on the night she was killed. I wouldn't be doing my job otherwise. Would you want me to not ask other people the same question? Even someone who might have killed her?'

Jens glared at her. But she could see the rage behind the eyes cooling. She waited.

'I was gaming.'

'Alone?'

'I was alone in my flat but I was gaming with mates. Online. That's good enough, right? An alibi? That's what you want from me, isn't it?'

Stella smiled. 'What are their names? These mates of yours?'

He reeled off three names and then sent their contact details to Stella's mobile. Tilde noted the names down while Stella focused on listening and trying to appear as unthreatening as possible.

'We'll contact them,' Stella said. 'Thanks again, Jens. I know you must be so upset. Tilde, can you escort Jens back to reception, please?'

Once Tilde had led Jens away, Stella picked up the phone. If telling a boyfriend his girlfriend was dead was bad, it had nothing on performing the same unpleasant duty with the parents.

25

Like a lot of overworked, underpaid middle managers, Ulf Sörenstam tried to avoid anything that might occasion him more stress than he already had loaded onto his narrow shoulders.

But that was hard. For some unfathomable reason of her own, the company's corporate social responsibility director had decided that recovering addicts deserved a second chance. As employees in the warehouse. Under his supervision.

Great.

And now one hadn't shown up for work.

Again.

Ulf had let it go the first few days. Made excuses for his own inaction while two more passed. After all, these people were always falling off the wagon, weren't they? That or going back to their dealers for a little pick-me-up that turned into a knock-me-down. Mikael wasn't the first. No way he'd be the last, either.

But now a week had gone by. Even a habitual stress-avoider like Ulf knew when the gig was up. He informed

ANDY MASLEN

HR in a short, badly spelled email that Mikael Matthiasson had now been absent without explanation for seven days.

The reply came a lot faster. He'd never liked the snotty cow who managed the weekly paid staff and her tart email made him want to throw something. That or sink a good hard belt of the O.P. Anderson aquavit he kept in the bottom drawer of his desk.

Someone called to him from across the warehouse. He looked up. One of the older guys, Per Sundling, was standing on a gantry waving down at him.

'Hey! Ulf! Matthiasson's on the damned lunchtime news. Come and see.'

What now? Ulf crossed the floor, narrowly avoiding being sideswiped by a forklift shifting a wobbling tower of crates.

'Hey watch it, you damned idiot! Shit-for-brains immigrants can't even drive a damned forklift without causing an accident.'

Puffing and red-faced from the effort, he hauled himself up the caged ladder and emerged onto the gantry, pressing a palm to his chest.

'What is it then, come on, show me. I haven't got all day.'

Wordlessly, Sundling turned his phone towards Ulf.

He peered at the screen. A presenter was asking the public to come forwards if they recognised the man in the photo that occupied the left side of the picture.

Ulf did.

'Damn him to the devil!'

'Too late.'

Ten minutes later, back in his office, Ulf called the police.

* * *

'And you're sure it's him?' Stella asked.

'Of course I'm sure! Unless the alkie who worked here has an identical twin brother also called Mikael Matthiasson, it's him. What, you think I like calling the cops for fun? Got a pen? I'll give you our address. I'm too busy to come into the city centre.'

She stuck her pistol in its holster, and headed down to the parking garage.

The warehouse stood among a half-dozen others on an industrial park to the west of the city. Not, in fact, a million miles from where the unfortunate Mikael Matthiasson had met his end on the grille of a Scania eighteen-wheeler.

The warehouse manager was striding across the vast space, barking orders and, to Stella's eye, acting like a total arsehole to his workers. His red face suggested hypertension at the very least and an imminent heart attack as a very real possibility.

She called out.

'Ulf Sörenstam?'

He turned and opened his mouth, ready, she could see, to hurl another foul-mouthed insult. Then he clocked the ID she was holding up. His eyes flicked to the pistol on her belt. The mouth closed.

He walked over.

'Was it you I spoke to on the phone?' he asked.

'That's right.'

'Yeah, well,' he ran a hand over his face, 'I'm sorry if I, you know—'

'– if you were rude to a homicide detective who was just doing her job?' Stella finished for him, smiling sweetly.

'I've been under a lot of stress recently,' he said with a shrug, then pushed a snus pouch under his top lip.

'I'm sorry to hear that,' Stella said. 'What can you tell me about Mikael?'

'He's like all of them. Here one day, gone the next. Why we can't just employ regular people, I don't know,' he said. 'It's either immigrants or bloody addicts. I mean, surely there must be a couple of honest Swedes who'd like a secure job out of the rain?'

Her senses quickened. 'Addicts?'

'Well, *recovering*,' he said, making air quotes. 'You know, junkies, alkies, meth-heads, speed-freaks. I tell you, Stella, some days it feels like I'm running a rehab centre instead of a warehouse.'

The complaint sounded rehearsed to Stella. She imagined her hypertensive witness sounding off in a bar somewhere.

'Do you employ a lot of recovering addicts here?'

'A lot? There's a revolving door between us and every bloody halfway house from Stockholm to Uppsala.'

'Who's in charge of this employment programme?'

He snorted, dislodging the snus, which he caught deftly in his left hand and reinserted under his lip.

'That would be Berta Fallingsby, our esteemed corporate social responsibility director. She works in the firm's nice headquarters in the city. Not this rainbow nation shithole.'

Leaving Ulf to his snus and unpleasant opinions, Stella drove back into the city.

Both in the UK and in Sweden, Stella had had occasion to interview business executives in their workplaces. And it always amazed her, the moment you stepped out of the public sector, just how much money was available for artworks, huge indoor plants up to and including real living trees, plush, leather-upholstered furniture, and high-speed computers.

The e-commerce firm's headquarters was no different. The reception area felt more like an art gallery than a place of business.

A black woman wearing a beautifully-cut turquoise linen suit came to collect her.

'Hi, Stella, I'm Berta Fallingsby,' she said. 'Director of Corporate Social Responsibility. Come up to my office.'

In the lift, Stella caught the other woman's perfume, a mixture of orange blossom and Earl Grey tea.

'I love your perfume,' she said. 'Do you mind if I ask what it is?'

'Not at all, and thank you! It's by Henrik Vibskov. Lotus Dust Red. My husband loves it,' she added with a smile.

'Yeah, I think my boyfriend might feel the same way.'

In Berta's office, they sat facing each other at a pale wooden table in which the grain twisted and turned beneath a thin skin of satin varnish.

'I spoke to your warehouse manager earlier today,' Stella began. 'Ulf Sörenstam. He identified one of the victims in the homicide case I'm currently investigating. The man's name was Mikael Matthiasson.'

Berta's hand flew to her open mouth.

'That's awful. His poor family.'

'Would you have a file with his next of kin, things like that?'

'I won't but our HR director will. Hold on. I'll call her.'

'Wait!' Stella said, more sharply than she meant to. 'Sorry, but could you also ask if she has a record of a Sara Marksson?'

It was a long shot. Jens had told her and Tilde that Sara was a TV presenter. But maybe that was before her demons got a proper hold of her.

Five minutes later, the door opened and a woman seemingly composed of angles and straight lines, eyes red as if she'd just been crying, came in.

'Hi, I'm Rosa Jacobsson, HR Director. This is just terrible.' She handed Stella two sheets of A4 paper stapled together. 'That's Mikael's personnel record. It has his address but I'm afraid he had no living family. We've no Sara Markssons working here, though.'

Stella scanned the first page then turned it over. On the back, under Next of Kin, was typed Sven-Arne Jonsson and, in brackets, (Ingrid's Way).

Rosa spun round and left. Stella heard a single loud sob before the office door closed.

'I'm sorry about that,' Berta said. 'She takes it very personally whenever one of our employees dies.'

'Does it happen often, then?'

'Oh, no. Not really. Hardly at all. But with colleagues like Mikael, well, sadly sometimes they relapse and yes, on occasion it's fatal,' she said. 'They are quite vulnerable, you see.'

Stella nodded. Inwardly, she was sighing with regret. The potential connection between the two victims had come apart before it had even solidified into a lead. Or had it? A thought occurred to her.

'As part of your community programme with the charities, do you ever do any outreach work? Maybe visiting the halfway houses or, I don't know, offering training or mentoring of any kind?'

'Absolutely! We give every colleague one day off every month to work on volunteering projects with our partner charities.'

Stella asked for a list of every employee who'd volunteered with the charities in the previous year. Perhaps the connection lay there.

* * *

After the following day's morning briefing, Stella was at her desk when the list of employee-volunteers came in from Rosa Jacobsson. It ran into the hundreds. No way was she about to add that to the growing total of people who theoretically could be involved. With Malin still choking off resources, she needed a smarter way to solve the case.

What about Mikael's entry under Next of Kin? Sven-Arne Jonsson? She'd Googled him. He was the founder of Ingrid's Way, one of the addiction charities with whom Mikael's employer had links. And it was the group Sara had been attending, too.

An hour later, she was on her way to see him.

'I'm dropping in to one of our meetings,' he'd said when she called him. 'Could you meet me there afterwards, say 11:00 a.m.? It's the Arts Club in Östermalm, do you know it?'

'I'll find it.'

As Stella drove into Stockholm's swankiest district, traffic-choked streets gave way to shady avenues lined with broad-leaved trees, many smothered in fragrant white blossoms. Chain stores, banks and fast-food joints were replaced by upscale retailers and chic cafes and brasseries, the latter's tables spilling across the pavements.

The Arts Club was housed in a majestic building occupying a corner plot between the two roads. A handsome, six-storey nineteenth-century structure in red brick and sandstone with ornate Dutch gables, wrought-iron balconies and turrets finished with leaded roofs and patinated bronze weathervanes.

She parked round the back, beside a bright-red Ferrari occupying a spot nearest the rear doors.

In a corner of the reception area, a small whiteboard on an easel bore the words 'Ingrid's Way' and an arrow pointing to a carved wooden staircase.

The young man at the desk offered Stella a sympathetic smile. Feeling the need suddenly to distinguish herself from the recovering addicts attending the meeting, she held up her ID.

'Police,' she said, returning the smile.

Downstairs, several unmatched armchairs in scuffed brown leather were grouped around a coffee table bearing arts magazines. To the left of the seating group, double doors bore another sign indicating that a meeting of Ingrid's Way was taking place beyond. She took one of the chairs and waited.

At five past the hour, the doors opened. In ones and twos, people emerged, some smiling and chattering, others more subdued, looking down or consulting their phones.

Stella recognised one young woman, a politician known for her outspoken views on climate change. When the last of them had gone, she got up and went inside. Sven-Arne was talking to a bearded man. The group leader, she assumed. They were shaking hands. Sven-Arne looked over.

'Ah, Stella, hi.' He turned to the bearded man. 'Bye, Tom. See you in a few weeks.'

He came over, hand outstretched again.

'Let's talk outside, shall we?'

Seated in one of the armchairs, he leaned forwards.

'This is about those dreadful killings, I'm guessing.'

Stella nodded. Wishing, as she increasingly did, that she could work under the radar, rather than directly in front of the scanning dish.

'One of the victims was a man called Mikael Matthiasson. He listed you as his next of kin. I know you weren't family but I'm sorry for your loss.'

Sven-Arne's mouth turned down, although his forehead remained smooth. Was he frowning? Botox was the most likely explanation. He was an actual celebrity, after all, possessed of real fame, rather than Stella's small measure of renown.

'Mikael Matthiasson?'

'Yes.'

'I don't think I know him. You're sure he meant me? There are seven other Sven-Arne Jonssons in Sweden on Facebook alone.'

'He put the name of the charity you founded in brackets so I'm pretty sure he meant you,' she said. 'In any case, we've established that he used to attend meetings of Ingrid's Way. And so did the female victim. Sara Marksson. Does that name ring a bell at all?'

He shook his head. Smiled. 'I'm sorry. Look, I founded Ingrid's Way, and I get around to a lot of the meetings. But it's all confidential. People are free to use a made-up name if they want to. In any case, we have thousands of members. No way could I remember even a fraction of them.'

'Would anyone else have a list of your members?'

'Sorry, no. We don't keep lists. For pretty obvious reasons.'

'How about your group leaders? You must have a list of them, surely?'

'Of course. It's held centrally. There are all kinds of

issues: safeguarding, diversity and inclusion, ethics, sensitivity training. We couldn't operate otherwise.'

'Could I have a copy of that list?'

He scratched behind his ear. 'Not a chance. I mean, not without a warrant.'

'Even if it would help us catch a serial killer?'

'Well, you don't *know* it would do that, do you? I mean, it *might* help you, but you can't be certain.'

Stella found herself taking a dislike to Sven-Arne in his studiedly casual rig of open-necked chambray shirt, distressed jeans and boat shoes worn without socks. Everything looked too expensive to be genuine. And she had a shrewd idea she knew who owned the blood-red Ferrari outside.

'No, I can't. But somewhere on that list might be someone who could help me make progress in my investigation.'

He smiled. 'Look, Stella, I know the game, OK? Before all this?' He swept his hand round in a wide arc. 'I was a best-selling author of serial killer novels. Still am, technically, though I don't write them anymore. I talked to homicide detectives all the time, including your predecessor. I'll happily turn over my list to you. When you come back with a warrant.'

'It's quite the coincidence, isn't it?'

'What?'

'Two murder victims mutilated by their killer are connected to an author of serial killer novels. Maybe you killed them, Sven-Arne?'

It was a desperate ploy. She knew even as the words escaped her lips she shouldn't have said it.

He smiled lazily, the expression falling well short of anything genuine. 'That's a pretty wild accusation to throw out with no evidence to back it up. If you're hoping I'll be intimidated, you'll have to try harder.'

'I'm sorry, I shouldn't have said that.'

'No, you really shouldn't. Because I could probably find half a dozen connections between Mikael and Sara if I spent an hour or two online. Sweden's not such a big place as you might think. Hardly more than ten million people,' he said. 'That's what, a seventh the size of the UK? If there's nothing else, you'll have to excuse me. I have work to do. Let me know when you get that warrant. If you can't find me, contact my lawyers.'

And then he left without a backwards glance. Stella sat on in the armchair, cursing her clumsiness.

26

Two weeks passed. With no new leads and, mercifully, no more victims, the temperature in Major Crimes began to cool. The Icarus Killer's two victims slid off the front pages and the journalists stopped calling for updates.

Oskar had produced a report from the ornithologists at the university. The wings attached to Mikael came from a cinereous vulture, to Sara, a martial eagle. He'd had a team reviewing CCTV from the raptor sanctuary, wildlife park and zoo, but so far they'd come up with nothing.

Malin called Stella into her office.

'I'm going to redirect most of your resources onto our other live cases,' she said. 'Maybe this was just a deranged artist after all, and not a serial killer. I still want you on it, Stella, but you have other open investigations running and I can't afford for us to get tunnel vision.'

Stella bit her lip in frustration. She'd known this was coming. It didn't make it any easier to swallow, though.

'Look, Malin, I get it. But you have to believe me. It's a serial. I can feel it.'

'Yes, well, I can't afford to keep spending the Swedish taxpayer's krona on *feelings*,' Malin sniffed. 'And this doesn't fit the pattern, does it? Serials accelerate. This time he kills two almost on top of each other, then, what? Nothing for two weeks? No. I think we should be considering other angles. Maybe go back and look at Mikael again. A disgruntled spouse. A drug dealer who didn't get paid.'

Stella couldn't stop herself. The words were out before she had a chance to think.

'Malin, he cut their arms off and sewed wings on instead. Does that really look like the work of a pissed-off drug dealer to you?'

Malin pursed her already thin lips. 'Please don't raise your voice to me in my own office, Stella,' she said in an infuriatingly calm voice. 'And I don't know *what* it looks like, to be honest. Drugs do strange things to people. It's why they take them, after all, isn't it?'

Stella spent a few more minutes trying to persuade her boss to keep the purse strings loosened but Malin was immoveable. Stella left promising to review all the other open cases.

That night, she and Jamie were sitting out on her balcony, sharing a cold bottle of wine. Below them, a street parade was in full swing, filling Mariebergsgatan with samba music, the clangorous rattling of thousands of drums, and the whistles, cheers and off-key singing of many times that number of drunken, though good-natured, revellers.

'They're having a good time,' Jamie said.

Stella wrinkled her nose. 'Yeah.'

'You're not?' he asked.

'Malin slashed my budget for the Icarus investigation

to the bone. She's got this stupid idea it's just a regular murderer with an artistic bent.'

Jamie put his wine glass down so hard on the table the base snapped clean off. 'Damn it!'

Stella fetched a paper napkin and had the broken pieces wrapped and a fresh glass in Jamie's hand in under a minute.

'What was that about?' she asked, once she'd resumed her seat.

'It's bloody bureaucrats, Stel. They're the same everywhere. You don't need to be a forensic psychiatrist to see that we're dealing with a serial killer. Even your rookie, what's her name?'

'Tilde.'

'Even Tilde can see that. She's bright, by the way. Unlike your boss.'

'Malin's not stupid, though. She's just got the usual concerns the brass always have.'

He grunted. 'Money.'

'Not just money,' Stella said. 'Taxpayers' money. No, wait. "The Swedish taxpayer's krona",' she added in a passable imitation of Malin's precise Stockholm diction.

'You have to persuade her, Stel,' Jamie said. 'He's going to do it again. I know it. You know it. Breaking up the team would be a huge mistake.'

'Any and all suggestions you have on changing Malin's mind gratefully received.'

Jamie smiled. 'That's where my expertise deserts me, I'm afraid.' He jerked his chin down at the brightly coloured revellers in the parade. 'Looks like they're enjoying themselves, at least.'

'Mm, hm,' she said distractedly, wondering what she could do, what argument she could advance that would convince Malin to reverse her decision.

'Talking of having fun, I was thinking,' Jamie said. 'Now we're back together, how about I move in with you? I could save the money I'm paying for the Airbnb and, I don't know, contribute to the food shopping or something.'

Stella shook her head. What had he just said? She'd been deep in thought, running lines of argument past an imaginary Malin.

'Sorry, darling, what?'

Jamie frowned. 'I was just saying, maybe I should move in with you here. Seems pointless keeping two places when we're together again.'

'Oh. That would be…'

She found she didn't know how to finish the sentence. Jamie was looking at her expectantly, perched on the edge of the chair. He took a sip of wine, then another. Yes, what *would* it be if he moved in with her? Exciting? Fun? Convenient? Efficient? Hardly the most romantic of reasons to move in together. And she'd got used to her new apartment being just the way she liked it. How would she cope, living with someone again? Two toothbrushes in the holder.

'Darling?' Jamie prompted. 'Is everything OK? I didn't mean to put you on the spot. If you need some time to think about it…'

She sighed. 'I don't know, Jamie. With the case and everything, my mind's not really focused on my home life. Could we maybe wait a little while?'

'Of course we could. I just thought, you know, it would be nice, that's all.'

'It would be. I just need some time to get used to the idea. I've been living on my own a long time.'

He smiled.

'And you get used to it, don't you? I'm in the same

boat, remember? You put a book down and it's exactly where you left it next time you want it. Not been tidied away or reshelved.'

Stella grinned. 'Toothpaste squeezed from the end...'

' – like it's supposed to be! Recycling box emptied out regularly—'

' – not stamped down so you can fit one more juice carton in.'

They laughed at the same time. Jamie refilled their glasses, emptying the bottle.

'I can wait,' he said. 'Just know that I'm serious, Stel. I love you.'

'I love you, too.'

'Can I still stay the night?' he asked.

She put her finger to the tip of her nose and looked upwards, pretending to think hard about it. Then back at Jamie, a grin on her face.

Later, while Jamie slept soundlessly beside her, she retrieved a book from her nightstand, *D'Aulaire's Book of Greek Myths*, careful not to clink it against the day-old glass of water. She'd bought it a few days earlier from a second-hand place at the end of her street.

As she read the story of the overexcited youth who flew too close to the sun, melted his wax-bound wings, fell into the sea and drowned, she became convinced of one thing.

This had nothing to do with the killer operating right now in Stockholm.

For a start, Icarus *wore* his wings, like those beered-up 'birdmen' (and a few 'birdwomen') who strapped wings on and attempted to fly across the river every autumn at IcarusFest.

And what about the lesson of the tale? It was either a warning against excessive pride or against youthful recklessness. Neither of those, as far as she could see, applied to either Mikael Matthiasson or Sara Marksson. Not now, at any rate.

She flipped through the pages, until her eye settled on an illustration of a man wearing some very fetching leather underpants, straining his shoulders (also fetching) against a massive rock. Sisyphus, she read, outsmarted death twice. For the sin of thinking himself cleverer than Zeus, he was punished by having to push a boulder up a hill, reaching the top only for the boulder to escape his grasp and roll back down to the bottom. For ever.

Her eyes drooped. Poor old Sisyphus. She knew how he felt.

* * *

The following day, Stella left Jamie sleeping while she went for a run with Jonna.

'What's the plan?' Jonna said as they cut through the park, weaving through mothers pushing prams and strollers, nodding to other Lycra-clad joggers.

'We keep going. Juggle all the other cases but you and I stay focused on Icarus.'

Later that morning, while Stella and Jonna reviewed all the case files, a TV crew was setting up in the austere but beautifully furnished living room of Anders Elklund, a film director. Books and old film cans in battered aluminium were stacked on interlocking white shelves, interspersed with glossy-leaved houseplants.

The interviewer, Louisa Tännander, checked her

makeup and adjusted the band holding her long blonde hair out of her face in a mirror held up by an assistant.

'Thanks, Ana,' she said with a smile.

When they were ready, Louisa took a chair opposite Elklund.

'Ready?' she asked him.

He nodded. 'Whenever you are, Louisa.'

She smiled. Nodded to the soundman holding up a boom mike, and then, over her shoulder, at the camera operator, who was focusing his lens on Elklund's craggy features.

'Anders Elklund, you directed the controversial film *Icarus Unbound*, in which an insane surgeon is obsessed with creating a perfect being. A man with a bird's wings. How do you feel about the speculation on some film forums that the killer was directly inspired by your film?'

Elklund nodded. Stared into the camera.

'You don't want to believe too much those people say. Anyway, the first thing I should say is that my film *wasn't* controversial. In fact, most critics were pretty sure it would win big at the Stockholm International Film Festival. Cannes, maybe. Even the Oscars.'

'But the lead actor, Peter Brandt, was killed during production, wasn't he? You were blamed for his death.'

'Well, Peter, my poor, dear Peter, was killed after principal photography was done. It was a tragic accident. His rig was faulty, as the police investigation concluded.'

'Indeed. But you attracted a lot of criticism on social media.'

Elklund spread his arms along the back of the black leather chair he was lounging in. 'Listen, baby, everybody who does anything more than go to work and collect their monthly pay cheque ends up getting shit thrown at them on social media. It's jealousy. Pure and simple. Haters achieve nothing, so they try to bring down people who've got off their arses and dared to fly higher.'

If Louisa was offended by his attitude, she prided herself too much on her professionalism to ever let it show. And Anders was nowhere near the worst interviewee she'd ever had sitting opposite her.

'There's been speculation online that you yourself are the Icarus killer,' she said, with a smile. 'Any truth in it?'

He laughed. 'I could tell you, but then I'd have to kill you and take your still-warm body down to my basement where I keep my collection of power tools and vultures' wings.'

She swallowed. Exchanged a nervous look with the sound guy.

Elklund frowned. 'Too much?'

'A little. I mean there are two dead people in the city morgue, after all.'

'Yeah, you're probably right. Sorry. It's not the first time my dark sense of humour's gotten me into trouble,' he said. 'Can we shoot that question again?'

'Of course.'

Louisa repeated her question.

'None at all. Mind you, there's been speculation online that I'm also, variously the antichrist, a communist, a fascist, a sellout and a plagiarist. I guess people project their fantasies onto me whether I like it or not.'

Louisa smiled. 'Anders, thank you very much.' She signalled for the camera guy to stop filming. 'Is it OK if we just film a few reaction shots, then we'll be out of your hair.'

'Sure, take your time. Just call me when you're done.

I'll be in the basement dissecting a condor,' he said with a wink.

After returning to the TV studio, Louisa sat with the editor reviewing the footage. When they reached the part where Elklund had joked about being the killer, before rerecording his answer, she stabbed the pause button on the desk.

'Can you make me a copy of that segment, Lars?'

'Sure. But you want to use the second answer for the broadcast, yes?'

'Yes.'

With the footage waiting for her on a secure server, she went to the canteen and found a quiet corner where she could make her call.

27

A cold cup of coffee at her elbow, Stella stared at the sheets of paper in front of her and sighed.

Each sheet bore a list. Longer lists required two or more sheets, which someone had helpfully stapled together for her.

Sweden was home to forty-nine orthopaedic surgeons, including ten at the most senior pay grade. Another 357 general surgeons practised in state and private hospitals.

Then there were the vets. As Tilde had discovered during her research, 245 people were either employed in vet practices in the Greater Stockholm area, or studying veterinary science at university.

The national police computer had records for 711 individuals who had convictions for animal cruelty, including fifty-five where the offences specifically related to birds.

With each cast of the net, she'd hauled in more people who needed to be traced, interviewed and eliminated. Tilde had found ninety-three people who'd either written blog posts, made TikToks or uploaded digital artwork to the web featuring winged humans as the principal theme.

Taking Carola's suggestion onboard had yielded a further 978 people who either had qualifications in aerospace engineering or who were actively employed in the sector in that role.

In all, 2,433 people.

Facing this monumental task, 811 individuals apiece, were *Kriminalinspektörs* Cole, Carlsson and Enström.

On balance, she thought she'd rather swap places with Sisyphus.

Her desk phone rang and, grateful for the interruption, she snatched it up and answered.

'Hi, Stella, I have a Louisa Tånnander on the phone for you.'

'That name rings a bell.'

'Yes! She's on TV. Cultural Sweden. They cover everything: art, literature, film, architecture, even. It's very highly regarded.'

Marvelling at the calibre of receptionist employed by the SPA, Stella waited for the call to be put through.

'Hello,' she said. 'This is Stella.'

'Hi, did your receptionist tell you who I am?'

'Yes, Louisa. How can I help you?'

'I hope it's the other way around. I have some video footage I really think you should see.'

'Footage of what?'

'An interview I conducted earlier today. It's to do with the Icarus murders. At least, I hope it is. Well, not hope, because that would mean I just interviewed a serial killer, but—'

'Where are you, Louisa? Can you come into SPA headquarters? We're on Kungsholmsgatan.'

'I can be there in fifteen minutes if you have time to see me now.'

A quarter of an hour later, Stella was showing Louisa into an empty meeting room. The younger woman pulled out her phone and played the footage. Stella watched as the man being interviewed grinned wolfishly, then laughed.

'I could tell you, but then I'd have to kill you and take your still-warm body down to my basement where I keep my collection of power tools and vultures' wings.'

Stella returned the phone.

'Can you send me a copy of that please?'

'Sure.'

'Was there anything else about Anders that made you suspicious, or was it just that answer?'

Louisa shrugged. 'Just that, I guess, although, I don't know, he came off as pretty glib. I mean, we were discussing whether a serial killer might have been inspired by his work and he just laughed it off.' She bit her lip. 'Did I do the right thing? Bringing it to you?'

'Absolutely, yes. And thank you. Do you have a number for Anders?'

Louisa handed her a sheet torn from a notebook. It looked to Stella as though she'd come expecting to be asked. Stella thanked her and, once she'd shown her out, returned to her office and called the director's number.

'This is Anders. But I'm not seeing a caller ID. Who is this?'

His voice was low and throaty. Gruff with a friendly edge.

'Detective Inspector Stella Cole. I'm lead investigator

on the two killings involving birds' wings. I wondered whether I could come to see you today, Anders?'

'Of course, Stella!' He sounded pleased. 'You'll be the second attractive young woman to beat a path to my door in one day. I should mark it on my calendar. Have you eaten lunch yet?'

Stella checked the time: 2:00 p.m. 'No, I haven't.'

'Can't solve murders on an empty stomach. Come now and I'll prepare something. We can talk while we eat.'

'Where do you live?'

He gave her an address a few kilometres to the south of the city in a suburb called Trångsund, which was bordered on its south side by Magelungen lake.

She arrived twenty-five minutes later. The house was a wooden villa painted in the distinctive deep, flat red the Swedes called falun. For Stella, the similarity to the colour of dried blood was too close to find it pretty.

Nevertheless, contrasting white woodwork around the doors and windows gave the house a cheerful look. A battered off-white Volvo estate covered in bird shit and detritus from an overhanging birch tree sat in a patch of mossy gravel. She rang the doorbell and waited.

The man who answered might as well have had 'famous art-film director' hung on a sign around his neck. He was in his sixties and dressed, apparently, for a rodeo.

His lanky six-foot-plus frame was draped in faded jeans and a black Western-style shirt with white piping, and embroidered cow skulls and cacti. The top three mother-of-pearl press studs on the shirt were undone, revealing a beaten-brass pendant on a leather cord that nestled in a mass of iron-grey curls on his scrawny chest.

Broken-down cowboy boots fashioned, apparently, from snakeskin rounded off the outfit.

His mane of silver-grey hair was swept back from a high, virtually unlined forehead. He had hooded eyes of a deep blue – almost purple. The way he looked at Stella made her feel simultaneously nervous and flattered. She didn't think anyone had ever looked at her with quite such intensity.

'You must be Stella,' he said. 'No need for the ID. I don't get so many visitors it could be anyone else.'

He held his hand out. When she shook it, the soft skin surprised her: she had been expecting work-roughened fingers. Then, smiling inwardly, she reminded herself Anders spent his time behind a camera or an editing computer, not riding bucking broncos or roping steers.

He led her through the house and onto a wooden deck. A plank jetty extended twenty metres out into the water. At its far end bobbed a blue-and-white, clinker-built rowing boat.

'You have a beautiful view,' she said.

'Paid for with the proceeds of *Icarus Unbound*. I assume that's why you're here?'

She nodded, observing him closely: his non-verbal reactions would say as much about him as the spoken part of his answers. What she was picking up was a mood she described to herself as extreme relaxation. It could mean he was a man with nothing to hide. Or a man with everything to hide but who really didn't feel fear. Time would tell.

'I made spaghetti puttanesca,' he said. 'I bet your new countrymen and women have been filling you with gravlax and reindeer meat and herrings. Swedes are so desperate to show off their national cuisine. I thought you might like something a bit dirtier. You know how it translates?'

She looked him in the eye. 'Whore's spaghetti.'

He burst out laughing, showing large uneven teeth.

'Exactly! Not that I'm casting aspersions. It was actually my second wife's favourite,' he said. 'Mind you, she *was* a whore, bloody Italian bitch. She took me to the cleaners despite being the one spreading her legs for the pool boy while I was away filming. Anyway, have a seat. I'll bring the food out. Can you drink while you're on duty?'

'Water would be fine, unless you have a diet Coke.'

'Filthy stuff! I wouldn't drink it if I was dying of thirst. But I've got something you'll enjoy a lot better.'

He went inside and reappeared five minutes later with a tray bearing two bowls of spaghetti tossed with olives, tomatoes, capers and anchovies, a glass of red wine and a tall tumbler of sparkling water.

He set the food down and pushed the glass of water towards Stella.

'Taste it,' he said.

She brought the glass to her lips, and took a cautious sip. It had a flinty taste and she felt she was drinking something very old. Old, and somehow health-giving.

'What is it?' she asked with a smile.

'Lake water.' He roared with laughter as Stella wrinkled her nose involuntarily. 'Don't worry, it's purified and carbonated. I specced the system myself. It comes straight from the lake fifty metres out where the water's deep. You could drink it unfiltered and it wouldn't do you anything but good. Some of the old folks hereabouts do just that. Swear by it, in fact.'

Mentally checking she had digestive remedies in her medicine cabinet at home, she twirled her fork into the spaghetti, from which savoury steam curled upwards into her nostrils. It was delicious: a rich blend of flavours from salty to sour, herby to fishy.

'Your ex-wife should just have taken the recipe,' she said, after swallowing. 'She could have made a fortune from it.'

He smiled. 'Very kind of you to say so. Now, ask me your questions, Stella, and let's see if I can help you catch a serial killer.'

She forked a little more of the pasta into her mouth and took her time chewing. Then she took another sip of the water. Watching him all the time. No change. He was either genuinely unbothered about her presence or just didn't know that normal people were generally on edge when visited by an SPA homicide cop.

'You called me attractive on the phone. How did you know what I looked like?'

'Maybe I've been stalking you. Taking long-lens shots of you from the SPA car park, or maybe outside your apartment building.'

She adjusted her position on the chair to introduce a little more space between her right hip and its wicker side. Felt, yet again, that maybe the Swedish had got it right when it came to arming their police officers.

'*Have* you been stalking me, Anders?'

'Nothing so…interesting. No, but I have seen you on the devilbox from time to time. The production team on Aktuellt seem to love you.'

'You don't like TV then?'

'Oh, it's fine, I suppose. But Netflix? All that? It's killing the industry. People don't want to go out to see films like mine anymore. They want everything there and then on their shit-damned TVs instead of getting the proper experience in a movie theatre.'

'Films like *Icarus Unbound*.'

'Yes.' His brow furrowed suddenly. 'Wait. Did that woman from STV1 tell you to call me? Is that why you're here? What did she say about me?'

'I found your film online while I was researching leads,' she said. 'A dead man with wings where his arms should be? Icarus sprang to mind immediately.'

'Oh, OK. It's just, I've learned over the years that you can't always trust people.'

'In the myth, Icarus's wings were attached with a harness. Why did you portray him as actually having wings where his arms should have been?'

Anders smiled. 'A good question. An *astute* question. In my vision, the character of Icarus is not escaping from Crete, but from the limitations imposed upon him by his very biology. He is not a man *wearing* wings,' he said, then paused dramatically. 'He is a man *with* wings. A flying man, do you see?'

Stella nodded. 'I do see. I see very clearly. Tell me, Anders, where were you on the 14th June?'

'I was here.'

'Alone?'

'Probably, yes. I am currently enjoying a period of solitude.'

'How about the 16th?'

'Again, the same. Though I would have to check in my diary. Hold on.' He pulled out his phone and swiped around the screen for a second or two. 'Yes. Here, alone, both days. Am I a suspect, because of my film?'

She shook her head. 'Not at all. It's a reflex. I ask everyone.'

'Well, as you can see, I have no alibi,' he said with an easy smile.

'Do you have a basement here?'

'I do. It's my editing suite. Would you like to see it?'

'Sure.'

As he led her inside and down a narrow flight of steps, Stella touched the butt of her pistol.

Anders opened the door.

'Welcome to my domain,' he said.

She took a breath and stepped inside.

28

The basement reeked of nothing but the faint tang of static electricity. Generated, she supposed, by the vast amount of sophisticated electronics that cluttered the low-ceilinged space.

The walls were spattered with nothing but film posters, including one for *Icarus Unbound*.

From the ceiling hung nothing but a large pendant lamp salvaged from a movie set.

She scanned the walls, looking for doors, but they were all plastered smooth. No looming cabinets or floor-to-ceiling shelving behind which a serial killer might have concealed an entrance to his torture chamber.

It wasn't him. She could tell.

She suggested they return to the deck, where the sun and the air were kinder than the closed-in atmosphere of the editing suite.

'What did you think when you heard a serial killer was sewing wings onto his victims?' she asked, when they were seated by the water once more.

His eyes flashed.

'It *was* young Louisa, wasn't it? She told you I made an off-colour remark.'

Stella shook her head. 'People are scared, Anders. Can you blame them?'

'Blame them? No. But consider this, Stella. Every year, several hundred Swedes are killed in traffic accidents. Roughly one thousand die in falls. Five die in hunting accidents. But people aren't scared of staircases, or their family Volvo, are they? They don't recoil in terror from their rifles. Why? Because they're the everyday, and the everyday is not frightening. But the outlier? The statistically minuscule risk you might be eaten by a shark or dismembered by a serial killer? That scares the shit out of people. It shouldn't. But it does.'

'I looked you up on IMDB,' she said. 'You've made several films that explore the concept of deviancy. What do *you* think's going on in the killer's mind?'

'I'm a film director, not a psychiatrist,' he said. 'Though, didn't I read in Svenska Dagbladet that you have a famous British shrink helping you on this case?'

'You did, and we do. But Doctor Hooke is a clinician. You are an artist,' she said. 'Sometimes it's easier to understand the deviant mind through the imagination, not the casebook.'

He smiled, ran his fingers down the leather thong holding his pendant.

'Do they teach flattery at detective school, Stella?'

'Do they teach mortality statistics at film school, Anders?'

'Touché. OK, first of all, forget Icarus. It's a dead end. Or what do you Brits call it?' He switched to English. 'A blind alley?'

'Why?'

'Like I said, Icarus is an academic's wank fantasy. It's

too far removed from our basic urges. I would imagine your killer dreams of flying like a bird. Or an angel. He wouldn't fantasise about having anything as basic as a harness. Why not just fantasise about hang-gliding? No, he sees himself as having wings.'

'Like in your film.'

'Yes. No! Maybe he wishes he could be a birdman but he is practising on his victims until he gets it right. He never will, of course, but then, he is as nutty as a fruitcake, isn't he? Otherwise he'd be working in an office or in an aeroplane factory.'

Stella's heart stuttered in her chest. 'Why did you say that? About a factory?'

'Because it's true! He'd just be normal.'

'But why did you say aeroplane factory, specifically?'

He shrugged. 'I don't know. Because we were talking about flying, I suppose. Is it important?'

'It could be. Why do you think he removes the arms? I've been looking online. In paintings of angels, the wings always come out from the shoulder blades.'

'Oh, well that's easy. The whole point is that the wings should *replace* the arms. Frankly, all the images on the web, all those dumb Facebook groups dedicated to the subject, every Old Master painting, sculpture, vinyl model, comic book, T-shirt and children's book illustration have got it wrong.

'No creature on the planet has wings growing out of its shoulder blades. Think about it! That makes it technically six-limbed. It's the same with dragons. Four legs plus wings. Six! Bats? Two legs, two wings. Birds? Two legs, two wings. So, no. The wings need to attach to the shoulders. It's how I would do it. Your man's a creative genius.'

There was a long silence after Anders made that

claim. Having been so sure just a few minutes earlier that he wasn't the killer, a part of Stella's hindbrain, the part that dealt with threats from predators, had just fired up.

She was sitting opposite a fit and healthy male, who had joked about cutting up a TV journalist. Who had no alibis for the two murders. And who had just asserted that he approved of the killer's MO. Called him a genius, no less.

Anders stared at her with the same intensity as he had used when he'd opened the door. Only now, instead of feeling like an aspiring actress being scrutinised by a famous film director, she felt like a potential victim being weighed up by a serial killer.

She stood.

'You've been most helpful, Anders. Thanks.'

He unfolded his long, loose limbs from the chair, moving from a seated to a standing position without apparent effort.

'I didn't kill them, Stella,' he said quietly.

'I have to go. Thanks for lunch.'

She turned and walked on stiff legs back to her car, right hand hovering beside her pistol. Sweat had broken out on her chest and under her arms. Her ears were straining to catch the slightest sound above the whispering of the breeze in the leaves of the birches. One scuff, one scrape of those ridiculous cowboy boots and she'd whirl round, gun levelled and Nik Olsson be damned to hell.

She reached the car, yanked on the door handle. It didn't budge. A wave of fear broke over her. Then she cursed herself. Took out the keys and blipped the fob to activate the central locking.

Inside she locked the doors and only then did she let out a breath.

Anders was standing on the deck, his hand raised in farewell.

'See you,' he mouthed.

Not if I see you first.

* * *

Stella spent her days chasing down leads, reading reports, urging her diminished team not to lose heart, even as she herself was doing just that. Malin was pushing for her to downgrade the two murders to cold cases and 'work on some of these damned everyday homicides clogging up my spreadsheets' instead.

Then, one morning, Stella arrived in Major Crimes to find the place thrumming with energy. Jonna hurried over as soon as Stella made her way through the crowded desks to their patch.

'You're not going to believe it.'

'Try me.'

'Icarus sent you a letter.'

Stella's stomach fizzed. This might be the breakthrough they'd been waiting for.

'Where is it?'

'Malin's got it. For safe-keeping, she said.'

Stella hurried over to Malin's office, knocked and entered. Malin looked up from her keyboard. Wordlessly, she pointed to an A4 glassine bag on the top of her old-fashioned wooden in-tray. It contained a white envelope with a thirteen-krona stamp and a handwritten address, and a single sheet of paper.

Stella grabbed it, sat back in the visitor chair and stared at the killer's missive. The paper was bright white. Lightweight. Cheap, all-purpose office paper for sale in thousands of shops all over Sweden. Not to mention online. And it was handwritten. Blue Biro by the look of it.

Stella,

So, how are you enjoying my work?

People these days are so concerned about 'growth'. About 'transformation'. About their Goddamned, shit-the-devil 'journeys'.

I am merely helping them on their way.

In death they are flying higher than they ever did in life. Like angels, you might say. Or maybe Icarus?

I have more planned for you. If you're as good as they say you are, I expect you will turn up at my door sometime soon, pointing your gun at me and waggling a pair of handcuffs.

If.

Or are you just a third-rater like Mikael and Sara? Content to sit on your arse and ride whatever luck life throws your way?

You will never catch me like that. You need to work at it. Every waking hour. (Maybe in your sleep, too. Are you getting any? Or do you lie there naked under the sheets, sick with nerves that this case will break you?)

Keep watching the skies!

Your friend,

Icarus

P.S. Maybe you were hoping it was a one-off plus a copycat? No such luck. I am the real deal. In the next twenty-four hours I will leave you a gift somewhere appropriate.

'Shit! He's going to do it again. We've got less than a day to find him or someone else is going to die. Give me more people, Malin, please.'

Malin nodded. 'Take Jonna and Oskar, a couple of civilian investigators, and as many uniforms as you can lay your hands on. I'll smooth things out with my counterparts in General CID, Response and Patrol. What about the rest of it?'

Blowing out her cheeks, she placed the letter on Malin's desk.

'We should send it over to the crime lab, but if there's a fingerprint or DNA on it I'll buy you and David dinner at Operakällaren,' she said, then immediately worried Signe and her team might come through. The Michelin-starred restaurant boasted a dining room like something out of a royal palace. Wood panelling up to the intricately carved ceiling, oil paintings everywhere and chandeliers dripping with crystal. And bills you needed a deep breath and even deeper pockets to settle. Stella had seen the website.

Malin offered a wintry smile.

'That confident, eh?'

'Read it, Malin!' Stella said, exasperatedly. 'It's typical psychopathic bullshit. Equal parts look-how-clever-I-am taunts and narcissistic boasts. Plus a smidgen of boilerplate God-baiting.'

'He mentions you being naked in bed. That's interesting, don't you think?'

Stella shook her head. 'Even if he's not deriving direct sexual pleasure from the killings, and, by the way, I wouldn't rule it out, so what? It's just crude sexual innuendo. Trying to put me off.'

'Or someone with a thing for you.'

'Oh, come on, Malin, really?'

Malin shrugged. 'Why not? It's right there in front of you. "Do you lie there naked under the sheets?"'

Stella snatched up the letter again and glanced at the final couple of paragraphs.

'Even if he is, so what? It doesn't help me catch him, does it? Unless you're thinking I should start wandering round Stockholm in my underwear hoping he's stalking me.'

Malin's smile was broader this time. 'Do you think it would work?'

'Malin!'

Malin held her hands up. 'Seriously, just think about it, all right? Maybe this individual thinks of you as, I don't know, an object of desire. Maybe we could find a way to use that against him. Lure him into making a mistake. Talk to Jamie. He might agree with me.'

Stella nodded. It wasn't, actually, a bad idea. She imagined Jamie suggesting they conduct 'a field trial'. Blushed. Caught Malin's gaze on her, interested, appraising.

'What?'

'Oh nothing, Stella. Is it too hot in here?'

'It's fine. I'll get this to Signe. Maybe dig up a forensic linguist, too. I have a contact at the university.'

Malin nodded and went back to her report-writing. Stella rose to go, aware as she turned that Malin was still smiling.

She found Jamie in the little box-room he'd converted into his office for the investigation and showed him the letter. He smiled at her and, just for a second, she felt the burden of the case lift a little.

'Ah, the famous letter. This place has been abuzz with it since it arrived. Can I see?'

She passed him the glassine bag and sat opposite him. He read in silence. She noticed his lips twitching, soundlessly forming the words. She knew what he was doing. Try out the killer's language for himself. Feeling the words in his mouth. He finished and looked up at her.

'I'm going to read it aloud. Tell me if you get anything different from reading it yourself.'

She closed her eyes. Waited. Jamie began reading, his voice a perfect match for the words written down. Smug, playful, arrogant and, when he reached the phrase that had so interested Malin, lecherous.

When he finished, she opened her eyes to find him watching her intently.

'Well?'

She shrugged. 'Like I told Malin. Same-old, same-old. A twisted fucker getting off on taunting the cops.'

Jamie pursed his lips. 'I wouldn't be so sure.'

'Oh God, not you, too? Malin thinks he has the hots for me. She's basically trying to stake me out on Stortorget as bait.'

He grinned. 'I'm sure she isn't, but anyway, I agree with her.'

Stella shook her head. That was all she needed. A serial killer writing her love-letters.

29

I feel bad for stringing Stella along like that.

The letter, I mean.

For myself, I wouldn't have bothered writing it. But it's expected. It's the form. I want to give her every chance. I even wrote it with a pen, so that she can see my handwriting.

Will it help her? I don't know. I doubt it. As far as I can remember, I've never committed anything to paper that I didn't type first.

Of course, there's always a chance I've forgotten something trivial. A note, perhaps. Or a jotting on a report.

It adds to the thrill. That she might figure it out – figure out my true identity, that is. Then we would have to have a showdown. Obviously I can't let her arrest me. I have no intention of going to prison, still less a secure psychiatric unit. All those loonies!

I got the idea for Peter from a postcard. Jacob Epstein's sculpture for Coventry Cathedral: St Michael's Victory over the Devil.

Although, obviously, in my version, the Devil (me) is absent.

30

Peter Lukasson had been a finalist in Mr Sweden two years running – 2010 and 2011. He'd parlayed his profile and TV-friendly good looks into a profitable sideline opening supermarkets and doing personal appearances at health and fitness shows.

But the brief flaring of his fame – at one time he'd envisioned himself as a Swedish Arnold Schwarzenegger – had brought not just money, but temptation.

After a decade of avoiding alcohol, tobacco and every drug except for a few carefully masked steroids, he finally gave in, figuring that outside the world of competition, he could afford to ease up on his self-discipline. After all, what would a few drinks do?

It turned out he had precisely two settings on the control mechanism in his brain.

On.

And off.

The bookings dried up as fast as his face bloated and his muscles withered, turning to fat and rounding off the sculpted body that was his only source of income. Finally, after having been dumped by his agent, he returned to the welding trade he had apprenticed in as a teenager, when pumping iron was something he did for fun after a long day in the workshop.

At 1.95 metres and eighteen stone, he was built like a Viking, as his former agent always put it in contract negotiations.

A Viking who came round in the middle of some sort of cockeyed surgical procedure in excruciating pain, strapped to a table. His arms were on fire: it felt as though someone were playing an oxy-acetylene torch over his shoulders. Thrashing his shaggily bearded head from side to side, he struggled to process what his eyes were telling him. How could his arms be on fire when he didn't seem to have any? Instead, huge tawny wings that flopped and twitched like he was roadkill.

Screaming in terror and agony, he caught sight of an overalled figure wearing a red rubber apron like a slaughterhouse worker.

'Help me!' he screamed. 'For pity's sake, help me!'

The figure turned and came over to the head of the table. As Peter took in the face behind the transparent plastic visor, his voice died in his throat.

'I must have miscalculated the dose. You are a big fellow, after all. No matter. Are you ready to fly?'

'What? No! Let me out! Oh, Jesus!'

The screwdriver that swam into view before his panicked eyes had a long, narrow blade. And in that moment, Peter understood the dread purpose to which it was shortly to be put.

He thrashed harder, flexing his back, his thighs, exerting every muscle in a desperate attempt to get free.

He felt one of the leather straps start to give. It was going to be fine. He could escape, beat this twisted fuck to a pulp and then, what? Get himself to hospital somehow.

He inhaled a huge breath, inflating his massive chest against the wide strap around his ribcage, and strained every sinew in an attempt to burst free from his bindings.

The masked figure bent over him and leaned against his face, crooking an elbow under his chin. With so much weight pushing down on him, he felt the strength drain out of his neck muscles. The tip of the screwdriver jabbed against his right nostril. He snorted and spat, frantic not to let it find a home inside his nose.

Jab, jab, jab, went the shiny steel blade, skidding off the wings of his nose, ripping the delicate flaps of skin and cartilage.

With one last, great effort he bucked against the restraints and yelled with triumph as he felt one give way. The effort caused him to tip his head back. Just a little.

And the screwdriver slid home, travelling fast up his right nostril, smashing its way through the thin bones at the back of his sinuses and into his brain before jamming into the underside of the frontal bone of his skull.

Panting, his killer walked a slow circuit around the table, holding out each vast brown wing in turn before letting it drop. A single primary feather, almost forty centimetres long, detached from the right wing and glided to the floor in a lazy spiral.

The hook and winch made moving the body easy. A child could have done it. The van stood ready, its rear doors open, the load bay sheathed in heavy-duty clear plastic sheets.

* * *

At 8:15 a.m. the following morning, reaching her junction on the E4, Carola Vilks flicked on her car's indicator. The stalk was fabricated from a single piece of billet aluminium, milled to a sensuous, sculpted shape and engineered to slot into each position with a satisfying click beneath her fingertips. It was one of the things she appreciated about the hand-built Dutch supercar. Attention to detail. Precision. Flair.

Smiling to herself, she dabbed the brake pedal and took the slip road. The sky, the blue of cornflowers, just a moment ago, darkened as she entered the outskirts of Norrköping. She glanced upwards. Charcoal-grey clouds were massing over the industrial park where Vilks Luftrum had its factory.

Fat drops of rain spattered the windscreen. The wipers activated, describing an arc so perfect it cleared every necessary part of the screen in a single efficient sweep. Thunder rumbled. A bright spark of lightning flashed against the clouds, earthing somewhere over the town.

By the time she drew up at the rear of the building, in the spot reserved for her exclusive use and where no employee was permitted, the rain was lashing the tarmac, bouncing upwards in milky coronets.

Back when she'd ordered the car, she'd specified a collapsible umbrella that slid into a leather-lined tube beside the steering wheel. She pulled it free and stuck it out of the door, popped the catch, then stepped out into the storm.

She locked the car, and turned towards the building. Looked up at the body suspended from a window-cleaning gantry overhanging the roof. Pursed her lips.

Inside, once she'd shaken the water off the umbrella

and stuck it in a perforated aluminium basket by the door, she stood in the centre of the steel-floored space and took out her phone.

31

Stella looked at her phone. Carola Vilks. *Now* what did she want?

'Carola. How can I help?' she asked, trying to keep the irritation out of her voice.

'I think it is more a case of how I can help you, Stella. Although perhaps "help" isn't quite the right word.'

Stella sensed it, lying in wait beneath Carola's dryly sarcastic tone. The killer had done it again.

'What is it?'

'It would appear Icarus has taken flight once more.'

'Sorry, Carola, could we not talk in riddles, please? Do you mean you've found a body?'

'Oh, I think we can safely say I've found a body.'

'Where?'

'It's currently dangling against the north-west wall of my factory,' Carola said. 'Looks like you'll be paying a visit to Norrköping after all.'

Pulse racing, Stella started calculating her next moves even as she answered.

'I'm on my way. I'll call your local police station and get them out there. Until they arrive, can you do your best to prevent anyone getting close or even taking pictures?'

'Of course. See you soon.'

She ended the call. Stella frowned. She'd taken a few calls from members of the public who'd found corpses before. Everyone from elderly dog-walkers to teenage kids playing truant. Their reactions varied hugely, but within a range of emotions from gabbling shock to screaming fits. None had ever told her in such calm, borderline-amused tones that they were looking at a dead body. Especially one that she knew would be grotesquely mutilated.

Jonna and Tilde were at their desk, the former peering at her computer screen, the latter on the phone.

'Jonna, with me, please. He's done it again.'

Jonna looked round, eyes bright. It was weird, how homicide cops got excited about murder, Stella thought. But then, that's why they went in for it. Tilde ended her call.

'What was that?'

'We've got another one,' Stella said. 'Down in Norrköping.'

'Do you want me along, too?'

'I want you here with Oskar in my absence,' Stella said. 'Things are about to get hectic. You can start by rousing the locals.'

Tilde's mouth turned down. Her disappointment was just as natural as Jonna's excitement. But there was no need to turn up mob-handed. And Oskar would need all the help he could get. She found him in the kitchen and filled him on the latest development.

'I'll get going on things from here,' he said. 'Start

locating CCTV. If it's a factory, there'll be approach roads, tonnes of security. We might get lucky and catch his vehicle.'

In the parking garage, Stella sweet-talked the transport manager into letting her have the keys to the fastest car in the fleet: a month-old Volvo hybrid, tuned beyond its already rapid performance until it could outpace everything on the road bar a Ferrari like Sven-Arne Jonsson's.

'*Polismästare* Andersson booked it out himself. He was hoping to have it for the weekend,' he said with a grin. 'I'll just have to tell him it was needed in the Icarus investigation.'

Stella smiled and patted his shoulder. 'Thanks, Dylan. I owe you a beer.'

'And a pizza!'

They left Stockholm, sirens wailing, blue lights flickering, heading into a summer storm that was rolling up-country from the south. Stella joined the E4 at 80 kilometres per hour and took the sleek black hybrid up to 160.

'We'd better not meet anyone from Traffic,' Jonna said.

Stella grinned. 'We might *meet* them,' she said. 'But I'm pretty sure we can outrun them.'

'Stel! That is so un-Swedish! Who are we, Cagney and Lacey?'

Stella raised her eyebrows as she shot past a banana-yellow Audi RS4 estate doing well over 120.

'How do you even *know* that show? It barely made it into colour.'

'I loved it when I was a little girl. They were so cool. It's why I wanted to be a cop.'

'Seriously? An American cop show from the eighties?'

'Why not? They were smart. Feisty. They carried guns and they were always better than the bad guys,' she said.

'Fair enough.'

After a pause, Jonna said, 'What did Richard think about you being a cop?'

'He was fine about it. He knew I could take care of myself. You didn't mean because he was a human rights lawyer, did you?'

'Maybe. A little. But I was mostly thinking, because I think men find it hard when the woman has a job like ours.' She paused. 'Women, too, sadly.'

'You mean Emmelie?'

'I put my job on my dating profile, but it just said police officer. She was OK about that, but obviously I had to tell her what kind once we were seeing each other.'

'She couldn't cope?'

'Not at all! She made an effort, but this one time? We were in bed, and she said I smelled of death. Can you believe it?'

Jonna sniffed and Stella realised she was crying.

'I'm sorry, Jonna. You never told me that before. I thought it just didn't work out.'

'Well, that about sums it up, doesn't it? Am I ever going to find someone?'

Stella replaced her hand on the wheel.

'Of course you are! You're smart, you're brave, you're resourceful…'

'Not hot, then?'

Stella grinned. 'And you're *super*-hot.'

'Like how, for example?' Jonna asked in a flirtatious tone.

Stella widened her eyes. 'Jonna Carlsson! Are you fishing for compliments?'

'A girl just needs her confidence building up from time to time, that's all.'

'Well, you've got that cute smile for a start, a lovely pixie face and your bum is a work of art.'

'God, it's a pity you're not gay, Stel,' Jonna said with a sigh. 'I think we'd be great together.'

Stella flashed on a memory from her time at university. A brief but enjoyable relationship with a girl in the year above her. A sign for Junction 119 flashed by, dispelling the memory. She started braking and indicated. 'Afraid our romantic prospects will have to take a back seat for now. We're almost there.'

Arriving at the Vilks Luftrum factory, Stella had to switch the windscreen wipers to their fastest speed. The rain was thundering down on the car's roof, the sky had darkened to a deep, bruised-looking purple and lightning forked down every five or six seconds. Thunder boomed and crashed, further adding to the disorientating effect of that summer's worst storm, which Jonna informed her, after checking her phone, had been named Nina.

The local cops had arrived in three marked cars, probably their entire complement, which were parked on three sides of a square with the factory forming the fourth. Blue lights flickered, their reflections splintering off rain-soaked tarmac and refracting through raindrops the size of hazelnuts.

Six bedraggled uniformed officers stood in a loose cordon outside a yellow crime-scene tape perimeter.

Stella parked. She turned to Jonna.

'Wait here a second, I'll check the boot for waterproofs.'

Jonna nodded. 'Fine by me.'

Taking a deep breath, Stella exited the car and was drenched in seconds. Blinking through the rain that ran into her eyes, she rounded the car and opened the boot. It held a set of golf clubs and that was all. Apparently the police master had packed early for his weekend.

She leaned into the Volvo's cabin, watching as a thin stream of water dampened the seat cushion.

'Looks like it's wet T-shirt time. Hope you're wearing a decent bra under that.'

Jonna rolled her eyes.

They strode through the puddles and sheets of standing water that had transformed the concrete apron into a miniature replica of Stockholm's dozens of lakes, bays and canals.

By the time they reached the cordon, Stella could feel the rain soaking right the way through her trousers and into her knickers. Wincing, she held up her ID for the uniformed cop, who at least had a hat to keep the rain out of her eyes.

The cop nodded and lifted the tape. Stella led Jonna inside.

A low-slung sportscar, Carola's, she assumed, sat in the centre of the taped-off space, like a tropical beetle caught out in a monsoon. Its metallic-orange paint job might have been dazzling under the sun that until recently had been baking southern Sweden like a kanelbullar. As it was, it glowed like an ember against the dark-grey factory walls.

She looked up.

Suspended from two ropes attached to the cantilevered arms of a window-cleaning gantry, a man's naked corpse twisted slightly in the gusting wind – a few degrees clockwise, then anti-clockwise, and back again. The vast wings, speckled brown this time, were outstretched – more aluminium? – the long primary feathers shedding steady streams of rainwater from their tips.

The corpse's legs were held apart somehow. It was impossible to see through the driving rain, but Stella suspected another aluminium rod. The pose reminded Stella of something. Something from England. She frowned. That was interesting. She hadn't just thought, something from *home*.

Jonna squinted upwards and pointed.

'Something's happened to his face, look.'

Stella refocused away from the wings and onto the face. Jonna was right. The nose appeared to have been mutilated, too. The rain had washed every trace of blood from the injuries, leaving the torn flesh stark and pink like an anatomical illustration in a medical textbook.

She turned back to Jonna.

'This is hopeless. Even if he got careless, the rain will have washed every last trace of physical evidence away. We might as well just get the fire service out here to bring him down. Come on, let's get out of this. You can call them from Reception while I find Carola. God knows what she'll think of me looking like this.'

Jonna gave Stella a frank, appraising stare. She smiled, an odd expression given the horrific display dangling some ten metres above their heads.

'I think she might find you quite sexy.'

Then she winked. Stella looked down.

'Oh God. I need something to cover them up.'

Five minutes later, having borrowed jackets from two

of the uniformed officers and, in return, sent them back to their car, Stella and Jonna were standing, dripping, in Reception.

Carola strode towards Stella and Jonna, her heels clicking on the brushed-steel floor tiles. She looked at their feet and raised her eyebrows.

'My God, did you swim here?'

'No umbrellas,' Stella said.

'Or waterproofs,' Jonna added.

'Come with me,' Carola commanded, before turning and marching back towards the lifts.

As the lift car travelled upwards, Stella watched as small pools of water gathered around her and Jonna's feet.

'You might want to get a cleaning crew in here, Carola,' she said. 'Your health and safety people would have a fit if they saw this.'

Carola smiled. 'Quite honestly, I'd have thought slipping in rainwater probably isn't the highest risk for one of my employees today, wouldn't you agree?'

'Does the man outside work for you, then?' Jonna asked.

Carola shrugged. 'I don't know. I didn't recognise him, but then he's not in what you might call tip-top condition, is he?'

There it was again. That sardonic sense of humour. Stella found herself wondering afresh about Carola Vilks. The lift doors opened.

'Come with me,' Carola said. 'I've got some spare clothes you can wear. A shower, too. You can change while I order some coffee and something to eat, yes?'

Stella really wanted to get on with her investigation, but balanced against that was the extreme discomfort of interviewing a witness while sitting in rain-soaked clothes. In any case, something told her Carola would brush aside any suggestions of urgency.

Twenty minutes later, she and Jonna were sitting at a round conference table in Carola's office, wearing dry clothes. High-quality cotton T-shirts in plain grey and navy sweat pants, plus sports socks. Their own clothes and shoes had been taken away by one of Carola's staff.

'Hope you didn't spend too long doing your hair this morning,' Jonna said with a grin.

Stella rolled her eyes. 'That good, eh?'

'You both look fine, given the circumstances,' Carola said. 'We have some specialist drying equipment in our materials testing bay. Your clothes will be ready for you before you leave.'

Sipping mugs of excellent coffee, and eating croissants, the three women watched as members of the Norrköping Fire Department took down the body.

'Do you have any security cameras covering that side of the factory?' Stella asked.

'Sorry, no. Only I am permitted to park there and I like my privacy.'

'You don't even have a camera pointed at your car?' This was Jonna.

'The car is equipped with its own,' Carola said. 'They're motion-activated and start whenever the ignition is turned off. The footage is stored on one of our cloud servers.'

'Impressive,' Jonna said.

'Isn't it? So what else can I tell you about our unexpected guest?'

'Why do you think the killer displayed him on your factory wall?' Stella asked.

Carola gave her a cool look then sipped her coffee.

'I have been asking myself the same question,' she

said. 'It seems to me that our man is interested in flight, yes? Where better to display one of his creations than at an aerospace company?'

'Are there any other spots unobserved by security cameras?' Jonna asked.

It was a clever question. Stella looked at Jonna and signalled with her eyes to keep going.

'No. The rest of the plant is completely covered with ten-degree overlaps.'

'Strange that the killer would know the one place where he, or she, could work without being filmed,' Jonna said.

Carola nodded. 'Do you think it could be one of my employees?'

'Apart from you, who would know about the blind-spot?' Jonna asked.

'I'm not sure. Our head of security, of course. His team. Nobody else, really. Not unless someone from security told them.'

'We'll need to speak to them,' Jonna said. 'And review what footage they do have from last night.'

Carola nodded. 'Of course. Hold on.'

She made a call.

'Jonas, it's Carola. I have two detectives from Stockholm with me. They'll be coming to see you shortly. Please cooperate fully with their requests.'

She put her phone down on the table.

'Was there anything else?'

'Where were you last night?' Stella asked.

If Carola was surprised by the question, she didn't show it.

'I left here at 6:59 p.m. and I arrived home at 7:32 p.m.,' she said. 'Then I was at home, alone, until 9:00 p.m. when I went for a run, returning to my house at

10:00 p.m. I was there for the rest of the night before leaving for work this morning at 7:41 a.m. And I arrived here to find my own personal birdman at 8:15 a.m.'

'You're unusually precise with your timings,' Jonna said.

'As an engineer, I dislike approximations,' Carola replied.

That seemed to be it. She didn't bluster about the injustice of having to explain her whereabouts. Of being suspected of murder when all she'd done was perform her civic duty. It was odd. In Stella's experience, most members of the public showed at least some sort of reaction at being asked to provide an alibi. Jonna might just as well have asked Carola what she ate for dinner or what she watched on TV.

'If it's OK with you, we'll go and talk to your security team now,' Stella said. At the office door, she turned. 'Could you check whether your car's cameras were activated at any point during the night, please?'

Fifteen minutes later, Stella knew one thing. The cameras at the gate had picked up a dark Ford transit van arriving at 3:46 that morning. The driver, presumably the killer, wore a baseball cap pulled low over their face. The plates, when she ran them, were registered to a similar van that had been scrapped eleven months earlier. The footage only lasted for a few seconds and had, as far as Stella was concerned, zero evidential value.

She called Tilde and asked her to start identifying dark Ford Transits on the E4 and in Norrköping Central for the previous twenty-four hours, but, realistically, it was just more box-ticking.

32

Stella got a call from Henrik at 2:30 p.m. that same day.

'Hey, Stella, you might want to come over to take a look at the latest victim,' he said. 'Things have changed up a gear.'

The body on Henrik's dissection table bore the brutal Y-incision of all post-autopsy cadavers: two diagonals from the outer points of the collar bones meeting at a point just below the sternum, then descending in a straight line to the pubic bone. Thick black sutures closed the wounds. But it was the face and neck that held her attention.

Numerous livid bruises disfigured the pale flesh of the throat. More mottled the cheeks and forehead. The lower lip was swollen and the face bore numerous lacerations and scrapes.

The nose had suffered the most damage, however. The right nostril was split for a centimetre and a half up from the tip. Henrik held the flap of flesh up with a steel rod. The septum was damaged and the skin on the inside of the nostril was cut.

'What do you think?' Henrik asked her.

'It looks like he's been in a fight. Did you find the same imprint of a screwdriver on the underside of his skull?'

'Exactly the same. A PZ2 Pozidrive.'

'He tried to fight off the killer,' Stella said. 'In the struggle, the screwdriver gashed his nose before being jammed home.'

'That's consistent with the other abrasions and contusions to the face and neck,' Henrik said. 'I think the killer eventually managed to get him in a headlock then dealt the coup de grâce.'

'How, though?'

'Our victim is a big fellow,' Henrik said. 'I'm only speculating, but I would guess that the killer didn't use enough ketamine to keep him under for the duration of the operation. He must have woken up halfway through.'

'Oh God, the poor man,' Stella said. 'Can you imagine what he must have been feeling?'

Henrik nodded and pushed his glasses up his nose.

'Not being a psychopath, unfortunately I can. He would have been disorientated, terrified.'

'But he still had enough left in him to at least try to fight back.'

'What about his arms and legs? They looked as though they were held up and apart somehow. More aluminium?'

Henrik went to a side bench and returned with three narrow aluminium rods, each about fifty centimetres long.

'Inserted between the ribcage and the triceps brachii of each arm, and between the semitendinosus and biceps femoris muscles of each leg. The tips were prevented from further travel by the humeruses and femurs.'

'It reminded me of something,' Stella said. 'The way he'd been posed. I'm sure I've seen it somewhere before.'

Henrik grinned. It was an expression she'd come to know. It meant he was pleased that a cop had come to the same point of enquiry he had.

'Me, too. Do you know the British sculptor, Jacob Epstein?' Stella shook her head. 'I'm a fan of his work. I knew it straight away. Come to my desk. I'll show you.'

Stella skirted the dissection table and went to join Henrik at his desk. He jiggled the mouse and there it was on screen. A sculpture, covered in a green patina, that eerily echoed the pose of the killer's third victim. A long-faced angel, clad in Roman-style military garb – breastplate, flowing cape and sandals – arms outstretched, one holding a spear, legs wide. Beneath him, chained at the ankle and groin, a supine devil.

'It's called St Michael's Victory Over the Devil,' Henrik said.

'Coventry Cathedral!' Stella exclaimed. 'That's where it's hanging, isn't it?'

Henrik nodded. 'On the east wall.'

'What about his internal organs? Any sign of alcohol or drug abuse?'

'Plenty. His liver was thirty per cent cirrhosed, and there are signs of alcoholic hepatitis, pancreatitis and cardiomyopathy. I also found several stomach ulcers and what appeared to be a nascent tumour in his colon.'

'Wow.'

'Yeah, wow. Basically, in non-specialist talk, he'd really shitted up his body. Even without the DIY lobotomy, I wouldn't have given him more than a couple of years if he carried on drinking at that level. The tox results won't be back for a few days, but I expect they'll show near-suicidal level of blood alcohol.'

'Maybe not.'

'No?'

'If he'd started attending Ingrid's Way meetings, maybe they'll come back clean.'

'Maybe. It's all a bit academic now, sadly. Poor guy's beyond her help now, or anybody else's.'

Once Henrik had repaired the damage to the dead man's nose, using finer sutures than those closing his Y-incision, Stella had him send her a full-face photo. She went back to the e-commerce firm and showed it to Rosa Jacobsson, the HR director.

'Do you recognise him?' Stella asked.

White-faced, Rosa took another look at the photo Stella was displaying on her phone.

'I-I'm not sure. It's so difficult to look at, you know. And his nose—'

'If you don't mind, I'd like to show it to your warehouse manager, Ulf Sörenstam.'

'Of course. Shall I take you?'

'I know my way.'

Reaching the warehouse, Stella approached the first person she came to, a young woman wearing an olive-green hijab.

'Where's Ulf?' she shouted above the noise of the rattling conveyor belts.

In answer, the young woman pointed upwards. A gantry ran along one side of the vast space. Halfway along, Stella saw Ulf leaning on the railing and looking down at the pickers, packers and forklift drivers who scurried this way and that like ants in a colony, each with a specialised job to do.

Keeping her eye on him, Stella walked towards a set of metal steps that rose to the mezzanine floor. Ulf caught her eye. His own widened in surprise and then he did something that surprised her. He ran.

Taking the steps two at a time, she reached the gantry, swung herself round onto the mesh walkway using a vertical beam that stretched towards the roof, and sprinted after him.

He looked over his shoulder, then tore off again. He was heading for another set of steps at the far end of the metal gantry. She could see it led down to the loading bay where huge double doors stood open. Her boots clanging on the perforated floor, she put on a spurt of speed and closed the distance between her and the clearly panicked warehouse manager.

But he'd reached the steps and took them at a flying pace, his feet barely touching more than one in four as he hurtled groundwards.

Stella reached the top of the steps as Ulf hit the bottom, swung himself round as she had just done, stumbled, righted himself, and ran for the open doors.

Reaching the ground floor, Stella dashed after him, dodging left and right as wide-eyed warehouse workers tried to get out of her way. In his panic, one dropped an armful of flat-packed cardboard boxes that spread out in front of Stella like an obstacle in a particularly bizarre video game. *Dodge the forklifts! Hurdle the packaging! Catch the fleeing manager!*

Ulf disappeared through the open loading bay doors. She heard a loud, insistent beeping. A truck making a delivery. Yellow flashes bounced off the interior of the entrance.

She made the doors and flicked a glance left and right before seeing Ulf, his head twisted round to see if she was still following him.

'Ulf!' she yelled. 'Look out!'

He looked ahead and screamed, before tripping and rolling beneath the truck's rear axle. Stella put on a burst of speed, grateful for her daily run with Jonna, and leaped up onto the running board on the passenger side before hauling herself up to the door and hammering on the window.

The driver turned and reared back in shock. Out of a reflex that probably saved Ulf's life, he hit the brakes, which activated with a monstrous hiss and a stink of hot metal.

The window buzzed down.

'I'm a cop,' Stella panted, holding up her ID. 'Don't move. There's a man under your truck.'

The driver killed the engine and cupped a hand round his ear.

'What?'

'There's a man back there. I think he went between your rear wheels. Just don't move the truck, whatever you do. Stay here.'

She climbed down and ran to the side of the truck. She got down onto her hands and knees and peered under the trailer. Ulf lay face down and apparently unconscious. His limbs were splayed, but they didn't look broken. No white spear-points of bone poking through his clothing, or unlikely angles at knees or elbows.

'Ulf!' she called. 'Can you hear me?'

Silence.

Swearing to herself, she got onto her belly and commando-crawled out of the sun and into the deep shade beneath the eighteen-wheeler.

When she reached Ulf, she saw blood beneath his head. Had he sustained a skull fracture? She prayed not.

She could already hear Nik Olsson's disapproving tones as he accused her of *recklessly endangering the life of a member of the public through outlandish paramilitary techniques.* That or something similar.

Close enough to examine Ulf, she sighed with relief. The blood was coming from his nose, which bore a deep cut across its bridge. His eyes were closed.

She pushed two fingers into the soft place under his jaw, searching for a pulse from his carotid artery. At first she felt nothing, but then located the blood vessel, and with it, a steady *bump-bump* beneath her fingertip.

Good, he was alive. She was debating the rights and wrongs of pulling him clear when his eyes opened.

'Where the devil's shit am I?' he groaned.

'Oh thank God,' Stella exclaimed. 'You're under a delivery truck, Ulf. Remember? You ran off when you saw me. Can you move your toes? Your fingers?'

Frowning, he closed his eyes. Stella saw the fingers on his right hand flex and curl, before opening again. His legs twitched and the toes of his work boots lifted.

'Yeah,' he said. 'I guess my spine's in one piece, eh?'

'Lucky for you. You could have been killed. Come on, we need to get you out from under here.'

Stella grabbed him under his shoulders and heaved. Ulf backpedalled with his heels and, inch by inch, they made their ungainly way out from under the trailer.

Other employees had gathered to watch and one woman, large and motherly-looking, now brought a swivel chair out into the sunshine.

'Here you go, Ulf,' she said. 'Park yourself on that. Mila's getting you a coffee and a cookie.'

'Thanks, but I don't need anything to eat.'

'Nonsense! You're in shock,' she said, folding her

arms under a generous bust. 'It's dangerous to let your blood sugar go too low.'

Mila turned out to be the young woman who had pointed Ulf out to Stella in the first place. She offered Ulf a white china mug and a chocolate cookie. He grunted his thanks then took a bite. As he chewed, a little colour re-entered his cheeks; greenish-white just a moment earlier.

'Thanks, everybody,' Stella said, turning to address the small group of onlookers. 'Ulf's going to be fine. If you could all just go back inside, I'll take it from here.'

Alone with Ulf, whose face looked almost as bad as the third murder victim's, Stella asked the obvious question.

'Why did you run, Ulf? You could have been killed.'

His eyes flicked left and right. His mouth worked, but no sound came out. Sometimes repeating the question helped, but with Ulf, she could see that he was resisting a decision he had already taken.

Stella waited. It would be just a little time before his conscious and unconscious minds reached an agreement.

— *We're in trouble.*

— *Yeah, but we can style it out.*

— *No, we really can't.*

— *But…*

— *I said no.*

He took a gulp of coffee and finished the cookie in two snatching bites, like a stray dog faced with the removal of a discarded kebab. He sighed.

'I'm dealing drugs, that's why I ran. I panicked. When I saw you back here again, I thought you'd found out,' he gabbled. 'I take orders online and send them out from here like regular deliveries. It's nothing major. Just retail, you know?'

Stella cocked her head on one side.

'I'm investigating a series of brutal killings, Ulf, as you ought to remember, given we've already had one conversation on the topic,' she said. 'Are you telling me you had nothing to do with the murder of Mikael Matthiasson and Sara Marksson?'

'Of course not! Like I said, I was dealing and I thought you'd rumbled me.'

'So, you can't be a murderer because you're a drug dealer. Is that it?'

'Yes! I mean, no.'

'Another body was found this morning.'

His eyes widened. 'When did it happen? Because I was at home with my wife all last night. Ask her.'

'We will, Ulf, believe me. What are you dealing?'

'What? Why?'

'Why? Why the hell do you think, Ulf? Because it's a crime.'

'But I thought you were Homicide, not drug squad.'

'Oh, Jesus, are you serious? Yes, I'm Homicide, but—'

Suddenly she remembered why she'd been looking for Ulf in the first place. She took out her phone and brought up the photo of the dead man.

'Recognise him?'

Ulf squinted at the phone and turned it a little so the sun wasn't shining directly onto the screen. He nodded.

'Yeah, I recognise him. Name's Pete. Lukasson. Been working here for a couple of months. Attendance was a bit patchy but you know, no worse than any of the others they send us. Looks like he met his Maker.'

Stella pocketed her phone. 'Thanks.'

'You're welcome. Always happy to help the police. You know, be a good citizen and all that —' Stella heard the *'crap'* even though he didn't voice it. 'So, are we cool?'

'Cool?'

'About the drugs, I mean? I'll stop today. I promise. It was just a sideline, anyway.'

She looked at him. Smiled. 'One of my colleagues from the *drug* squad will be in touch.'

Stella drove back to SPA headquarters turning over in her mind what she had. Three victims. All recovering addicts of one sort or another. All either employed by the e-commerce firm with links to Ingrid's Way, or attenders at the group's meetings. Or both. That made them vulnerable to all kinds of pressure, from blackmail to the lure of the substance that was killing them.

She felt sure that their killer was present somewhere in that world. A counsellor, group leader, meeting host, company manager. What she wanted was a link between one of her persons of interest and the charity of its corporate partner.

As she pulled into the car park on Kungsholmsgatan, Stella found she was repeating the three murder victims' names as a mantra.

'Mikael Matthiasson. Sara Marksson. Peter Lukasson. Mikael... Shit!'

Swerving to avoid a yellow-and-black painted bollard, she brought the car to a stop.

'Matthiasson, Marksson, Lukasson. Matthew, Mark, Luke. Shit the devil, it's the gospels!'

She hustled the car into a space and ran inside. Four minutes later, panting from racing up the stairs, she burst into Major Crimes. Nobody from her team was in.

She sat at the first empty desk and Googled the latest Swedish census. In 2012 there were almost 74,000 people with the surname Jonsson. Even if she cut a third on the assumption they were children, that still left a potential victim pool of 50,000.

No, it wouldn't, would it? Because Icarus was targeting addicts. Addicts with a connection with Ingrid's Way.

'Oh Christ!' she murmured.

33

Heart racing, Stella called Sven-Arne Jonsson. 'Come on, come on, answer your damn phone,' she said, staring at the screen and willing him to pick up.

'Hi, this is Sven-Arne. Leave a message. Yours in sobriety.'

'Sven-Arne, this is Stella Cole. Your life is in danger. Stay with other people, in public if possible. Call me when you get this. We need to take you into protective custody.'

Using the official driving licence database, she found the eight men with his name. Cross-referencing with his age, she narrowed the eight down to one.

She called Jonna.

'Get anyone and everyone over to 21 Värdshusbacken on Stora Essingen. It's Sven-Arne's place. He's in danger.'

'What? How do you know?'

'Just do it. I'll explain later.'

She ran back out of the office, praying she'd be in time to save Sven-Arne from Icarus. On the way down the corridor she bumped into Nik Olsson coming out of his office.

The IA chief rewarded her with a scowl of bottomless contempt.

'You may be wondering why I haven't made a formal complaint against you,' he said.

'No, Nik. And I really don't have time to discuss it with you.'

* * *

It was one of his iron rules. He turned his phone off when he was talking to another addict. People thought he was superficial, a self-promoting fraud. But they were wrong.

Sven-Arne had known the hell of addiction and he'd managed to drag himself out of the underworld and back to a normal life. He didn't seek them out, but if attenders at Ingrid's Way meetings came to him, he would give them as much time as he could.

He was used to dealing with celebrities. The worlds of TV, fashion and music were populated by people for whom fame wasn't the only drug they craved.

For some, it was the pressures of the job, for others the fear of losing their precarious grip on the ledge where their idols clustered. Still others saw it as part of the role, until it began to consume them and they realised no amount of followers, streams or paparazzi shots could pry their addiction's cold, scaly fingers from around their necks.

The woman sitting opposite him in his expensively furnished lakeside house was different. For a start, she wasn't part of celebrity culture. Oh, perhaps in the business pages or the serious monthly magazines she was.

But she could walk down the street without being asked for a selfie or an autograph every ten metres. He appreciated her understated jewellery and elegant, tasteful clothes: a navy linen dress that just skimmed her knees, low-heeled tan loafers.

'Tell me your story,' he said.

Maybe because of his former life as a writer, a teller of tales, he'd found this was the question that unlocked the truth.

Hers differed in the specifics, but the tide that had washed her onto his shore was the same as for all addicts. Alcohol to cope with the stress of running the business. Then sleeping pills to knock her out when it wore off at three in the morning. Uppers to get her moving the next day. She'd been able to cope…until she hadn't.

'And you want my help, Carola?' he asked.

'No. I'm dealing with the problem privately.'

He frowned, unsure now for the first time since she'd rung him.

'Then, forgive me, but why are we having this conversation?'

'I became interested in your organisation after learning of its connection to two of Icarus's victims,' she said. 'I am friendly with the detective leading the investigation. I researched the work you do and I would like to help Ingrid's Way expand. The inevitable negative publicity as the bodies keep piling up is going to call for expert media relations. I could help there, too. These things take money, of which I have plenty.'

Sven-Arne felt a flash of irritation at her offhand attitude. He'd built up Ingrid's Way on his own without any help from patronising industrialists. But then again, she *was* right. He'd already been fielding a growing stream of enquiries from journalists, not all of them friendly.

'First of all,' he said, 'I'm not sure we should talk about bodies "piling up". I've met Stella too and she seems pretty on it to me.'

'Of course. I apologise. A poor choice of phrase,' she said with a half-smile. 'Does this mean you aren't interested in my proposal?'

He shook his head. 'No! Not at all. It's a very generous offer. And the chance to partner with such a successful woman in business would be something of a coup for Ingrid's Way.'

Carola smiled. 'Good. I think so, too.'

The meeting took a further half-hour, with Carola ending it promising to bring her general counsel next time along with some papers to sign.

Sven-Arne showed her to the door, intoxicated as much by the heady perfume she wore as her promised help for Ingrid's Way. As she stepped out onto the pavement, a gleaming black Jaguar limousine drew up at the kerb with a whisper of rubber on tarmac.

A forest-green-liveried chauffeur emerged to hold open the rear door for her. She slid inside, onto a white leather seat, her dress riding up a little over her thigh as she did so. Sven-Arne offered a wave at the blacked-out privacy glass then turned away, wondering whether the rest of her was as toned as her legs.

Five minutes later, the doorbell rang.

He smiled to himself. She'd probably forgotten something.

He opened the door.

* * *

The fastest route to Stora Essingen led Stella back through Östermalm. She rounded a bend to find herself at the end of a long tailback. Tyres squealing, she pulled around the last car and sped to the head of the queue. The delay was caused by temporary traffic lights, which were on red. Coming towards her was an open-topped Mercedes. She pulled in ahead of the car at the head of the queue just in time to avoid a head-on collision. Östermalmers might be polite, but their command of Swedish swearing was at least as well developed as their less affluent neighbours.

Hand raised in mute apology, Stella tore down Linnégatan, slamming through the gears and praying she'd be in time to save Sven-Arne.

34

Stella was almost at the junction with Banérgatan; a pretty, grassed island on which a lone sycamore tree spread its shade. As she braked, she saw a man strongly resembling Jamie step out from a door on the other side of the street. No. Not 'resembling' Jamie. It *was* Jamie.

A curvaceous blonde in tight jeans and a white spaghetti-strap top followed him onto the pavement. Smiling, they embraced, then the blonde kissed Jamie full on the lips. What the hell?

Head turned, mouth gaping, Stella almost missed the turn. Swearing, she hauled the wheel over, dabbing the brakes just enough to stop the car sliding into the kerb. Like a lot of junctions in the capital, the junction wasn't controlled by traffic lights. Each intersecting street ended in a zebra crossing, and the theory was that you gave way to pedestrians.

The theory.

Still trying to process what she'd just seen, she rounded the corner, tyres screeching, and screamed, 'No!'

In front of her, a crocodile of elementary school children in fluorescent yellow hi-vis bibs were crossing the road. Sweet, innocent little kids, smiling gap-toothed grins, singing, laughing, playing games with teddy bears held loosely in pudgy fingers, unaware their short lives were about to be cut short.

Slamming the brakes on, wrenching the wheel over to the right, Stella brought the car to such a sudden halt, she stalled it. A cloud of blue smoke stinking of burnt rubber drifted over the roof and enveloped the children and their teachers.

The children stopped and stared, open-mouthed, and in several cases, crying. At the head of the procession, two young women with coloured lanyards round their necks whirled round, their arms reaching protectively for the children Stella had almost just run down.

Their expression changed from fear to anger. They gesticulated at the zebra crossing, the children, at Stella herself. Even without lip-reading skills, she could tell more or less exactly what they were shouting.

She buzzed the window down.

'I'm really sorry! It's a police emergency. Hurry, please.'

Looking barely mollified, they led the children across. The two adults at the rear of the crocodile stood, arms akimbo in the centre of the road, until every last child had made it to the safety of the opposite pavement. Still glaring at Stella, they sauntered over to the far side of the road.

Almost crying with frustration, and the shock of seeing the fear in the children's eyes, Stella restarted the engine and put her foot flat on the floor. Jamie and the blonde kissing hovered in mid-air front of her as if projected a metre or so beyond the windscreen. She shook her head to clear the unappealing head-up display; she didn't have time for this now. Whatever the fuck that was between Jamie and his busty new ladyfriend would have to wait.

Stora Essingen was due east of Östermalm, but the direct route would involve an endless series of surface roads and dense Stockholm traffic. Instead, Stella headed north, up to the E20 motorway, with its flyovers and uninterrupted eastwards progress towards the island.

She flipped on the radio.

'This is Stella. Report in, please.'

The responses crackled in.

'Tilde. I'm in Segeltorp. Ten minutes out.'

'Jonna. I'm in the mother of all jams in Vasastan. Someone's broken down. Nothing's moving.'

'Oskar. Fifteen out. Roads are clear.'

Stella drove fast through the light motorway traffic. Her thoughts performed a jerky somersault and she found herself thinking of the elementary school children. How old were they? Five? Four? Younger?

Lola was just a baby when she had been mown down by a hit and run driver. Behind the wheel, a High Court judge named Leonard Ramage. She'd never made it to nursery, let alone infant school. *Oh, Lola. Why did you have to die?* Stella's eyes misted over and she wiped the moisture away with the back of her finger.

'We paid him out, though, didn't we?'

She whirled round, looking for the source of the voice. But the back seat was empty. Of course it was. Because Stella was alone in the car. A loud rumbling filled the cabin. She'd strayed over onto the corrugated strips at the side of the road. She jerked the wheel over to centre the car, but not before a wave of panic washed over her, bringing a greasy film of perspiration to her forehead and making her guts churn.

'You're gone!' she shouted into the empty cabin. 'You're dead! I killed you!'

She flicked her eyes to the rear-view mirror. The rear seat was empty. No blazing-eyed version of Stella twirling a pistol around her index finger, or testing the blade of a hunting knife against her thumb.

The voice was in her head. That was all. Just like Alyssa had said. But it wasn't even supposed to exist *there*. She swallowed. It must have been the shock of seeing Jamie in a very public embrace, then almost crashing into the line of elementary school kids. It had triggered all those old, old emotions: grief, anxiety, depression, yes, all of those...and murderous, all-consuming, vengeful rage.

'I don't have time for this,' she muttered, and pushed her foot down harder on the accelerator pedal.

Twelve minutes later, Stella crossed the wide motorway bridge that connected Lilla and Stora Essingen islands. The sun sparkled off the water, and even as she sped on, she couldn't help but be amazed at the sheer number and variety of the city's waterways, studded today with the sharp-pointed white triangles of pleasure yachts like a child's folded-paper models.

Then she was onto the island, lights and sirens clearing a path through the sleepy summer traffic to the beginning of Sven-Arne's road. Värdshusbacken snaked down the side of the island's southern edge in a swooping series of S-bends. With each turn, the lake came into view through broad-leaved trees that turned the sunlight a soft greenish-gold.

The residents of this gently wooded hillside had one of the best views in Stockholm, and also the most private. The houses were set back from the road. They varied in style from contemporary architect-designed villas to traditional timber-framed cottages in falun red. All looked well maintained and, Stella imagined, would cost the thick end of a couple of million krona apiece.

As she negotiated the last, and tightest, bend she saw flashing blue lights. Two cars were parked in a V outside the black-painted steel gates of a house set in its own walled garden. Unless Jonna had escaped the traffic jam, this would be Tilde and Oskar.

The house was a striking modern building. A series of interlocking pale-grey cubes, with black-framed windows. A tree smothered in creamy flowers smelling of honey spread its shade over the gravelled parking area.

The side door was open and she ran through, calling out for the other two. There was no answer.

She emerged from the shadowy hall into a bright, airy living room facing the lake. A gently sloping lawn, mown in perfect stripes, led to the waterfront, where a matching boathouse sat beside a wooden dock.

Two figures were standing shoulder to shoulder at the far end of the dock, beyond which the sun bounced off the water in dazzling flashes. With the sun in her eyes, Stella couldn't be sure, but the outlines looked like Tilde and Oskar. One had her bulk, the other, his bony, angular frame.

Shading her eyes with a raised hand, she stepped out through the sliding-glass doors.

'Guys, is that you?' she called.

The figures turned, their faces in deep shadow. Stella blinked as the wind-ruffled lake surface threw scattered splinters of sunlight into her eyes.

'Hi, Stel,' Oskar called as they walked back to meet her. 'We're too late. He's dead.'

'Same way?'

He nodded, glumly. 'With a twist.'

She accompanied them back to the dock, their footsteps amplified by the silvered wooden planks. Reaching the end, she looked down and shook her head. All thoughts of Jamie and of the children she'd almost mown down vanished.

'My God.'

About five metres out from the dock, bobbing gently on the crystal-clear water, Sven-Arne was kneeling on a white paddle board, his forehead resting on the ridged surface of its deck. Vast white wings drooped down onto the water, where they floated, outstretched, at least four metres from tip to tip. A pool of blood had spread out beneath his face. Stella knew, without having to wait for Henrik, that the cause of the haemorrhage would be the forcible insertion of a PZ2 Pozidrive screwdriver into the brain.

'I think they must be from an albatross,' Tilde said.

Oskar nodded. 'Or a pelican, maybe? We can cross-check with the team investigating the zoo break-ins. Actually, I think you're right, Tilde. The shape is more albatross-like. Narrower.'

'It's just a guess. I saw a documentary on migratory birds last month and they had a camera that was flying alongside one.'

'Look, can we just drop the ornithology seminar for a moment?' Stella snapped. 'We've got another dead body floating in the lake and I really want him out of there and under cover before people start taking videos. Is there anything we can use to drag him in?'

Tilde flushed. 'Of course. Sorry, Stella.' She pointed. 'There's a boathouse. I'll see if there're any hooks.'

While Tilde marched across the lush, velvety lawn

towards a pale-blue wooden outbuilding, Stella looked back at the body. A wind had sprung up, tugging the surface of the lake into busy wavelets that set the paddleboard bobbing.

Horrified, Stella watched as the wind caught one of the vast white wings and lifted it free of the surface, its soft feathers ruffling as if the birdman that had once been Sven-Arne Jonsson were shaking them dry. The board swivelled slowly, counter-clockwise, and began to drift away from the dock.

'Oh, Christ, that's more than any boathook's going to reach,' she said.

Oskar pointed off to their left.

'Look.'

A pleasure cruiser, its double row of windows glinting in the sun, was steaming straight across the lake towards them. Stella only gave the tourist boat a quick glance. She was already sitting to remove her boots.

'You're not going in, are you?' Oskar asked, incredulously.

'Well I'm not going to stand here while Sven-Arne goes viral, that's for sure.'

She pulled her jeans down and stepped out of them, then removed her T-shirt. Without hesitation, she dived off the dock. The water was so cold it made her gasp. She felt her muscles seize up and had to force herself to start swimming.

Her daily jogs with Jonna meant she was running-fit, but using unfamiliar muscles and fighting the bone-cold water of the lake had her slowing down to the pace she'd last managed in primary school swimming lessons.

After what felt like minutes, but was probably only seconds, she reached the paddleboard and seized the nose. This close she could see that the killer had lashed Sven-Arne down using thin white cord.

She tried to turn the board for shore, but a gust of wind slid beneath the right-hand wing and lifted it clear of the water again. The breeze was dragging her further away from the dock and she felt the first cold fingers of fear encircle her chest.

Her legs were heavy, and they were refusing to obey her when she urged them to kick out. Her teeth were chattering, whether from the cold, or panic, she neither knew nor cared. She managed to turn the board round again and, struggling to make headway, towed it a metre or two towards Oskar. Tilde had joined him on the deck. If she'd found a boathook, she'd discarded it. It wouldn't have been any use, anyway; Stella was at least fifteen metres from the dock.

Then she lost her grip on the paddleboard's nose: her fingers were too cold to maintain enough pressure. It started to slide away from her.

Stella wanted to cry for help, but it felt so stupid. Maybe they could throw her a life buoy, though. She opened her mouth and caught a wavelet instead of air. Coughing, she missed a stroke and sank beneath the surface just as she was gasping in a breath.

She splashed her way to the surface, retching and trying to clear her airways to take a breath before going under again. She saw a splash from beneath the water: a beautiful inverted flower of greenish-white bubbles striped from above by the sunlight. Someone had dived in after her. She struck out for the surface, but at some point she'd become inverted. After two strokes she realised she was swimming downwards.

Breath running out, she was seized by panic.

35

Strong hands closed on her left hip and right shoulder and spun her around until she was facing upwards. As she turned, she caught a glimpse of a third figure, deep down where the water was a dark jade-green. Dark hair swirling around her head, a sardonic smile on her face: on *Stella's* face. Then it was gone, and Stella was on the surface, lying on her back, with Tilde's left hand cupping her chin as she swam powerfully back to the bank.

Stella had no reserves left. She allowed Tilde the freedom to get them both back to the dock in the best way she saw fit. Oskar, his bony, unshaven face creased with concern, was waiting. He reached down and grabbed Stella's wrists, helped her to spin round and then hoisted her bodily from the water and sat her on the warm wooden planking.

'Are you OK?' he asked, handing her her clothes.

'Yeah, yeah, I'm fine. I just feel so stupid.' She looked round. 'Where's Tilde?'

'She's gone back for Sven-Arne. Look!'

Stella watched as Tilde, without apparent effort,

dragged the paddleboard and its grotesque passenger back towards the dock. Behind her, the pleasure cruiser was still a good few hundred metres away, but Stella could make out the flashes of sunlight reflecting off upheld phones. She prayed their zooms would render anything they did capture a pixelated mess.

Oskar stood, leaving her to finish dressing. He picked up a wooden-shafted boathook and poked it under one of the wings. With Tilde at the back pushing, and Oskar pulling, they manoeuvred the monstrous floating object up to the dock.

Dressed now, Stella ran for the shed and found a grey nylon cover shrouding a couple of mountain bikes. She pulled it free and raced back to the end of the dock, throwing it out and over Sven-Arne's body to shield it from the tourists' lenses.

Tilde climbed out of the water in a single flowing move, despite the weight of her soaking clothes. She sprawled on the deck, chest heaving.

Holding the paddleboard in tight to the dock with one hand, Oskar reached into his pocket and pulled out a penknife. He held it up to Stella.

'Can you cut him free? Between us we should be able to get him off that board and onto the dock.'

Teeth still clacking like castanets from her recent immersion, Stella accepted the knife. She pulled out the larger of the two blades and stuck the upper half of her body under the cover to start cutting the para cord. Beneath the nylon, her nose was assailed by the sudden stink of a dead body, mixed with the oily smell from the feathers. She felt her gorge rising and swallowed hard to keep from vomiting.

Once the last strand was severed, Sven-Arne sagged to the left and, for one horrible moment, Stella thought he was going to topple off into the water. She grabbed the nearest wing and felt her stomach lurch as something gave in the join between bird and human anatomy.

'Quick!' she shouted. 'He's slipping.'

Together, she and Oskar dragged Sven-Arne off the board and onto the dock. Stella snagged a corner of the nylon sheet and replaced it over the body.

Out on the water, the pleasure boat motored past. Although a handful of curious passengers were looking in their direction, Stella was confident there was nothing to see beyond the bedraggled group on the dock gathered round a grey-sheeted mass.

Heart thumping from the exertion, Stella turned to Tilde.

'You saved my life, Tilde. Thank you. I had no idea the water would be so cold.'

Tilde looked down, then back at Stella and smiled shyly. 'I could see you were in trouble. And I was always a strong swimmer.'

'It was a brave thing to do, especially fully dressed. I'm going to put you forward for a commendation,' Stella said. 'But now, we really need to get everybody down here.'

'They should be here any moment. I called it in on my way over,' Oskar said, sitting on his heels, hands flat on the tops of his thighs.

Stella looked up as a wailing siren shattered the silence. Blue lights flickered through the trees above Sven-Arne's house, the white van on which they sat disappearing then reappearing as it negotiated the tight bends.

Jonna arrived before the CSIs. She raced across the lawn and down onto the deck.

'Hell! What happened?' She looked from Stella to Tilde and back again. 'Why are you both soaking wet?'

'We had a little trouble recovering Sven-Arne from the lake,' Stella said. 'He was tied to a paddleboard. Tilde rescued us both: she's a pretty strong swimmer.'

'Well done, Tilde,' Jonna said.

Tilde smiled. 'Anyone would have done it.'

'No, really, that was impressive.'

'Well, maybe being what my mom always called a big ox isn't such a handicap after all.'

Jonna's mouth dropped open.

'Your mother called you that?'

Tilde looked down. 'She did, yes.'

'My God, you must have been so hurt.'

Tilde shrugged. 'Kids are very resilient. She didn't mean any harm by it. It was just her way.'

'Well, it's a funny kind of way if you ask me,' Jonna said.

'Can we get on, please?' Tilde asked Stella. 'I don't want to be the centre of attention when there's another victim we have to process.'

'Of course. Come on. Let's get a closer look.'

Jonna crouched and lifted a corner of the nylon sheet, then let it fall.

'Is that it, then? Four gospels, four victims. Has he finished?'

Stella sighed. 'Honestly, I have no idea. I hope so, but we just lost another potential suspect, so we're back at square one.'

Tilde stood. 'Anyone want a coffee? I saw a pod machine in the kitchen.'

'I don't think the forensics guys will be happy,' Oskar said.

'I'll wear gloves,' she said. 'Anyway, I'm taking an

executive decision. It's coffee or you'll be dealing with at least one case of hypothermia.'

She trotted off towards the house, her soaked clothes clinging to her muscular limbs. Seized with a sudden fatigue, Stella lay on her back, not caring that the fourth victim's body lay not half a metre from her shoulder.

'You OK?' Jonna asked.

'Yeah, I just need a minute.'

'We'll be in the house, then.'

Stella closed her eyes. Felt the sun warming her skin. The hideous apparition that had grinned up at her from deep in the lake swam into view. She knew who it was. And it terrified her. But why was she back? What was Other Stella trying to tell her?

Stella agreed with Alyssa: her mental health was fine. Her vengeful drama was all played out. Had been for over a decade. And there was something different this time, too. Other Stella didn't feel real in the way she had before. Stella never felt in the presence of another person. These were more like visions. No out-of-body experiences, no lost time, no coming round from a fugue state dripping in blood.

She opened her eyes, suddenly wanting that cup of coffee very much indeed. Maybe some caffeine would help her grasp the thought that danced so enticingly out of reach.

She joined the others in the kitchen, to find Oskar had already made coffee. She accepted a mug gratefully.

The rest of the day passed in a blur of meetings and paperwork, as Stella expanded the investigation yet again. But every time she found herself alone, her mind returned to the sight of Jamie kissing the voluptuous Swede on her doorstep.

She spent the evening at Jamie's place, dreading the

moment she'd have to confront him. The Airbnb apartment was small but decorated so tastefully it hurt. The owners had gone for a restrained palette of pale creams, beiges and, as an accent colour, a deep petrol-blue. Scatter cushions all in blue used texture rather than colour for variation: everything from plaited suede to extravagantly furry numbers and silken tassels.

In brief, unemotional language, Stella told Jamie about the scene that had greeted her out on the lake. He asked her about the body, the wings, the way Sven-Arne had been posed and she supplied the answers. But after kicking ideas around for another thirty minutes and draining most of a bottle of wine, they were no further along.

'Come on,' Jamie said, finally. 'Enough talking for now. Let's eat.'

Jamie had cooked couscous with roasted Mediterranean vegetables, on top of which he'd drizzled a fiery, plum-red sauce. Harissa, he'd said, when she asked.

Sitting at a table made from a single rough-edged plank of pale wood with a beautiful swirling grain, Stella took a bite. It was delicious. The couscous was fragrant, studded with caramelised onions and plump raisins, and lightly spiced with cinnamon and ground coriander.

Ignoring the fluttery feeling in her belly, she swallowed, then put her fork down. Took a swig of the red wine he'd opened.

'Everything all right?' Jamie asked, looking concerned. 'It's not too hot is it? I haven't used this brand of harissa before. They can really vary. I bought it from this really great Moroccan minimarket on—'

'Who was that woman I saw you kissing today?' Stella blurted out.

Jamie's eyes widened.

'Pardon?'

Now she'd let the genie out of the bottle, she found she didn't want to stuff it back in. It was as if the stress of the case had become distilled into this moment.

'She's kind of hard to forget, I'd have thought. Blonde, tits out to here. Lives on Linnégatan near that little park on the road junction.'

Jamie smiled, which infuriated Stella. He held his hands out.

'Look, it's not what it looked like.'

Stella gulped some more wine.

'Really? Why, what really happened? Did she lose an earring down your throat and was using her tongue to get it back?'

'If you saw me with Freja then you know that's not what happened.'

'Oh, well, forgive me for misinterpreting the evidence of my own eyes. Because from where I was sitting, what you and *Freja* were doing looked pretty bloody unambiguous.'

Jamie's eyes narrowed. 'Where exactly *were* you sitting? Were you spying on me?'

'No! Of course not! I'm trying to catch a serial killer, in case you'd forgotten.'

'So he was on Linnégatan, the killer?'

'I was in my car. On my way to Sven-Arne's place.'

'You must have been in a hurry, then.'

'I saw what I saw, Jamie.'

'OK, look. Here's what you saw, Stel. Freja's been giving me Swedish conversation lessons. I wanted to surprise you. You must have noticed I've been trying it out in the office.'

'Yes, but I thought you'd been memorising stuff off the internet.'

'I have, a bit, but Freja's been helping me with my everyday Swedish. I thought I was going to need it, but now I'm not so sure.'

'Fine,' Stella said, feeling her pulse slowing down. She took another sip of the wine, a smaller one this time. 'But she kissed you. Properly! I *saw* Jamie!'

He shrugged. 'Did you see me pull away?'

'What?'

'When she kissed me. Did you see my reaction?'

'No. Like I said, I was in a bit of a rush to stop a murder. I needn't have bothered, as it turned out.'

Jamie smiled. 'She took me by surprise. Up until today she's been friendly, I suppose you'd call it. Just a double-kiss on both cheeks like normal,' he said. 'Then, today, she planted one right on me. I really wasn't expecting it, darling, I promise. I practically jumped back into the traffic.'

'I didn't see that. I was too busy avoiding wiping out about a hundred nursery school children.'

Suddenly she felt her cheeks heating up. Jamie's teasing smile wasn't helping. He poured more wine. She drank some. He held her gaze, a smile just curling the edges of his mouth.

'You wouldn't, by any slight chance, be jealous would you?' he asked, finally.

Stella grinned, her outrage of a few moments ago dissipated.

'Her boobs *are* enormous, though.'

Jamie grinned back. 'I'm pretty sure they're implants.'

She dropped her mouth open in mock horror, able

now to see the funny side of things. 'Oh, you were close enough to tell, then?'

'Call it masculine intuition.'

'So what has the lovely Freja been teaching you to say then? "Hello, can I press up against your amazing fake breasts?"'

Jamie smiled and shook his head.

'Jag saknade dig så mycket när du var borta. Låt oss aldrig låta det hända igen.'

He'd just told Stella he'd missed her so much when they were apart and to not let that happen again. She felt tears pricking at the corners of her eyes.

'Jag älskar dig, Jamie Hooke,' she said, smiling.

'Jag älskar dig också, Stella Cole.'

So they loved each other. In Swedish, no less. If only it weren't taking place in the grotesque shadow of winged human beings.

36

Three weeks after the episode at Lake Mälaren, Stella sat at the head of the table in the meeting room. She looked around at the officers gathered there to discuss the case. She saw it in all their faces. Resignation. Fatigue. Even boredom. The case had become what they used to call, back at the Met, a 'runner'.

No suspects, but thousands of people to be TIEed. DNA samples by the hundred as they swabbed everyone they could identify who had any connection to either Ingrid's Way, its halfway houses or the e-commerce warehouse where two of the four victims had been working.

Malin had been making increasingly loud noises about the commitment of resources to a case that was going nowhere. And, thanks to a terrorist outrage on Stockholm's famous Vasa Bridge, in which a radicalised Muslim youth had stabbed five people before being shot dead by police, the Icarus case was no longer in the news.

It had slipped, first off the evening news and the

front pages, and then out of public view altogether. Now and again it turned up in occasional 'Did the police miss a vital clue?' pieces on late-night TV news.

And it wasn't as if Stockholm's common-or-garden murderers had agreed amongst themselves to give the homicide squad some space to do their job. Husbands were still drunkenly battering their wives to death. Drug dealers were still shooting each other, and the odd passerby, in turf disputes. Business partners were still falling out, murderously so.

Stella desperately wanted to inject some renewed enthusiasm into the gathered detectives. She'd invited Jamie in to lead a brainstorming session. He spoke now.

'This killer is a strange one.'

'No shit,' Oskar drawled, his habitually gloomy expression deepened to something approaching terminal depression.

His response drew a low chuckle from the room. But there was no mirth in it.

Jamie nodded, smiled. 'I know, I know. You didn't need a forensic psychiatrist to tell you that, right? Let me try again. Four victims. All mutilated in the same, unique way. And I have checked the literature thoroughly, ladies and gentlemen. You're dealing with the first recorded case ever of a serial killer creating bird-human hybrids. Yet, they're really not that similar. Three men, one woman. Ages ranging from thirty-two to fifty-five. Different social class, different jobs, personal backgrounds—'

'Yeah, but that's not what connects them, is it?' Oskar complained. 'They're addicts, we know that.'

Jamie nodded. 'Absolutely. And I'll get onto that. Then there are the wings. The university's zoology department has confirmed the species from which the wings were taken. A martial eagle, a cape vulture, a cinereous vulture and a great albatross. Four different birds.'

'How about the poses?' Tilde asked. 'Sara was mock crucified on a roundabout. Peter, posed like a sculpture of Saint Michael on the wall of a British cathedral. Sven-Arne folded into a rough approximation of a swan.'

Stella sat forwards. This was exactly the question that had been niggling at her since the episode at Sven-Arne's dock.

'Nothing connects them,' Jonna said. 'Apart from the wings, obviously.'

'Exactly!' Jamie said with a smile. 'It's almost as if the killer is trying on a persona, or an attitude. More like an artist than an obsessed serial murderer. Believe me, I have spent many hundreds of hours talking to psychopaths. Not all of them serial killers, but enough. And what I can tell you is, their fantasies? Their drives? Their modes of thinking, of behaving, of killing? They're rigid. Fixed.

'A man who wants to create archangels only creates archangels. A man who wants to turn human beings into swans, turns them into swans. He doesn't think, "Oh, I think today I might go for a greylag goose or maybe a pelican." If swans turn him on, then swans are what he does. He doesn't chop and change; a crucifixion here, a triumphant angel there, a fairground swan-boat over there.'

'What about the names?' Jonna asked. 'We thought this was about the gospels. And he hasn't done any more since Sven-Arne Jonsson, so maybe that's it.'

'It's possible he's suffering from a religious delusion, but apart from the correlation of the names, I don't see it. Where's the message? He's made no overt references to the victims as sinners or unworthy of God's love in some way.'

'There was nothing in his letter, either,' Stella said.

'Anyway, weren't they more like reformed sinners?' Oskar asked. 'After all, that's how he was picking them.'

As she sipped the coffee Tilde had brought her just before the meeting, Stella's ears pricked. Oskar had just used the past tense. She didn't like it. No way would a serial killer just stop like that. *You did*, a quiet voice echoed in her head. *When I was finished*, she replied, then shook her head trying to rid herself of the irritation.

'You don't agree, Stella?' Oskar asked, turning to her.

'Sorry, no. I mean, yes, I agree with you. I think religiously motivated murderers think they're either killing saints or sinners. Saints if the killer is violently anti-religious, sinners if they're hyper-religious. Our four victims were neither.'

'So where does that leave us?' Tilde asked.

'You know where, and I'm sorry to say this, folks,' Stella said, then drew in a breath. 'We have to go back over every single piece of evidence. Every witness statement, every second of security video. The killer's clever, cunning, even, but he's not invisible. He can't fly or teleport. He uses a physical workshop somewhere. He drives a van from there to the deposition sites. He buys aluminium rods, surgical tools, para cord. He gets blood on him and he leaves traces of himself behind.'

To a chorus of groans and sighs, she closed the meeting. She felt about as enthusiastic as the rest of her team. But only she would have to face the consequences of a failed investigation.

As it turned out, there were other actions of hers that

were already having consequences. Malin called her into her office.

* * *

Later that afternoon, having missed both breakfast and lunch, Stella's stomach finally protested so loudly that Jonna grinned and suggested she might like to go out and eat because it was too hard to think with 'that racket'.

She walked to a pavement cafe facing a small city park a couple of blocks over from the station and ordered an open sandwich with goat's cheese and roasted beetroot. While she waited for her food, she sipped an excellent coffee and stared at the mums and toddlers playing in a sandpit or on the swings. The hot late spring air smelled of lime blossom.

She sighed.

Something didn't add up. No, scratch that. Nothing added up. This was a serial killer who apparently wasn't a sexual sadist, yet who took perverse delight in inflicting gruesome mutilations on his victims. He'd displayed two of them in quasi-religious poses – but not Sven-Arne – and matched all four to the gospels. Yet he eschewed the typical MO of a religiously inspired killer.

* * *

As she was leaving that evening, Tilde hurried over, a travel mug of coffee in her outstretched hand.

'Here you go, boss. You look like you need one.'

'Thanks, Tilde,' Stella said. 'You're a star.'

Half an hour later, Stella and Jamie were sitting out

on her balcony. A half-empty bottle of wine sat between them.

'What you said in the briefing about the lack of a pattern,' she said.

'Yes? What about it?'

'It's what's been bothering me about it.'

She outlined the discrepancies that had come to her in the cafe earlier.

Jamie steepled his fingers under his nose.

'You know, one of the problems with my field is that we are only as good as the last piece of data,' he said. 'Sorry, that was really vague, even for me. Let me try again. Everything we know about psychopathic serial killers, we know from those who've been caught, yes?'

'Yes,' Stella said, already seeing where Jamie was going.

'So we build models. Religiously inspired killers act like this, sexual sadists like that.'

She nodded. 'But every time there's a new, and as-yet-unapprehended killer, he could be unique. Off the wall. Random.'

'He could.'

'If we throw out the accepted wisdom, then what do we have?'

'That's an excellent question. I can see why you're such a good detective.'

Stella inclined her head, accepting the compliment.

'Can I try and answer it myself?'

He shrugged. 'You're the boss.'

'Number one, let's turn everything we think we know on its head. It's not a man, it's a woman.'

Jamie gave her a searching look. 'We know that under extreme stress, women can kill.' He paused. 'More than once.'

'We do,' Stella said, trying to ignore the wavering form sitting behind Jamie and nodding vigorously in agreement. She blinked. It disappeared. 'The religious angle is either a coincidence or deliberate but under control. A game, rather than a compulsion.'

'Meaning what?'

'Meaning, they're playing with us. They're saying, "I'm so much further ahead than you. I can set up these blind alleys and you all go rushing down them while I'm over here, laughing at you."'

'Speaking from experience?' Jamie asked, his eyes turning from brown to red, leaking blood-coloured light that wavered in the air between them.

Stella knew she should find the vision troubling. But her pulse remained steady. It wasn't as if it were real. It was just stress, she knew that. Yes. Just stress. And the effect was not, actually, unpleasant.

'Stel? Are you all right?' Jamie asked.

'I'm fine,' she said, smiling. She had to fight down an urge to trail her fingers through the scarlet vapour coiling in the two feet of air between them. So pretty. But Jamie wouldn't understand. 'I'm just saying, it's like a bad imitation. Something Sven-Arne Jonsson might have come up with in one of his books.'

He was replying. She could see that. His lips were moving. Not completely naturally, but they were doing that…thing…when people speak and their mouths aren't in sync with the sounds coming out. That.

While he chattered on…dissociative states… personality disorder…disordered thinking blah blah blah…she explored her own ideas…

…the class is anxious to hear what she has to say

i mean they ought to be, given how many people i've

slaughtered

no! i didn't mean to say that, what i *meant* to say was *caught*, how many killers i've *caught*

thirty eager-beaver young detectives here to hear – oh, that's funny, it rhymes

anyway, where was we, oh yes, to hear

moi on the subject on catching cereal packets oops serial killers, sorry, sorry everybody

so, point number uno, when you're a homicide detective the thing you have to be careful of is
gnitteG
otnI
A
tuR
you find something that works and you stick with it because, you know, it's how you caught the last guy
but what if *this* guy isn't like *that* guy

what if he is a she or an it you know like…

…a bear…

…or something

…well all your old tried-and-testeds aren't going to be much help are they? Hmm?

what do you think other me?

i point a finger at myself and smile like i know something

me? no

no they are not

So we are not going to catch Icarus by focusing on the MO.

OK, that came out surprisingly coherent. Is this whatever-it-is wearing off then? Better work fast.

Quick sip of wine to lubricate the old synapses. Or, maybe not. Not wine. Maybe that's where the thing is. You know, the drug. Because I'm pretty sure that this is a hallucination. Or an altered state of some kind. Yes, I'm in here. The real me. I just need to finish that thought before I leave.

The killer has to find their victims somewhere. And it's connected to Ingrid's Way. I need to go back there. That's where I'll find Icarus.

Jamie's still talking. I'm amazed he hasn't noticed I've been gone.

37

What the *hell* had just happened? Had she just drunk the wine too quickly on an empty stomach? It had gone down fast, but even heavy drinking had never produced the kind of effect she'd just been buried in.

She looked at her empty wine glass. A horrifying thought crossed her mind. Had Jamie spiked her drink? Roofied her? No! It couldn't be. Why would he? But then what had just happened? She felt anxious. Wanted, suddenly, to be running as fast as she could out of the city, along one of the waterways, until she reached the birch forest and she could disappear into its welcoming green.

She felt clammy. Off-centre somehow. But Jamie appeared not to have noticed. She forced herself to remain calm, suddenly not wanting him to notice.

'…an interesting idea, Stel, I'll give you that,' he said, though his tone suggested he didn't rate whatever it was she'd just said.

What was an interesting idea? She needed to ask

without giving the game away. Something subtle, that he wouldn't notice.

She smiled. '*What* was an interesting idea?'

Well *that* didn't work.

He frowned. 'That it's a bad imitation.'

OK, that came as a surprise. Apparently she hadn't lost time at all.

'Enlighten me.'

'The person you're hunting – and, for the record? I still think it's a man – is doing it because he's *compelled* to do it. Just because you haven't discerned a pattern, doesn't mean there isn't one,' Jamie said. 'Serial killers often contact the police to jeer or to boast, but I can't accept that his entire,' he shrugged, '*programme* of killings is just a glorified version of a look-at-me letter. I just can't.' He picked up the wine bottle. 'Refill?'

She placed her hand over the rim of her glass.

'Better not. I need to eat.'

He emptied the bottle into his own glass and twisted to place it on the floor. The movement revealed a piece of white fluff sticking into his shirt under his arm. Stella leaned forwards and plucked it free. Her heart started hammering in her chest. It wasn't fluff. It was a feather.

Jamie turned back to her, laughing.

'Are you tickling me?'

She held up the feather, forcing herself to smile. 'This was stuck on your shirt.'

'Must have floated onto me at work today. I took my coffee up to the roof. Two gulls were scrapping over a fast-food wrapper. God, the racket!'

'It was under your arm, though.'

He shrugged. 'OK, maybe it came off the duvet this morning.'

'How?'

Smiling, he said, 'I don't know. Is it important? Wait. You're not...' His face changed. 'Stel, you don't think *I'm* Icarus, do you? Because that would be taking paranoia to a whole new level.'

'Is that a professional diagnosis, Doc?' she asked, trying to smile. Failing.

'You're just tired, darling. This case. It's a bastard. Come on, let's go inside and eat. You'll feel better with something inside you.'

* * *

In bed, after they'd turned out the lights, Jamie snaked a hand over her belly and nuzzled into the back of her neck. A memory of the weird trip she'd taken earlier came back to her. She swallowed down a sudden surge of nausea.

'I'm a bit tired, Doc,' she whispered. 'Do you mind if we just sleep?'

The mattress bounced as Jamie pulled away from her. The skin on the back of her neck, warm just a moment earlier, felt cold as he withdrew his lips. She could hear precisely nothing. The nothing of a person controlling their breathing so firmly not a whisper of sound escaped. She knew he'd be lying on his back, maintaining a corpse-like stillness *the better to alert her to his displeasure.*

She frowned. Jamie wanted to have sex and she didn't. And now he was pulling up the drawbridge. But it wasn't as simple as that, was it? The signs were so easy to read. Every man she'd ever been involved with, and God knew it wasn't many, but they'd all, at some point, behaved in exactly the same way. Because for all their play-acting, they really wanted to be noticed. Noticed and then mollified. *'Oh, baby, don't be upset. I'm just tired, that's all. Shall I just give you a wank? That'll make it better, won't it? You just lie there.'*

She sighed. She really *was* tired. The kind of bone-deep fatigue that even one good night's sleep would only partially remedy. Maybe Jamie was enjoying his role as a pro bono consultant to the SPA while filling his leisure time learning conversational Swedish with the lovely Freja, but the case was making her ill. This one had really got under her skin and *shit the devil!* what she really wanted to do was sleep.

'Let's try in the morning,' she murmured.

'It's fine.'

Well, that was easy enough to translate.

She rolled over. Through the dim light entering the bedroom through the curtains she saw he was lying on his back.

'You know,' she whispered, *'some people* might say you're a little bit old to be sulking just because you didn't get your end away.'

He propped himself up on his elbow.

'Oh, really? Who would they be, exactly? Your girlfriend?'

'What?' That was not the response she'd been expecting.

'Jonna, of course! You two seem pretty cosy together. Always out for your early morning runs. Sharing confidences. Do you tell her about us? About me? "Bloody men!" Is that what she says? Does she offer to comfort you because I'm too demanding?'

'Jamie! What *are* you talking about? Jonna's a colleague. A friend, too, but seriously, you're not telling me you're jealous, are you?'

'Should I be?'

'No! Of course you shouldn't. Look, I'm tired. Can this wait until morning? I really need to sleep.'

Jamie got out of bed and walked to the window, pulled the curtain aside and stared down at the street. Orange light from the streetlamps below flooded the bedroom.

'I've seen how she looks at you, Stella. I'm not blind. And, believe me, you don't have to be a forensic psychiatrist to read her body language. She fancies you.'

Stella sat up, pulling the sheet up to cover her breasts. She could feel her temper rising.

'So fucking what? She's gay. Maybe she *does* fancy me. Anyway, what about when I saw you kissing Frida?'

'Freja.'

'Whatever the fuck she's called! Are you telling me I should be worried about you running off with your Swedish teacher? Or any of the other attractive women I've seen you ogling while you've been here?'

'Of course not!'

'Well then?'

'You know that's not the same. Men are just wired like that. It doesn't mean anything. But this is different.'

'Oh, it's *different* is it? How very *convenient* for you. So what you're telling me, Jamie, basically...and forgive me because I'm just a silly little lady cop and not a forensic fucking psychiatrist...but what I *think* you're trying to explain to me is that when *I* feel jealous of you, it's nothing. Just a man being a man. But when *you* feel the green-eyed monster rearing its ugly head, that's something we all have to take seriously. Well, guess what? We don't! I'm tired, as I think I may have already said, and I need to sleep. So either come back to bed or...'

'Or what?'

He turned towards her and put his hands on his hips.

The pose might have looked more impressive had his penis not been caught in a band of light from outside the window, turning it a delicate shade of pink.

'Or you could always put that in a hot dog bun for me,' she said, laughing. 'All this arguing has made me hungry!'

Jamie glared at her for a second. Then he walked to the chair where he'd draped his clothes and started dressing.

'What are you doing?'

'What does it look like I'm doing?'

'Jamie! Don't be silly. Come back to bed.'

'Maybe this was a mistake,' he said, shoving one foot down into his jeans.

'I did say it might have been a bit early to be moving in together.'

'That's not what I meant.'

'What did you mean, then?'

'Chasing after you.'

'But you said you loved me. Come on, Jamie, don't let's turn this into something bigger than it needs to be.'

He yanked his belt tight and straightened his shirt.

'You need your space, I see that now. I should go.'

Stella felt her energy and enthusiasm for prolonging the conversation ebbing.

'Maybe you *should* sleep at yours tonight. Let's get dinner tomorrow though, yes? Have a proper talk. This is just tiredness talking.'

Buttoning his shirt, Jamie looked over at her.

'I meant I should go back to England.'

'What? What about the case?'

He pushed his feet into his shoes, shrugged on his leather jacket and then rounded the end of the bed.

'Jamie!'

'I've done all I can do from here, Stella. Call me if you need anything.'

And then he was gone. Too stunned to move, Stella sat up in bed, listening to the sound of Jamie leaving. The front door closed with a soft click.

What the hell had just happened? She lay back, trying to keep her breathing soft and slow, when every nerve was screaming at her to get up and go after him. Then she thought about the trippy episode that had engulfed her after Jamie had poured them both some wine. Was there something she was missing? Something right under her nose? They said love was blind, after all.

She'd brought Jamie into the case, not the other way round, hadn't she? She'd asked him to get involved? Hadn't she? She cast her mind back to their first night together in Stockholm. They'd been in bed. But…she'd asked him for his help. His opinions.

Hadn't she?

But he was working pro bono. That was a little odd, even for Doctor Strange. He'd said he was at a loose end. That he had some savings to live off while he worked out what he wanted to do next. Was he really? Had he really resigned from the private sector job, or was he sacked? And what about that little feather? Innocent debris from a bird-on-bird food fight or something more sinister? And the episode after drinking her wine? *Had* that been him after all?

With these thoughts spinning round in her mind, she fell asleep. Seconds later, she was awake again. For a moment, she believed she'd woken at that dreaded, unholy time – 3:00 a.m. – destined to spend the rest of the night tossing and turning and unable to sleep. But when she grabbed her phone she saw it was 6:37 a.m. A night without dreams. It made a pleasant change.

She flung out an arm, to find Jamie's pillow cold to the touch. Frowning at the memory of the previous night's row, she got up and padded into the kitchen to make coffee. Something told her it was going to be another long day.

With a mug steaming in front of her, she picked up her phone. One text. She swiped to open it.

I pushed too hard. We both need space. I'm flying back tonight. Speak soon. x

She called Jamie. It went straight to voicemail.

She wanted to say something, But not to apologise. She had nothing to apologise *for*. She took a deep breath.

'Jamie, it's me. Look, about last night. Let's not leave it like that. Call me.'

Ninety minutes later, after checking in with Oskar, Jonna and Tilde, she was standing in front of another crowd of journalists, trying to explain why they hadn't arrested anyone yet. Even *she* didn't find her words convincing.

38

In a white Tyvek CSI suit, hood, facemask, gloves and bootees, Ronny Halvorsson bent over the vast white wing laid out on the table in front of him. Beside him, similarly attired, the female detective from Homicide stood watching his every move. She'd called first thing, telling him she wanted the body and wings from the Sven-Arne Jonsson crime scene re-examining.

Ronny hated working while people watched. And it was hardly as if the Jacks didn't have enough to do. But Tilde had been most insistent.

She'd arrived at the National Forensic Centre first thing, lugging the wing with her in a gigantic brown paper evidence bag. After signing the relevant documents, she'd watched as Ronny loaded the wing, in its brown paper sack, onto a trolley and pulled it into one of the fourteen inspection bays in the basement.

In his left hand, he held a cream-handled acrylic magnifier, its lens scratched here and there but otherwise perfectly functional. In his right, a pair of his own long-handled stainless-steel tweezers. He'd found them on a website for tropical fish keepers. They were designed for retrieving debris from the bottom of fish tanks, but they were perfect for probing among the long off-white feathers.

The basement was cool, which helped to counter the heat building up inside the forensic suit. Thankfully he wasn't sweating, which made his job easier.

The smell of putrefaction was strong, despite the wing having been kept refrigerated. He imagined it would be worse on those recovered from the first three victims.

'Remind me why I'm going back over this?' he asked the chunky blonde detective.

'It stands to reason. If the killer is going to make a mistake,' she said in an infuriatingly patient voice, like he was a seventh-grader and not an experienced CSI, 'it will be as he progresses in his demonic plan and begins to lose control.' She paused. 'Plus Stella Cole wants me to.'

He shrugged. 'You're the boss.' *A boss with a weird way of treating colleagues, but still, if it's for the Queen of Weirdness…*

After an hour, during which he lifted and examined each off-white feather under the powerful halogen lamp clamped to the edge of the inspection table, he turned his attention to the aluminium rod protruding from the bone.

The original CSIs had left the aluminium rod embedded in the bone. Maybe they'd had it out, but here it was, its shiny surface smeared black with dried blood, whether human or avian he couldn't tell.

But Tilde had been clear. Her boss, the British super cop, had ordered them to go back over *everything*. Everything!

Wishing she'd give him more space, Ronny grasped the humerus in his left hand and took hold of the rod in his right, then gave them a counter-twist. At first, nothing moved. He gripped tighter, inhaled and held it, straining to produce even a fraction of give between metal and bone.

Gritting his teeth inside the stifling mask, he grunted with effort. Then something cracked. Audibly. A bright, sharp-edged sound in the sterile, echo-free confines of the inspection bay.

He looked down. The bone in his left hand had splintered, needle-pointed shards scattering onto the stainless-steel bench top.

'Shit!'

'It's fine. Keep going,' Tilde said, as if she were in charge of the lab.

Ronny bit his lip with frustration. But at least it meant the aluminium rod was loose. With a third and final twist, it came free.

He laid it on the bench and picked up an LED torch. Angling the humerus, he played the bright-white beam into the cavity left by the rod.

'There's nothing there,' he said.

'Please, Ronny,' she wheedled. 'It's my last chance. I really need a result I can take back to Stella. Did you *really* look?'

Sighing, he angled the beam down into the bloody recess. Maybe he'd found a fractionally better angle, or perhaps it had been dislodged during handling. But there, reflecting the torchlight like a silver wire, was a hair.

'I've got something,' he breathed, feeling, as he always did at moments like these, like Indiana Jones on the brink of discovering another priceless ancient artefact.

Smiling to himself with satisfaction, he reached for the long-handled tweezers and inserted them into the hole. He withdrew them with the hair clamped between their serrated tips. Under the magnifier, he saw the translucent waxy bulb that held the donor's DNA in all its double-helixed glory.

He sealed it in a transparent plastic evidence bag, then dated and signed it.

'You're a star, Ronny,' Tilde said, then kissed him lightly on his masked cheek. It was an oddly erotic moment that left him feeling confused and gratified at the same time.

Once the wing was resealed, dated and initialled in its own bag, Tilde took it back to the evidence locker. Her next stop was the forensics lab itself. Her route took her along a covered walkway enclosed by geometric white tubes. She stopped at the midpoint, and got out her phone. She called Stella.

'Yes, Tilde, what is it?'

'I've been at the NFC all morning. Looking at Sven-Arne's wings.' She hesitated. 'I mean, not *his* wings, but the ones the killer—'

'I get it, Tilde,' Stella said. 'What have you found?'

She sounded stressed. Tilde hoped her news might take some of the pressure off.

'A hair. It was embedded deep inside the socket the killer drilled in the wing bone.'

'Sorry, Tilde, the line just broke up. Did you say a hair?'

'Yes! It looks human. I think it must be the killer's.'

'Tilde Enström, you're a fucking legend,' Stella said, in English.

Tilde felt pride swell in her breast. Fought down the unfamiliar emotion.

'Cheers, guv,' she replied, also in English, before switching back to her mother tongue. 'But can you authorise budget for a fast turnaround on the DNA analysis? It'll take weeks otherwise.'

'Yes, of course! I don't know where from, but I'll find the money. You leave that to me. Just get it done on tonight's run OK? If anyone gives you grief, tell them I'll come up there and tear them a new one.'

Tilde grinned at the image Stella's word conjured up.

'Thanks. I'll see you later.'

Completing the paperwork took no time at all, and after impressing on the lab technician the urgency of the job, she left her with the hair. Stella was going to be pleased. No question.

* * *

Sitting on the bed, his open suitcase beside him, Jamie stared at the photos, one after the other. He could have viewed them onscreen, but he was, he admitted to himself, old school. There was something about handling a sheet of glossy photo paper that enabled him to appreciate what he was looking at in greater depth. To see as a killer saw. To feel as a killer felt. To live as a killer lived.

Stella had asked him how he could work with 'those people', as she put it, without going crazy himself. Didn't it drive him to murderous thoughts of his own? To take revenge on them for the evil they'd done?

And each time, he'd explain, patiently, that he didn't believe in the concept of evil.

'I'm a doctor, darling,' he'd say. 'I treat people. I don't condemn. That's for the courts.'

And each time, she'd try to argue him round, pointing to a cannibal, a child-killer, or a sexual sadist at the hospital he worked in, and asking why they deserved compassion and not a noose round the neck.

And he'd reply, 'Because a judge said so.'

It had led to more than one ding-dong of a row. After the most serious of them, Stella had actually staged a sex-strike, suggesting that if Jamie cared so much for his patients he could, 'go and fuck one of them. I'm sure they'd enjoy it'.

Jamie smiled at the memory. The strike hadn't lasted. Cordial relations between the warring parties had been resumed. Just like they would be this time. He lifted up a photo of Sven-Arne Jonsson that Oskar had taken on his phone. The dead man looked like the sort of pleasure boat one might hire for one's children at a seaside waterpark. Apart from the blood leaking from his nose onto the paddleboard's deck, obviously.

He was aware, as he perused the grotesque images, that normal people might be revolted by them. But then, if you went into forensic psychiatry as a career, the grotesque and the repellent quickly became the commonplace and the anodyne. To react otherwise was to risk one's sanity. And then, who knew, maybe one would end up as twisted as the people one was treating.

Sighing, he replaced the photos in the cardboard folder and slid it inside the mesh pocket in the suitcase lid. He checked his phone. The Uber was ten minutes away. Time to be gone. Soon he'd be sipping a gin and tonic in an air-side bar at Arlanda. After all, Stella was right: they *should* take a break. A little time apart would do them both good. It had been an intense time since he'd arrived in Stockholm, and back in her life. And the case was so stressful.

He'd write to her to apologise. Not an email. A letter. Handwritten, to show her how much he truly cared. He'd been stupid. Arrogant. He loved her and had only wanted to help.

Smiling, he zipped the suitcase closed.

39

At 7:55 p.m. that evening, Stella, Tilde and Jonna were sitting in Stella's office, waiting for the email from the DNA lab, which was due at 8:00 p.m.

Oskar had stayed as long as he could before leaving, pleading 'dad-duties'. His son, Gustav, was now twenty months and apparently not happy with just 'stinky mummy' in the evenings.

Stella suspected that Hedda might have been coaching her son to say that so she could get a few evenings off. She didn't blame her. A sudden physical pain pierced her chest as she thought of how much she would have liked to be 'stinky mummy' to Lola, who'd never reached twelve months, let alone twenty.

Coke cans and coffee mugs littered the desk. Pizza boxes were piled haphazardly in one corner, their bottoms grease-stained, crusted with solidified scraps of melted cheese and black olives that Tilde had fastidiously picked off her slices.

Every time Stella's PC emitted its little bong, the

three cops jumped. Each time, Stella sighed, or swore, as the message revealed itself to be about nothing more vital than a new training course, community awareness programme or drugs outreach scheme.

'Surely it should have come in by now,' Jonna complained, stifling a belch with a fist.

Stella checked the time.

'It could be late if there's been a lot of requests from other counties.'

'Yeah, but we're the only ones investigating a serial killer, damn-him-to-hell,' Jonna said feelingly.

'It'll be here,' Tilde said. 'Any time now.'

Stella got up.

'I need to pee. I'll be right back.'

Alone in the ladies, Stella stood at the sinks, staring at herself in the mirror. Daring herself – her *other* self – to come out of the shadows.

Maybe Alyssa was right. Maybe it was simply the stress of the case. After all, so far she'd had a pretty good run with the SPA. Major homicide cases wrapped up, not with the minimum of effort, quite the contrary. With a *huge* amount of effort. But until now she'd always felt that she had the case by the scruff of the neck and just needed to bring it down.

This one was different. And the confused, and confusing, relationship with Jamie wasn't helping. She wanted him to come back to Sweden. Come back to her. But it had to be the result of something more considered than just chucking his job in and saying, *Well, I've got nothing else to do, so I might as well try Stella again.*

The woman standing behind her nodded in agreement.

'Sounds like a plan, babe.'

Stella's heartrate exploded. She gasped as *she* – Other

Stella – placed her hands on her shoulders, long red fingernails digging in slightly, and began to massage her tight-wound muscles.

Shaking all over, Stella turned. Other Stella put up no resistance, but when she'd spun round completely it was to discover she was alone in the room.

She bent her head to the tap and scooped several mouthfuls of cold water up, swallowing hastily and choking as some ran down her airway.

No. This could *not* be happening. Not now. Not in the middle of a case. She couldn't succumb. Not again. She needed to be sharp, focused, *alone*.

Shaking, she returned to the toilet stall she'd just vacated, locked the door and called Alyssa.

'Hey, Stella, is everything OK?'

Well, *that* was a good question, wasn't it? How in hell did she answer it without getting herself sectioned, or whatever the Swedes called it?

'Yeah, fine. Well, mostly fine, anyway. But I'm having the occasional panic attack. I just wondered whether you could prescribe me something to take my anxiety levels down a notch or two.'

And send my alter ego back to oblivion where I thought I'd already put her.

'Of course. But I do have to warn you, anything in that line carries a high risk of addiction. Benzodiazepines have a less than perfect reputation as a long-term fix,' Alyssa said. 'Or we could try you on an antidepressant. SSRIs have been shown to be quite successful in treating some forms of anxiety. Although there's a two- to three-week latency period when your symptoms might actually increase in severity.'

Picturing Other Stella assuming potent corporeal form and taking over as she had before, Stella fought down the urge to scream, *No!* If her symptoms increased any further, she'd be checking herself into a psychiatric unit.

'I kind of need something faster-acting than that, to be honest,' Stella said, striving to keep her voice light. 'And I wouldn't be taking them regularly or anything. More of a break-glass-in-case-of-emergency type of thing, if you see what I mean?'

Alyssa laughed lightly. Presumably she never had to worry about murderous versions of herself coming to life and sawing people up with kitchen implements.

'That's a very good analogy. I might borrow it for my next lecture on psychopharmaceuticals, if you don't mind?'

'Be my guest. So, can you help?' Stella asked, acutely aware of the risk of displaying what she knew doctors called 'drug-seeking behaviour'.

'Sorry, yes. I'll email you a script. You can take it to the SPA pharmacy. But come and see me soon, OK? I'd like you to check in with me.'

Stella had forgotten the in-house pharmacy. Useful when prisoners were brought in off their faces on everything from ketamine to angel dust and needing stabilising, tranquilising, putting to sleep, waking up and everything in between.

Her phone pinged with Alyssa's email. She thanked her and ended the call, then left the bathroom for the ground floor.

Fifteen minutes later, Stella was chasing down a small white tablet with a mouthful of water from a drinking fountain. She'd had to queue behind a uniformed officer who was filling in the duty pharmacist on the story behind his need for tranquilisers. He and his partner had pulled in a coked-up Stockholm housewife who'd been wandering the streets wearing a pink fluffy bathrobe and carrying a loaded shotgun. On reflection, Stella thought he'd have had it easier with Mrs Twelve Gauge than the person *she* carried inside her.

Feeling calmer, she walked back into the CID office to find Jonna and Tilde looking at each other with shocked expressions. As they turned in unison to face her, she caught something else. Guilt? Sympathy?

She had a sick feeling something had just gone very, *very* badly wrong with the case. Stella looked from one to the other. Neither Jonna nor Tilde could meet her eye. An email was open on her screen.

'Come on, then,' she said. 'One of you better tell me what happened. Did we not get a hit? Is that why you both look like somebody ran over your puppy?'

Jonna swallowed. She was pale.

'No, Stella, we *did* get a hit. That's the problem.'

'How is that a problem?' Stella asked.

She knew that she ought to be feeling nervous, but the tranquiliser had kicked in hard and she felt pleasantly relaxed. It was an odd sensation, like standing at the very end of the high board at a swimming pool but feeling like you were at ground level.

'It's Jamie,' Jonna whispered.

Stella quirked her mouth to one side. 'Sorry, Jonna, what's Jamie?'

'The hit. It's a direct match.'

Stella frowned, then she smiled. They were playing a practical joke on her. Admittedly a practical joke in very bad taste, but that was cops for you.

'Very funny. So who is it really?'

'It really is him,' Tilde said. 'Look.'

She pointed at the screen. Stella bent forwards to

read the brief email and felt a wave of nausea rush over her.

MATCH

Subject: James Hooke.

Level of confidence: 99.99%

This couldn't be happening. Jamie was a forensic psychiatrist, not a serial killer. He helped catch them, for God's sake. It was literally why he was in Stockholm.

'How is Jamie's DNA even on the system?' Stella asked, finally.

'That was me,' Tilde said, looking sick herself. 'Back when the investigation was just getting started, you said to take reference samples from everyone working on the case. Jamie had just come on board. I swabbed him myself.'

'I don't remember asking you to do that,' Stella said, feeling a sense of disconnection with the world around her.

Christ! Why had she chosen this moment to pop a tranquiliser? Her head felt like it was stuffed full of cotton wool. Maybe she *had* asked Tilde to screen the staff. It was standard practice in case someone shed a hair or nicked themselves at a crime scene. She couldn't remember. But she *ought* to be able to. She was the lead investigator.

Tilde looked panicked. She turned to Jonna, but Jonna was staring at Stella, her forehead crinkled, doubt written on her skin as clearly as if she'd used marker pen.

Stella dragged in a short, sharp breath.

'No, you're right, Tilde. I remember it now,' she said, wishing it were true. 'It's just been a difficult case, that's all. Start again. What happened?'

As Tilde spoke, in clear, simple sentences, Stella tried to process what she was hearing.

Tilde had taken a cheek swab from Jamie.

She'd sent it to the national DNA lab as part of a routine elimination file.

The DNA on the hair retrieved from the feather taken from Sven-Arne Jonsson was a direct match to Jamie's.

Therefore the hair in the hole drilled in the wing bone belonged to Jamie.

Therefore, Jamie had, *at the very least*, been present at the moment Icarus was mutilating Sven-Arne.

Tilde stopped short of the logic-train's engine bearing down on Stella as she waited on the platform at Comprehension Central.

Stella didn't.

'Jamie's the killer,' she whispered. And that little white feather had come, not from a seagull, or a duvet, but a bird's wing he was busily stitching onto a living human being.

Then she collapsed into a chair and, for a moment, black curtains swung shut over her vision. She sagged forwards and let her head drop between her knees. She stared at her feet, and the worn blue institutional carpet they rested on.

She felt a hand on her back, between her shoulder blades, rubbing lightly. She looked up. It was Jonna, bent low beside her.

'We have to arrest him, Stella,' she said. 'Urgently.'

Stella jerked upright, shrugging Jonna's hand off.

'Oh my God! I told him to go back to England. We had a row last night. His flight's tonight.'

'Call him,' Jonna said.

'What?'

'Call him! Say you're sorry about the argument and you want to make it up to him in person. You can ask if he's left Stockholm yet and he won't suspect anything. In fact, tell him you've changed your mind. Say you don't want him to go after all.'

Stella nodded. This was all wrong. She felt as if she were dreaming. Damn that Xanax or whatever the pharmacist had given her. But she had no choice. It had been Jamie all along. Witnesses could be unreliable. CCTV could be blurry. But DNA didn't lie.

She called Jamie.

'Hi, this is Jamie Hooke. Please leave a message.'

She stabbed at the end call icon.

'Shit! Straight to voicemail. We need to get over to his Airbnb. Blue lights, no sirens. I'll drive, Jonna. Tilde, you head for Arlanda in a second car.'

Jonna frowned.

'You can't be there, Stella! No way. You're in a relationship with him,' she said. 'Tilde and I will go. You handle the airport end of things from here.'

Stella shook her head. 'No. I can help. If he, you know, becomes…agitated, or something.' She glanced at Jonna's hip. But her gun was in its holster on her desk. 'I can talk to him.'

'Jonna's right,' Tilde said, firmly. 'You have to stay out of the arrest. We'll bring him in. Call Arlanda. See if he's listed on any of the London flights since last night. The last evening flight is the British Airways direct at 21:10. If he's not on it we've got until 06:50 tomorrow. And you should tell Malin.'

Stella sighed. Because they were right. Of course they were. What was she thinking? Because her on-off-on-again boyfriend was a fucking serial killer! Ha! Snap! Maybe they could get adjoining rooms in the psych ward. Discuss the best way to joint a human body. She felt a maniacal laugh dancing on her tongue, milliseconds before it erupted from her lips and consigned her to a stay somewhere with no sharp edges or opening windows.

She stood. 'Go and get him. I'll make the calls.'

With a sick feeling in her belly, and the continuing fluffy-headedness from the tranquiliser, Stella called Arlanda, giving her police ID number. Once she was speaking to the right person, she explained what she needed.

'So, that's passenger Hooke, with an "e", initial J, travelling to London, yes?'

'That's right.'

'Hold on, please.'

Stella listened distractedly to the sound of a keyboard being tapped. Very efficiently, to judge from the speed of the clicks.

'Come on, come on,' she murmured.

'I'm going as fast as I can. The system's been a bit glitchy today.'

'Sorry, not you. It's just urgent, that's all.'

'Yes, here we are. James Hooke travelling tonight on BA783. Scheduled to depart on time at 21:10, arriving London Heathrow at 22:40. Was there anything else?'

Stella checked the time on the big station clock mounted on the wall opposite her. Below it sat a whiteboard on which colour photos of Jamie's four victims were attached with multicoloured magnets. It was 8:15 p.m.

'Has he checked in yet?'

More keyboard clicks.

'Ah, no, not yet.'

'OK, thanks. Can you transfer me to the police station there, please?'

Moments later, Stella was talking to an Inspector Albie Skinnet.

'How can I help you, Inspector?' he asked her in the thick Skåne accent many of Stella's Stockholmer colleagues derided as that of a country bumpkin.

'I need you to prevent a passenger from boarding a plane.'

She gave him Jamie's details and then hung up, fighting down an urge to scream. Had Jamie always been a killer? All the time she was spilling her guts to him about her own misdeeds, was he laughing at her? She couldn't believe it. Didn't *want* to believe it. Had no choice *but* to believe it.

Except that was wrong, wasn't it? You *always* had a choice. Lord alone knew, Stella had made some questionable decisions in the past, but she'd never let down the people she loved. Never betrayed a friend. Never deviated from a path she felt was good and true.

This was a mistake. She didn't know how it could have happened. But Jamie was no more a serial killer than she—

No. Better not go there, Stel, she thought. That path led into some very rocky territory indeed.

But Icarus was sadistic, deranged. A psychopath with less empathy it was hard to imagine. And then there was the man she loved. Jamie Hooke was *made* of bloody empathy! He'd written the *book* on empathy – literally. She had a copy on her shelf at home. *Empathy and the Narcissistic Mind: Why Sorry Really is the Hardest Word for Psychopaths*. Not the catchiest title, admittedly, but she'd been so proud when he'd brought her one of his author copies, so fresh off the press it felt warm to the touch.

Her thoughts were a mess of contradictory impulses and ideas. On the plus side, the hallucinatory visions of

Other Stella had not reappeared. And the burst of adrenaline had, to a degree, counteracted the Valium.

She called Malin next.

'Stella, what is it? Do you have a suspect?'

Stella sidestepped her boss's question, desperate to buy time.

'Jamie Hooke's DNA was found on one of the wings attached to Sven-Arne.'

The seconds she'd bought ran out.

'Where on the wing? He wasn't at the crime scene, was he?'

'No. He wasn't. Look, Malin, it was found inside the drilled-out socket,' Stella said. 'But it has to be a mistake. Jamie's not a killer. He's our consultant.'

Malin didn't answer for a few seconds. Stella could feel her heart bumping in her chest. Had time to imagine a pitched battle between the adrenaline and the benzodiazepine coursing round her bloodstream.

'What's the statistical likelihood of a match?'

It was a good question. And Stella had no place to hide.

'Ninety-nine point nine-nine.'

'And you've sent an arrest team?'

Such a simple, operational question. And yet, concealed inside it, like a flick-knife in a curled palm, a more insidious enquiry. *Can you reassure me your relationship with the suspect won't cloud your judgement?*

'Yes, Malin. Jonna and Tilde are on their way now. And I've spoken to the duty inspector with the airport police. They won't let him board the plane.'

'Good. I expect you to keep me informed from now until you have him in custody.'

'Yes. Of course.'

'And, Stella?'

'Yes?'

'I'm sorry.'

Malin ended the call before she could hear Stella's sob, which burst from her suddenly, racking her whole chest and doubling her over.

40

We're in the endgame. I can feel it.

Soon, she and I will be together. Properly. No secrets. Everything open between us. Two superior beings striding the Earth on a completely different plane to those ordinary human beings who call themselves 'normal'.

What a joke! Normal!

Sure, if by 'normal' you mean mentally flat-lining, unable to see beyond the most basic daily concerns. Eat this, buy that, go here, work there, post this, share that, like her, fuck him.

Yeah, OK, be normal. Just don't expect me and Stella to be like you.

I've killed enough now.

I have her attention.

And soon, I'll have her all to myself.

41

Nik Olsson's phone pinged with an incoming message.

His wife tutted. He and Rosanna were watching a tennis match on TV. She hated it when his work intruded into their 'together time', as she called it.

He glanced at the screen; he could always read it later. But when he saw who it was from, he opened it at once.

As he scanned the brief text – **Stella's bf = Icarus** – he shook his head. He'd fooled them all.

This was like Midsommar, Christmas and his birthday all rolled into one. He had her now, for sure. He would conduct the investigation personally. He started running through a list of questions he would throw at Stella. Had she colluded with Hooke? Facilitated his kills? Had she deliberately led the investigators away from the very man she should have been pointing to?

He envisioned a bare interview room. Once the professional courtesies had been observed, he would lean towards the woman who'd come to dominate his thoughts, day and night.

'*Well, Stella. It looks as though we're going to be spending quite a bit of time together, doesn't it?*'

'What's that, Nik?' Rosanna asked from her own armchair. 'You know the together time rule.'

'I do, darling, I do,' he said. 'It's a just a little work thing, that's all.'

She harrumphed. 'Martinsson just played a tactically brilliant point. You missed it.'

'No I didn't. I saw it. I have to say, it looked like she was winging it to me.'

As Rosanna watched the match, Nik felt his awareness leave the room altogether. The white-clad women in their skimpy dresses and those tight, bum-hugging shorts they all wore nowadays continued scurrying left and right, forwards and back, producing little pops and cracks as they smacked seven bells out of the ball.

Nik was back in the interview room.

Stella would be trying to wriggle off the hook, but he was about to jam it so deep she'd never get free.

* * *

Jamie smiled at the woman on the check-in desk as she sent his cases juddering off on their conveyor-belt journey into the hold. He hoped nobody would decide to inspect them. They might get more than they'd bargained for.

'*Tak tak,*' he said, in his best Swedish accent, as she handed him his flight documents and passport.

She rewarded him with a gap-toothed smile of her own before saying, in perfect English, 'You're welcome, Dr Hooke. Have a good flight.'

He checked the time. More than enough for a drink.

The choice of bars at Arlanda was narrow. An Irish-themed bar called O'Leary's. Or a branch of The Famous Bar, which seemed to be everywhere and were either owned or sponsored by The Famous Grouse whisky. He opted for the latter.

With a large gin and tonic and minor heart palpitations at the number of krone he'd just paid for it, he took a sip and leaned back against the brown leather banquette.

He began surveying his fellow passengers.

It was his favourite game at airports, and far more diverting than reading or listening to music. He wasn't on social media, having seen its addictive effects on colleagues and patients alike. So the endless scrolling through other people's opinions and images was, thankfully, not available to him.

A fat businessman in a generously cut suit waddled left to right across his field of vision. He was yammering into his phone via a Bluetooth earpiece, gesticulating with one chubby hand while the other towed a wheeled carry-on bag behind him. Jamie wondered if he realised that, a few decades earlier, such behaviour would have had him sectioned.

The thought made him smile. A young woman, catching his glance, smiled back at him before looking away. The minor exchange of flirtatiousness gave him a little thrill. Even though he was in love with Stella, he couldn't deny the most basic of human emotional urges. The need to be recognised as a sexual being, capable of giving and receiving love.

Here came someone who would definitely have Jamie either crossing the road if it were a dark night, or pushing an alarm button if they were in a clinical setting.

A young man, tall, rangy. Ripped and grimy jeans:

the result of poor hygiene not fashion. A scrim of whiskers, too thin to be a beard, too long for designer stubble. Red-rimmed eyes flicking left and right. His lips moved ceaselessly, but this time, Jamie saw no evidence of earbuds, a mic or any device at all.

Jamie took another pull on his drink. Winced at the thought he'd just swallowed about two pounds' worth of very average spirit.

Now that he was leaving Sweden, he had some distance to consider how he'd left things with Stella. Despite his best efforts, she was no closer to catching Icarus.

It was inevitable that would put her under enormous strain. After all, she'd had a pretty good run so far. Not that he'd tell her quite how closely he'd been following her career since leaving the Met. She'd probably give him a shocked expression and ask if he was stalking her. Which was only true if you considered following the woman you loved online as stalking.

He sighed. Because he knew Stella would be thinking the case would get solved eventually. But he'd spoken to, worked with, and even counselled, too many homicide detectives not to know that a second outcome was a distinct possibility. That the serial killer would escape. Trails went cold. Murderers died of natural causes or got murdered themselves. They moved country, got imprisoned for other offences, got smarter, or more cunning. It happened.

How would it affect Stella? She was resilient, that much he knew for sure. And once they'd got through this little rough patch, he knew he could support her better. Help her move past it.

Sure, there'd be media flack for a while. The news outlets that had been trumpeting the British super cop as a breath of fresh air in the stale world of Swedish policing would no doubt be first in line to start throwing stones. But they'd lose interest and then they could focus on the future. A future he hoped would see them living together permanently; married, even.

Icarus might get lucky and escape Stella. But that would only bring them closer together.

The young man with the wild eyes had marched off across the highly polished floor, barging through knots of passengers who rolled their eyes or frowned at his passage. Jamie followed him until he was out of sight.

Among the crowds of milling people, one figure was striding in the opposite direction. She was moving as fast as the troubled-looking young man, but with a fixity of purpose evident in her long strides and the way people moved out of her way ahead of time.

Jamie tried to focus on the figure coming across the departure lounge towards him. She looked familiar.

He blinked. It was Jonna. What on earth was she doing here? And why was her hand resting on the butt of her service weapon? She seemed to be heading directly towards him. He got to his feet as Jonna neared the open front of the bar. For a brief, worrying moment, he imagined Stella had told her about his ill-considered jab at Jonna's sexuality.

'Jonna,' he said, smiling, 'what are you—'

A woman yelled from right behind him.

'Police! On the ground, hands behind your head!'

This made no sense. He was transfixed by the sight of Jonna drawing her pistol.

Then something hit him hard in the back of the right knee. He yelped and collapsed forwards, aided by a shove in between his shoulder blades. He just had time to take in the astonished looks of his fellow drinkers before

309

Jonna came to a stop above him, aiming the pistol at his face.

'Keep still,' she yelled.

'But—'

'Quiet!' she shouted.

The other cop – because it had to be a cop, didn't it? – yanked his hands behind him and slapped on a pair of handcuffs. The steel edges bit painfully into his wrists. He heard the ratchets snickering closed. And he recognised her voice. It was Tilde. The brawny rookie detective Stella had taken under her wing.

'James Hooke, you are under arrest for murder. We're taking you to the police station where you'll be informed of your rights.'

'Let's go,' Jonna said.

Together the two cops hauled him to his feet and frogmarched him between them towards the plate-glass doors. He was dimly aware of his fellow passengers gawping, some with phones upraised.

'You're making a mistake,' he said, pulse racing. 'I haven't murdered anybody. I'm here to help.'

Tilde snorted.

'Help? By killing and mutilating Swedish citizens? The only person you can help now is yourself, by making a full admission when we interrogate you.'

42

Stella sat at her desk, staring out of the window without seeing. They'd arrested Jamie the previous night and his interrogation was due to restart at 9:00 a.m.

He'd asked for a British lawyer, but that had proved fruitless. So a Swedish public defence lawyer had been appointed for him. Malin had driven in and told Stella in straightforward language that she was on no account to even think of taking part in the interrogation.

In truth, Stella had only briefly entertained that thought. The conflict of interest would sink the prosecution. In any case, she felt unable to look Jamie in the eye right now, let alone put questions to him about a series of horrific murders.

Black thoughts swirled in her head, making logical thought impossible. Guilt that she hadn't seen what was right under her nose. Disbelief that the man she loved could be capable of the evil crimes she'd been investigating. And, lying beneath those, like a huge black eel lurking in the muck on the bottom of a freezing lake, the terror that Other Stella was on her way back.

Beyond the pane of bird shit-spattered glass, a fine Stockholm summer's day was encouraging tourists and residents alike to shed layers of clothes down to the minimum socially permissible. Stella felt she was enclosed in a shroud, in mourning for a new life with Jamie in Sweden that was over before it had even begun.

Malin stopped by her desk.

'Are you coming?'

Stella looked up. Malin's face bore an expression of concern that made her want to weep.

'Coming where?'

'To the observation room. I thought you would want to listen in.'

Stella nodded and pulled herself upright. She traipsed behind Malin out of the Murder Squad's accommodation, down a brightly lit corridor and then into a dim room lit by a pair of computer monitors and the light coming through the one-way glass that faced the interrogation room.

Jamie sat on the other side of the glass beside a bespectacled woman in a dark-grey suit. His lawyer. He was wearing grey prison sweats. Dark circles framed his eyes above unshaven cheeks.

Stella took the swivel chair Malin pulled out for her and waited for the process to begin.

Jonna and Tilde walked in and sat in a move so coordinated, she wondered whether they had rehearsed it. Jonna's voice crackled out from the observation room's ceiling-mounted speakers. She spoke in English. For one surreal moment, Stella wondered whether any of her old colleagues at the Met would have been able to interview a Swedish suspect in their own language.

'James Hooke. You have been arrested on suspicion of the murders of Sara Markusson, Peter Lukasson and

Sven-Arne Jonsson. Also of exceptionally gross assault on Mikael Mathiasson,' Jonna said. 'You have already been informed of your rights under Swedish law in both Swedish and English. But, in the presence of your lawyer, and because you are a foreign national, I am going to read them to you again.'

Once Jonna had recited Jamie's rights, she asked him if he understood.

He leaned forwards a little and croaked out a, 'Yes'. Frowning, he cleared his throat and repeated himself. 'Yes, I understand.'

'Last night, we asked you if you could account for your whereabouts on four dates. On each date, you claimed to be alone in your Airbnb in Stockholm. Overnight, have you remembered anyone who might be able to corroborate your story?'

Jamie went to spread his hands but the chain linking them through his handcuffs to a ring-bolt set into the tabletop prevented him from completing the movement. The chink of the links rattling through the bolt set Stella's teeth on edge.

'No, but it doesn't matter. I didn't murder anyone,' he said. 'My lack of an alibi can hardly be seen as damning evidence. Why are you holding me? There must be something more, I don't know, compelling.'

'They've got your DNA on a murder victim!' Stella wanted to scream through the glass.

Beside him, the lawyer was making copious notes in a yellow legal pad. From time to time she'd glance across at him, but for now she seemed content to let him answer Jonna's questions.

Jonna looked down and adjusted the papers in the file in front of her. Tilde leaned forwards. Stella had time to admire the slick signal they'd agreed between them, even as she feared what was coming next. But there was also a part of her copper's brain that wanted to see how the suspect would handle the revelation that Tilde was about to sledgehammer into him.

'You deal in people's motivations, don't you, Jamie? Why they do what they do? Where we can find the roots of their deviant behaviour?'

'I do, yes,' he said cautiously.

'Which is all very well, in its way. But *we* deal in hard evidence. Fingerprints, blood-spatter, phone records. DNA. Harder to argue with, wouldn't you say?'

'Well, yes. Although even physical evidence can be corrupted or misinterpreted.'

The lawyer opened her mouth for the first time.

'We're not here to discuss criminalistics, Detective Inspector. Do you have a question for my client?'

Tilde smiled sweetly, a curiously girlish expression from such a strongly built woman.

'I do, yes. Talking of roots, we found a hair at one of the crime scenes, complete with its root. Our scientists isolated DNA from that root. The DNA is a direct match to yours, Jamie. To within one one-hundredth of one per cent. My question is, how did one of your hairs find its way onto the body of Sven-Arne Jonsson?'

Jamie looked genuinely shocked. Stella had interviewed plenty of murderers, of both the psychopathic and everyday varieties, and she reckoned herself a shrewd judge of the degrees of acting skill they employed. Jamie's face, pale beneath the stubble, flushed then whitened as the blood drained away like a tide. His mouth dropped open and then clamped shut again, while his Adam's apple bobbed in his throat.

He looked at his lawyer. She leaned towards him and whispered behind her hand. Stella knew she'd be advising him to go 'No comment'. Even though it was the sensible course of action, she desperately hoped he'd ignore it.

He did.

'I don't know. It must have been cross-contaminated somehow. I've been in and out of the station. I may have left a hair on a piece of furniture, or in the carpet. It could have been transferred onto the corpse by a police officer.'

It wasn't a bad answer. And as an explanation, it would ordinarily stand a decent chance of being accepted in court. But Tilde was merely giving Jamie more rope with which to hang himself. Tilde looked down at the sheet of paper she had just lifted clear of the file in front of her. Then back at Jamie.

'Cross-contamination. I see. So, tell me, Jamie. This hair that you claim you shed onto the carpet in SPA headquarters. Can you explain how cross-contamination would have caused it to find its way inside an albatross wing bone that had been attached to Sven-Arne Jonsson's own arm?'

She leaned back and folded her arms.

Jamie's mouth open and closed. He blinked twice. Frowned.

'Sorry,' he said finally. '*Where* did you find it?'

'In a hole in the wing that, until our CSI conducted a more thorough investigation, had been plugged by an aluminium rod. We also found traces of the victim's blood on the hair, which links you to Sven-Arne as well as the wing you attached to his body.'

Jamie looked at Tilde, then at Jonna, and finally at his lawyer. Stella's stomach was knotted as she watched him trying to wriggle free of the chains Tilde had wrapped round him.

'No. This can't be. Someone put it there to incriminate me. I'm being framed.'

Jonna took over the questioning with another smoothly choreographed move.

'Jamie, can't you hear how desperate that sounds? Why would anyone do that?'

'I don't know! Why would I kill and mutilate four people? It doesn't make any sense.'

He shuddered violently, as if suppressing a sneeze. Then he leaned forwards and scrubbed at his face with his chained fists, bringing his head close to the table top and obscuring his face. When he straightened again, Stella saw that a change had come over him. He looked different. Purposeful.

'Are you all right, Jamie?' Jonna asked. 'Would you like a break?'

He shook his head.

'No. I'm good, thanks, Jonna. But I want to say something.'

Stella's stomach squirmed with anxiety. Oh, Christ! This was it. He was going to confess.

43

Jamie straightened in his chair. Stella caught a glimpse of the professorial clinician who could patiently explain the difference between various personality disorders to sceptical cops and hold their attention while he did it.

'You have my DNA on a murder victim,' he said. 'Or do you?'

Jonna frowned. 'Well, yes, we do. My colleague just explained where we found the hair.'

Then Jamie did something that shocked Stella. He smiled. Not the tight, borderline-hysterical expression that flashed across the faces of the guilty when their lies became too much to hold straight in their heads. This was genuine. She'd stake her reputation on it. Where the hell was he going?

'Yes, she did,' he said, turning to Tilde. 'You did, Tilde. You told me exactly where you found it.'

'Yes. On Sven-Arne's body.'

He shook his head. 'No, you didn't. You found it on the wing that was attached to his body.'

'It amounts to the same thing. They were joined by an aluminium rod in their humerus bones.'

The lawyer's pen was skittering across page after page of lined yellow paper.

Stella could hear Malin's breathing beside her.

'It doesn't amount to the same thing at all,' Jamie said. 'You see, I *am* being framed. And that means the murderer needed to put my hair where it could be found. Where has Sven-Arne's body been stored since he was retrieved from the lake?'

'In the RMV mortuary,' Jonna answered, seemingly unaware she'd swapped roles with Jamie. She'd committed the basic error of letting the suspect dictate the direction of the interrogation.

'Which is a secure facility with armed guards and heavily restricted access, yes?'

'Yes, but—'

'Where was the wing stored?'

'In the evidence room here in Kungsholmsgatan.'

'To which any cop has access? In fact, anyone who works here with the right ID and a little bit of sweet-talk could probably manage it.'

'Yes, but there are protocols. You can't just wander in and ask for something without signing it out. There'd be a record.'

Jamie shook his head. 'Protocols can be bypassed. Records can be faked, or tampered with. Especially by someone who knows what they're doing.'

'You're not seriously suggesting a police officer tampered with evidence to frame you for the Icarus killings, are you?' Jonna asked.

'Maybe not a police officer. But a secretary. A civilian investigator. Someone in IT, Human Resources, the mailroom,' Jamie said. 'Look at the bigger picture. Tilde, you say you deal in hard evidence, not what you no doubt think of as my fluffy psychological BS. But you'd agree with me that these four murders are the work of a psychopath, yes?'

'Yes. Clearly,' Tilde said, though Stella detected a quaver of doubt in her voice.

'Exactly. They're not domestic murders, bar brawls gone wrong or drug-related killings. You're not looking for a violent husband, a drug dealer or a drunk. You're looking for someone with a very specific personality disorder,' he said, hitting his stride. 'Lacking in empathy, incapable of showing remorse. Shallow affect. That isn't me. I'm in a relationship with your boss. Ask Stella, she'll tell you! I am not a psychopath, I'm a psychiatrist!'

'So was Hannibal Lecter,' Tilde said.

'Hannibal Lecter's a fucking character in a book!' Jamie burst out.

Beside Stella, Malin pushed her chair back so hard it banged into the wall behind her.

'Right, this has gone on long enough. They're losing control,' she snapped before leaving.

Twenty seconds later, Malin entered the interview room.

'This interrogation is suspended.'

She reached over and snapped off the digital recorder. Stella lip-read her next words. *'You two, with me.'*

Stella got to her feet. Wondering what was about to happen.

Malin's head appeared round the door.

'My office, Stella.'

A few minutes later, the four women were sitting round a conference table in Malin's spacious, if sparsely furnished office.

'What the hell just happened in there, Jonna?' she asked.

Jonna frowned. 'What do you mean? We had him. He was just spinning us a line. That DNA evidence will see him convicted.'

'It's true, Malin,' Tilde said. 'When the prosecutor stands up in court and puts it before the judges, there's no way they won't convict.'

'Then why did you allow him to totally take over the interview? That was a complete shitshow in there. He was asking questions and you both were answering.'

'Malin, if I can answer here,' Stella said. 'Jamie can be extremely compelling. I've seen him hold a roomful of hard-bitten detectives in the palm of his hand. It wasn't their fault.'

Malin tightened her lips until they disappeared into a thin line of disapproval.

'I'm afraid your opinion has to be considered tainted here, Stella, for obvious reasons.'

'I understand, Malin, I do. But I'm not trying to defend Jamie, I'm just saying it wasn't on Jonna and Tilde. And I do agree the DNA evidence looks compelling.'

Malin arched a blonde eyebrow

'Only *looks* compelling?'

'I've known Jamie for years. We've caught serial killers together. And before you talk about what's *obvious* again, yes, I am in a relationship with him,' she said, realising as she spoke where she was going to have to go and feeling a lump forming in her throat. 'Jamie is capable of deep emotion. He can be loving, kind, and I have seen him completely distraught when I broke up with him in England. I know how much I hurt him. He was crying, Malin. That isn't the behaviour of a psychopath.'

'Then how do you explain the presence of one of his hairs *inside* the wing bone?'

'I can't. Not at the moment. But I know it can't be him. I *know* it!'

Malin said nothing for several seconds. Stella felt the air thickening around her. Finally Malin shook her head.

'No. He stays in custody here. I will speak to the prosecutor about having him moved into a remand centre. He presents a risk to the public *and* a flight risk. We'll move ahead to a trial at the earliest opportunity. This is good work, you three. Tilde, you especially.'

Tilde bowed her head. 'Thank you, Malin. But it was a team effort, really. Stella's been the one urging us all to put in the extra effort.'

'Yes, well. Stella, I think you need to take a couple of days away from the office. Get your head clear. Focus on something else for a while.'

* * *

The next morning, Stella woke not knowing what day it was. Only that she had slept incredibly badly, dreaming of Jamie being led to a gallows, bloody white wings dragging on the floor.

She intended to take Malin's advice. Just not in the way Malin meant it.

She ate a rushed breakfast of marmalade-smeared crispbreads and strong black coffee, then sat at the desk she'd installed in the flat's tiny second bedroom. Trying not think about how Jamie must be feeling, she took down a notebook from a bookshelf above the desk.

321

She paged back through the notebook where she'd recorded all her ideas about the case. This wasn't the formal document – that was her SPA-issue investigation record: the *Utredningsprotokoll*. This was her private system. A place where she allowed herself to capture any thought, however outrageous, un-Swedish or just too damned expensive to pursue. She bought the cheap blue notebooks from a stationery shop around the corner from the flat. There were ten of them now, one per investigation.

She flipped back to the beginning of the case and started reading. Carola Vilks had dismissed the idea of a connection to aerospace engineering because the aluminium was solid not honeycombed. But what about the most glaring fact? That he – *or she, because this is the left-field notebook, Stel* – was turning human beings into birds. Or at least trying to. Didn't that speak to at least an interest in flight, if not an obsession?

And where would you learn to be an aerospace engineer?

She called Carola Vilks. Carola's voice was warm, friendly.

'Stella, how can I help you?'

'I wanted to ask your advice about aerospace engineering courses.'

'Are you considering a change in career?' She sounded amused.

'I'm just tying up some loose ends.'

'What sort of loose ends? I thought you'd made an arrest.'

'How do you get to be an aeronautical engineer? Where do you study, I mean?'

'Well, first you do a bachelor's degree in engineering. Then you specialise by doing a master's. There are only two: Linköping and KTH Royal Institute of Technology in Stockholm, which is the better of the two.'

Forseeing a painful round of stonewalling from officious university admissions departments, Stella decided to try Carola one more time.

'Do you have contacts at either of those?'

'Of course I do! In fact I am a guest lecturer at Linköping and a visiting professor at KTH. It also helps that I personally, and Vilks Luftrum corporately, make regular large donations to them both. We even endowed a chair at KTH last year in advanced materials research. Why do you ask?'

It was cards on the table time. Stella wasn't working against her own team's investigation. Not precisely. But she could imagine Malin's reaction if she were to learn of Stella's activities. A mixture of icy calm and a slow-burning then volcanic eruption, like her namesake, *Grímsvötn*.

Stella inhaled sharply and began speaking on the outbreath, fearful that if she hesitated she might stall before she'd started.

'The man we've arrested. He's my boyfriend. I know that sounds almost childish, but I don't know what else to call him.'

'And you don't believe he's guilty.'

'He can't be.'

'I watched the press conference last night though,' Carola said. 'I must say your boss seemed pretty sure of herself. She said they had DNA evidence linking him directly to the crimes.'

Stella was about to argue, then changed her mind. And she didn't want to continue this conversation on an open line.

44

Stella pulled up in the spot next to Carola's bright-orange sportscar, as the CEO had instructed her. Then she waited.

Five minutes later, the unobtrusive door in the side of the factory opened and Carola was striding across the tarmac towards her. Today, she was wearing a white trouser suit. Her just-tanned skin glowed in contrast. Her mouth widened into a smile of welcome.

'So nice to see you again, Stella. Let's take a walk, shall we?'

Carola led Stella away from the factory towards a distant corner of the car park. There, a gate in the fence yielded to a palm-print and Carola was standing aside to usher Stella through.

Beyond the plant, it was as though nature had been waiting to reclaim the land from Swedish heavy industry. Birches and low-growing, yellow-flowered shrubs grew in profusion. Stella caught the faint tang of pine and raised her eyes to the horizon. Across the motorway, a thickly forested hill glowed blue-green.

'This is beautiful,' Stella said, as Carola walked beside her through the trees and then out onto a gorse-covered common.

'Isn't it? I thought, given the sensitive topic of your enquiry, we might do better to talk out here. I do a lot of my best thinking on the common.'

Stella looked around. Sunlight flashed off car windscreens on the distant motorway. At this distance, the roar of engines and the hiss of rubber on hot tarmac was reduced to a soft hum.

'It must be nice to have somewhere you can come to get away from the pressures of the business,' she said, turning a full circle and not seeing a single soul.

Carola laughed. 'I'm afraid they accompany me wherever I go. Sometimes I wish I could leave it all behind me. Just climb into my plane and fly away.'

'What sort of plane do you have?'

'Several, actually. But my baby is the Saab Gripen E.'

Stella pictured the boxy convertible her first boss had driven. 'Saab?'

Carola smiled indulgently at her. 'As well as somewhat boring cars, Saab makes rather wonderful jet fighters.'

'And you can fly it?'

'Uh-huh. If you've consulted my resume, which somehow I imagine you might have, you'll see I worked as a test pilot for a number of years before inheriting Vilks Luftrum from my father.'

Stella looked at Carola with renewed interest.

'Aren't you frightened?'

'Why would I be? I know the aircraft. I know its tolerances. Its limits.'

'How about yours?'

Carola frowned. 'My what?'

'Your limits.'

Something she'd read in the introduction to Jamie's book about psychopaths had come back to her now. Jamie talked about the professions in which people scoring highly in the Hare Psychopathy Scale were over-represented. One of the surprising occupations, to Stella, at least, was test pilots.

Carola flapped a hand. 'Limits are for little people, Stella. You of all people should know that.'

'Little people.' There was a phrase to prod a detective's brain into action.

Jamie had written about how psychopaths had great difficulty in understanding that other people were, well, just that: people. They saw themselves as superior beings, not just able but entitled to gratify their needs however they pleased. That might simply mean flying an experimental jet beyond the limits stipulated in the test-flight protocol. Or cutting a living human being's arms off and replacing them with bird's wings.

And what had Carola meant by, 'You of all people'? Surely she couldn't know of Stella's own, colourful CV. Could she? Ought Stella to ask? Suddenly the common seemed a very lonely place. She looked around, wondering whether a dog walker or a hiker might have come this way.

They were alone among the yellow flowers and sharp, unforgiving spines of the gorse bushes.

Carola was bestowing on her an appraising glance. Stella imagined she might look at an aircraft the same way. As a thing. A *play*thing.

'What do mean, "You of all people"?' she asked, adjusting the distance between them to a little over an arm's length.

Carola grinned at her, showing her teeth.

'I said I'd been following the case. I wasn't being strictly honest with you, for which I apologise.'

Carola's tone was flirtatious, playful. It did not reassure Stella. She tensed. Fight or flight: that was what the tight, squirmy feeling in her gut was telling her. She'd run tens of thousands of miles in the years since Lola and Richard were murdered. And she'd taken down bigger and more physically imposing people than Carola Vilks.

'What do you mean?' she asked, striving to keep her voice light.

'I've followed your progress since you first arrived here,' Carola said. 'It has been dramatic, wouldn't you say? Especially that business up in Söderbärke last year. I knew Jenny Freivalds.'

Carola was speaking about the charismatic leader of a Swedish nationalist party who'd been murdered by a serial killer. Jenny had tried to befriend Stella, too, before her untimely death.

Stella pictured the two powerful women sharing a bottle of wine in a quiet bar somewhere. *Was that how it was done at that level of society?* She chided herself. *Of course it was! Cops networked the same way, and the more senior they became, the wider their circle of contacts became.*

Another thought occurred to her. She was just another contact to Carola. A prominent woman, with an intriguing back story, whom the industrialist could add to her circle of acquaintances. Perhaps she found it amusing to be so close to the heart of the investigation into her own crimes. It wouldn't be the first time.

She kept her eyes on Carola's hands, which were currently stuck into the pockets of her immaculately tailored white jacket. If one came out wrapped around anything except air, Stella would strike first. No way was she going to allow herself to be knocked cold by a fat dose of ketamine.

'You seem on edge, Stella,' Carola said. 'Is everything all right?'

'Do you ever have dreams where you can fly?'

Carola batted away a fly that was buzzing around her head. 'Pardon?'

'You know. You just stretch out your arms and flap them and away you go, up into the air. Free as a bird.'

Carola took her hands out of her pockets. Stella tensed. But they were empty. She raised them out from her sides and gave them a little wiggle.

'Like this, you mean? No. I never dream. Or if I do, I don't remember them.'

'Do you think Icarus wishes *she* could fly?'

The use of the female pronoun was deliberate. A baited hook. Carola didn't bite.

'It's possible, I suppose. Most people have indulged in that fantasy at least once in their life, don't you think? And I'm sure all pilots have. I think, for many of us, it's the primal force that drives us to take up flying in the first place. That or designing better aircraft.'

'You said you had contacts at the two universities that run masters' programmes in aerospace engineering,' Stella said, wanting to drag their discussion earthwards again. 'Could you introduce me? Perhaps suggest that they would be providing a vital public service if they would let me look at their alumni records?'

Carola inclined her head. It was a gracious expression, a queen acquiescing to a request from one of her subjects. *One of the little people*, a quiet voice in Stella's head whispered. She ignored it.

'Of course.'

Stella thanked her and suggested they walk back to the factory. She relaxed a little, although she kept at least a metre of space between her and Carola and never once took her eyes off the woman's hands.

45

I killed because I felt like it.

And because I wanted her to notice me, of course. But I am efficient. I am diligent. I am focused. I permit them to find only what I want them to find.

Let them believe they have me. They'll pat themselves on the back, go to a bar for celebratory drinks. And it will all be over.

And if, at some point in the future, once Stella and I are together, I feel the need to scratch the itch again, I'll do it as I have always done it. Carefully. Methodically. And, this time, invisibly.

All that silly performative rubbish with the wings? Too risky. Plenty of easier ways to kill without pushing myself into the limelight.

46

Back at her apartment, Stella called the aerospace engineering departments of the two universities. Neither head of department was available and, frustrated, she left messages asking them to call her back urgently.

What now? Time was draining away through the hourglass and Jamie's arraignment was getting closer. She experienced a momentary flash of doubt as she brewed another pot of coffee. What level-headed homicide detective would go out of her way to ignore DNA evidence – the gold standard – placing a suspect literally inside a murder victim's remains?

The answer came to her just as the kettle clicked off like a hypnotist's snapped fingers. One who knew that they'd arrested the wrong man.

Evidence got cross-contaminated all the time. Probabilities got screwed up by bad bits of code. And, yes, despite its sounding like a crime novel cliché, people did get framed for crimes they hadn't committed.

But who would want to do that? she asked herself as she carried the coffee through to her study. It was possible, *entirely* possible, that there were people who might enjoy seeing Jamie fall from grace professionally. Maybe even personally. No human being could live for forty-plus years and not make at least one enemy, especially not one as successful as Jamie Hooke.

But there was a huge gap between a little light *schadenfreude* at a colleague's career hitting a bumpy patch and framing him for murder.

No, the person who stood to gain the most from Jamie's arrest and probable conviction was the person who had really been committing the murders. Icarus.

That took Stella straight back into troubled waters. Because it pointed a finger of suspicion not at an outsider like Carola Vilks, but inwards. At the SPA itself.

She took a sip of the coffee and rubbed her temples, trying to ease the headache rumbling between her eyes like a distant thunderstorm.

Grabbing a piece of scrap paper out of the bin, she doodled a triangle on it and labelled the corners.

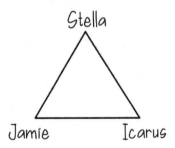

What were the links between the three players?
Stella was hunting Icarus.
Icarus had framed Jamie.
Jamie was in a relationship with Stella.

There was another relationship there. One that remained tantalisingly out of reach. She tried approaching the puzzle from a different direction.

Who benefited from Jamie's incarceration? And why? That was the crucial question. Was there something beyond simply getting away with their crimes?

In a domestic murder, a husband who murdered his wife then framed her lover got off scot-free, but also had the satisfaction of seeing his sexual rival jailed.

In a gang-related hit, a mobster who framed a rival for a third's murder could take not one but two enemies off the board.

She tried to find relationships between the three players in this unholy love triangle by running around the perimeter in the other direction: not clockwise but anti-clockwise.

Stella was trying to exonerate Jamie.

Jamie was trying to help her catch Icarus.

Icarus was…what, exactly? What was this demented killer trying to do to Stella? Or for her? Or with her?

Multiple answers presented themselves at once. She murmured as she jotted them under the triangle.

'Icarus wants to outwit me. Clearly. Psychopaths always think they're cleverer than the police. Icarus wants to use me to magnify his fame. Because he – or she – is a narcissist. Icarus picked Jamie because he knows we're together and this destroys my love life.'

As the words left her lips, she paused, the pen hovering above the paper. Her thoughts went back to her last, massive row with Jamie. Each had accused the other of sexual infidelity. Surely this wasn't some twisted kind of sexual jealousy playing out in the most grotesque way imaginable? She forced herself to consider it. After all, every one of the standard approaches they'd tried so far had drawn a blank, unless you counted the damning DNA evidence against Jamie.

But who would feel enough sexual jealousy towards her to murder and mutilate four people and then frame her boyfriend?

Since arriving in Sweden she'd had precisely one relationship. The short-lived but pleasurable few months she'd spent going out with Magnus Larsen. And it had ended with neither a bang nor a whimper. Instead, a growing, mutual realisation that it was never going to work. They'd parted amicably and still saw each other around on what both referred to as the homicide beat.

In any case, she had no need to consider Magnus as a potential serial killer. He didn't have the access to the evidence locker he'd need to interfere with the wing attached to Sven-Arne.

Was it professional jealousy, then? A fellow officer angered by her rapid rise to prominence in the SPA? She quickly ran through the members of her team. Tilde was too new and neither Oskar nor Jonna had ever shown even the slightest sign of resenting her. She counted both as friends. Yes, she was aware of sour locker-room talk: end-of-shift grumbles about the British super cop getting the juiciest cases, or the biggest budgets. But that was par for the course in any station. She'd heard the same, or worse, at Paddington Green.

And then a face – cadaverous, shaved so close the skin shone, pierced by deep-set eyes that could fix you with an intensity that felt physical – swam into view.

The face belonged to the 'brother' officer who, she was sure, would rejoice in an uncharacteristically buoyant way if she were to be sent home in disgrace.

Nikodemus Olsson was probably digging into her background, looking for an incriminating link between her and Jamie. Her gut roiled. Because he'd find one, wouldn't he? She'd brought Jamie onboard with minimal due process. Skirted the inevitable questions about budget because Jamie had offered to work for nothing. She could hear Nik's crowing voice in her head.

Not only does she allow this psychopath to misdirect the investigation, she gives him unfettered access to the case files, thus allowing him to cover his tracks. And he would have succeeded, but for the diligent work of a lowly Swedish *police officer,* gobbets of sarcasm dripping from his lips.

Nik. A man who would like nothing better than to see Stella's Icarus-like rise in Swedish law enforcement come to a bloody end.

Nik. A man so mentally traumatised by a knife attack perpetrated by a homicidal maniac that he'd had to forgo active investigative duty for the hated role of Internal Affairs.

Nik. A man with high-level security clearance, forensic awareness and access to every file in the SPA.

Oh God. *Was* it him? Had she been played? Manoeuvred into a position where he could don his 'human mask' and see her kicked out of the SPA?

Her mind reeled. She was seeing suspects everywhere. Sven-Arne, until he'd been murdered. Then Carola. Then Nik. She felt panic washing through her. Abruptly she got up from her desk and went into the bedroom. She changed into athletic gear and was out on the street and racing to outrun her fears.

As she dodged pedestrians, who regarded her with amused smiles as she yelled out apologies in English-accented Swedish, she forced herself to concentrate. Little by little, her mind stopped whirling around on itself like a dog chasing its tail.

As her heart and lungs came on song, allowing her to

drop into the semi-meditative state she craved, she felt the street fade into a sort of physical background noise to her thoughts. She made turns, ran on the spot at traffic lights, and picked quieter streets until she reached the waterfront where she could flow across the running track put there by thoughtful city planners.

It wasn't Jamie. But it wasn't Nik, either. It couldn't be. While she waited for the aerospace professors to get back to her, what could she do to anchor her personal investigation in reality? The old training mantras came back to her. *Who benefits?* (No point: it was a dead end.) *Follow the evidence.* (She didn't like that one.) *ABC: Assume nothing, Believe nobody, Check everything.* Maybe that was the place to start. Go back to the beginning. Again. But on her own this time.

Ingrid's Way was the connection. The wellspring. The killer would be a group leader or another attender at their meetings, one with connections to law enforcement.

After Sven-Arne had refused to help, she'd assigned Tilde to get a warrant for his charity's records. In a briefing that felt like it had happened years ago, she'd reported that nothing had stood out. But Tilde was an inexperienced homicide cop. Maybe she'd missed something. And Stella was anything but inexperienced when it came to homicide.

Sven-Arne and his lawyers had done all they could to obstruct the investigation, citing everything from privacy law to commercial confidentiality. But Sven-Arne was dead. And Stella saw a way in.

47

Ingrid's Way occupied a single floor in a nondescript office block in the commercial district.

On the way in from the car park, Stella passed a group of kids practising skateboard tricks in a concrete underpass decorated from ground to ceiling with splashy graffiti. One turned to look in her direction, but spotting someone he no doubt thought of as a boring adult, he'd turned back to his mates. She found it came as a relief not to be recognised, called out to by her Christian name or harried for a comment by a journalist thrusting a digital recorder under her nose.

The charity's chief operating officer was Ida Graf: it said so on a slender piece of brushed aluminium slotted into a wooden rail on the outside of her door. She wore a harried look. Suddenly finding yourself running a charity whose charismatic founder had just been murdered would do that to a person, Stella thought.

'I know you've already cooperated with our team, but I need to take another look at your records,' Stella said.

'I'm assuming you're happy to oblige, given we already have the warrant.'

The woman frowned, as if Stella had asked her to perform a complicated piece of mental arithmetic.

'I'm not sure I understand,' she said. 'Nobody has come here with a search warrant.'

Now it was Stella's turn to look puzzled.

'Are you sure? Could it have been one of your colleagues who dealt with it?'

'No. It would have been me. I'm sort of the general manager around here. Sven-Arne, he handled all the public-facing things,' she said. 'Everything to do with the charity and how it's run comes through me.'

Stella wanted to call Tilde and ask her straight out what had happened. It was a crucial oversight that might have delayed the investigation. Hell, Sven-Arne might still be alive otherwise. Was the young woman from the sticks a glory-hound? Happy arresting people and getting stuck into forensic evidence, but bored with routine enquiries? That would never stick in court, let alone on Stella's team. She parked the thought. She'd talk to Tilde later.

'I'm sorry about that,' she said. 'A miscommunication within my team. But I do really need to consult your records.'

'I'll do my best, but this is highly irregular. Which ones are you interested in? Financial? Promotional? Operational?'

Stella shook her head. 'Personnel. I want to know who works here, who runs your groups, who volunteers, and, if possible, who attends your meetings.'

Ida looked away, as if an adviser might materialise at her shoulder to tell her what to say.

Still avoiding eye contact, she said, 'You really do

need a warrant then. Swedish privacy laws are very strict, as I'm sure you know. I could lose my job.'

Stella did know. It made no difference. She was here now and determined not to leave without the information she'd come for.

'Ida, you surely don't need me to remind you that your founder, Sven-Arne Jonsson, is currently lying in the mortuary because Icarus murdered him,' she said.

She felt bad for the woman now on the verge of tears, her eyes glistening but not yet leaking water down her plump, pale cheeks. Bad, but not so bad she'd be deflected from her purpose. She continued.

'I asked Sven-Arne for this information, too. He refused and I really hope that the delay didn't end up costing him his life. So, I am asking you once again. Do you want to help me prevent anyone else suffering the same, dreadful, fate as poor Sven-Arne?'

A sob escaped Ida's throat, a low, animal sound. Now the tears did flow, coursing over her cheeks and plopping onto the desk. Stella offered her a packet of paper tissues. Ida tore two free and mopped her eyes. While she blew her nose, which had turned red at the end, Stella heard Nik Olsson's voice rising indignantly as he addressed an invisible disciplinary panel.

To cap it all, she made an illegal request to an executive at Ingrid's Way, using emotional blackmail to obtain access to confidential information protected under Swedish human rights law.

'Do you really think it will help?' Ida asked, sniffing and dabbing at her eyes with another tissue.

'I do, yes,' Stella said, meaning it. 'And I'm sure it won't cost you anything but a few minutes of your time.'

Ida drew in a shuddering breath and spoke on the exhale.

'Then I will agree. For Sven-Arne's sake. But you

341

have to keep this just between the two of us. I will be in a great deal of trouble if the board of trustees finds out.'

Stella nodded. 'Of course. Anything I find out as a result I can claim came from a tipoff. Perhaps a group member who wished to remain anonymous for obvious reasons.'

Ida smiled a little. 'Yes, yes. I can see that would hold water. There's only one thing, though.'

'What's that?'

'Well, maybe Sven-Arne mentioned this, but we don't keep records of who actually attends our meetings,' she said, able now to look Stella in the eye. Her own were a soft grey, like pigeon feathers. 'I'm pretty sure AA doesn't either. It's sort of the whole point.'

'But you have a list of staff, and group leaders?'

'Of course. Volunteers, too. Lots of them are recovering addicts, as a matter of fact, so there might even be an overlap with attenders that way.'

'Let's start with those, then,' Stella said.

'Would it be OK if you just looked at them here, in my office? I'd really rather not have anything printed out and taken away.'

Stella offered a reassuring smile. 'Of course. I understand. Here is fine.'

'It will take me a few minutes,' Ida said, already intent on her computer screen, her right hand clicking and swerving the mouse on its pad while she typed with her left.

Stella got up from her chair and wandered over to the window, looked down. The skater kids were still zooming around on the concrete, flipping their boards, sliding down steel rails, or just sitting smoking – joints, she assumed – watching appreciatively as their friends executed tricks.

She turned to look at Ida, who was still busy with her PC. She raised her head and smiled. 'Won't be long now.'

Stella nodded and paced over to the wall opposite Ida's desk, which was covered with framed photographs. The largest, almost half a metre square, was a montage of smaller shots collaged together. In the centre of the picture, rainbow-coloured text spelled out a headline:

Ingrid's Way Summer Picnic 2021

The picnic had taken place on a gloriously sunny day. Above the various groups of people, wispy white clouds scudded across a sapphire-blue sky. Judging from the short, intensely dark shadows, the majority of the photos had been taken around noon.

Stella leaned closer. In one, smiling staff members were gathered behind a long smörgåsbord table. She could make out rose-pink slices of smoked salmon and its darker, salt-and-sugar-cured cousin, gravlax. Hard-boiled eggs, bowls of salad and baskets of dark and pale breads dotted the white tablecloth.

Looking straight at the camera with a serious expression on his face was Sven-Arne. Or was he merely squinting into the sun? He was holding a glass full of a blush-pink liquid. Rosé, she assumed, before mentally slapping herself. *Wine? At an addiction charity's summer party. Of course, Stel! And while we're at it, why not put out bowls of coke to dip the hard-boiled eggs into?*

To his left and right, young attractive women looked inwards at their founder. Had he attracted the killer's attention at the party, or one like it, for flying high on all that adoration?

She stooped a little to search him out in some of the other photos. He popped up in about half of them.

'Here we are!' Ida said from behind her.

Stella was turning when a photo in the bottom-left corner of the montage caught her eye. Or, rather, not the photo, but someone in it.

A young woman stood half in shadow beneath a weeping willow. She was much taller than her companions, overtopping them by at least a full head. Her build was solid where theirs were slender, an oak among birches. And there was something about her posture. Stella knew someone else who stood like that, one hip cocked, feet turned slightly inwards. She looked closer, trying to make out the woman's features.

'Is that you, Tilde?' she whispered in surprise.

'Stella? I have the lists for you,' Ida said. 'I put them into a spreadsheet.'

Frowning, Stella turned away from the photo montage and returned to her seat. Ida swivelled the PC round to face her and pushed the keyboard and mouse across the desk.

Rather than start reading down the rows of personal information, Stella clicked the magnifying glass icon and entered a two-word phrase. Her fingers trembled as she typed the surname and she misspelled it. Tutting, she backspaced and tried again. **Tilde Enström**.

A cheerful bong sounded from the PC's speakers and the software informed her that it couldn't find the information she was searching for. She scratched her head, wondering whether Tilde was short for something. She tried again. **Matilde Enström**.

Once more, the PC shrugged its shoulders.

'What is Tilde short for?' she asked Ida, who was chewing a fingernail that looked wet and ragged.

'Oh. Well, Matilda, usually.'

Nodding, Stella tried spelling the name with an 'a' at the end instead of the 'e' she'd started with. Still nothing. She sighed. Maybe she was chasing a ghost and what she needed to do was buckle down and start reading through the entire list. Except that would take too long, and time was the one thing she was short of.

Could she shortcut the software by using the human source sitting directly opposite her?

'Does the name Tilde Enström mean anything to you?'

Ida frowned. 'She's certainly not on the staff. I suppose we might have a volunteer with that name, but I generally know most of them and it doesn't sound familiar to me.'

Stella pulled out her work mobile and scrolled through her contacts, each complete with a portrait image in a circle the size of a one-krona coin. She found Tilde's profile and held the phone out to Ida.

'Do you recognise this woman?'

Ida fumbled in a desk drawer and pulled out a pair of black-framed reading glasses, the sort available for a few krone in a pharmacy or bookshop. She placed them on the bridge of her nose and peered at the picture.

Then she smiled broadly.

'Oh, of course! Her name's not Tilde, though. It's Teresa. Teresa Ekdahl. I'm so sorry,' she said, taking off the glasses. 'I'm being a bit dim today. I'm not used to helping the police with their enquiries,' she said, putting air quotes around the final phrase.

Stella's pulse picked up. She pointed over her shoulder at the photos of the summer picnic.

'Would that be Teresa in the photo at the bottom left? The tall one under the tree?'

Ida walked round her desk to check the photos, then came back to sit again.

'Yes, I think so. You can't see her face but she's a big girl. It's quite hard to miss her. She's very in demand with our group leaders because she has such an inspiring story to tell. Do you know her?'

'How long has she been a volunteer here?'

'Let me check. Not long. I think she started just this year.' Ida tapped a few keys and then nodded. 'Yes, here we are. She started volunteering last year. Initially over in Söderbärke, but then here in Stockholm.'

'What does she do for a living?'

Ida clicked the mouse. Then smiled. 'You'll never guess. She works at a bird sanctuary. Even at work she's helping those who have fallen from their true path.'

Stella felt it, then. The growing certainty that she'd been right to suspect someone inside the SPA all along. Keeping her voice neutral, despite her elevated heartrate and the excitement making her fingertips tingle, she pushed ahead.

'You said she was popular with the group leaders?'

'That's right. You see, alongside the leaders themselves, we like to invite people who have fought their demons and won to address our groups. Sort of like testimony from the other side, if you know what I mean.'

'So she would have been speaking at different groups each week? Each month?'

'Yes, probably. Shall I check?'

Stella could only nod. Her mind was whirling.

Ida was speaking again, listing half a dozen Ingrid's Way groups by their venues, which were mostly churches.

'Now I need the names and phone numbers of the leaders of those groups,' Stella said.

Stella noted down the information Ida read out.

'I need to call them,' she said. 'But I'd really like to do that in private. Would you be OK with lending me your office to make the calls?'

Ida had gone so far in her cooperation, Stella felt certain this request would be granted. 'I can always take them away with me if you'd prefer?'

Ida shook her head.

'No, no. Stay here. I'll go out and buy us a couple of coffees, shall I?'

With Ida gone, Stella called the first group leader, a Marty Andersson.

'Yes, can I help you?'

His voice sounded calm, compassionate. Whiskery somehow. She pictured a rugged, outdoorsy type in a red plaid shirt and a bushy red beard.

'My name is Stella Cole. I'm a detective. I'd like to read you out a list of three names. Can you tell me if any of them attended your meetings?'

'I'm sorry, but that would be breaking a confidence,' he said. 'No way can I answer your question.'

'The people I'm going to name are all dead. Does that change things?'

'Wait. Is this about Peter?'

'Do you mean Peter Lukasson?'

'Yes. He was murdered by Icarus. We were devastated. The group was in tears.'

'So he attended your meetings?'

'Yes. Right up until the week he died.'

'Did you ever have a volunteer speaker address one of your meetings? A Teresa Ekdahl?'

'Sure. Tilly gave a totally inspiring presentation,' he said. 'What's this all about, anyway? Haven't you got somebody in custody already? That English psychiatrist?'

347

'We're just tying up loose ends. Thank you, Marty.'

She ended the call before he could ask any more questions. Not that she would have answered them. Fifteen minutes later, she had her answers.

'Teresa Ekdahl' had also spoken at a *St Johannes Kyrka* meeting where Mikael Matthiason was a regular attender. And at *Hedvig Eleonora Kyrka*, where Sara Marksson had been among the rapt listeners. And as a volunteer, she'd have known all about Sven-Arne. Had even been introduced by him at a couple of meetings.

Was Tilde Icarus?

Stella felt a queasy wave of nausea run its slippery fingers over her stomach as she considered the possibility. She swallowed, hard.

Tilde was linked to all four victims. But so, indirectly, was every staff member at Ingrid's Way. She also had access to the evidence locker, which none of them did. She was strong enough to haul a human body around like a sack of grain. And she'd lied to Stella's face, and in her written reports, about searching the staff records at Ingrid's Way. Why?

Stella thought the answer was obvious. Because she didn't want to reveal her connection to the victims. If it was all just an innocent piece of volunteering, why not admit it? She could have come to Stella in private to explain if she was embarrassed to do it in front of her colleagues. Stella would have understood. Tilde would hardly be the first cop with addiction issues.

She made a mental note to contact the police station up in Söderbärke.

She sat back and closed her eyes, rubbing her temples in a vain attempt to dispel the headache that had taken up lodgings behind her eyes. The trouble was, it was circumstantial evidence at best. Never mind a lawyer, if she confronted Tilde herself, she'd just laugh it off and say she was doing her bit for her community. The pseudonym was just to protect her identity, given the sensitive nature of her job.

As to the lying over the records check, she could just admit it. *Confession time, Stella. I was stressed over work and I took a shortcut to try and catch myself up. It won't happen again.* Stella could – would – boot her off the team and write her up for unprofessional conduct. Worst case, she'd get demoted and sent back to Söderbärke and a uniform. But her old desk in a centrally heated copshop was hardly the same as a cell in a high-security prison.

No. This was merely a start. It made Tilde a person of interest, nothing more. Although that was shocking enough in itself. What Stella wanted now was proof.

Ida knocked on her own office door then entered carrying two takeaway coffees. Stella thanked her but left her cup untouched on the desk. She had work to do.

* * *

Malin liked to keep office hours. Callie had been just the same. She'd explained it to Stella, when they were attending a meeting with the Mayor of London in full dress uniform.

'See this lovely costume jewellery on my epaulettes, Stel?' she'd said, tapping her left shoulder board. 'You might think they stand for chief superintendent. But the actual translation is "Nine",' she tapped the crown, 'to "Six",' she tapped the pip. 'Oh, I think about the job all the bloody time, but at least I get to do it in the comfort of my own home, eh?'

Stella appreciated her current boss's punctuality as she entered SPA headquarters at six-thirty that evening.

She made her way down to the cells, officially the Prisoner Accommodation Suite – so Swedish. Nodding to the officer on duty she flashed her ID and asked to speak to the prisoner in Room Six.

48

Jamie's skin had the grey cell-pallor that afflicted prisoners wherever they were being held. It wasn't merely the absence of daylight: Jamie's room actually had a small window just below the ceiling. It was a combination of factors ranging from institutional food to persistent anxiety.

'How are you holding up?' she asked him, once the door was closed behind her.

He rubbed a hand over his face, clean-shaven she was pleased to notice.

'Oh, you know,' he said with sigh. 'Trying to stay positive. All that mindfulness crap.'

'Not very right-on for someone in the mental health game,' she said, aiming for a cheerfulness she didn't feel.

'Yeah, well to be honest I'm not feeling particularly right-on at the moment.' He spread his arms wide. 'What with my current accommodation.'

She leaned towards him and took his hands.

'Look, Jamie,' she said in a low murmur, 'I know it wasn't you, OK? But I think it might be Tilde.'

'What?' he said, overloud in the hard-walled cell. Then, quieter, 'How? Why?'

'She lied to me. To all of us. She falsified a report about getting a warrant for the Ingrid's Way records. And she's been volunteering there as some sort of motivational speaker, but using a false name. She's connected to all the victims, she's got access to the evidence room, forensics, everything. But I need your help.'

Jamie's eyes, dull and lifeless a moment or two earlier, now danced with energy.

'What do you need?'

She explained her plan. To gain access to Tilde's apartment. Conduct an illegal search. Find evidence damning enough to arrest Tilde. Get a confession so the evidence wouldn't matter. Secure a warrant for her apartment, storage space and lock-up. Discover more evidence that would see her put away for good.

'How do I get under her skin?' she finished.

Jamie frowned and rubbed a hand over his face.

'Aren't you getting ahead of yourself here?'

'What do you mean?'

'Think about it, darling,' he said.

'What do you mean, "think about it"?' Stress making her angry. 'What the fuck do you *think* I've been doing?'

He shook his head.

'There's an innocent explanation for all of that. It's hardly a smoking gun, is it?'

'Do you *want* to get out of here or not?'

'Of course I do! But you trashing your career on the basis of circumstantial evidence is hardly going to do that, is it?'

Stella folded her arms. 'So that's it then, is it? You're just going to sit here in your, your fucking...*prisoner accommodation* and let them send you down for life?'

'No. But we need to do this legally. You can't go back to your old way of doing things.'

They both knew what he meant.

'I'm not going to,' she said quietly, after a long silence. 'But I'm not leaving you to rot in a Swedish prison when I know you didn't do it. Look, assume I get something more concrete against Tilde. I arrest her and I need her to confess. How do I press her buttons? How do I get under her skin?'

'Assuming you do all that, and assuming it really is her, you find out what the wings mean to her. Because it's something huge. Something that has come to define her,' Jamie said. 'And you find out who the person is she's trying to kill, over and over again.'

'There's something else.'

'Go on.'

Stella visualised the triangle she'd doodled with Jamie and Icarus at its corners.

'I was trying to work out what the relationship is between me and the killer. From my perspective, it's easy.'

'You want to catch her.'

'Clearly. But how about from her perspective? I was wondering if there was some sexual jealousy there.'

'And that's why she framed me,' Jamie said, smiling for the first time. 'To get me out of the way, clearing the path for you two to be together.'

'My thoughts exactly, Sherlock.'

'If that's true then you need to be extremely careful when you do confront her. If she's built this fantasy around you, showing her the reality won't go down well, to put it mildly.'

353

'It could break the illusion she's built about us.'

'Yes and that would be incredibly dangerous. She could turn on you.'

'Fit me for my own set of wings,' Stella said.

'Stel, please! Don't joke about it. I'm deadly serious.'

'So am I, Doc. You're saying that if I shatter Tilde's dream about us wandering off into the sunset hand-in-hand, she could start to decompensate.'

'Nice use of the jargon, but yes. And if she does start to come apart at the seams, you'll be in the firing line.'

'Ignoring your mixed metaphor, I think it sounds like a plan.'

Jamie's eyes flash-bulbed.

'Are you crazy? Did you even hear what I just said?'

'I did. And what I heard was a way to get Tilde to drop her defences. I can get into her head and that's when I can get an admission out of her.'

With Jamie still protesting, loudly, she kissed him on the cheek and left the cell. She had work to do.

49

Tilde's apartment was on the fourth floor of a ten-storey block on one of Stockholm's scruffier streets. Finding the address had been the work of moments.

Stella called Tilde from the car.

'Hey, Stella, are you enjoying your time off?'

'Yeah. Just catching up on laundry, house-stuff, doing a bit of running. How are things at the station?'

'Oh, busy with preparing the case. Jonna and I are just about to go into a meeting with Jan Harkin actually, so…'

It was exactly what Stella wanted to hear. Tilde would be kept busy with the prosecutor for at least an hour.

'Go, go,' she said. 'I was just checking in, that's all.'

She pocketed her phone and donned dark glasses. She tucked her hair under a black baseball cap, pulled up her hood then got out and locked the car. As she approached the front doors, a young guy in running gear was leaving. He smiled shyly as he held the door for her.

Stella walked down the long, narrow corridor on

Tilde's floor to the apartment at the end. Lockpicks already in hand, she crouched and was inside ten seconds later. With the front door closed quietly behind her, she could relax. A little. She pulled on a pair of nitrile gloves and added a surgical facemask to her protective gear.

She started her search in the bedroom. In any house, even that of a person living by themselves, the bedroom was the most personal space. Sure, you could leave your sex toys, porn or collection of Barbie dolls on the coffee table in the sitting room. You could festoon the kitchen with bondage gear or cosplay outfits if you really wanted to. You just didn't. You kept them in the bedroom.

If Tilde did have any dirty secrets, they were well hidden. Stella had the uncanny feeling she'd stepped onto a movie set, or, more prosaically, the master bedroom in a show home. The bed was neatly made, a creaseless floral duvet cover smoothed over plump and undented pillows.

She dropped to her hands and knees and peered under the bed. The polished wooden boards gleamed in the light reflected from the mirrored wardrobe door. Not so much as a single dust bunny marred their pristine surface, which smelled of floor polish. Stella lay flat, turned on her back and wriggled under the wooden frame. Nothing lay sandwiched between the mattress and the pale, unvarnished slats a few centimetres above her face.

She slid back out. The wardrobe, then. Plenty of space for trophies. Jewellery in a pull-out rack, perhaps. Photos taped to the front of a drawer. With a flush of revulsion she realised that they'd never found the missing arms. She inhaled, braced herself mentally, and slid the heavy mirrored panel to the left.

If there was a gruesome display of body parts in the apartment, it wasn't here. Stella riffled through the clothes on hangers. Tilde's tastes ran in a narrow groove. Most of the garments were in shades of grey or brown, with the occasional white shirt or pair of black trousers. The kind of smart things cops wore to court.

The drawers held entirely predictable collections of underwear, socks and tights and T-shirts. Stella had similar stuff in her own bedroom, though in smaller sizes. Boots and shoes stood in neat pairs in a three-tiered white wire rack.

She looked up. A sleek, brushed-aluminium suitcase lay on the shelf above the hanging space. Standing on tiptoe, she curled her fingers around the handle and pulled. The suitcase didn't move. She twisted her torso slightly and adjusted her grip. Holding her breath, she jerked the case into motion, dragging it towards her. As its centre of gravity moved over the lip of the shelf, the case crashed downwards, wrenching her arm painfully.

What the fuck was inside it? The image of a tangled skein of human arms rose unbidden into her mind once more. She laid it on the bed and then swore. She'd have to be extra-careful about re-plumping the bedclothes when she'd finished.

She popped the catches and lifted the lid, braced for a gust of putrid air to billow out and envelop her.

'Oh, you have to be kidding me!'

The objects crammed inside the case weren't limbs, although they would bulk them up.

For some reason, Tilde kept a set of brightly coloured weights in a suitcase on a high shelf. Why not put them under the bed or keep them in a corner like a normal person? But then, if Stella's assumption about her newest recruit was correct, Tilde Enström was anything but a normal person. Did her obvious hatred of clutter lead her to keep her fitness equipment on a high shelf? Or was it a part of her routine? It would certainly be extra work putting them up there at the end of a session.

Stella fastened the latches and lifted the case off the bed. Or tried to. The case slipped out of her grasp and fell onto the floor again, the corner scraping painfully down her right shin.

* * *

Tilde frowned with annoyance. The prosecutor's assistant had called to cancel the meeting.

'Jan's held up in court. He'll let you have a new date as soon as he can. I'm sorry.'

'What's up?' Jonna asked.

'We got dressed up for no reason,' Tilde said. 'Apparently Jan Harkin is stuck in court.'

Jonna pulled a face.

'Enjoying one more glass of wine at some fancy restaurant in Östermalm, more like.'

Tilde checked her watch. It was getting towards the end of the afternoon and the smell emanating from her armpits had been disturbing her all day.

'Jonna, is it OK if I pop home? I'm up to date with my paperwork and I could really do with a shower and a change of clothes. I could come back if you need me?'

Jonna smiled. She was friendly to Tilde where some of the other Stockholmers had made little effort to hide their amusement at this oversized country cousin come to play homicide cop in the big city. Tilde liked her all the more for it.

'No need. You've been working your tits off on this

one. Go home and relax. We'll see Jan in the morning, hopefully.'

* * *

Rubbing her shin, Stella stared at the silver suitcase lying at her feet. Her blurred reflection glared back at her: it was as if the suitcase had a malevolent personality of its own. *'Come on then. Get me back up there or you're going to have some explaining to do.'*

Tilde was six inches taller than Stella at least. Her limbs were longer and she was physically stronger than Stella. The laws of physics worked in her favour. Clearly she had no trouble lifting the weight-laden case back up to its resting place on the high shelf.

Stella fetched a side chair from the kitchen. Then she discovered another problem. The gap between bed and wardrobe was too narrow to fit the chair in. Feeling the first irrational proddings of anxiety, she sat on the bed and looked between the suitcase and the shelf.

'Come on, Stel,' she said aloud. 'Think.'

Thinking got her nowhere. She realised what she really needed was half of the famous double-act, Brute-Force and Ignorance.

She knelt on the bed and hauled the case up and back onto the duvet. Then she squatted in front of it, her thighs either side. She swung it up in a clumsy arc then snapped her hand around and grabbed it top and bottom. Her hands were sweaty and the smooth aluminium slid under her palms.

The mattress sank beneath her feet, moving her away from the shelf. Maybe she could use that. She adjusted her grip again and started bouncing on the balls of her feet.

359

She started counting.

'One, two...'

On a grunted 'Three!' she heaved the case up and away from her, using every ounce of strength to send it curving towards the narrow gap between the ceiling and the floor of the upper storage area. The edge of the case cleared the lip of the shelf, and she began to relax. Just keep shoving and it would slot home. But the demon inhabiting the suitcase had one more trick waiting for her. It spun through twenty degrees and started sliding back out.

'No!' she shouted, immediately regretting the loss of control.

She pushed with all her remaining strength and the case, finally, accepted its destiny and rumbled back into position.

Stella dropped back to the bed and swivelled round until she could place her feet on the floor. Head down, she took a few steadying breaths before smoothing the bedclothes and returning the chair to the kitchen.

There had to be something connecting Tilde to Icarus's crimes. Because otherwise, Stella had an unpleasant truth to face. What if Jamie really were the serial killer she'd been hunting all this time? What then?

'Obviously moving in together is off the agenda,' she croaked, her throat suddenly dry.

She decided to leave the bedroom. Maybe she'd have better luck elsewhere. The second door off the corridor opened onto a much smaller bedroom.

The room was barely big enough for the rowing machine that sat dead-centre on the bare laminate floor. Taped to one wall was a sheet of paper, on which Tilde had been keeping detailed records of the... Stella peered at the neat rows of numbers. Jesus! The *thousands* of kilometres she'd covered just sliding backwards and forwards on that moulded plastic seat. Ten a day? When did she have time?

She scanned the rest of the wall space and, as she completed her circle, she found herself looking at a pair of postcards, one above the other, Blu-tacked dead-centre on the wall behind the door.

An antique engraving of a human arm, reduced to its skeleton.

A pen and ink drawing of a dissected bird's wing.

Cold prickles broke out along Stella's forearms. She rubbed the skin, which felt as though she'd brushed against nettles.

* * *

Normally Tilde walked to work. She didn't have to worry about keeping fit by running, like Stella and Jonna: she did enough exercise at home. Besides, she emulated Stella in other, far more important ways. Mainly, she hoped, professionally. Putting Jamie Hooke in a cell had to count as the highlight of her life so far. She was sure Jan Harkin would have no trouble convincing the judges to send Hooke to prison for life. Maybe some of the Stockholmers would be laughing on the other side of their faces after that. And Stella? She'd be pleased.

No.

Pleased was for mothers watching their children get their lines right at a school play. Pleased because you tidied your room nicely. Pleased that you got your breakfast every day this week and put your clothes through the washing machine on your own even though you were only eight, and surely that was her job. Pleased because you let her sleep in and while she snored like a pig you collected up the bottles and put them in the green recycling crate in the kitchen and then out on the street, careful to share a few out with the neighbours so the men in the shiny green and white collection truck didn't make more nasty remarks about 'that drunk bitch' in flat 31.

No. Stella would be proud. Stella would promote Tilde. She'd see her for what she really was. Who she could really be. The role she could play in her life.

She smiled to herself, ignoring the man coming in the opposite direction who smiled back at her, imagining her expression was for him.

The sun came out from behind a cloud, turning the apartment buildings on her street from a muddy brown to a rich, warm terracotta. It wasn't a great address. Stockholm rents were stupidly high. But with her promotion, she'd be able to afford something in a better neighbourhood. Maybe in Mariebergsgatan. Maybe she wouldn't even need to cover the whole of the rent on her own.

She fingered the keys in her pocket, selecting the long brass one and inserting it between her index and middle fingers. She never really felt any threat from the assorted weirdos, predators and drunk guys who fancied themselves. But it would be kind of fun if one tried anything. The Swedish penal code permitted a person to use reasonable force in self-defence. And if that person happened to be a strong, fit, tall, female law enforcement officer, with training in unarmed combat, well, that could hardly be laid at her feet, now could it?

The door was in sight now. She glanced back, over her shoulder. Nobody there. Sadly. She pocketed her keys.

50

Stella stared at the postcards. On their own, they proved nothing.

Malin would look at them and then back at Stella. Raise one finely plucked eyebrow in a questioning arch. *You brought me here to show me these?* the eyebrow would ask.

Jan Harkin, one of the more creative-minded prosecutors in the justice department, would shake his head. *'I'm not going into court with a police officer's art postcards when we have a suspect's DNA on the murder victim.'*

And Tilde would look as though Stella had slapped her. Not angry, but hurt. An eager-to-please rookie put down by her overbearing superior. Fat, wobbling tears would bulge at the corners of her eyes. *I bought them to remind me to keep focused,* she'd say. *I can't believe you didn't trust me, guv.*

Stella leaned against the opposite wall and stared at the two cream-and-sepia images. She became aware that the room smelled of sweat. Tilde would generate gallons of the stuff as she rowed furiously back and forth, going nowhere as she racked up all those thousands of kilometres.

But if it wasn't Tilde, that left her with only one conclusion to draw. Jamie was Icarus. She forced herself to consider it seriously. And it made a weird kind of sense. Had he been drawn to work with the very group of which he was a member?

He knew his way around the dark, labyrinthine passageways of the deviant mind. He had flown to Sweden and inserted himself into the investigation with the precision and determination of a mortician driving a razor-pointed trocar into a femoral artery to drain a corpse of its blood.

Jamie knew all about forensics. Not his field, but he had worked alongside detectives for long enough. Maybe he was doing it to get back at Stella for the way she'd left him. But then why act so lovingly towards her? Why talk about love with her at all?

Because he knows your history. Offering love is the best way to torture you, an internal voice spoke up.

Interesting. Not Other Stella's barbed, dry sarcasm. Just the regular inner speaker everyone heard from time to time, even talked to when nobody else was available.

And it would have worked, until he slipped up. The way they all did. Dahmer, Nielsen, Shipman, Sutcliffe, the Wests. Serial killers so supremely confident, arrogant, or just unbothered that they grew careless and left a clue behind them. In Jamie's case, one of his own hairs, which had come loose, follicle and all, and drifted down into the bloody socket he'd just drilled in a humerus.

'No!' she shouted in the empty room. Then again, louder. 'No! It's not him.'

* * *

Tilde pulled the stairwell door open. Her fourth-floor neighbours all took the lift. That was lazy. The fat lady in the next-door flat really ought to take the stairs. It might give her a few extra years before a stroke, or Type 2 diabetes got her. And the young black guy with the dreadlocks and the easy smile? Well, he was skinny, so what was his excuse? Probably being stoned all the time. She could smell the weed on him if she passed him on her way home from work.

She hit the first flight of concrete steps with a loping bounce. Taking them two at a time, she cruised up to the half-landing, swinging herself around the two ninety-degree angles using the plastic-covered handrail for leverage.

As she lifted her right foot for the next flight, she caught her toe against the lip of the step and stumbled, barking her shin on the next sharp-angled edge.

'Shit-in-hell!' she hissed, rubbing at the painful spot of thin skin over flat bone before resuming her climb at a walk.

Breathing easily, one in for three steps, one out for the next three, she passed the second floor, then the third. As she turned at the final half-landing before her floor, she caught the whiff of weed drifting down and into her flared nostrils. She canted her head back and met the gaze of the black stoner guy. He was heading down, earbuds in, bopping his head to the jazz she knew he liked.

He saw her looking and pulled out the right earbud. Gave her that lazy grin.

'Hey, neighbour,' he slurred. 'Back home early today, I guess?'

She nodded. 'Our case is pretty much closed now.'

'Yeah, I saw on the TV. Like, you caught the Icarus

guy. An English shrink, right? That's crazy. Maybe, like, with Brexit we should stop them even coming here.'

She took in his pink-tinged, unfocused eyes. What a stupid thing to say.

'Not every Brit who comes here is bad,' she said. 'My boss is British and she's a genius.'

He shrugged and replaced the earbud.

'Whatever, man,' he said as he descended, squeezing over to the wall as he passed her.

Tilde grabbed him by the shoulder, momentarily surprised by the rounded hardness of the deltoid muscle beneath cotton shirt. He whipped his head round, frowning, mouth open.

She shoved him back against the wall so hard one of his earbuds flew out. His eyes widened in shock, and now the pink-tinged whites were visible all the way round his deep-brown irises.

'No! It's not "whatever". And it's definitely not "man",' she said, right into his face. 'I'm a woman, and so is she. We nailed that bastard before he killed anybody else. So maybe try showing some respect. And, by the way? If I smell weed on you again, I'll pull you in.'

She pushed him again then leaped up the last eight steps, chest heaving and slammed through the fire door into the corridor.

Behind her, she heard him fire a volley of coarse insults her way. The weed gave them a drawling fuzziness that drew their sting. Even so, she imagined him tripping just as she'd done, only he'd tumble down the entire flight before cracking his skull against the wall, brains splattering onto the concrete floor.

She walked along the centre of the narrow passageway, her shoes squeaking lightly on its painted surface. At her own front door she pushed a hand down into her pocket for her keys. Then she paused. Cocked her head and pressed her ear to the painted wood.

She'd heard a sound from inside. Something faint. If she'd had a cat, she'd have imagined it knocking over a plant pot or a book from a shelf. But she didn't have a cat.

She closed her eyes. Heard a second sound. A door closing.

Her pistol was back at the station. It didn't matter. Swedish burglars almost never carried firearms. No need, really, except maybe out in the country, where farmers all had shotguns and hunting rifles. Worst case here? A knife, or maybe a screwdriver. Neither weapon frightened her.

As silently as she could, she slid the key into the lock and twisted it to the right. Tilde was houseproud, even though she lived in a street where the other residents clearly didn't give a shit. For example, she squirted a little fizz of WD-40 into the lock every Sunday morning. She felt, rather than heard, the tumblers align and the barrel start to rotate: the lock didn't emit so much as a click.

When the key reached the stop on its clockwise turn, she took a steadying breath and pushed.

* * *

In the kitchen, Stella opened closed drawers and cupboards. Not because she expected to find a saw or a container of drill bits clotted with dried blood and gore – this was just so she could move on.

As she turned to go, a key-rack caught her eye. It had been hidden by the door when she entered the room. Keys were interesting. Keys promised admission, or denied it. Keys could keep secrets – or unlock them. Tilde had labelled them all.

Flat Bike Storage Car Workshop

Stella ran her index finger along the keys, all present except for 'Flat'. What did 'Storage' belong to? Probably a locker or room in the basement of the apartment building.

Stella had one, too. A dingy, one-by-two metre concrete box stuffed with things she had no room for in her flat. Her crash helmet, long disused since selling her last ride and not replacing it. A few cartons from her move she'd never got round to unpacking. Not junk. Not exactly. Just things that occupied that ambiguous space between everyday necessities and distant memories.

Not useful enough to keep close at hand, but still carrying enough value not to get rid of. Was that how she felt about her relationship with Jamie? Could she ever rescue it? Would he even want her to? After all, it was her team who'd arrested him.

She needed to check out the storage space. But the key shouting louder than all the others – *Turn me!* – was the small silver Yale at the end. 'Workshop.' It hung from a split-ring alongside a green plastic fob enclosing a slip of paper marked *Självförvaring Barkarby* – 21.

The name rang a bell. Not the first word – it translated as self-storage. But *Barkarby*: she knew she'd seen it before. It looked as though Tilde was renting a lock-up somewhere. Probably on one of the industrial estates or retail parks on the outskirts of the city. Was that it? Was that where she was creating her bird-people?

She took a photo of the key on her phone. She

wanted to just slide it off the hook and pocket it, but this way was better. Leave no trace.

'Stella!'

She whirled round, heart stuttering in her chest, adrenaline flooding her bloodstream.

Tilde was standing in the doorway, staring at her. But she didn't look angry. Surprised, maybe. But she was smiling widely.

51

Stella needed to say something. Fast. Anything to explain her presence in Tilde's kitchen. It was obvious she'd broken in, so what the hell would work?

'Hi,' she said, her mouth desert-dry, her mind racing. 'I wanted to see you. I came by and saw the door was unlocked. I was worried something had happened.'

It was a lie. Of course it was. A huge lie. Maybe it would work. Its very magnitude so improbable as to be capable of only one interpretation. It was the truth.

Tilde put her head on one side, like a blackbird spotting a worm peeping incautiously from a lawn.

'That's odd. I always double-check it when I leave for work.' She spread her hands. 'Oh, well. There's a first time for everything, I suppose. But as you can see, I'm fine. No burglar tied me up and raped me then stabbed me to death, so we're all good. Coffee? A cookie? Actually, no, what am I saying? It should be wine. After all, we have something to celebrate, no?'

Stella swallowed the saliva that had flooded her

mouth, turning the desert to a swamp. 'Yes,' she choked out. 'Wine would be great.'

'Excellent! Sit, sit!'

Tilde fetched a bottle of white wine from the fridge and opened a bag of crisps, then, her back to Stella, busied herself with a corkscrew.

Stella did as she was told and sat at the table. Her pulse had steadied. Tilde's reaction to finding her in the kitchen was way off. Who would be that accepting? Even a colleague of many years' standing might be expected to express a little more in the way of shock. And given the suspect currently languishing in a cell was their boss's boyfriend, surely they'd be sympathetic rather than glibly upbeat?

What were her options? Let it play out as an accidental meeting or start asking Tilde difficult questions?

'Here you go,' Tilde said, placing a wine glass in front of Stella, then sitting opposite her with a tumbler of sparkling water. 'Cheers,' she said in English.

They clinked glasses. Tilde took a sip from her glass. Stella raised her own to her lips. Tilde was watching her avidly, reminding Stella again of how a bird might watch something it wanted to eat. She probably didn't realise she was doing it, but Tilde was moving her own lips and tongue as if it were her drinking. From nowhere, Stella remembered how she'd tried to encourage baby Lola to gum a piece of pear or banana by miming chewing it. *Yummy banana, Lola. Num num num.*

Why did Tilde want Stella to drink?

Casually, Stella put the glass down on the white laminate tabletop. Tilde's lips tightened and for a micro-second Stella saw disappointment mixed with anger flicker across her face.

'Not going to toast our success?'

'*Have* we been successful, Tilde?' she asked.

Tilde smiled. 'You know we have. Jamie's in custody. Game over.'

'I'm not sure it is,' Stella said, leaning back, putting as much distance between her and Tilde as she could without actually leaving the table.

'But we found his DNA on one of the victims.'

'I know.' A second lie came to her then. Bigger than the first. And knocking on the door marked 'unprofessional conduct'. 'But he was with me when Sven-Arne was murdered. It can't have been him.'

Tilde smiled. Took another sip of her water.

'You're lying, Stella. You would have said something when we arrested him. Anyway, I know he wasn't with you.'

'How?' Stella asked, knowing, as the word left her lips that she knew the answer.

'I've been keeping an eye on you. I had to, you see, in case Jamie decided to kill you to derail our investigation,' she said. 'He's played you, Stella. He's *used* you. Psychopaths are cunning. You must know this. They think nothing of using people to get what they want.'

Stella focused on keeping her breathing regular. Her next move was going to escalate things. Aiming for a nonchalance she didn't feel, she put her hands in her pockets.

'Speaking of lies, why didn't you mention that you were a volunteer – a *celebrity* volunteer, it seems – with Ingrid's Way? Why did you lie in your report and say you'd already followed up that line of enquiry, Tilde?'

Tilde flicked at an imaginary crumb on the table. She looked back at Stella and in that moment, Stella was sure she was face-to-face with Icarus. The look in her eyes was so empty of emotion, there was no other way to explain it.

'I'm an addict, Stella. Pure and simple. I'm recovering. But I didn't want my addiction to hamper my progress in your team,' she said. 'I have more to offer you than you know, Stella. So much more.'

'You could have come to me in private. Explained. It's not as though you're the only cop in Sweden with problems. Why do you think we have departmental shrinks like Alyssa?'

Tilde's eyes flicked down to Stella's wine glass. A smirk appeared on her face. She made a visible effort to wipe it off, like swiping at lipstick with a makeup remover pad.

'Oh, I know I'm not the only cop with problems, Stella. Believe me.'

Stella flashed on a conversation she'd had with the SPA psychologist before their brief follow-up session. *'Sorry, Stella, your file wasn't in its usual place.'* And in that moment, she saw a pattern of events unfold like a wing.

'You burgled Alyssa's office, didn't you? You found out about my background. My hallucinations. Have you been drugging me? In my coffee?' She pointed at the untouched wine glass in front of her. 'Is it in that wine?'

Tilde said nothing. Not at first. Then she leaned forwards and fixed Stella with an unwavering gaze that made the hairs erect on her bare forearms.

'I only want what's best for you.'

Stella ignored the endearment. Jamie's words floated in the air between them, about how dangerous it could be to shatter Tilde's dreams of the two of them being together.

'Did you plant Jamie's hair inside the bone, Tilde?'

'Of course not,' Tilde said with a puzzled smile. 'I watched Ronny Halvorsson pull it *out* of the bird bone.'

Stella could feel the unfolding wing stretching wider until it encompassed them both.

'But you could have put it there first, for Ronny to find.'

'I could have, but I didn't.'

They could go on fencing like this all night, Stella realised. She needed to push Tilde harder. She wracked her brain trying to remember anything from Jamie's book that might help her. A common factor in most serial killers' childhood's was an abusive parent, most often the mother.

'Was your dad an addict, Tilde?' she asked.

Nothing from Tilde. Not a flicker.

Stella inhaled. 'Your mum?'

This brought a twitch of the lips. Nothing else. Another fleeting micro-expression. Stella was ready for it though. Had trained long and hard not to miss those lightning flashes of emotion that disfigured an interviewee's face for less time than it took to blink an eye.

'My mum's dead,' Tilde said flatly. 'She drank herself to death. Not before time.'

'Is that why you developed problems with alcohol, Tilde? I checked with the police in Söderbärke. Kennet told me you were drinking heavily there.'

'Children of addicts tend to go in one of two directions, Stella,' Tilde said, adopting a scholarly tone as if she were addressing a roomful of trainees. 'One, they become teetotal, or completely anti-drug. Whatever their parents were hooked on, they push it away. That's the best outcome,' she said, with a lopsided grin. 'But on the *other* hand…they follow Mama or Papa down the same sad road to the bottle or the pills or the needle, or wherever the fuck they go to get their fix. Guess which way poor little Tilde went?'

Stella's heart was bumping along like a car with a flat tyre, with her as the driver wrestling with the steering wheel to keep herself on the road. It felt like Tilde was on the brink of giving in and confessing, but she sensed a reluctance in her. And Tilde was, as various people had mentioned, some cruelly, a big girl. A powerful girl. With a killer's reflexes and a psychopath's lazy enjoyment of causing pain.

Maybe she could push another button by taking an indirect route.

'Jamie's going to go free,' she said. 'I persuaded Malin he's been set up. We're reopening the case. We're looking at all the cops involved in the investigation. I told her I thought you were involved. You've got a workshop out at Barkarby. I was looking at the key when you came home. What will we find if we look inside? Boxes of old clothes? IKEA furniture you grew out of? Or a freezer full of body parts and birds' wings?'

Tilde's features remained immobile for a couple of seconds. Then a series of expressions chased themselves across her face like gulls scrapping over a French fry in mid-air. Her mouth quirked to one side then relaxed. Her eyes narrowed, flicked left and right, back to Stella. She wrinkled her nose and sniffed, loudly. She rubbed her cheeks with both palms then took a swallow of water. Put the glass down carefully on the table.

'I did it all for you, Stella.'

'Did what for me, Tilde?' Stella asked, wishing she'd thought to bring a pair of cuffs, or even some heavy-duty cable ties.

'Catching Icarus would make your career. After that,

who knows? You could go on to be anything you wanted. The national police commissioner, or a TV personality, or even an MP. Maybe even the prime minister. You still can!' she said. 'I don't think you did talk to Malin. And even if you did, she's not going to ignore DNA evidence. How could she? It's what the Americans call a slam-dunk. Let Jamie go to prison. Then you and I can be together. I'll always be there to help you solve cases.' Tilde jerked forwards across the table. 'And I'll never let you down.'

Stella reared back but she was trapped between the table and the wall behind her chair. A memory rose from a place in her mind she had shut away behind padlocked gates. The psychopathic serial killer Mim Robey racing around a vast storage tank of black oil towards her, a wickedly sharp machete raised over her head.

'Jamie is innocent, Tilde. I'll prove it,' she said, trying to stay calm as she tried to anticipate an attack from Tilde. 'I'll find out how you got hold of his hair and how you planted it inside the bone. It won't be hard. And when I do, I'll arrest you and you'll be tried and convicted.' Then she took the final step in her attempt to break Tilde. The step Jamie had warned her was too dangerous to try. 'We're not going to spend our lives together. You're going to spend the rest of yours in a maximum security prison. Somewhere nice, like Helby.'

Tilde swallowed convulsively, as if trying to stop herself vomiting. She blinked. Her head twitched, this way and that.

'No. You can't do that. You mustn't.' Her voice switched to a girlish whine as if somebody had swapped settings on a voice-changing app. 'Why, can't you see how much I love you? Why? It's not fair!' Her face contorted and for several seconds she said nothing.

Finally, she glared at Stella from beneath lowered eyebrows. 'I hate you, Mama!'

Stella's flesh crawled. Could this be an inner version of Tilde like her own demon, Other Stella? Maybe this was something she could exploit.

'Did you kill those people, Tilde?' she asked, looking Tilde straight in the eye and injecting a motherly sternness into her voice. 'You can tell Mama. I won't be cross.'

Tilde pouted. She folded her arms across her chest.

'So what if I did? They didn't matter,' she muttered. '*You* didn't matter, Mama. Only Stella matters. Her and me.'

Slowly, Stella slid her body out from between the edge of the table and the chair. Getting to her feet, she stood over Tilde.

'I'm arresting you for murder. Come with me to the station and let's get you somewhere to stay. You're tired, I understand.'

Tilde looked up at her and Stella was surprised to see she was crying.

'I *am* tired,' she said, pushing back from the table.

She stood, towering over Stella. If she made a move now, it was going to be a fast, dirty fight. Stella hadn't forgotten the moves she'd had a former police unarmed combat instructor teach her. Dark, dangerous strikes no police service would sanction. Designed to maim, to disable, and to kill.

But Tilde seemed passive. Docile. She stood in front of Stella, looking at the floor.

'I want you to behave yourself, Tilde,' Stella said, keeping the maternal firmness in her voice. 'You're not going to try anything silly, are you? Mama wouldn't like that.'

'No, Mama,' Tilde said. 'I'll be a good girl.'

'Come on, then. Let's go. You first.'

Tilde nodded, sniffed once and wiped her nose with the back of her hand, then shuffled towards the hallway and the front door. Stella followed, keeping a small gap between them, far enough away that a back-kick wouldn't connect.

On the landing, still jacked on adrenaline, Stella turned to shut the apartment door.

All she heard was the scuffing of Tilde's boots on the landing's smooth flooring. She whirled round to see Tilde sprinting towards the fire door at the far end of the corridor.

52

Stella was fit, but Tilde was fitter. Arms pumping, she raced down the echoing hallway, her boots clumping on the hard surface. By the time Stella reached the fire door, Tilde had straight-armed it like a rugby player fending off a tackle, slamming it wide and barely breaking stride as she powered into the stairwell.

Through the wire-reinforced porthole in the door, Stella caught sight of Tilde's lower legs heading up the stairs. She dodged around the slow-closing door, catching her shoulder on the edge and grunting with pain as a muscle tore.

'Tilde, stop!' she shouted as she hit the stairs, but the younger woman was already onto the next landing.

Taking the stairs two at a time, Stella swung herself round on the half-landing, chasing Tilde's heels as they flashed up and onto the next flight. She desperately wanted to catch Tilde, but the younger woman had the advantage of height, leverage, strength and her position on the stairs. If she turned and lashed out with a booted foot, she could send Stella tumbling back down those unforgiving concrete steps or, worse, haul her up and over the handrail to plummet five floors to her death.

The oversized floor numbers were painted in bright primary colours, as if the developers were building a nursery school. Red, orange, green, yellow. Breath came in painful rasps now as Stella staggered at the final half-landing before the tenth floor.

Tilde had been gaining on her the whole way up through the stairwell and now Stella could only hear her footsteps as she raced unstoppably towards the top of the block.

She reached the final landing. The fire door was slowly shutting on its pneumatic closer and Stella barged through, careful to avoid her damaged shoulder.

Tilde was almost at the far end of the corridor. She'd run straight past the lifts. Where was she going? Did she know of another way down?

No. Stella realised Tilde's – and her – destination just before Tilde kicked out at a door that gave with a splintering crash. The roof.

Her chest was pierced with a vicious stitch that ran like a knife wound from her throat to her pelvis. Jogging with Jonna had kept her in great shape, but those were even-paced runs, mostly on the flat, not this adrenaline-fuelled sprint up multiple flights of stairs. She bent, hand on the tops of her thighs, taking a second or two to drag in some deeper breaths before racing to the burst-open door.

A short, narrow flight of steps led upwards and when Stella cautiously pushed through the final door, she found herself on the enormous flat roof of the apartment block.

Tilde was picking her way over wide steel pipes that criss-crossed the flat expanse of grey roofing material.

Girders and water tanks, even a couple of what looked like pigeon cages, were dotted about like an obstacle course.

Stella called out again, but Tilde didn't even turn her head. Just kept heading towards the far end of the roof, where a low rail marked the edge.

Swearing to herself, Stella ran across the roof, vaulting the array of obstructions like a steeplechaser.

She got to within five metres of Tilde, who'd almost reached the edge, and stopped.

Tilde turned, slowly. 'Don't come any closer, Stella.'

Panting, Stella held her hands out, palms outwards.

'I won't, Tilde. I'm staying right here. Just come towards me a little, OK? Just one step. We can go to the station together. I'll help you.'

Tilde shook her head.

'I need to tell you something. Then I'll go.'

Breath burning in her chest, Stella nodded. 'Tell me, then. I'm listening.'

Tilde took a half-step back until her calves bumped against the rail. Stella had visions of her toppling backwards, falling. An odd sensation, half pain, half itch, spread outwards from the backs of her knees. A gull wheeled above them, crying loudly. Tilde looked up and smiled, then lowered her head and looked back at Stella.

'It's the story of a little girl,' Tilde said. 'Her mom was an alcoholic. The little girl didn't know that was the name for what was wrong with her mom. She only knew that when she was drunk, she forget she even had a daughter. Used to pass out on the sofa or in her bed and leave the little girl to cook her own meals, make her own lunches for school, do her own laundry.

'Her mom didn't look after the house they shared, either. The little girl did the cleaning, but the house itself was only made of wood and after a few years it started to fall apart. The eaves outside the little girl's bedroom were rotten and crows found their way inside. Probably they were attracted by the mice.

'Every night, when the little girl, Tilly, tried to sleep, she could hear the crows hopping about on her ceiling. Their claws made scary ticking noises and sometimes she thought she could hear the mice screaming when the crows snapped them up in their long, black beaks.

'She used to have nightmares and run to her mom's bedroom to get under the covers. Even though her mom was unconscious and stank of wine, Tilly could cuddle up to her and feel a little bit safer until morning.

'One day, near Midsommar, when it was so hot Tilly kept her windows open at night, a crow came right into her bedroom. She screamed, but the crow didn't fly away. It was a young one. Maybe it was lost. It hopped onto Tilly's bed and just stood there, its head on one side, its shiny black eye like a bead looking at her.

'Even though she was frightened, Tilly stretched out her hand and the crow hopped closer and tapped her finger with its beak. She held onto her fear and stroked its feathery wing. The crow seemed to like it.

'The next night Tilly waited for the crow and when it came back she stroked it again. She'd kept a piece of crispbread from supper and she broke it into pieces and fed it to the crow. Little by little, night after night, they made friends, and she even gave it a name. She called it Odin.

'But one afternoon, when Tilly came home from school, she saw Odin lying in the yard in a great pool of blood. She ran to him and when she got close she saw that he had no wings. They'd been torn clean off and thrown onto a flower bed all overgrown with weeds.

'Her mom came out of the house, holding a bottle by the neck. She was smiling but her face was all messy and Tilly could smell the drink on her like a sickly yellow cloud. "Hey, Tilly," she said. "I caught the crow that was giving you nightmares. Look! He won't be bothering you anymore".

'Tilly was crying so hard snot was coming out of her nose. She screamed at her mom. "I hate you, I hate you, I hate you!" She ran upstairs to her room and slammed the door and she cried until her tummy hurt so much she was sick.

'But that wasn't the worst of it. Because crows are very clever birds. They look out for each other. When the other crows saw Odin's dead body with his wings pulled off, they decided to take revenge. The next day, Tilly's mom was passed out inside the house and Tilly was playing outside in the yard with her doll. The doll had a soft cloth body with hard plastic arms and legs. Her name was Pippi. You know, like in the story? Pippi Longstocking.

'Tilly got a funny feeling on the back of her neck, like a ghost was tickling her and she looked up. All around the yard, the crows had landed on the clothes line, the shed, the hedge at the end, and on the ground. They all flew at Tilly and pecked and scratched her. She screamed and ran inside, batting at her head to try to keep the crows off her. Only she dropped Pippi Longstocking.

'She watched the crows through the window in the kitchen. They crowded over Pippi, their big black wings over her like funeral umbrellas, and they pecked her. They pecked and pecked and pulled and tugged and tore and then I saw poor Pippi's arms come off and the crows flew off with them in their beaks and I—

Tilde blinked and resumed speaking in her normal voice.

'I hated my mom, Stella. From that moment on. Not for what she did to me. But because she killed Odin. And then Odin's friends killed Pippi Longstocking. Then I had nobody to play with. Nobody who loved me.'

Despite the fact she was listening to a violent psychopath who had murdered four people, Stella felt a lump in her throat. She could visualise Tilly, barely making it through each new day, caring for her alcoholic mother while trying to look after herself, too.

But right now, she needed to get Tilde away from the edge of the roof and all the way back to Kungsholmsgatan and a cell. She'd be evaluated by a departmental psychiatrist, that was for sure. Whether she ended up in a prison or a secure hospital would be for the courts to decide. Keeping her talking for now seemed like the best option.

'Is that why you gave them birds' wings, Tilde?' she asked. 'Because of Odin?'

Tilde nodded. 'And because of what his friends did to Pippi.'

'How did you get Jamie's hair?'

'I went to his apartment. I said I wanted to understand more about serial killers. You know, because I was the rookie on your team. He was very kind. He spent ages explaining. And then I did the old trick. I asked to use the bathroom. I found a hairbrush and just took what I needed,' she said, smiling slyly. 'I was going to steal his toothbrush from the bathroom if I couldn't get a hair. I put the hair into the wing bone when I killed Sven-Arne.'

Stella thought back to the hallucinations of Other

Stella. And the way Tilde had watched her so closely when she'd poured the wine earlier.

'Did you break into the psychologist's office, Tilde? Did you read my file?'

Tilde shifted her stance a little. Stella's breath caught in her throat.

'I did. But only to understand you, Stella. To find out all I could about you. But when I read about your, you know, problems, I realised if you were a little unstable, it could help us both,' she said. 'I was microdosing you with LSD. I took it from the evidence locker. Just a tiny amount in the coffees I made you. It wasn't enough to hurt you. I made sure of it.'

Hurt me? Stella wanted to scream. *I thought I was losing my mind!*

She kept the thought inside. She couldn't afford to say anything that might spook Tilde. Not with her standing with her back to a ten-storey drop. But she still had questions. Questions she thought Tilde would be happy to answer. And while she was talking, she wasn't jumping.

'Tilde, did you kill anyone before Matthias?'

Tilde bit her lip. Stella read the body language immediately. A little girl's guilty tell. She envisioned a string of bodies, maybe winged, or maybe just slaughtered like Odin.

'Tilde?' she prompted.

'Only one.'

'Can you tell me who? Who did you kill, Tilly?' she asked, deliberately using Tilde's childhood nickname in a desperate effort to reconnect with her inner child. The person she'd been when she was innocent, before she'd turned into a serial killer.

'Who do you think?' Tilde said, pouting.

387

Stella reckoned she didn't need to be a Freudian psychoanalyst to answer *that* particular question.

'Was it your mom?' she asked, using the American word, just like Tilde had.

Tilde nodded. 'You're so clever, Stella. We'd have made such a good team.'

'What happened?' Stella asked.

'She finally got clean, can you believe it?'

In that moment, Stella saw it with a blinding clarity. Not just why Tilde had targeted addicts and alcoholics, but why she'd selected them from Ingrid's Way and not AA or NA.

'She went to Ingrid's Way meetings, didn't she?'

'Yes, the fucking bitch did!' Tilde hissed out savagely. 'Tried to contact me to tell me she forgave me. Forgave *me*! She'd got her life together, she said, and now we could be a proper mom and daughter. Well,' Tilde emitted a brittle laugh, 'you can see that I couldn't allow that to happen, Stella. But it did give me an idea for how I could build myself a new family, with you. I'd rid the world of a few more selfish addicts like Mom and win your heart at the same time. You'd have solved your greatest case with my help.

'I know it would have taken you a little while to get over Jamie,' Tilde said. 'But I would have been there for you, Stella. I would have cared for you. Made you breakfast, made sure you had clean clothes to wear, the sheets were laundered even after you wet the bed because of the crows. And stroked you when you had the nightmares.'

Stella fought back the grimace of revulsion that slid around behind her cheeks. Why hadn't she thought to bring a gun and a pair of cuffs? She could have ended this without having to sweet-talk Tilde. Maybe there was one last way she could reach her. Despite the danger Jamie had warned her about.

'Come to me, darling,' she said, reaching towards Tilde. 'Let's get you somewhere safe. Somewhere nobody can ever hurt you again. Somewhere with no crows, no mom, just kind people who want to help you.' She steeled herself. 'Then, when you're better again, maybe we can plan our life together after all.'

Tilde smiled. A guileless expression in which Stella saw the traumatised little girl whose only friend had been torn apart by her mother.

'You mean it? You *do* love me?'

Stella forced herself to smile. 'Of course I do, silly! I just couldn't admit it to myself.'

Tilde held her hands out, like a child asking for a cuddle. Stella finally felt herself relaxing. It was over. She closed the distance between them and stretched her hands out to take Tilde's.

Tilde's hands shot forwards and enveloped Stella's in a grip so powerful it made Stella gasp. The small bones in her hands were being ground together like twigs, ready to snap at any moment.

'You're a liar! You don't love me at all! ' Tilde screamed into Stella's face. 'So if we can't live together, we'll die together.'

She yanked Stella towards her, stepping over the low rail with her left foot. Stella felt her weight shifting forwards. Another few centimetres and her centre of gravity would start working against her, dragging her deeper into Tilde's fatal embrace before she took them both over the edge and down onto the road so many floors below.

'No!' she yelled, tugging her hands back.

Tilde simply leaned backwards and managed to lift

her right foot over the rail. Her hands held Stella's like a pair of steel cuffs. Now her heels were overhanging the roof and she was leaning back, dragging Stella inexorably to her death.

Stella's vision telescoped down to Tilde's brawny forearms and the clawed fingers encircling her hands. A voice from far away called out at her. A voice she recognised, gratefully this time.

The dead bird, babe! Show her the dead bird!

'Look, Tilly,' Stella screamed as she felt her feet scraping over the gritty roof towards the rail. 'It's Odin!'

Tilde's head snapped up and for a split second her grip on Stella's right hand loosened. Stella jerked her hand free and punched Tilde as hard as she could, right over the larynx. Eyes bulging out of their sockets, whooping in shock and pain, Tilde let go of Stella's left hand as well to clutch her throat.

And in that moment, she toppled backwards.

'Tilde, no!' Stella screamed, lunging for her.

But Tilde was already falling, her arms spread wide as if what was waiting for her ten storeys below wasn't the hard, unforgiving concrete of the pavement, but a feather-soft cloud into whose maternal embrace she could float.

Stella ran to the parapet and looked down.

Tilde was still falling. The rush of air rippled the material of her shirt.

Then, with an echoing bang, she slammed onto the white roof of a delivery truck parked outside the front entrance. Stella clapped her hand over her mouth.

Slowly, blood emerged from beneath Tilde's broken body, filling in the spaces between her outflung arms and her rib cage before flowing away, left and right, over the sides of the roof and onto the ground.

53

Jamie was released as soon as Stella got back to Kungsholmsgatan. When she'd put her hands in her pockets in her talk with Tilde, she'd turned on the voice-activated recorder she'd brought with her. The recording was muffled, but enough of Tilde's confession was audible to convince Jan Harkin and Malin.

Stella and Jonna visited the self-storage facility on the retail park in Barkarby. The interior of unit 21 stank. Blood, and an unpleasant, oily smell she couldn't place until Jonna said a single word: 'Feathers.'

Tilde had assembled a rudimentary operating table complete with an overhead lamp. All the kit she'd needed was arranged neatly on wooden shelves from IKEA. Bottles of ketamine and syringes. A small baggie containing squares of blotting paper that would turn out to be impregnated with LSD. Cylindrical aluminium rods, 12mm in diameter. Knives, power saws, drills, all meticulously cleaned but which would, under the forensics investigators' alternate light sources and chemical reagents reveal traces of Tilde's victims' blood.

Just as Stella had predicted, a large chest freezer contained six folded wings, one pair white, one black, the third a pale grey. Of the dismembered arms, there was no physical trace, bar blood stains.

That night, she, Oskar and Jonna celebrated with champagne and seafood at a new bar everyone was raving about.

But not everyone was as quick to congratulate Stella as the remaining members of her team. Malin had raised her eyebrows, and a score of difficult questions, about how, precisely, Stella had found herself at Tilde's apartment building and been able to get a confession out of her. The lack of notes in her investigation folder complicated matters.

'We also have a dead police officer,' she said. 'She should have stood trial.'

Nik Olsson also came calling, the inquisitorial light burning even brighter behind his eyes. She had no intention of letting him make the running in the conversation. Not after what she'd been through in recent weeks.

'What can I do for you, Nik?' she asked, neither rising from her seat nor offering him coffee.

'Maybe stop killing police officers?' he replied, with a nasty edge in his voice.

It was a cheap shot, aimed clumsily. Stella had plenty of time to dodge the incoming fire. He wanted to provoke her into claiming one less psychopath in the world was a price worth paying. He might as well have brought a placard.

'I did everything in my power to save Tilde,' she said. 'I regret not being able to take her into custody. No doubt you've read my report. It's all in there.'

'Is it? I wonder,' he said, a tight, predatory smile creasing the lower half of his face.

Stella got to her feet. Now she knew Other Stella's brief reappearance had been generated by Tilde's microdoses of LSD, she'd stopped worrying. She'd been to see Alyssa again. The psychologist had confirmed that the drug could have amplified Stella's natural anxieties about the case until they assumed scarily realistic form. But Other Stella as a *persona*? That was a woman Stella enjoyed being once more.

She took a step towards Nik. Close enough to see the fine pores on his smooth-shaven cheeks. To smell his aftershave.

He took a reflexive step backwards, bumping into Jonna who was walking behind him, coffees in hand.

'Hey! Watch out!'

'Sorry.'

'Nik?' Stella said. He turned back to her. 'I don't know why you don't like me. And, honestly? I don't care. So do your job and let me do mine. There'll be fewer killers on the streets and we'll all be able to sleep a little easier at night. Now, you'll have to excuse me, but I'm having a drink with the prosecutor.'

She left him standing there, mouth agape.

Unlike Nik, Jan Harkin was on her side. They met in a busy pub a few blocks from his office. The place was full of cops and justice department staffers.

'Listen, Stella,' he said over beer and pickled herrings in onions. 'The evidence is overwhelming, and it was obtained perfectly legally. If you, ah, took a slightly unorthodox route before then, well, it was a problematic case from the start. A serving SPA officer murdering people like that? A trial could have been a public relations nightmare. This way, I can close the case with a satisfactory outcome. Guilt established, and proven. There'll be some fallout in the media, but nothing like on the scale we would have seen if she'd gone to court. Shit, she could have pleaded not guilty. Then where would we have been?'

* * *

In the last stages of the investigation, Oskar looked into Tilde's background for the report they would send to Jan and Malin. Her mother had died earlier in the year, but not from drinking. She'd been sober for ten years, although Tilde had had no contact with her. Stella had to fight back tears as Oskar outlined the circumstances. Cause of death: a hit and run.

The driver had never been found, but when they examined Tilde's car, which was otherwise spotlessly clean, they found a single blood spot on the radiator. It matched Erika Enström's DNA.

* * *

On the day Jamie was due to fly back to England, Stella drove him to Arlanda and signalled for the short-term parking. Jamie put a hand on her right arm.

'Just the drop-off will be fine.'

'You're sure? I was going to come in with you. I thought we could have a beer before you went through.'

He shook his head.

'It's easier this way.'

There was something in his voice she didn't like, but she pulled back into the left-hand lane anyway. Two minutes later she was bringing the car to a stop in a slot between two taxis.

Jamie retrieved his luggage from the boot. She joined him behind the car.

'Is everything OK?'

He ran a hand over his face and sighed. The sound seemed to come from a place so deep inside him she felt it physically: a well into which you could drop a stone and not hear the splash for a long time.

'You arrested me, Stella.'

'That was Tilde and Jonna,' she said, knowing she was deliberately missing the point. Also that Jamie would know she was doing it. And why. Bloody headshrinkers.

'You know what I mean,' he said. 'I came out here to help you and I ended up in a cell.'

'But we couldn't know Tilde had planted it, Jamie. Your DNA was literally inside a murder victim's body! No detective on the planet would have done anything different,' she said. 'I went straight to Malin. I defended you! I told her it was a mistake. She wouldn't listen. That's why I disobeyed her. I spent every hour that I could stay awake trying to discover what really happened. It's how I found out about Tilde.'

'I just wonder how good of a fit we really are. I need some time to think.'

'No, you don't!' she said, gripping his upper arm. 'We've done too much thinking. I love you. And I think you love me, too. And look at everything we've got in common. I'm a serial killer and you were arrested for being one. We could write a book together. Call it *Serial Killer Spouses*. It'd be a best-seller.'

She was gabbling, and unable to stop. Gently, Jamie disengaged her arm.

'Come back to England with me, then. Get yourself transferred back to the Met,' he said. 'I'm sure Callie would welcome you with open arms. We could buy a place together. Write that book, even, though we might have to use pen names.'

'You know I can't do that,' she said, feeling a weight descend into her belly like the onset of a cramp. 'Or have you forgotten what Gemma Dowding said to me?'

'I know what you told me she said.'

'What? What do you mean "told" you she said? She *did* say it.'

Janie shrugged. He looked at his watch.

'I should be going. I need to check in.'

A uniformed airport official was strolling down the line of parked cars towards them. He caught Stella's eye and tapped his own watch.

'Sorry, folks, five minutes maximum. Do you need to go park?'

'We're nearly finished,' Jamie said in passable Swedish.

'Jamie, please,' she said, hearing the pleading note in her voice and not caring. 'Don't let's leave it like this.'

He leaned towards her and kissed her on the side of the mouth, then drew back and pulled up the handle on his suitcase until it clicked into place.

'I'll call you.'

He turned and walked away from her, raising a hand to acknowledge a taxi driver who stopped to let him cross the next lane over before he disappeared into the terminal building.

Stella drove back to her flat feeling lost.

Back home, depressed and angry, she opened a bottle of wine and took it out onto the balcony.

What she wanted to shout to the city spread out before her was, 'It's not fair!' She'd single-handedly caught Icarus, and freed an innocent man— her boyfriend, no less — in the process. But she felt as though she'd lost everything. Was she really this shallow? A successful professional woman brought low because her boyfriend was having doubts?

But it *wasn't* fair. And Jamie *was* being unreasonable. If he truly loved her, surely he'd understand she'd been in an impossible position. He was a psychiatrist, for God's sake! Understanding people was supposed to be his stock-in-trade.

Her phone rang. She took it out and glanced at the screen. Jonna.

'Hey.'

'Hi, Stel. I was in the neighbourhood. Don't suppose you fancy a drink?'

'I've just opened a bottle. Why don't you come round?.'

Stella went back into the kitchen and brought another wine glass out to the balcony.

Above her head, a V of geese wove on a sinuous flight-path towards the water.

397

READ ON FOR AN EXTRACT FROM
SHALLOW GROUND, THE FIRST
BOOK IN THE DETECTIVE FORD
THRILLERS...

PROLOGUE

Summer | Pembrokeshire Coast, Wales

Ford leans out from the limestone rock face halfway up Pen-y-holt sea stack, shaking his forearms to keep the blood flowing. He and Lou have climbed the established routes before. Today, they're attempting a new line he spotted. She was reluctant at first, but she's also competitive and he really wanted to do the climb.

'I'm not sure. It looks too difficult,' she'd said when he suggested it.

'Don't tell me you've lost your bottle?' he said with a grin.

'No, but . . .'

'Well, then. Let's go. Unless you'd rather climb one of the easy ones again?'

She frowned. 'No. Let's do it.'

They scrambled down a gully, hopping across boulders from the cliff to a shallow ledge just above sea level at the bottom of the route. She stands there now, patiently holding his ropes while he climbs. But the going's much harder than he expected. He's wasted a lot of time attempting to navigate a tricky bulge. Below him, Lou plays out rope through a belay device.

He squints against the bright sunshine as a light wind buffets him. Herring gulls wheel around the stack, calling in alarm at this brightly coloured interloper assaulting their territory.

He looks down at Lou and smiles. Her eyes are a piercing blue. He remembers the first time he saw her. He was captivated by those eyes, drawn in, powerless, like an old wooden sailing ship spiralling down into a whirlpool. He paid her a clumsy compliment, which she accepted with more grace than he'd managed.

Lou smiles back up at him now. Even after seven years of marriage, his heart thrills that she should bestow such a radiant expression on him.

Rested, he starts climbing again, trying a different approach to the overhang. He reaches up and to his right for a block. It seems solid enough, but his weight pulls it straight off.

He falls outwards, away from the flat plane of lichen-scabbed limestone, and jerks to a stop at the end of his rope. The force turns him into a human pendulum. He swings inwards, slamming face-first against the rock and gashing his chin. Then out again to dangle above Lou on the ledge.

Ford tries to stay calm as he slowly rotates. His straining fingertips brush the rock face then arc into empty air.

Then he sees two things that frighten him more than the fall.

The rock he dislodged, as large as a microwave, has smashed down on to Lou. She's sitting awkwardly, white-faced, and he can see blood on her leggings. Those sapphire-blue eyes are wide with pain.

And waves are now lapping at the ledge. The tide is on its way in, not out. Somehow, he misread the tide table, or he took too long getting up the first part of the climb. He damns himself for his slowness.

'I can lower you down,' she screams up at him. 'But my leg, I think it's broken.'

She gets him down safely and he kisses her fiercely before crouching by her right leg to assess the damage. There's a sharp lump distending the bloody Lycra, and he knows what it is. Bone.

'It's bad, Lou. I think it's a compound fracture. But if you can stand on your good leg, we can get back the way we came.'

'I can't!' she cries, pain contorting her face. 'Call the coastguard.'

He pulls out his phone, but there's no mobile service down here.

'Shit! There's no signal.'

'You'll have to go for help.'

'I can't leave you, darling.'

A wave crashes over the ledge and douses them both.

Her eyes widen. 'You have to! The tide's coming in.'

He knows she's right. And it's all his fault. He pulled the block off the crag.

'Lou, I—'

She grabs his hand and squeezes so hard it hurts. 'You *have* to.'

Another wave hits. His mouth fills with seawater. He swallows half of it and retches. He looks back the way they came. The boulders they hopped along are awash. There's no way Lou can make it.

He's crying now. He can't do it.

Then she presses the only button she has left. 'If you stay here, we'll *both* die. Then who'll look after Sam?'

Sam is eight and a half. Born two years before they married. He's being entertained by Louisa's parents while they're at Pen-y-holt. Ford knows she's right. He can't leave Sam an orphan. They were meant to be together for all time. But now, time has run out.

'Go!' she screams. 'Before it's too late.'

So he leaves her, checking the gear first so he's sure she can't be swept away'. He falls into an eerie calm as he swims across to the cliff and solos out.

At the clifftop, rock gives way to scrubby grass. He pulls out his phone. Four bars. He calls the coastguard, giving them a concise description of the accident, the location and Lou's injury. Then he slumps. The calmness that saved his life has vanished. He is hyperventilating, heaving in great breaths that won't bring enough oxygen to his brain, and sighing them out again.

A wave of nausea rushes through him and sweat flashes out across his skin. The wind chills it, making him shudder with the sudden cold. He lurches to his right and spews out a thin stream of bile on to the grass.

Then his stomach convulses and his breakfast rushes up and out, spattering the sleeve of his jacket. He retches out another splash of stinking yellow liquid and then dry-heaves until, cramping, his guts settle. His view is blurred through a film of tears.

He falls back and lies there for ten more minutes, looking up into the cloudless sky. Odd how realistic this dream is. He could almost believe he just left his wife to drown.

He sobs, a cracked sound that the wind tears away from his lips and disperses into the air. And the dream blackens and reality is here, and it's ugly and painful and true.

He hears a helicopter. Sees its red-and-white form hovering over Pen-y-holt.

Time ceases to have any meaning as he watches the rescue. How long has passed, he doesn't know.

Now a man in a bright orange flying suit is standing in front of him explaining that his wife, Sam's mother, has drowned.

Later, there are questions from the local police. They treat him with compassion, especially as he's Job, like them.

The coroner rules death by misadventure.

But Ford knows the truth.

He killed her. *He* pushed her into trying the climb. *He* dislodged the block that smashed her leg. And *he* left her to drown while he saved his own skin.

DAY ONE, 5.00 P.M

SIX YEARS LATER | SUMMER | SALISBURY

Angie Halpern trudged up the five gritty stone steps to the front door. The shift on the cancer ward had been a long one. Ten hours. It had ended with a patient vomiting on the back of her head. She'd washed it out at work, crying at the thought that it would make her lifeless brown hair flatter still.

Free from the hospital's clutches, she'd collected Kai from Donna, the childminder, and then gone straight to the food bank – again. Bone-tired, her mood hadn't been improved when an elderly woman on the bus told her she looked like she needed to eat more: 'A pretty girl like you shouldn't be that thin.'

And now, here she was, knackered, hungry and with a three-year-old whining and grizzling and dragging on her free hand. Again.

'Kai!' she snapped. 'Let go, or Mummy can't get her keys out.'

The little boy stopped crying just long enough to cast

a shocked look up into his mother's eyes before resuming, at double the volume.

Fearing what she might do if she didn't get inside, Angie half-turned so he couldn't cling back on to her hand, and dug out her keys. She fumbled one of the bags of groceries, but in a dexterous act of juggling righted it before it spilled the tins, packets and jars all over the steps.

She slotted the brass Yale key home and twisted it in the lock. Elbowing the door open, she nudged Kai with her right knee, encouraging him to precede her into the hallway. Their flat occupied the top floor of the converted Victorian townhouse. Ahead, the stairs, with their patched and stained carpet, beckoned.

'Come on, Kai, in we go,' she said, striving to inject into her voice the tone her own mother called 'jollying along'.

'No!' the little boy said, stamping his booted foot and sticking his pudgy hands on his hips. 'I hate Donna. I hate the foobang. And I. Hate. YOU!'

Feeling tears pricking at the back of her eyes, Angie put the bags down and picked her son up under his arms. She squeezed him, burying her nose in the sweet-smelling angle between his neck and shoulder. How was it possible to love somebody so much and also to wish for them just to shut the hell up? Just for one little minute.

She knew she wasn't the only one with problems. Talking to the other nurses, or chatting late at night online, confirmed it. Everyone reckoned the happily married ones with enough money to last from one month to the next were the exception, not the rule.

'Mummy, you're hurting me!'

'Oh, Jesus! Sorry, darling. Look, come on. Let's just

get the shopping upstairs and you can watch a *Thomas* video.'

'I hate *Thomas*.'

'*Thunderbirds*, then.'

'I hate them even more.'

Angie closed her eyes, sighing out a breath like the online mindfulness gurus suggested. 'Then you'll just have to stare out of the bloody window, like I used to. Now, come on!'

He sucked in a huge breath. Angie flinched, but the scream never came. Instead, Kai's scrunched-up eyes opened wide and swivelled sideways. She followed his gaze and found herself facing a good-looking man wearing a smart jacket and trousers. He had a kind smile.

'I'm sorry,' the man said in a quiet voice. 'I couldn't help seeing your little boy's . . . he's tired, I suppose. You left the door open and as I was coming to this address anyway . . .' He tailed off, looking embarrassed, eyes downcast.

'You were coming *here*?' she asked.

He looked up at her again. 'Yes,' he said, smiling. 'I was looking for Angela Halpern.'

'That's me.' She paused, frowning, as she tried to place him. 'Do I know you?'

'Mummee!' Kai hissed from her waist, where he was clutching her.

'Quiet, darling, please.'

The man smiled. 'Would you like a hand with your bags? I see you have your hands full with the little fellow there.' Then he squatted down, so that his face was at the same level as Kai's. 'Hello. My name's Harvey. What's yours?'

'Kai. Are you a policeman?'

Harvey laughed, a warm, soft-edged sound. 'No. I'm not a policeman.'

'Mummy's a nurse. At the hospital. Do you work there?'

'Me? Funnily enough, I do.'

'Are you a nurse?'

'No. But I do help people. Which I think is a bit of a coincidence. Do you know that word?'

The little boy shook his head.

'It's just a word grown-ups use when two things happen that are the same. Kai,' he said, dropping his voice to a conspiratorial whisper, 'do you want to know a secret?'

Kai nodded, smiling and wiping his nose on his sleeve.

'There's a big hospital in London called Bart's. And I think it rhymes with' – he paused and looked left and right – 'farts.'

Kai squawked with laughter.

Harvey stood, knees popping. 'I hope that was OK. The naughty word. It usually seems to make them laugh.'

Angie smiled. She felt relief that this helpful stranger hadn't seen fit to judge her. To tut, roll his eyes or give any of the dozens of subtle signals the free-and-easy brigade found to diminish her. 'It's fine, really. You said you'd come to see me?'

'Oh, yes, of course, sorry. I'm from the food bank. The Purcell Foundation?' he said. 'They've asked me to visit a few of our customers, to find out what they think about the quality of the service. I was hoping you'd have ten minutes for a chat. If it's not a good time, I can come back.'

Angie sighed. Then she shook her head. 'No, it's fine
. . . Harvey, did you say your name was?'

He nodded.

'Give me a hand with the bags and I'll put the kettle
on. I picked up some teabags this afternoon, so we can
christen the packet.'

'Let me take those,' he said, bending down and
snaking his fingers through the loops in the carrier-bag
handles. 'Where to, madam?' he added in a jokey tone.

'We're on the third floor, I'm afraid.'

Harvey smiled. 'Not to worry, I'm in good shape.'

Reaching the top of the stairs, Angie elbowed the
light switch and then unlocked the door, while Harvey
kept up a string of tall tales for Kai.

'And then the chief doctor said' – he adopted a deep
voice – '"No, no, that's never going to work. You need to
use a hosepipe!"'

Kai's laughter echoed off the bare, painted walls of
the stairwell.

'Here we are,' Angie said, pushing the door open.
'The kitchen's at the end of the hall.'

She stood aside, watching Harvey negotiate the
cluttered hallway and deposit the shopping bags on her
pine kitchen table. She followed him, noticing the scuff
marks on the walls, the sticky fat spatters behind the hob,
and feeling a lump in her throat.

'Kai, why don't you go and watch telly?' she asked
her son, steering him out of the kitchen and towards the
sitting room.

'A film?' he asked.

She glanced up at the clock. Five to six. 'It's almost
teatime.'

'Pleeease?'

She smiled. 'OK. But you come when I call you for tea. Pasta and red sauce, your favourite.'

'Yummy.'

She turned back to Harvey, who was unloading the groceries on to the table. A sob swelled in her throat. She choked it back.

He frowned. 'Is everything all right, Angela?'

The noise from the TV was loud, even from the other room. She turned away so this stranger wouldn't see her crying. It didn't matter that he was a colleague, of sorts. He could see what she'd been reduced to, and that was enough.

'Yes, yes, sorry. It's just, you know, the food bank. I never thought my life would turn out like this. Then I lost my husband and things just got on top of me.'

'Mmm,' he said. 'That was careless of you.'

'What?' She turned round, uncertain of what she'd heard.

He was lifting a tin of baked beans out of the bag. 'I said, it was careless of you. To lose your husband.'

She frowned. Trying to make sense of his remark. The cruel tone. The staring, suddenly dead eyes.

'Look, I don't know what you—'

The tin swung round in a half-circle and crashed against her left temple.

'Oh,' she moaned, grabbing the side of her head and staggering backwards.

Her palm was wet. Her blood was hot. She was half-blind with the pain. Her back met the cooker and she slumped to the ground. He was there in front of her, crouching down, just like he'd done with Kai. Only he wasn't telling jokes any more. And he wasn't smiling.

'Please keep quiet,' he murmured, 'or I'll have to kill Kai as well. Are you expecting anyone?'

'N-nobody,' she whispered, shaking. She could feel the blood running inside the collar of her shirt. And the pain, oh, the pain. It felt as though her brain was pushing her eyes out of their sockets.

He nodded. 'Good.'

Then he encircled her neck with his hands, looked into her eyes and squeezed.

I'm so sorry, Kai. I hope Auntie Cherry looks after you properly when I'm gone. I hope . . .

* * *

Casting a quick glance towards the kitchen door and the hallway beyond, and reassured by the blaring noise from the TV, Harvey crouched by Angie's inert body and increased the pressure.

Her eyes bulged, and her tongue, darkening already from that natural rosy pink to the colour of raw liver, protruded from between her teeth.

From his jacket he withdrew an empty blood bag. He connected the outlet tube and inserted a razor-tipped trocar into the other end. He placed them to one side and dragged her jeans over her hips, tugging them down past her knees. With the joints free to move, he pushed his hands between her thighs and shoved them apart.

He inserted the needle into her thigh so that it met and travelled a few centimetres up into the right femoral artery. Then he laid the blood bag on the floor and watched as the scarlet blood shot into the clear plastic tube and surged along it.

With a precious litre of blood distending the bag, he capped it off and removed the tube and the trocar. With Angie's heart pumping her remaining blood on to the kitchen floor tiles, he stood and placed the bag inside his jacket. He could feel it through his shirt, warm against his skin. He took her purse out of her bag, found the card he wanted and removed it.

He wandered down the hall and poked his head round the door frame of the sitting room. The boy was sitting cross-legged, two feet from the TV, engrossed in the adventures of a blue cartoon dog.

'Tea's ready, Kai,' he said, in a sing-song tone.

Protesting, but clambering to his feet, the little boy extended a pudgy hand holding the remote and froze the action, then dropped the control to the carpet.

Harvey held out his hand and the boy took it, absently, still staring at the screen.

DAY TWO, 8.15 A.M.

Arriving at Bourne Hill Police Station, Detective Inspector Ford sighed, fingering the scar on his chin. *What better way to start the sixth anniversary of your wife's death than with a shouting match over breakfast with your fifteen-year-old son?*

The row had ended in an explosive exchange that was fast, raw and brutal:

'I hate you! I wish you'd died instead of Mum.'

'Yeah? Guess what? So do I!'

All the time they'd been arguing, he'd seen Lou's face, battered by submerged rocks in the sea off the Pembrokeshire coast.

Pushing the memory of the argument aside, he ran a hand over the top of his head, trying to flatten down the spikes of dark, grey-flecked hair.

He pushed through the double glass doors. Straight into the middle of a ruckus.

A scrawny man in faded black denim and a raggy T-shirt was swearing at a young woman in a dark suit. Eyes wide, she had backed against an orange wall. He could see a Wiltshire police ID on a lanyard round her neck, but he didn't recognise her.

The two female civilian staff behind the desk were on their feet, one with a phone clamped to her ear.

The architects who'd designed the interior of the new station at Bourne Hill had persuaded senior management that the traditional thick glass screen wasn't 'welcoming'. Now any arsehole could decide to lean across the three feet of white-surfaced MDF and abuse, spit on or otherwise ruin the day of the hardworking receptionists. He saw the other woman reach under the desk for the panic button.

'Why are you ignoring me, eh? I just asked where the toilets are, you bitch!' the man yelled at the woman backed against the wall.

Ford registered the can of strong lager in the man's left hand and strode over. The woman was pale, and her mouth had tightened to a lipless line.

'I asked you a question. What's wrong with you?' the drunk shouted.

Ford shot out his right hand and grabbed him by the back of his T-shirt. He yanked him backwards, sticking out a booted foot and rolling him over his knee to send him flailing to the floor.

Ford followed him down and drove a knee in between his shoulder blades. The man gasped out a loud 'Oof!' as his lungs emptied. Ford gripped his wrist and jerked his arm up in a tight angle, then turned round and called over his shoulder, 'Could someone get some cuffs, please? This . . . gentleman . . . will be cooling off in a cell.'

A pink-cheeked uniform raced over and snapped a pair of rigid Quik-Cuffs on to the man's wrists.

'Thanks, Mark,' Ford said, getting to his feet. 'Get him over to Custody.'

'Charge, sir?'

'Drunk and disorderly? Common assault? Being a jerk in a built-up area? Just get him booked in.'

The PC hustled the drunk to his feet, reciting the formal arrest and caution script while walking him off in an armlock to see the custody sergeant.

Ford turned to the woman who'd been the focus of his newest collar's unwelcome attentions. 'I'm sorry about that. Are you OK?'

She answered as if she were analysing an incident she'd witnessed on CCTV. 'I think so. He didn't hit me, and swearing doesn't cause physical harm. Although I am feeling quite anxious as a result.'

'I'm not surprised.' Ford gestured at her ID. 'Are you here to meet someone? I haven't seen you round here before.'

She nodded. 'I'm starting work here today. And my new boss is . . . hold on . . .' She fished a sheet of paper from a brown canvas messenger bag slung over her left shoulder. 'Alec Reid.'

Now Ford understood. She was the new senior crime scene investigator. Her predecessor had transferred up to Thames Valley Police to move with her husband's new job. Alec managed the small forensics team at Salisbury and had been crowing about his new hire for weeks now.

'My new deputy has a PhD, Ford,' he'd said over a pint in the Wyndham Arms one evening. 'We're going up in the world.'

Ford stuck his hand out. 'DI Ford.'

'Pleased to meet you,' she said, taking his hand and pumping it up and down three times before releasing it.

'My name is Dr Hannah Fellowes. I was about to get my ID sorted when that man started shouting at me.'

'I doubt it was anything about you in particular. Just wrong place, wrong time.'

She nodded, frowning up at him. 'Although, technically, this *is* the right place. As I'm going to be working here.' She checked her watch, a multifunction Casio with more dials and buttons than the dash of Ford's ageing Land Rover Discovery. 'It's also 8.15, so it's the right time as well.'

Ford smiled. 'Let's get your ID sorted, then I'll take you up to Alec. He arrives early most days.'

He led her over to the long, low reception desk.

'This is—'

'Dr Hannah Fellowes,' she said to the receptionist. 'I'm pleased to meet you.'

She thrust her right hand out across the counter. The receptionist took it and received the same three stiff shakes as Ford.

The receptionist smiled up at her new colleague, but Ford could see the concern in her eyes. 'I'm Paula. Nice to meet you, too, Hannah. Are you all right? I'm so sorry you had to deal with that on your first day.'

'It was a shock. But it won't last. I don't let things like that get to me.'

Paula smiled. 'Good for you!'

While Paula converted a blank rectangle of plastic into a functioning station ID, Hannah turned to Ford.

'Should I ask her to call me Dr Fellowes, or is it usual here to use first names?' she whispered.

'We mainly use Christian names, but if you'd like to be known as Dr Fellowes, now would be the time.'

Hannah nodded and turned back to Paula, who handed her the swipe card in a clear case.

'There you go, Hannah. Welcome aboard.'

'Thank you.' A beat. 'Paula.'

'Do you know where you're going?'

'I'll take her,' Ford said.

At the lift, he showed her how to swipe her card before pressing the floor button.

'If you don't do that, you just stand in the lift not going anywhere. It's mainly the PTBs who do it.'

'PTBs?' she repeated, as the lift door closed in front of them.

'Powers That Be. Management?'

'Oh. Yes. That's funny. PTBs. Powers That Be.'

She didn't laugh, though, and Ford had the odd sensation that he was talking to a foreigner, despite her southern English accent. She stared straight ahead as the lift ascended. Ford took a moment to assess her appearance. She was shorter than him by a good half-foot, no more than five-five or six. Slim, but not skinny. Blonde hair woven into plaits, a style Ford had always associated with children.

He'd noticed her eyes downstairs; it was hard not to, they'd been so wide when the drunk had had her backed against the wall. But even relaxed, they were large, and coloured the blue of old china.

The lift pinged and a computerised female voice announced, 'Third floor.'

'You're down here,' Ford said, turning right and leading Hannah along the edge of an open-plan office. He gestured left. 'General CID. I'm Major Crimes on the fourth floor.'

She took a couple of rapid, skipping steps to catch up with him. 'Is Forensics open plan as well? I was told it was a quiet office.'

'I think it's safe to say it's quiet. Come on. Let's get you a tea first. Or coffee. Which do you like best?'

'That's a hard question. I haven't really tried enough types to know.' She shook her head, like a dog trying to dislodge a flea from its ear. 'No. What I meant to say was, I'd like to have a tea, please. Thank you.'

There it was again. The foreigner-in-England vibe he'd picked up downstairs.

While he boiled a kettle and fussed around with a teabag and the jar of instant coffee, he glanced at Hannah. She was staring at him, but smiled when he caught her eye. The expression popped dimples into her cheeks.

'Something puzzling you?' he asked.

'You didn't tell me your name,' she said.

'I think I did. It's Ford.'

'No. I meant your first name. You said, "We mainly use Christian names," when the receptionist, Paula, was doing my building ID. And you called me Hannah. But you didn't tell me yours.'

Ford pressed the teabag against the side of the mug before scooping it out and dropping it into a swing-topped bin. He handed the mug to Hannah. 'Careful, it's hot.'

'Thank you. But your name?'

'Ford's fine. Really. Or DI Ford, if we're being formal.'

'OK.' She smiled. Deeper dimples this time, like little curved cuts. 'You're Ford. I'm Hannah. If we're being formal, maybe you *should* call me Dr Fellowes.'

Ford couldn't tell if she was joking. He took a swig of his coffee. 'Let's go and find Alec. He's talked of little else since you accepted his job offer.'

'It's probably because I'm extremely well qualified.

After earning my doctorate, which I started at Oxford and finished at Harvard, I worked in America for a while. I consulted to city, state and federal law enforcement agencies. I also lectured at Quantico for the FBI.'

Ford blinked, struggling to process this hyper-concentrated CV. It sounded like that of someone ten or twenty years older than the slender young woman sipping tea from a Spire FM promotional mug.

'That's pretty impressive. Sorry, you're how old?'

'Don't be sorry. We only met twenty minutes ago. I'm thirty-three.'

Ford reflected that at her age he had just been completing his sergeant's exams. His promotion to inspector had come through a month ago and he was still feeling, if not out of his depth, then at least under the microscope. Now, he was in conversation with some sort of crime-fighting wunderkind.

'So, how come you're working as a CSI in Salisbury? No offence, but isn't it a bit of a step down from teaching at the FBI?'

She looked away. He watched as she fidgeted with a ring on her right middle finger, twisting it round and round.

'I don't want to share that with you,' she said, finally.

In that moment he saw it. Behind her eyes. An assault? A bad one. Not sexual, but violent. Who did the FBI go after? The really bad ones. The ones who didn't confine their evildoing to a single state. It was her secret. Ford knew all about keeping secrets. He felt for her.

'OK, sorry. Look, we're just glad to have you. Come on. Let's find Alec.'

He took Hannah round the rest of CID and out through a set of grey-painted double doors with a well-kicked steel plate at the foot. The corridor to Forensics was papered with health and safety posters and noticeboards advertising sports clubs, social events and training courses.

Inside, the chatter and buzz of coppers at full pelt was replaced by a sepulchral quiet. Five people were hard at work, staring at computer monitors or into microscopes. Much of the 'hard science' end of forensics had been outsourced to private labs in 2012. But Wiltshire Police had, in Ford's mind, made the sensible decision to preserve as much of an in-house scientific capacity as it could afford.

He pointed to a glassed-in office in the far corner of the room.

'That's Alec's den. He doesn't appear to be in yet.'

'*Au contraire*, Henry!'

The owner of the deep, amused-sounding voice tapped Ford on the shoulder. He turned to greet the forensic team manager, a short, round man wearing wire-framed glasses.

'Morning, Alec.'

Alec clocked the new CSI, but then leaned closer to Ford. 'You OK, Henry?' he murmured, his brows knitted together. 'What with the date, and everything.'

'I'm fine. Let's leave it.'

Alec shrugged. Then his gaze moved to Hannah. 'Dr Fellowes, you're here at last! Welcome, welcome.'

'Thank you, Alec. It's been quite an interesting start to the day.'

Ford said, 'Some idiot was making a nuisance of himself in reception as Hannah was arriving. He's cooling off in one of Ian's capsule hotel rooms in the basement.'

The joviality vanished, replaced by an expression of

real concern. 'Oh, my dear young woman. I am so sorry. And on your first day with us, too,' Alec said. 'Why don't you come with me? I'll introduce you to the team and we'll get you set up with a nice quiet desk in the corner. Thanks, Henry. I'll take it from here.'

Ford nodded, eager to get back to his own office and see what the day held. He prayed someone might have been up to no good overnight. Anything to save him from the mountains of forms and reports that he had to either read, write or edit.

'DI Ford? Before you go,' Hannah said.

'Yes?'

'You said I should call you Ford. But Alec just called you Henry.'

'It's a nickname. I got it on my first day here.'

'A nickname. What does it mean?'

'You know. Henry. As in Henry Ford?'

She looked at him, eyebrows raised.

He tried again. 'The car? Model T?'

She smiled at last. A wide grin that showed her teeth, though it didn't reach her eyes. The effect was disconcerting. 'Ha! Yes. That's funny.'

'Right. I have to go. I'm sure we'll bump into each other again.'

'I'm sure, too. I hope there won't be a drunk trying to hit me.'

She smiled, and after a split second he realised it was supposed to be a joke. As he left, he could hear her telling Alec, 'Call me Hannah.'

DAY TWO, 8.59 A.M.

The 999 call had come in just ten minutes earlier: a Cat A G28 – suspected homicide. Having told the whole of Response and Patrol B shift to 'blat' over to the address, Sergeant Natalie Hewitt arrived first at 75 Wyvern Road.

She jumped from her car and spoke into her Airwave radio. 'Sierra Bravo Three-Five, Control.'

'Go ahead, Sierra Bravo Three-Five.'

'Is the ambulance towards?'

'Be about three minutes.'

She ran up the stairs and approached the young couple standing guard at the door to Flat 3.

'Mr and Mrs Gregory, you should go back to your own flat now,' she said, panting. 'I'll have more of my colleagues joining me shortly. Please don't leave the house. We'll be wanting to take your statements.'

'But I've got aerobics at nine thirty,' the woman protested.

Natalie sighed. The public were fantastic at calling in crimes, and occasionally made half-decent witnesses. But it never failed to amaze her how they could also be such *innocents* when it came to the aftermath. This one didn't even seem concerned that her upstairs neighbour and young son had been murdered. Maybe she was in shock. Maybe the husband had kept her out of the flat. Wise bloke.

'I'm afraid you may have to cancel it, just this once,' she said. *You look like you to could afford to. Maybe go and get a fry-up, too, when we're done with you. Put some flesh on your bones.*

The woman retreated to the staircase. Her husband delayed leaving, just for a few seconds.

'We're just shocked,' he said. 'The blood came through our ceiling. That's why I went upstairs to investigate.'

Natalie nodded, eager now to enter the death room and deal with the latest chapter in the Big Book of Bad Things People Do to Each Other.

She swatted at the flies that buzzed towards her. They all came from the room at the end of the dark, narrow hallway. Keeping her eyes on the threadbare red-and-cream runner, alert to anything Forensics might be able to use, she made her way to the kitchen. She supported herself against the opposite wall with her left hand so she could walk, one foot in line with the other, along the right-hand edge of the hall.

The buzzing intensified. And then she caught it: the aroma of death. Sweet-sour top notes overlaying a deeper, darker, rotting-meat stink as body tissues broke down and emitted their gases.

And blood. Or 'claret', in the parlance of the job. She reckoned she'd smelled more of it than a wine expert. This was present in quantity. The husband – what was his name? Rob, that was it. He'd said on the phone it was bad. 'A slaughterhouse' – his exact words.

'Let's find out, then, shall we?' she murmured as she reached the door and entered the kitchen.

As the scene imprinted itself on her retinas, she didn't swear, or invoke the deity, or his son. She used to, in the early days of her career. There'd been enough blasphemy and bad language to have had her churchgoing mum rolling her eyes and pleading with her to 'Watch your language, please, Nat. There's no need.'

She'd become hardened to it over the previous fifteen years. She hoped she still felt a normal human's reaction when she encountered murder scenes, or the remains of those who'd reached the end of their tether and done themselves in. But she left the amateur dramatics to the new kids. She was a sergeant, a rank she'd worked bloody hard for, and she felt a certain restraint went with the territory. So, no swearing.

She did, however, shake her head and swallow hard as she took in the scene in front of her. She'd been a keen photographer in her twenties and found it helpful to see crime scenes as if through a lens: her way of putting some distance between her and whatever horrors the job required her to confront.

In wide-shot, an obscene parody of a Madonna and child. A woman – early thirties, to judge by her face, which was waxy-pale – and a little boy cradled in her lap.

They'd been posed at the edge of a wall-to-wall blood pool, dried and darkened to a deep plum red.

She'd clearly bled out. He wasn't as pale as his mum, but the pink in his smooth little cheeks was gone, replaced by a greenish tinge.

The puddle of blood had spread right across the kitchen floor and under the table, on which half-emptied bags of shopping sagged. The dead woman was slumped with her back against the cooker, legs canted open yet held together at the ankle by her pulled-down jeans.

And the little boy.

Looking for all the world as though he had climbed on to his mother's lap for a cuddle, eyes closed, hands together at his throat as if in prayer. Fair hair. Long and wavy, down to his shoulders, in a girlish style Natalie had noticed some of her friends choose for their sons.

Even in midwinter, flies would find a corpse within the hour. In the middle of a scorching summer like the one southern England was enjoying now, they'd arrived in minutes, laid their eggs and begun feasting in quantity. Maggots crawled and wriggled all over the pair.

As she got closer, Natalie revised her opinion about the cause of death; now, she could see bruises around the throat that screamed strangulation.

There were protocols to be followed. And the first of these was the preservation of life. She was sure the little boy was dead. The skin discolouration and maggots told her that. But there was no way she was going to go down as the sergeant who left a still-living toddler to die in the centre of a murder scene.

Reaching him meant stepping into that lake of congealed blood. Never mind the sneers from CID about the 'woodentops' walking through crime scenes in their size twelves; this was about checking if a little boy had a chance of life.

She pulled out her phone and took half a dozen shots of the bodies. Then she took two long strides towards them, wincing as her boot soles crackled and slid in the coagulated blood.

She crouched and extended her right index and middle fingers, pressing under the little boy's jaw into the soft flesh where the carotid artery ran. She closed her eyes and prayed for a pulse, trying to ignore the smell, and the noise of the writhing maggots and their soft, squishy little bodies as they roiled together in the mess.

After staying there long enough for the muscles in her legs to start complaining, and for her to be certain the little lad was dead, she straightened and reversed out of the blood. She took care to place her feet back in the first set of footprints.

She turned away, looking for some kitchen roll to wipe the blood off her soles, and stared in horror at the wall facing the cooker.

'Oh, shit.'

KEEP READING

NEWSLETTER

Join my no-spam newsletter for new book news, competitions, offers and more…

Follow Andy Maslen

Bookbub has a New release Alert. You can check out the latest book deals and get news of every new book I publish by following me here.

BingeBooks has regular author chats plus lists, reviews and personalised newsletters. Follow me here.

Website www.andymaslen.com.
Email andy@andymaslen.com.
Facebook group, The Wolfe Pack.

ACKNOWLEDGMENTS

I want to thank you for buying this book. I hope you enjoyed it. As an author is only part of the team of people who make a book the best it can be, this is my chance to thank the people on *my* team.

For sharing their knowledge and experience of The Job, former and current police officers Andy Booth, Ross Coombs, Jen Gibbons, Neil Lancaster, Sean Memory, Trevor Morgan, Olly Royston, Chris Saunby, Ty Tapper, Sarah Warner and Sam Yeo.

For helping me stay reasonably close to medical reality as I devise gruesome ways of killing people, Martin Cook, Melissa Davies, Arvind Nagra and Katie Peace.

For her wonderfully detailed information and advice about Swedish forensic science and law enforcement, Brita Zilg.

For their brilliant copy-editing and proofreading Nicola Lovick and Liz Ward.

For his super-cool covers, especially this new look for Stella, my cover designer, Nick Castle.

The members of my Facebook Group, The Wolfe Pack, who are an incredibly supportive and also helpful bunch of people. Thank you to them, also.

And for being an inspiration and source of love and laughter, and making it all worthwhile, my family: Jo, Rory and Jacob.

The responsibility for any and all mistakes in this book remains mine. I assure you, they were unintentional.

Andy Maslen
    Salisbury, 2022

ABOUT THE AUTHOR

Photo © 2020 Kin Ho

Andy Maslen was born in Nottingham, England. After leaving university with a degree in psychology, he worked in business for thirty years as a copywriter. In his spare time, he plays the guitar. He lives in Wiltshire.

Printed in Great Britain
by Amazon

22627373R00245